RED WET DIRT

Nicholas Grabowsky

BLACK BED
SHEET

Red Wet Dirt
Formally published by
Triad Publishing, September 2007
A Diverse Media/Black Bed Sheet Book
January 2008
Second (Special) Edition: July 2015

Interior illustration of Nicholas Grabowsky as a child by Ola Larsson,
copyright © 2008 by Ola Larsson.

Photograph of the author by Phyllis Haupert and copyright © 2008
by Nicholas Grabowsky and Diverse Media

The selections in this book are works of fiction. Names, characters,
places and incidents either are the product of the author's imagination
or are used fictitiously, and any resemblance to actual persons, living
or dead, events, or locales is entirely coincidental.

The following selections were previously published, with grateful
acknowledgement to those publishers: "The Yuletide Thing" in
Doorways Magazine Issue #4 (Doorways Publications), "The Freeway
Reaper" in the anthology *From The Shadows* (Triad Publishing Group),
and "Looks Like a Rat to Me" in the anthology *Echoes of Terror*
(Lachesis Publishing).

Visit Nicholas Grabowsky's official website at
WWW.DOWNWARDEN.COM.

Red Wet Dirt

A Black Bed Sheet/Diverse Media Book
Antelope, CA

Also by Nicholas Grabowsky:

Fiction:
The Everborn
Pray, Serpent's Prey (*as Nicholas Randers*)
The Rag Man (*as Nicholas Randers*)
Tale of the Makeshift Faire (*as Nicholas Randers*)
Halloween IV
Halloween IV: The Special Limited Edition
Sweet Dreams, Lady Moon (*as Marsena Shane*)
June Park (*as Marsena Shane*)
The Wicked Haze
Diverse Tales

Nonfiction:
Nick Reads & Reviews 2004-2007
Nancy (Biography of the First Lady) (*as Marsena Shane*)
The Easy Way to Great Legs (*as Marsena Shane*)
Your Heart Belongs to You (*as Marsena Shane*)
Diverse Arcanum

Children's:
Flatty Kat: Tales of an Urban Feline (*with Phyllis Haupert*)

Recent anthologies:
From the Shadows (*Triad Publishing Group*)
Echoes of Terror (*Lachesis Publishing*)
Fear (*Whiskey Creek Press*, introduction)
Satan's Holiday
Welcome to Your Nightmare
Read Us or Die
When the Night Darkens the Streets

After Red Wet Dirt, read The Everborn:

"My Dear Nicholas: You seem to me---in a way that's entirely admirable----a man out of time. You're writing horror epics when the audience has become increasingly numbed by cinematic hokum and stale ideas. I SALUTE YOU: your ambition, your dedication, your achievements. I have no doubt in my mind that there is much, much more to come from your fertile and blissfully complex imagination, and I'll await the next work with much anticipation!"
----**Clive Barker (***Hellraiser,* **director, producer, artist and bestselling author)**

"Grabowsky has melded Horror with Science Fiction with such expertise that I am left speechless. This is a novel of epic proportions and told in such a unique way that it defies explanation. By utilizing ideas from religious history, the reader is given a totally surreal reason for what UFOs really are and you will start to believe it's true."---*Gorezone Magazine*

"Grabowsky's writing is at times touching and emotional, however, his real talent is his ability to infuse his writing with a sense of dread and loathing that I have not experienced since H.P. Lovecraft..........(a)** unique and often terrifying world that Sacramento novelist Nicholas Grabowsky launches us into......(it) has the feel of an "X-Files" episode, at other very twisted turns it delves into the psychedelic. For those of us looking for something new in the alien horror genre, look not to the stars, but look to Nicholas Grabowsky's "The Everborn." --- *Tahoe Daily Tribune*

Nicholas Grabowsky has succeeded in creating an entire world that is situated over our own, shading our every move with darkness and its ghostly alien presence....leaving the reader in utter astonishment as to the amazing detail that Grabowsky's world has been created with. The detailed mythology that he creates with his alien forces ties together more than one earthly superstition, weaving a web that connects the world of the supernatural and the extraterrestrial.........the reader will be unable to get the terrifying and original visions out of their head! ------**Heidi Martinuzzi,** *E! Entertainment Television, Pretty/Scary.net*

"Grabowsky exploits (the story) to explore concepts such as being, death & immortality in a fabulist world where more than a half-dozen major characters shift identities with Cronenberg-like regularity....a solid storyline, fresh ideas on everything from relationships to religion and blood-chilling violence makes Grabowsky's latest offering a compelling read!"

----*Sacramento **News & Review***

***** 5 stars (highest rating) "ALL HAIL GRABOWSKY! .....a captivating plot completely unique...with a story so imaginative and profound, even I was astounded....satisfying a reader's interest in alternative science fiction, classic horror, suspense and yes, folks, even gore. The atmosphere is complex, murky and entraps you. The style of writing is blunt, audacious and head-on.....this book rises above the average horror/science fiction novel!"

------*Horror-web.com*

".....an amazingly original way to treat the done-to-death alien motif. (This) really is an outstanding book....."

----*Garret Peck (*Bram Stoker Award nominee, *Personal Demons)*

"Nicholas Grabowsky has been around a while and I have read several of his books but this one will always remain my favorite as it is with most of his "fans". I say "fans" because once you begin reading his novels you will get hooked. He has a style unlike any other writer in this genre. He is really not just good at what he does - he is great! "The Everborn" is a classic and will be long read after he is gone from the face of this earth."

-----*W. H. McDonald Jr., 128th Assault Helicopter Company (South Vietnam, 1966 & '67, awarded The Distinguished Flying Cross, The Bronze Star, 14 Air Medals and the Purple Heart*

"Forget sleeping, forget eating...you will live this book, every dramatic step, every action, every thought...this book will consume you from page one and the thing is.....you will be glad for it. Nicholas soars as one of the greatest Sci-Fi storytellers of all time.

Watch out Anthony and Asimov......this Sci-Fi king is here and he means business."

--*Twisted Dreams Magazine*

"...a well-crafted novel that seamlessly blends elements of horror and science fiction. This novel has it all: demons, apparitions, aliens, and serial killers. This novel will reach out and touch you on many levels and Grabowsky's compelling storytelling will have you reading well into the night, afraid to put it down........

------Holly Catanzarita, *Sinisteria Magazine*

"Spellbinding and utterly amazing......"

----*Garry Charles* (bestselling author, *Heaven's Falling* series)

Golden Award winner! Best Science Fiction novel of 2004.....

--*American Author's Association*

"A well-established author of horror/fantasy fiction...."

---*Scary Monsters Magazine, 2004 Yearbook*

"I don't know what else to say about this that has not already been said by some of the best writers of the genre. All I can do is join them in singing his praises. Grabowsky is a master of taking old legends and giving them new life...discover for yourself one of the best up and coming writers of our decade!"

--Eve Blaack, *Hacker's Source Magazine,* on *RED WET DIRT*

Ask for The Everborn everywhere books are sold.

For my sons, Jeremy and Charlie, with love.
To Art and Doris Grabowsky, my parents, for
always being there; and to the fans and readers
throughout the world.

Sincere Thanks to Garry Charles, Brian Yount, Carole Spencer, Diana Barron, Norm Applegate, Johnny Martin Walters, Giovanna Lagana, Mars Homeworld, Jonathan Morken for all his help filming the *Cutting Edges* movie trailer, The Ancient and Honorable Order of E. Clampus Vitus, Bob, Peggy, and Chris Horton, Mister Lobo, everyone who showed up to my *Festival of Fallen Souls* party/graphic novel photo shoot during the Sac Film Fest of '07, Tony Moran for his support, Clive Barker for believing in me, Phyllis Haupert for inspiring *The Yuletide Thing*, Vern Firestone for first publishing this collection before falling off the planet, Francy Weatherman for having me on her radio show to advertise this book which introduced us to each other, and everyone who put up with me while I was writing *Red Afterworld*.

CONTENTS

Dear Playboy Advisor, My Hamster Loo, The Adventure of Goldenfish, Russia Shocks World, You're a Pretty Boston Fern, Bepto Pismal, The Chloroform Angel, Sixth Grade Poetry, Story Going Nowhere and Left That Way, I Got Drunk and Wrote This, Class Autograph

Red Wet Dirt

Nicholas Grabowsky

THE YULETIDE

THING

It was a Monday Christmas, a *very* Monday Christmas, as not only did December twenty-fifth fall that year on the most notoriously dismal of all days of the week, but this day in particular was *particularly* dismal. The rising sun of Christmas Day's dawn hadn't yet begun to poke from out of the horizon like a *Kilroy was here* on my half of the globe yet, and I was already sure-as-shit certain this day was going to wreak havoc on me, really bring me down.

We were kicking back, nice and comfy, sharing two chaise lounge chairs at the end of a long dock jetting out from Yuletide Ranch & Cabins at Spark Lake, California, a beating human heart and I.

Looking out at the lake this time of morning, you wouldn't think its waters were murky and filthy, its shores full of seaweed, small but potentially lethal jagged rock, and duck shit. I wouldn't advise that you swim in it. I heard somewhere that Spark Lake used to be Sparkling Lake until a court order imposed a change in its name so it didn't intentionally deceive tourists, kind of like how Aquafina had to admit to its tap water resources on its labels.

The early morning air was chilly and clear, and though the weather forecaster on News 11 had well driven home how it was going to be a *green* Monday Christmas and just as green throughout the days surrounding it, I'd seen *plenty* of snow so far.

And not one flake of it fell from the sky.

Already, power boats and pontoons were livened at their docks and setting forth into the distance of the Lake, and I found myself paranoid that the pulsing mass of veined glistening muscle seated next to me would be noticed and consequently draw attention. Some of the boaters from the docks on either

1

side of us cruised by only twenty meters from where we sat, some rudely canvassing us and the waters with their spotlights and laughing. Not certain if they were laughing at us, at me, or at each other from merely enjoying themselves and in fact paying little attention to where their spotlights fell.

Upon my head I wore a generic dollar store Santa Claus hat I immediately thought to remove and place over the heart beside me in an attempt to conceal it. A difficult task, when a human heart is throbbing and pounding all by itself and you're struggling to hide it just enough so that it can still witness a Christmas sunrise with you.

***

Talia and I, each a stone throw past our thirty-somethings, packed our bags and set forth Friday morning up I-5 in my black Ford Focus to this place, a trip of over three hours north of the Sacramento home we shared with our 3-year-old son, Anthony, just after we dropped him off at her parents', with all of us to be reunited Christmas Day.

I'd scored online tickets six months prior to a *Toby Keith at Yuletide Christmas Concert/Winter Fireworks Extravaganza (weather permitting)*. The Yuletide Resort & Spa (where "*Every Day is Merry at Yuletide*") was regionally famous for concert venues, and throughout the entirety of our half-a-decade relationship, Yuletide came to be our refuge, our getaway for a weekend at a time, and at previous Yuletide getaways we rocked to Aerosmith, Big & Rich, Tom Petty, Bob Dylan, Alice Cooper on Halloween Night.

But the prospects of seeing the Big Dog Daddy of all big daddies balls-out live onstage with his red white and blue anthems and bluesy ballads, his bad-ass band, brass section and sax with his little whiskey girl on backups and blazing pyrotechnics, Toby was our ultimate conquest. Talia's brother was a United States Marine serving in Iraq and had met Mr. Keith on his tour there to support the troops. My best friend and his girlfriend road-tripped to Oklahoma just to visit Toby's *I Love This Bar & Grill* restaurant, and I bitch at him to this day of my jealousy. *Let's Get Drunk and Be Somebody* has been Talia's personal anthem for awhile, whereas mine has been *Weed with Willy*, as far as his songs were concerned, and we owned every last recorded and widely distributed one of them.

And what were *we* like? Talia was a raging alcoholic and I chronically smoked the Good Herb in an overall excuse to distance my emotions from the results of her drinking too much, like the numerous times I'd come home from work to find her passed out cold while Anthony had trashed the house and sat naked in a dirty dish-filled kitchen sink. Or the instances, altogether countless, of the times when she'd drastically change her personality for no apparent reason other than vodka and Natural Ice, on a dime, on a comment I'd give about a television commercial she was watching, on a disagreement as to whether the bread was so old that we should throw it away, when she'd lash out at me, cuss and swear and try to kick my ass like I was a priest and she was possessed with the demon of No Reason for This Behavior.

I was hoping this Yuletide concert getaway would be for us the ultimate retreat, where we could both of us chill and get along like we used to, and maybe keep the peace going long afterward. After all, this would mark our first Christmas together, the first time I was invited to spend the holiday with Talia and her relatives.

For ambiguous reasons which always rendered me with deep feelings of rejection, Talia, each Christmas, had to disappear for a few days with her family, sans me, and she never took Anthony with her either.

There was always something about that which never seemed quite right. Not to me, not to anyone close enough for me to confide in.

"*She turns into a creature that time of year,*" my younger brother by nine years suggested once in jest. "*She goes away, becomes a werewolf or some shit, kills a bunch of innocents and feeds their entrails piled high on plates like steaming hot bloated spaghetti pasta to her werewolf family on Our Lord's blessed birthday in a jolly frickin' feast, man.*"

"Zach," I remember telling him as we shared a joint, "I wouldn't put that past her. But she becomes a *creature* nearly *every other night....*"

***

3

When we first arrived at our cabin, we met with the grounds caretaker and his wife who showed us around and gave us our keys. Our cabin was a fully furnished cottage larger than any studio apartment I've lived in. It sported a front patio with a barbeque, a fire pit and chairs, and I was able to back my car right up to it and park it there just a few yards from the front door. Inside, its kitchen table was fully set and cabinets stocked with kitchenware and various sundries, a fridge and countertop appliances, 42-inch HD television in the corner of a forest-motif livingroom complete with pencils whittled out of Redwood branches one could use to fill out the "*how was your stay*" questionnaires, and a ghetto blaster stereo for our Toby Keith CDs.

Outside, our cabin shared the property with nine others situated in a lazy half circle a cabin's length apart from each other. Stretching out from the patio/fire pit sections of each of the cabins were long pebble-ridden pathways parted from between foot-high ivy islands that led through a forestland of evergreens reaching into canopies of branches that collectively sheltered the entire nest of cabins from the sky. A venture down each path would eventually bring you to one of two recreation room structures, where visitors could lounge, play pool, read regional magazines.

The beachfront was riddled with several lounge chairs surrounding a community fire pit with flower beds and redwood beams of rustic fencing separating it from both its neighbors. Out further was the dock, flanked by a few kayaks and two row boats further into the water for us to use free of charge. The first sixty or so feet of the dock was rickety and wooden and was situated on tree trunk pillars which kept it two yards above the water, until steps of stairs descended onto a floating dock the length of a school bus.

As the sun went down on our Friday, Talia and I really began to talk things out for the first time in a long time. Some of what she said I expected her to say, some thoughts and feelings were conveyed that I wasn't quite prepared for. It was a relaxing moment, a rare moment we never quite shared at home, though we brought with us our vices and indulged in them there as we sat on that cloud of heaven as private and peaceful as the occasional passing boat or canoe or the partiers on the beaches and nearby docks would allow. I'd been sober all day up until that point; Talia, soon as we arrived at our cabin several hours ago, broke into one of her four twelve packs of Natural Ice and what she brought to the dock was a Big Gulp cup I'd find out later was filled with half the fifth of whiskey we brought.

Though we were getting along at the time, we were extremely disappointed by the condition of the beach, where we had looked forward to swimming and sunbathing, perhaps fishing. Talia was beginning to weigh the pros against the cons of being here versus at the resort itself, where we could have stayed if I'd thought to reserve a room a lot sooner, where there was a swimming pool and a restaurant and a tiny store, where, for example, at Toby's concert she could readily exile herself to our room should she get too drunk to stand, and her tendency to dwell on the negative festered into ceaseless complaint and the pouring forth of woes. It burst our peaceful bubble. Our heart-to-heart chat dove into the murky Spark Lake water and strangled itself in seaweed like the dead floating fish we saw on our way down the dock to these chairs. At the tail end of a verbally abusive and heated exchange of words, Talia rose, spat *what do you know, you've never done anything for me but knock me up*, and lunged at me, shoving me off the lounge chair. The floating dock swayed, and as I got to my feet and faced her I found myself more fearful that she'd lose her balance and fall right into the water than of the loss of a potentially healing weekend.

The dock swayed as I rushed over to her, but I failed to catch her, and her body simply toppled over the side, plunged right into the water, and I fell to my knees, reached out my arms to grab at the shoulders of her denim jacket. Her confounding panic attack and a manic kicking and screaming forced me into a dive in after her, but she continued to fight against me and circumstance, and I lost her. As soon as she went under, my hands reached and arms flailed desperately. I submerged face-first over and over again, fighting for a feel for her through a congestion of confounding blackness and dense subaqueous growth and sludge as far into the depths as I could dive, as far around the general vicinity as I could swim without going completely mad and swimming further out to no end. Visions and heated notions bombarded my senses stricken sober by this desperate emergency, and, treading water, I began to cry out for help.

Calling attention to this was the last thing I wanted to do. I wanted to find her, pull her to safety, make the incident nothing more than a lesson for her without involving anyone else, hoping to hold on to the possibility that this would be a memory of momentary personal nightmare we'd keep between ourselves and nothing more, and that it would force us into a sobriety we'd swear to for the rest of our lives. Talia's drowning would be unthinkable, and given the way we got along, speculative fingers would point at me. I thought about our relatives, I thought about Anthony. I thought of 911, of police, a botched weekend, a burden I'd carry with me until my own vices brought me to my grave.

As I turned my gaze in all directions, keeping my head above water and calming down enough for a rational inspection of my surroundings and for any hint that Talia was near, I ceased my cries and noticed movement at the shoreline. With no other illumination but for the moon and stars, it was difficult to see.

***

I was certain what I saw wasn't any animal *I'd* ever seen, more certain when it crawled from the shallow shore waters and stood upright upon the rocks just barely beneath the bridge structure connecting our dock to the land. I called out Talia's name, sure as shit she'd turn and motion to me in an *I'm okay* acknowledgement to indicate that this obscurity was indeed my girlfriend and not some independent anomaly immerging onto the beach.

It collapsed and sunk into itself, becoming half the size that it was.

Debris began to float across the water towards me from the spectacle, and I grabbed the first object drifting to me that I could reach. It was leathery and heavy as I lifted it until I saw that it was a dripping wet pair of jeans. The thing on the shore cried out in the voice of something which sounded like Talia at her most heated and vocal moment, evolving next into a deafening screech and a violent thrashing about. I braved myself closer in stubborn determination to check it out more clearly,

6

keeping near to the dock, my shoes finally sensing a foothold upon the lake bottom before I found myself ankle deep in its sludge. I was several yards away from it when I halted and studied.

It was pale, naked, hairless but for long clumpy strands about its head, half the size of a person though for a wild animal quite sizeable. It rose upon all fours, shook itself rapidly like a dog emerging from a bath and hobbled up the rocky embankment. From what I could make of its facial outline in the dark, I found it appeared to have a possum-like snout, its eyes round and black and half the size of Frisbees, glistening and reflecting the moonlight in a greenish hue. Its attenuated forelimbs stretched impossibly long as it scaled the rocks and muddy terrain on talons which themselves were half the lengths of yardsticks and segmented like a spider's legs. Bony protruding indentations of skin from the spine and rib cage of its back down to its rounded posterior resembled the rear view of a scrawny elderly man having fallen and trying to get up.

Disallowing its reality to sink into me fully, it hopped over the rocks with cricket-like hind legs, gained its footing upon the smoothest surface of the beach, and methodically leaped onto the manicured grass, past the lounging area and over the fire pit, into the forest terrain and its eventide shadows.

As I pressed onwards to the shore, I felt like I was abandoning Talia, whose body was possibly lifeless and tangled in seaweed somewhere near the dock where she fell. As I passed the spot from where the creature immerged, I noticed clumps of articles of clothing washing up onto the rocks. I needed only to pass them a glance to know who'd been wearing them ten minutes prior. Exhausted, overwhelmed, and immediately in denial of the entire incident, I chose to return to our cabin, regroup my thoughts, shower all the funk off me, see what was left of our whiskey.

I was thinking, maybe Talia would return, very human and soaked to the bone, march right up to me and with a bold bitch slap curse me for leaving her to nearly drown, then pass out in the bedroom. I was hoping the thing that I saw which defied imagination was merely a figment of my own, or could otherwise be explained under sober circumstances.

I'd cleaned up in no time at all and was preparing two thick sirloin steaks for a barbeque, as planned. I didn't want to think about what happened. I wanted to keep myself busy. I popped Toby Keith into the livingroom stereo while I sat outside on a folding chair waiting for the charcoals to glow orange in the round Weber next to me.

The cabin next to me on the other side of my car was filled with several festive young women who congregated outside to share cigarettes every fifteen minutes or so before they went back inside, yelled and cackled and blared Kid Rock at full volume.

I waited up for quite a spell, feasted, drank some of Talia's beer when the whiskey and eggnog was gone. My obstinate disassociation with what happened at the dock was emotionless, distant, numb, like I'd been turned into a Stepford Wife, but I must've chain-smoked three packs of cigarettes that night. A scrawny man in a Santa outfit stopped by, passing out candy canes cabin to cabin compliments of Yuletide. I stretched out on the sofa, sucking on one of the canes till it was as sharp as a toothpick, watched local cable, surfed through news channels. *Year Without a Santa Claus* was on channel 5 and Heat Miser's jazzy melody melted away my worries for a few hundred seconds.

Until I heard the screams.

At first, I had to listen, listen again. I grabbed the television remote, muted the only inspirational source of Christmas joy I had, and the screams continued, originating from somewhere outside. I bolted from the sofa, ran for the front door, and as soon as I exited into outside air, the screams silenced. There were no signs of the girls, save for the bright inside lights of their cabin, front door open wide to silence, moths dancing about the spiraling energy efficient bulb of their porch light. Resigning myself to the assumption that whatever I'd heard was no big deal, I returned to my folding chair, settled into it and took a toke of my weed.

Then, something fleshy and globulous fell from out of the foot-high ivy island between our cabin and theirs and rolled to a stop onto the disheveled dirt about a yard in front of me. The way it wobbled when it rolled reminded me of The Blob, how it seemed at the start to be moving of its own accord, and

Red Wet Dirt

I freaked out inside though remained glued to my chair. Covered partially in the dirt it accumulated downhill, it resembled a breaded pork roast ready for frying in a pan the size of a toddler's swimming pool. It sat there, and I looked at it. I then rose from my chair, and rather than inspect it I thought better to take a look at where it came from.

The perimeter of the ivy fell just short of the line of my porch light, so when I stepped into the ivy patch itself my line of sight fell into a darkness in which my vision could only decipher outlines of shadow. I wished I'd brought my flashlight. Beneath the branches of a tall Redwood, just a few feet away from our patio area, was a sprawled, unmoving, human-sized blackness that I was immediately distracted from when I took notice of the woman lying beneath the porch light of the girls' cabin. I could see her all the more clearly with each step I took towards her, unmindful of the thick carpet of foliage against which I braved to reach her and completely abandoning my curiosities with the figure beneath the tree.

The woman was spread-eagled upon her back with her arms outstretched upon the dry ground between the front door's welcome mat and their fire pit, like she'd fallen over backwards trying to get in. But the entire section below her neck and above her abdomen was split open, like a shucked clam with no internal organs in her chest cavity, her rib cage split and splintered all the way to the ground like two racks of lamb fatty-side-up on both sides of her. Pools of blood draining from broken arteries pooled within and about her, trailing off like tiny rivers and branches of rivers that surrounded the fire pit and flowed into the night. The sight of it was so surreal and astounding to me that I doubted its authenticity fully, in spite of my experience at the dock. Yet, the conviction I had that what I was seeing was real made me sick inside, made me want to puke up the alcohol intake my system hadn't fully absorbed yet, and aside from the effects of the pot I needed that alcohol to numb me and keep me from freaking out. I turned to the opened front doorway of their cabin, took one single step inward, leaned forward, peered inside.

There were three young ladies, rib cages split down the middle and pulled open so wide they'd snapped, chest cavities hollowed out in like manner as the poor lass outside.

All were on their backs, limbs outstretched so that each of
them formed a human "X", one on the wooden coffee table,
one before the television on the hardwood floor, another upon
the throw rug before the kitchen area. It was as though hand
grenades had detonated from behind their breasts. I braved
a step inward, and my shoe fell into a blood flood as high as
the water on my bathroom floor when the toilet
overflowed something fierce, and beside a chunk of meat I
recognized as the same sort of fleshy mystery organ that rolled
from out of the ivy beside my fire pit. There were several of
these on the floor, I noticed, one not far from either side of
each girl, and the supposition that these objects might be lungs
evaded me until later.

Right then, I tried to close my mind against the gore and the
willingness to about-face and hide away from it all, smoke some
more weed and forget about everything, but my curiosity was
driven by a growing conviction that what I saw at the dock
was real, and, putting two and two together, the creature that
rose from the shore was Talia and that Talia was responsible
for this.

As I ventured across the room, mindfully
sidestepping around the two girls on the floor, I
approached a magazine-littered kitchen counter along which
stood two bar stools, and, passing this, I was able to not only
behold a fourth young woman lying with her back against the
floor, still alive though barely conscious, but the very
thing itself from the dock perched atop her waistline upon
its cricket-like hind legs. It bent over her in a manner
reminiscent of Henry Fuseli's famous painting's *Nightmare*
demon, holding the girl down with not much effort, and half her
size. Its claws, when pointed downwards, were the length of its
height and extended from each of its four fingers like jointed
concrete rebar that narrowed at the tips like sharpened
pencils. Upon its clumpy-haired head was a Santa Claus hat, the
floppy tasseled cottony 99-cents store kind, between two
pointed elfin ears. Its body was like that of a hairless cat, its
pinkish skin wrought with wrinkles and freckled blemishes like a
newborn hamster. With the end of the claw of one index finger
from the one hand facing me, it toyed with the buttons trailing
down the girl's jean-colored shirt, popping off one button

and then the other, before it found her exposed belly button and plunged into it deep. The girl heaved upwards, writhed and gyrated from obvious pain, as though the thing had popped a quarter into her for a storefront mechanical pony ride, then her motions subsided as the claws from her tormentor's opposite hand revealed a number of dark red swollen globs of tube-laced muscle the size of softballs impaled in shish kebob-fashion like the beads on a mathematical bead calculator.

Although the revelation concerning the lungs hadn't hit me yet, it immediately struck me that this creature wasn't hungry, wasn't indulging in a bloodlust spawned solely by blind rage, but that it was collecting human hearts. Perhaps for Christmas presents. It sported more than several, and it wore them like diamond rings. Then, raising the claws of both hands and in a matter of seconds, it plunged its talons straight into the center region of the young woman's breast plate, tore through her shirt and flesh and bone, ripping open wide her rib cage in a sudden broad sweep so powerful and precise that it splintered the rib bones about the sides of her spine and pulled apart both lungs which spilt and tumbled in opposing directions across the floor. Then, like a fork into a meatball around a spaghetti of arteries, it pierced the girl's heart and pried it from out her chest. The thing then used the claws of its other hand to force the heart further up to join its collection.

I wanted to turn away from it with a repulsion more powerful than when I'd stepped from beyond the curtains of my bathroom shower as a kid to catch sight of my dad's genitals just before he pulled up his trousers from taking a dump in the toilet. I froze where I stood, held my breath. I didn't want to disturb it. If it wasn't Talia, if this was a creature whose presence was altogether coincidental from when she fell over into the lake, I knew my life was over, weekend fucked beyond going home afterwards and sorting it all out in therapy.

And then it reared its head, positioned its greenish tea-cup-sized glossy fathomless eyes my way. Sans pupils, they resembled the round protruding windows of a deep sea submarine vessel. The tubular end of its possum-like snout seemed to cast a grin at me, and in a single backwards thrust

11

from its hind legs it abandoned the poor girl and hopped onto the kitchen counter, hopping then into the open window above the sink upon which it simply perched there, half its body in and half outside, its gaze in my direction. It then yawned open a small slit of a chinless mouth as if it were about to speak, took a deep breath, and then, astonishingly, began to exhale a heavy white pollen-like substance which resembled snow. It shot out this substance from the end of its snout like a nozzle for a high pressure washer snowmaking pump for off-season ski resorts, and I backed away at the magnitude of whiteness that swirled in the air about me and everywhere within the girls' cabin. I found myself in a turbulent blizzard that all at once subsided, and everything about me was suddenly drenched in the Christmas color scheme of red and white.

I retreated backwards, and then......there was something about the snow-like substance that began to give me a high very different than that of any pot I'd ever smoked, any drug I've ever indulged in, experimented with, incomparable to any sober feelings of bliss or fulfillment, jubilance, any positive feeling I've ever known. *Poppies will put them to sleep*, as the Wicked Witch in the classic *Oz* film had said, and this came to mind in a fleeting moment as I succumbed to a dark magic swirling about me, and I wondered if Dorothy and company actually felt *this* way when *they* dropped into the poppy field on their sojourn to the Emerald City, and though the snow which fell upon *them* through the Good Witch's wand wave awoke them to press onward, it was the snow spew from the creature's snout which made me feel this way.

The thing hopped into the outside night, abandoning the scene, leaving me alone in the midst of the snow- strewn aftermath of death.

And suddenly, as I stood, there arose from within me the compulsion to clean, to tidy everything up, all the remnants of its destruction, and I was hypnotically happy to do so, set forth right away without further ado. I remember only vague remnants of the process, but as the snow itself melted so too did the flesh of the girls' bodies, which made it all the easier to dispose of them. I remember trash bags. I remember mops and buckets and sponges, scrub brushes and abrasive household kitchen cleaner liquids, the smell of bleach, the brittle snapping of bones and how even the redness of the blood turned white and evaporated as I worked, which made the cleanup a very easy thing to do. I even remember the body of shadow beneath the tree whose lung rolled into my camp and beckoned my curiosities to venture over to the girls' cabin, how it belonged to the Santa- suited groundskeeper who'd passed around candy canes earlier that night.

I remember.........but, the following morning, and for a short while afterwards, I forgot.

***

I awoke upon the sofa in our cabin, quarter 'til noon as the clock on the wall read. I jolted upwards and fully alert, knowing there was much for Talia and I to do today and our scheduled shuttle pick-up for the Yuletide Resort and Toby's concert was five pm sharp. I parted the drapes to let the overcast sun shine in through the window, opened the front door, stepped outside for a cigarette. Remnants of snow fell from the trees like droplets of weary rain which the cold breeze picked up and splashed lightly against my face like one of those water spritzers with a fan at the nozzle you can buy at the state fair and wear on a string around your neck. I tossed my cig by way of the fire pit and withdrew inside, suddenly worried over Talia. Frankly, I wasn't even sure she'd returned, if she was alive, or of what had happened last night.

But I found her fast asleep beneath the covers of the bedroom bed, nude, partially wet as if she'd showered, a Santa Claus hat upon my pillow like complimentary hotel mint candy beside her. I went to her, attempted to wake her. I shouldn't have done that, for when she aroused from slumber, I had all hell to pay. She opened her eyes, immediately screamed at me something incoherent and fierce, and I begged her to come to her senses, for we had plans to drive out to the nearby town for thrift store shopping, to see a local Christmas parade, to be sober and eventually ready ourselves for the shuttle bus that would deliver us to the festivities of the main event at Yuletide Resort, to Toby, to fun times awaiting.

Regardless of my efforts, she would not remove herself from the bed, not make an ounce of effort to rise and say hello to the good times in store. An hour, two hours passed. Talia

13

Nicholas Grabowsky

still in bed, I gave up and went out to the end of the dock, smoked some herb. It made me feel better, brought to me a much-needed calm, just like back home. I thought about our son, what he was doing with the relatives, thought about a lot of things, foremostly a weekend of potential bliss being ruined before my eyes due to her goddamn drinking. Come four-thirty that afternoon, I stood alone at the paved road outside Yuletide Cabins waiting for the shuttle to take me, without Talia, to the concert, chain smoking, cussing under my breath.

God knew I'd be damned if I was going to miss the concert because she wanted to keep sleeping, and I'd be doubly goddamned if she was going to ruin my Christmas.

Maybe, just maybe, I was goddamned already. *She* sure as shit was, as far as I was concerned.

***

The concert was *incredible*, hands-downs, feet down, after I'd been feeling so *very* down myself.

Outside amphitheater, scores upon scores of happy holiday people all juiced up on watered-down high- priced beer they had to wait and wait and wait in long lines for, cowboy hats of diehard country music fans a-wavin' and good old southern rock bands opening to boot. I bought a t-shirt for twenty-five bucks and writhed into it, the bland generic Walmart-bought plain black one I wore on my way there slung over my shoulder, jalapeno nachos oozing with cheese in my hand and a cigarette in the other, a whiskey-Coke at my beckoned call in the cup holder in front of me. I was fifteen rows in, off to the side, and, standing with everyone else, the view was perfect for me. Toby came out in a blaze of glory, just after a movie screen the size of the stage presented a short film presenting him as a kick-ass super hero in a Ford truck dropped to the stage floor and fireworks spewed over the crowd. Song after rockin' song, the entire time, I couldn't help but glance my eyes into the direction of the empty seat beside me, and I found myself wondering what Talia was doing, if she'd fully awaked to find me gone, regretting for her the full-on spectacle she was missing. I tried not to think about that, convinced myself that I was having a good time, regardless, and I was.

14

I *was.*

Hell, I figured, *she knew where to find me.*

A plethora of Christmas numbers highlighted the show, and the promised firework extravaganza lit the sky with all the brilliant *'tis-the-season* kind of colors which decorated our tree at home. The concert's end was brought to all of us courtesy of the red white and blue, as Toby's grand patriotic anthem went in stylish encore, and soon afterwards I found myself shuffling towards the exits with everyone else, wanting more, but unlike most wanting my girl at my side with me as I left.

Concert over, feeling mighty lonely but tremendously inspired and full of Christmas spirit, I found my way down an endless sloping walkway towards the towering cluster of hotel rooms to the Yuletide Resort's famous restaurant and bar.

I shuffled inside with the crowd, made my way down the lengthy inner hallway past the front desk and the multitude of autographed mug shots of the countless bands and recording artists that had previously graced the Yuletide stages over the course of many years. I made my way patiently through the throng of shoulder-to-shoulder partiers, got my of-drinking-age glow-in-the-dark wristband at the door of the main bar, passed the two inner bars and writhing dance floor and onstage country rock band until I found my way outside again to a vast patio overlooking Spark Lake.

I desperately required a drink, and found myself waiting in a line so long a young girl offered me twenty dollars just to cut in front of me, and I let her. With that twenty, I purchased three well whiskey-Cokes and a double shot of Jack all at once, so I wouldn't have to soon wait again for more and could relax for awhile with no worries, no worries about booze, at any rate. Drinks in hand, I made my way down the very lengthy patio until I reached the end, just past an entrance to the swimming pool area guarded by two of the many bouncer-sized attendants to where I spied an empty table booth and bee-lined for it. With this crowd, I couldn't believe I scored an entire table all to myself, and I immediately sat down with my handful of intoxicating concoctions, proceeded to chain smoke and indulge in sip after slurp after gulp of the amber liquid courtesy of the desperate line-cutter. I sat there, watching the crowd, the people standing and smoking and drinking in clusters and the ones seated and conversing at the bar stools along the lengthy perimeter of the patio overlooking the water, mumbling to myself often aloud about my woes with Talia and regretting how I couldn't share my Saturday night experience with her like the rest of the couples here, but nevertheless relishing the experience I had thus far by myself, nodding to passers by and wishing them a heartfelt merry Christmas.

Looking out into the crowd, I began to notice tiny white flakes falling from the blackness of the sky, sprinkling the air, settling upon my table.

I extended one finger onto one of them that rested there beside my third full glass of whiskey, pressed against it, brought it before my eyes, to my tongue, tasted it. It was like snow, yet there was more substance to it, like flour sifting from the heavens.

And in the air also, my ears in the next instant became privy to the sounds of distant screams. They seemed to originate from within the restaurant's bar where the house band played, and then their music silenced, the screams grew louder, and as I stretched from my seat for a better view past the outside crowd towards the rear bar exit, a swarm of people issued forth from inside. They spilled onto the outer deck, collapsing against others and falling, the ones behind them in equal desperation to flee stampeding over them and tumbling face-first into others as well. The congested ocean of drunken humanity the outside crowd presented imposed a barrier against any escape from whatever terrified them so, and as quickly as all eyes upon the deck swung in their direction, the entire mass of everyone standing began to founder and buckle over backwards as from the force of an explosion, like they'd all congregated upon one gigantic carpet that was suddenly wrenched out from under them. I remained where I was in the midst of the pandemonium about me, my attention focusing on the exit from where the panic ensued. My experience of the night prior rapidly resurfaced to the forefront of memories, like the sudden recollection of a recent and profoundly disturbing dream. I dreaded what I would at any moment witness emerging from that exit, braced myself for a vision of the thing responsible for this mayhem, my girlfriend, the mother of my son, the collector of hearts and perpetrator of enough unspeakable carnage to devastate a thousand Christmases.

And she indeed presented herself from out of that exit, grasping with all fours the sides of the doorway just below the dangling mistletoe, snout stretching into the air and blowing forth tremendous amounts of the very same intoxicating pollen-like snowflake substance which seduced my awareness into suppressed memory before, blanketing the crowd before her. Her head tilted, swayed side to side and up and down until its glossy reflective gaze centered in on me, singled me out. It leapt into the air, and along the way of its approach towards me, the body-length forks of its claws randomly pierced clear through the upper torsos of the victims which it fell upon in no more an effort to keep itself upright than to simply kill, its grasshopper-like hind legs landing shoulder upon shoulder before taking off again to eventually plant itself right on top of my table.

It curved its snout downwards like a mosquito's proboscis, leaned into me, the fun-house mirrored duality of my reflection in her saucer-shaped glass-like eyes ironically reflecting the very duality of her identity into my own, for I knew who she was, and likewise she knew me. I maintained my composure, lifted the only remaining portion of drink to my lips that she hadn't already spilled, and, before I could say one word, she proceeded to tell me off rather heatedly for abandoning her at the cabin and seeing the concert without her, for leaving her all alone. She griped and bitched about everything concerning that, leaving me with no room to explain myself or to calm her, and before I knew anything else, she'd already pinned her weight against my body, driven the tips of those long-ass talons of hers into my abdomen, up and into my rib cage, extracted my heart and set it upon the table before me.

And I remained alive, felt no pain, saw very little blood in result, the cavity Talia'd made in my chest closing up over itself.

She exclaimed that I was to finally be just like her, and that I had no choice in the matter, that it was my destiny to know

17

the world as she knew it, and that perhaps by seeing things as she did I would understand. She implored me to leave this place, to meet her later that night at the dock for as long as it took to wait, and, before she retreated and disappeared over the side of the dock and into the waters of Spark Lake below, she charged me with making sure I take care of that ol' heart of mine, keep it close, or the Christmas magic she bestowed upon me just wouldn't work. I had no problem with that. Mostly.

I arose almost immediately, collected my still- beating heart and pack of smokes, made my way very nervously past the countless mass of snow-covered survivors which only then began to stagger languidly to their feet, suddenly unaffected by the onslaught, the way Jake and Elwood Blues would arise from below the cinderblocks of calamity's aftermath, wipe themselves clean and with a shrug continue with their lives. As I went, I overheard people requesting buckets and mops and hefty bags from one another, some already gathering body parts and dragging away those deceased. It wasn't exactly a brief sojourn reaching Yuletide Ranch & Cabins on foot, but, with determination and patience, I did. And at the dock, I waited for Talia to meet me. I waited there for forever, past the next day, the next night, and it was just like a woman to cause me to do so.

***

"Hey buddy."

A baritone voice with a slight southern drawl which to my ears resembled that of the groundskeeper who Friday afternoon had presented our cabin keys spooked me nearly out of my chaise lounge chair, and I immediately turned, careful to pull the Santa cap fully over my heart seated beside me. The groundskeeper man stood in shadow just far enough to maintain polite distance, and I had the feeling he'd come upon me wanting to be alone just as I did, didn't expect anyone to be there besides himself.

"I'm sorry," he continued, "it seems everyone wants to spend a moment in time alone before the Christmas sunrise. I've had a hell of a weekend, in a bad way it turns out, and I don't know why. Have a merry one."

"What do you know about women?" I blurted out, surprising even myself.

He hesitated. Then, "Well son, and this doesn't account for all of them, but some can just rip your heart right out from you. When a woman steals your heart, and gives it back to you, she's yours. And you have to deal with the good *and* the bad, for the rest of your life, and love her, understand her, against all odds. That's what commitment is all about. If she *doesn't* give your heart back to you, she'll save it for Christmas dinner man, I'm telling you. Hope it all works out."

He paused briefly to let me consider, and I did, before a thank-you from my lips would hopefully send him on his way to leave me in peace in the event Talia showed up with him there and had groundskeeper heart for breakfast.

He then left me alone to my thoughts and weary anticipations, but not before imparting words: "Enjoy your Christmas. And thanks for showing up at my concert, man. Means a helluva lot to me...."

Almost as soon as he ventured off, Talia *did* arrive, finally, in human form, sauntering up the dock to meet me as if nothing over the weekend had happened at all, and she took up my heart and surrendered it back to me. I was healed, and somehow, for the very first time, I understood that thing which swelled within her, her frustrations, her shortcomings, her tendencies to lash out at the world or to escape from it, especially at this time of year.

And I loved her.

And later that day, we shared a Christmas with her family like no other, without incident, us and Anthony, except to say that rather than the turkey dinner I expected, we all of us gorged ourselves upon a bounty of human hearts.

Nicholas Grabowsky

THE FREEWAY
REAPER

Suicide was the word of the day.

You'd think, on Valentine's Day of all days, the word would be.....well, it wouldn't be *suicide*. It would be *love* or *sex* or *money*, *flowers* or *chocolates*, or something along those lines. But for many people on this particular day, and *especially* for Jason Heigh, all of those things summed up together would *equal* the one word of *suicide*.

What a multi-faceted word, looking at it that way.

Jay had contemplated suicide to a degree where loved ones should be concerned in the months leading up to actually stepping up to the plate, but he never thought he'd go through with it. Really, he never even planned it, not even this time. It was a spur-of-the- moment kind of thing when it happened, when Jay decided *awe, fuck it* in a flurry of frustration, stepped out of his bucket of bolts AMC Gremlin in the afternoon rush hour bumper-to-bumper traffic of the eastbound I80 business loop in California's capitol city, just before the "P" Street off ramp, and spilled himself over the overpass railing, feet first, back against the wind.

If the resulting aftermath of his rapid decent into self-imposed doom occurred only a moment sooner or even later, he would have missed the windshield of the red Ford Aspire crossing the intersection way above the posted speed limit below completely, and Jay would have been less colorful in announcing to everyone what exactly the word of the day was.

Brenda Coubri had willed a lead foot into saving her and her highly-functional autistic seven-year-old son through a yellow-turning-red light and from the sedan that had been riding her ass since 12th Street. Both her and whoever was behind the sedan's wheel were in a hurry, for reasons no more or less

20

important than Jay's in trying to get somewhere fast, relatively speaking.

Only difference was, *they* were succeeding.

Partially because they didn't have to take the congested fucking freeway.

***

Let's revert to several months ago when Jay, an average 38-year-old poverty-stricken under-achieving bachelor, was regularly frequenting a local sports bar to suck up like a rubber water squeeze toy puffer fish all the intoxicating atmosphere any down-the-street pool hall dive such as what the Mississippi Moonshine Meat & Magic Company had to offer when you had a good twenty spot to spend and the guarantee that at least one or two acquaintances would be there to assist you in shmoozing for free drinks after that spot was spent.

For Jay, one of those acquaintances was Ray Man, Raymond Avery, a dude he'd brushed cordial shoulders with time to time but never knew outside of bar exploits away from the home he shared with Jay Heigh Senior and Gilda, his aging parents.

Jay dreaded how his lackluster life had led thus far to living again with his folks, and the pub had proven to be a blessed refuge between work and home, a sanctuary after work so he wouldn't have to *go* home just yet, and could take his time being there without Mom and Dad telling him how constantly disappointed they were with how he handled his life. Retail job after retail job and odd job after another in a successive line since high school graduation unleashed him into a life of not knowing what to do with himself other than living.

If there was anyone else Jay knew who in recent times was even less than half the man he himself was, it was Ray Man. Ray Man was a locally infamous belligerent alcoholic, a barfly in triplicate, married times six, thrown out of Mississippi Moonshine six times and wouldn't have kept showing up if the bar's ownership hadn't morphed throughout six months into so many different faces.

There's three sixes in that.

To some, Ray Man *was* the Devil. He always boasted with Jay about this bitch he raped, or that dude he pulverized to the point of death for laughing at how he resembled a body-building Carrot Top caricature whose buffered muscles languished in recent times like deflating balloons, or how he busted into an office building and stole computer equipment he didn't know how to use or sell, how he decapitated his cousin's poodle with an axe and threw it into a bonfire as an offering to Beelzebub.

For Jay, Ray Man had simply provided company and conversation, and if you would have asked Jay, he would have told you Ray Man was always talking out of his asshole.

Jay happened to have been socializing one-on-one with Ray Man in the rear outside patio of the pub one particular evening when a cavalcade of shit-faced individuals oozed out of the back doorway in an *I'm gonna size-you-up-then-fuck-you-up* stride, circling them, separated Ray Man into a corner, and proceeded to pound and kick and beat the ever-loving living shit out of him.

Poor Jay didn't know what to do. He stood, watching, witnessing the onslaught, figuring the bastard had a bad ass whooping coming his way, what with all Ray's mouthing off and wayward reputation and whatever else the dude had gotten himself into. Thing was, whatever it was, Jay had no business in his right mind playing any part in the situation other than the role of helpless spectator.

In the instance following the band of assailants casually escaping the premises without further drama, just before the police and ambulance arrived and Jay abandoned the bleeding broken body of the Ray Man because he knew full well that cops plus driving home from bars equals trouble, Jay Heigh decided it was time to skid addle promptly.

And he did, but not before Ray Man had a chance to call out to him, lay upon him a curse from one brother to a self-proclaimed other that he'll not readily forget what happened that night as he coughed up blood and lamented over the woes of a bar buddy's refusal to come to his aide when he needed him most.

Ray Man made good on his curse.

After a couple weeks of state-funded healing and with a bottle full of good prescription drugs and locally brewed meth in his veins and cocaine in his lungs, he got to asking around just where Jay resided and paid him a visit as a midnight prowler who left behind forensic signs of his presence everywhere and the bodies of Gilda and Heigh Senior sprawled atop their sleep number bed with their abdomens slit as wide open as cheap kitchen waste basket bags overfilled with nastiness that burst out the bottom when you lifted them.

The night that happened, Jay had been awake all along, beneath the quilts of his bed in his own room, filling his mouth with Wavy Lays potato chips and watching Yoda kick Sith ass on Encore. Ray Man had known Jay was home at the time of his nocturnal visit, his finger prints and an outline of his right ear upon Jay's bedroom door was later discovered by detectives dusting and waving print-revealing lights around in the dark.

In deciding to spare Jay's own life, Ray had thought it a good idea to rather kick Jay's loss of loved ones up a notch by paying a visit to the home of his most recent ex-girlfriend, Lisa Dove, whose address he was privy to simply by sifting through handwritten notes beside the telephone answering machine at the counter in Jay's folk's kitchen with a flashlight. And how many times at Mississippi Moonshine did Jay lament over Lisa? Lisa seemed pretty goddamn important. And she wasn't very far away.

Turned out she'd been living with her parents, too, but had recently moved out on her own to a studio pad somewhere downtown. By his hands, her folks were history.

It was all over the news the day following.

It became *national* news when Ray decided, in the proceeding days and weeks, to randomly invade susceptible homes in the middle of the night and slit a number of bellies open in slumber, family pets included, even children, just for the thrill of it, because he liked it so much the first time around.

Twenty-six victims in all.

***

And now, a word about freeways.

And angels.

Firstly, freeways suck serious ass when you're in your vehicle and cruising down one, trying to get somewhere in a hurry when traffic slows so suddenly that you pray to dear Jesus the driver behind you is paying utmost attention to your brake lights and abrupt determination to come to a halt. Legally speaking, it's his fault if he rear-ends you, but it doesn't matter if you're dead as a result. At least, not to you. Because you're dead.

And traffic slows to a languid bumper-to-bumper crawl on freeways, where you sit and sit for minutes at a time before you push out just a little more gas to move up a meter and then sit again, particularly during rush hour, for a variety of reasons. Could be due to merging traffic. Could be an accident. A stalled vehicle. A stray dog or naked homeless person streaking across the lanes. Anything.

But then there are times when traffic just stops and then inches along for apparently no reason, where you're stuck for a time long enough to pull your hair out by its roots or give in to road rage, and then when everyone starts to pick up speed and you get the feeling it's all smooth sailing from there you look around and find absolutely no signs of there ever having been a reason for traffic to have slowed down at all. You find yourself wondering about it for a minute, scratching your head about it, and then you place it in the back of your mind because you're happy that you've got yourself cruising along again and your thoughts have returned to where you're going and your business at hand.

Well.....

***

Suicide was indeed *not* supposed to be the word of the day for the angel Devilosa, as she placed herself dead center of bust-a-gut rush hour east-bound traffic of the Interstate 80 business loop in California's capitol city, just before the "P" Street offramp.

She'd been doing this sort of thing for under a year now, throughout numerous major U.S. cities, on an average of four times a year, standing out in the middle of traffic with a predetermined agenda and an utter absence of fear.

No one could see her, no one could hurt her.

She was a working girl, good enough at doing her job to avoid such mishap as being seen.

Devilosa belonged to an order of angelic beings whose existence was denied by both God and Satan, except in metaphors, kind of like a secretive branch of the most secretive branch of any organization ever established.

These very lower-class angels slept, most of the time, and after a few months of slumber they would suddenly find themselves awaked into action like from an irritating alarm clock noise, don their wings, and fly to retrieve a soul to bring up to heaven early, or to hell, however the case may be. They'd been at it since the first of these angels took up the biblical Enoch who, according to scripture, never saw death because God liked the dude so much He thought He'd take him early, *as is.* Another example was Judas Iscariot, whose unscheduled suicide caused the angel who came to take him to hell without dying to forfeit her wings for several hundred years as a penalty.

In society, a person on occasion sometimes simply *disappears.* You hear about one or two of these instances whenever the media chooses to sensationalize this report or that, but after awhile the cameras rush to the next big news event when the prior disappearance story runs dry. An x-number of those become completely forgotten when they disappear, aren't very much missed at all because there are very few of their loved ones left in the world to miss them or give a rat's ass. They become sixty seconds of air time, a single blip on a radar, a dead end in a dark alley where there once was a door.

They are those chosen few for whom God says *enough already, they're better off with ME. Take 'em,* and as for taking a soul to hell, Satan says the same thing.

And what better way to take 'em than from out of rush hour traffic, enroute between points A and B, when everyone around them is anxious and pissed off and distracted.

Freeways, and freeways only, proved the optimal landscape upon where to get this kind of business done successfully, extracting a worthy soul from society to be at heaven with the Lord at an early time. And it always meant plucking their vehicle and every trace of their presence up along with them, and to administer déjà vu to all those around....

***

Devilosa landed her bare angel feet upon the concrete of Business I-80 just short of "P" Street in Sacramento, naked yet invisible to the naked eye. Skin-pale wings the span of five meters at both her sides folded tightly against her back the way the *Mimic* roaches did when they wanted to look human. Not that it mattered.

25

She raised her right hand against the oncoming traffic and it slowed to her will.

She was looking for Jay Heigh, trying to single him out amongst the onrush of vehicles like a celestial *Price is Right* announcer, for Jay to come on *up* rather than *come on down*.

By her power, traffic slowed for no coherent reason among everyone else who knew no better, and a multitude of drivers were plenty peeved, wondering what the hold-up was.

***

Jay was pressed for time, running late so far over fifty minutes from the time he'd promised Lisa Dove he'd arrive at her apartment's front doorstep downtown.

No matter that Lisa was his *ex*; no matter that her *being* his ex was *his* fault.

On *this* Valentine's Day, they needed each other. Both their parents had been murdered by Ray Man, and through the course of time since that happened, they'd grown closer to each other.

Jay was well-equipped for the occasion, a dozen roses, a heart-shaped box of Bach's chocolate candies, dancing plush animatronic rooster singing *You Sexy Thang* when you depressed its right feather with your thumb and forefinger, except that he was running so low on fuel he was obsessively sweating out a gas gauge with the letter E glowing like a Sesame Street demon administering that particular letter of the alphabet straight from running-out-of-gas-on-the-freeway hell.

Devilosa was ready for him. Ready, with her right hand outstretched.

And then, with no warning, the fucker just.......just up and abandoned his vehicle and threw himself over the railing, as soon as she spotted him coming up in the fast lane and made his AMC Gremlin disappear, when he was supposed to have remained *inside* his car as she took him up t'ward heaven......

Suicide became the word of the day for her, too, after he did that.

And, just like the motorists on the freeway, she was plenty pissed off as well.

And so was the Good Lord.

***

26

When the combination of gravity plus Jay's sudden willingness to end it all resulted in a collision with Brenda Coubri's windshield, what happened next was as follows:

Brenda slams on the breaks of her red Ford Aspire with such an impulsive instinct that her foot would've responded the same way severed. The car doesn't swerve. Jay's body plummets into and through the glass, collapsing onto the hard plastic dashboard, shards of various sizes from the pulverized windshield projectile- vomit deep into Brenda's left eye and neck and instantly kill her.

Jay's body lands in such a way that his arms, through the broken glass, almost embrace her.

Her autistic son seat-belted otherwise safely in the front passenger seat slips down beneath his restraint and cowers into a ball in the crevice of foot room still available below the glove compartment. The collision with the falling object leaves him with no physical injuries, but seriously fucks up his world in so many other ways, and he wets himself.

The driver riding her ass since 12th Street has no time for breaks and collides into her rear, and the impact sends his body flying forwards through his own windshield, straight into and through Brenda's rear hatchback glass, his body thrown so far forwards that he arrives with his head an inch and a half away from Brenda's car's stereo and resting over the parking break in between the two front seats.

Concerned witnesses rush from the corner gas station, flood out of the Burger King, pedestrians inching cautiously nearer the wreckage. Motorists on the freeway above abandon *their* cars to gaze down over the railing, which further impedes traffic flow and pisses off many more commuters. Unnoticed by all, Devilosa casts her gaze down along with them. She almost weeps, but finds herself nearly as jolted as the autistic boy and unable to cry just yet from the sheer shock of it all.

This wasn't supposed to happen, she said to herself aloud, knowing no one would hear her. *I was supposed to whisk him away, car and all, like I always do when I'm summoned by the Higher Power to do so, easy as pie. No one told me he was going to all of a sudden up and get out of his car the very second before I pulled a Chris Angel on his ass. Now, after I made everything about him on the road*

27

today vanish, my powers missed the man himself. Cops are going to be scratching their heads over this one, and I'm wondering if the Almighty's going to treat this situation as if it was my *fault........*

The air was filled with the sounds of the sirens of emergency vehicles nearing.

And with something else only the angel could hear. A stirring of life within the wreckage.

Devilosa was stricken with the feeling that some form of the magic she'd invoked to steal away all traces of Jay there on the freeway hitched a ride with his soul and followed him to his doom.

Something was all amiss down there, and it went beyond what mortal men could see.

But then Devilosa was called back into her place of slumber in a brilliant flash of light that most people *did* notice but weren't much paying attention to, at the same moment Lisa Dove awoke in her apartment to an alarm clock announcing that it was time to get herself ready for Jay's Valentine's Day arrival.

She thanked God Jay was running late, because, well.....so was *she*......

***

Jay was conscious, but wasn't where he was supposed to be.

Wasn't *who* he was supposed to be either, for that matter.

He found himself inside Brenda's Aspire, face-down between the two front seats atop the parking brake and inches away from the stereo.

Lifting himself slightly and turning his head upwards to his left, he caught sight of a man wrapping his arms around a woman drenched in blood, his body sprawled across the opposite side of a bed of windshield shattered all to hell but largely sticking together, save for the gaping hole that spilled him on top of the woman. The woman was dead, the man was still alive and screaming, screaming at the top of his lungs the words *mommy mommy mommy* over and over again in ceaseless lament.

Turning to his right, a small boy emerged from beneath the dashboard in slow deliberation, his eyes never leaving Jay's, his mouth forming a widened "O" shape until his lips came together and released an outpouring of profanities as his left hand fumbled for the passenger door handle and found it. The door swung open. Jay struggled after him, no more to follow him than to get away from the vehicle and assess the situation from a distance, wait for the cops to hand him over to some mental institution's custody.

After a prolonged hospitalization, at least, because he *hurt like hell*.....

But as he crawled out and away, he was struck with the realization that the man weeping for *Mommy* through the broken glass was in fact *he*, clear as day, and that *his* soul, *Jay's* soul, was trapped within the body of the guy from the sedan, and that the soul of the *boy* was trapped in *his* own broken body.

Did that mean the soul of the man from the sedan was in the little boy?

The boy sprinted for the sedan the moment he freed himself from the wreckage, popped the sedan's trunk open with a determined kick and gathered into his arms a loaded AK-47, proceeded to fire it into the air, dispersing the accumulating crowd of onlookers and those looking to help. The sirens drew nearer, like some street skateboarder'd been perching a ghetto blaster atop his shoulders blaring out the very sounds sirens make, and emergency crews really weren't coming at all given how long they were taking to arrive.

The weapon-toting kindergartener made a fervent dash for a vacant lot beside the gas station consumed by tall yellow grass and Jay immediately followed suit, limping but managing nevertheless to walk upright, calling out after him, *"You son of a bitch, all our souls swapped bodies back there, and I've got yours! Get back here! All I wanted to do was* die, *goddammit........!"*

"Stay the fuck away from me!" the boy would occasionally spin around and yell out to him as if Jay was his own personal Ghost of Christmas Past, but he never fired his weapon towards him, just into the air, and when his ammo was spent he tossed the gun aside, scaled a wooden fence and disappeared into a residential district.

Jay was all too eager to run him down, and when he did, it took no time at all for him to wrestle him out of sight, pin him against a grassy stretch of somebody's side yard between

29

two rows of junipers for a quick discussion regarding just what the hell was going on.

***

Band on the Run by *Wings* was playing out Ray Man's illegally-acquired emerald green '87 Honda Accord's stereo system when it was cut off by a commercial for *Yours Card* from Providential Savings & Loan:

"KAFS Sacramento Daily Ten-in-a-row Nonstop Yesteryear Hits sponsored by *YOURS CARD. YOURS CARD. YOURS CARD* for living, *YOURS CARD* for life."

The commercial usually amused him into a chuckle because he knew what it sounded like, but he'd just figured out that the song he'd been listening to said "*Band* on the Run" and not "*Man* on the Run," because that's what the DJ said before the song had begun, and he for decades called himself a *man on the run* because of that song.

Damn how things never turn out to be what you thought they were.

He was a man on the run regardless, and a rather infamous one lately. He knew he was prison-bound since the night he decided to release the bowels of those Jay held dear and then some, had resigned himself to the fact that after the first life was taken, his days were numbered

.....and it would only be a matter of time before the law found him.

Once in custody, the system would swallow him up for the rest of his earthbound days.

So, he'd figured, *why not have fun with it, suck the marrow from the bone of freedom for all it's worth? Create more death?*

......and, as a consequence, be subjected afterwards to ceaseless cable news interviews and women pen pals until in years to come he'd escape the death penalty via one amended state law or another and ultimately die contented that the vengeful misery which compelled him to kill in the first place was heard around the world?

It was a sweet deal, the way Ray understood it.

All he needed was time, more time, and keeping himself hidden within city limits seemed to be a good idea so far, as long as he was "tricky like a Ninja," as a crank dealer he'd been staying with downtown kept telling him, and as long as the law

30

was looking outside Sacramento County because people who didn't know what they were talking about were reporting sightings of him that far away.

But today he hotwired this Honda Accord, needed money so desperately he'd just done a *stop 'n rob* (held up a convenience store), and his quick left-turn dash into an alley down 12th Street was impeded by a large flow of unforgiving traffic. His instinct was to follow the tail of a red Ford Aspire in a lane that was moving along faster than most.

The Aspire then sped through the yellow light of an intersection, and Ray wasn't about to let a red light stop him. He was obsessed with locating an opportunity to inconspicuously abandon the Honda, slip away down some narrow alley and quickly, escape with his loot and his stash of weapons accumulated inside the trunk in the event of a police show-down Old-Western-style. He planned on transferring his belongings into another vehicle luck would have him steal, because he was very good at breaking into cars almost as well as he was with killing people.

From that point, he'd haul his ass to his sister's in Del Paso Heights where he'd likely find months of Ann Frank-esque sanctuary, screw some crank whore who'd be happy to see him and who regularly took refuge there herself, and partake in some very good fuzzy purple rare Hawaiian home grown herb the entire time of his stay.

But when the word of the day became *suicide*, it affected even *Ray Man's* Valentine's plans, as his body burst from out of his hotwired Honda's windshield upon a very tumultuous impact with the rear of the Aspire.

The next thing he knew, he was beneath the dashboard of the Aspire, gazing upon a blood-soaked caricature of himself who returned his gaze from between the front seats. The son-of-a-bitch looked just like *himself*. And he.....he himself was so damn *small*, looking up at him....

He was freaked out, to say the least, but still he was a *man on the run*, regardless what the words the *Wings* song truly said, and he had to keep moving, however way he could

***

The two separated themselves and simply stared at each other between the two rows of junipers, upon their backs at first

31

in an attempt to catch their breaths, then they both managed to sit upright and scoot against the hedges opposite one another in silence.

People were searching for them, and neither wanted to be found just yet, so each thought it best at the moment to keep quiet and contemplate.

Ray Man found himself trapped within a terrible damnable plight, an almost incomprehensible identity crisis, unable to understand clearly *where* he was or even *who* he was. The man he'd known himself to be, at least in strikingly similar appearance, had chased him down, was now staring back at him, covered in blood from a deep crevice gaping down one side of his temple. And Ray himself was a boy, a little boy, in little boys' shoes and pants and little boys' racing car t-shirt with tiny white hands coming out the sleeves of a thin gray windbreaker jacket sporting a series of blue racing stripes from shoulder to wrist.

That was all *Ray* knew, aside from the series of events which got him into that outrageous predicament.

Jay had the advantage, as far as with knowledge of the situation.

He knew he *caused* the situation, for one thing, by up and taking his own life the way he did. The clearly apparent shuffling of souls and bodies within the Aspire he landed upon was likely a heavenly-ordained consequence, he figured, of his choosing to die. Throughout his years, he'd always been religiously *persuaded* but never truly religious. And also, people had told him that *karma was a bitch* long enough that he'd believed for some time that karma *really was a bitch.* Maybe he *was* dead, and this was all a test, karma being a bitch to him to see what he was made of before it was decided whether he should go to heaven or hell from there.

He just committed the unpardonable sin, that's what it was, and God decided to fuck everything up for him to see what he'll do afterwards with the circumstances now set before him.

Jay had no clue whose body it was he inhabited, or whose soul inhabited the boy.

If he knew *that*, he'd have failed the test completely, if there *was* such a test, probably would have killed the boy and done the world a favor, then killed himself to release his own soul out of the motherfucker's body regardless of the eternal price to pay.

Jay figured from the boy's machine gun antics that whoever this was, he must've been a bad-assed member of some local gang, some sort of *wanted* man.

While Ray Man remained preoccupied and increasingly overwhelmed with whatever was going on in his mind, Jay was developing a plan.

He knew the soul of the boy was trapped within his own body sprawled atop the Aspire's windshield, and God only knew what was going on with that. The sirens which filled the air just minutes ago had ceased, and Jay was certain authorities were assessing the situation with the fingers of witnesses pointing in the direction of the vacant lot where he and the boy had disappeared.

Jay made a quick, heartfelt decision, then and there.

He lifted himself up, inspected his wounds. His pullover hooded drawstring-at-the-neck sweat top was saturated with blood as if it had been dipped thoroughly in the macabre liquid, and the primary flow seemed to be originating out the side of his head. The pain in his right side up into his rib cage swelled excruciatingly, as did his left thigh and ankle, and he felt within his bowels a near-crippling build-up of gas and diarrhea. With no further hesitation or regards for his pain, Jay took the boy by the arm and, restraining him, wrenched off his striped jacket. He tied one arm of the jacket around his wrist into a knot, tied the other arm of the jacket around the neck and shoulder and armpit of the boy into a sling so tight that the kid virtually clung to his wrist, writhing and struggling and calling him a motherfucker throughout the whole ordeal.

"Sorry kid, or whoever you are," Jay repeatedly told him in varying versions of apology, "but I have to see somebody today, if it's the last thing I do, and for the sake of the possibility of saving this boy you're trapped within, and for the sake of my own soul, you'll have to come with me. We'll sort *us* out later. Today's Valentine's Day. I need to see Lisa "

Lisa Dove's apartment, conveniently enough, was only a block and a half away.

All Jay had to do was get there, out where everyone could see his bloody self limping along through the neighborhood like a *Die Hard* movie survivor before the end credits, hauling a struggling kid tied to his wrist with a jacket.

33

***

By the time the doorbell rang at Lisa Dove's apartment, Lisa had had enough time to ready herself for her date. He was more than an hour late, and for that she was pissed off, but she'd awoken out of the strangest dream and was in dire need of preparing herself for him, and his lateness gave her ample time to prepare, though until the ring of the doorbell he was so extremely late she was beginning to doubt he'd arrive at all. His flakiness was the dominant reason for her previously breaking up with him in the first place. Prick never even bothered to telephone her, as a courtesy, to apologize for running late.

Maybe he was stuck in traffic.

Maybe something terrible had happened to him.

By the time the doorbell rang at her apartment also, unbeknownst to Lisa, her date's desperate attempt to see her had attracted much attention. In the ten minute's time that it took for Jay in Ray Man's body to haul the boy across the street, between two houses and out onto another street and down the sidewalk the length of a dozen homes and two apartment buildings, the drivers of passing vehicles and pedestrians and housewives peeking out their kitchen windows had already made an accumulative eighteen calls to 911.

No one approached the screaming boy and the man covered in blood whose face was all over the news. Jay was aware of the scene his presence was causing, but he boldly ignored it and pressed onwards towards his goal. He even had time enough to stop beside somebody's flower garden to snap off some roses and daisies and carnations from their stems to accommodate for the gifts he'd left behind in his Gremlin on the freeway.

Lisa Dove was so certain that it was Jay ringing the doorbell that she didn't bother to check the peephole before she opened the door. She had no idea that cops had already sectioned off the street, nor heard the sounds of helicopters whipping through the air above her apartment complex, not even as she answered.

There, before her, smiling and presenting her with flowers, was.....

.....well............

She tried to close the door immediately, but Jay in Ray's body asserted himself before she could do so and stepped inside, hauling the boy in with him.

Lisa turned and ran for her very life's sake.

Ray Man had ceased trying to break free from out of his jacket restraints. After he caught sight of Lisa, and recognized who she was, he allowed himself to go limp and let his out-of-body-experience drag him along through the apartment landscape in pursuit of the girl without further protest. He might have been borderline-stupid-slow where mental faculties were concerned, but he'd gotten away with murder more than a dozen times over, constantly though successfully seeking refuge from incarceration, and, actually, the possible benefits of being trapped within the physical husk of a little boy started to appeal to Ray moreso than even hiding out at his sister's house in Del Paso Heights.

Jay called out to his date as she ran from him, as he pursued her, letting go of the flowers he'd picked for her and trampling over them.

"Lisa! Lisa, listen! It's *Jay*! Something terrible has happened, and no matter what I look like, it's *me*, honey, and let me *explain*.... ..."

Voices through megaphones called out from beyond the opened door. Neither of the three paid any attention, nor to the ringing telephone. They were busy at the moment.

The boy was a rag doll against Jay's assertive strength. Jay went for Lisa, grabbed her by the shoulders, pulled her down against the carpet of her livingroom, turned her body around, forced her to face him eye-to-eye. The boy flailed about, restrained increasingly tighter around Jay's wrist like a boy-sized wristwatch that couldn't possibly at this point tell the time of day from his own asshole.

Lisa clawed and kicked and grabbed hold of an eye socket and pushed her thumb right through, like pushing gelatin out of a shot glass, and her assailant screamed.

And then he began tearing at her.

In the room with them, images from the television set jumped from a series of current news clips depicting freeway chaos that Lisa hadn't been paying attention to, to a portion of the movie where Mickey Rourke puts Robert DeNiro's character of Louis Cypher and the name Lucifer together as being one and the same.

It was Devilosa's favorite part of *any* film.

During the livingroom struggle, Jay caught sight of his own image within a mirror the shape of a decorative crossword puzzle scaling down the livingroom wall. Upon the mortifying recognition that it was Ray Man himself who from the square tile reflection returned his gaze, minus one eye, Jay lost control of his faculties altogether and inadvertently whacked Lisa's head against the wall something fierce. Lisa's head hit the surface hard.

Knocked her out cold.

***

A soprano female voice called out directly to Jay from within the room, a surreal sort of *hey you* that wasn't expected at all and which was almost *sung* as it was spoken with the kind of off-the-tongue vibrato that cute bashful preteen girls would utter while batting their eyebrows at attractive boys, and it clearly didn't come from the boy he'd dragged through the door with him or from the megaphone voices outside.

"Jay. Jay Heigh. See me now."

An intense light engulfed the room suddenly, and, within the light, turning himself to face its source, Jay *saw*. One look upon the being was all it too for Jay, in disbelief, to return his gaze upon Lisa, pinned below him unconscious. He then reverted his gaze to the completely nude version of Lisa perched upon the antique oak arm of the velvety red sofa, fleshy newborn-mouse-pinkish wings coming out the small of her back and spreading as wide as the diagonal width of the room. The sight of her was both horrifying, perplexing, and utterly beautiful.

Ray Man remained quite conscious, himself beholding the vision of the spirit angel, blinking and speaking not a word, the body he inhabited as paralyzed as a UFO abductee in the process of being violated, as a deer in headlights.

"I suppose you have the answers to all this," said Jay to the entity. As overwhelming as her presence was, he'd already been through enough to readily accept the fact that she was there, but he couldn't get past h o w

36

"I may resemble the one you love, but I only exist when she sleeps," spoke the entity to him. "Most of the time, I sleep along *with* her, because I *am* her, even when she's awake. I'm the other side of the face upon the silver dollar of her existence, and she's unaware of me. Nor will she ever *be* aware, until she dies and we become one again, like the Mystics and the Skeksis did in the finale of *The Dark Crystal*. Now *that* was a damn good film."

"Who the hell are you?" Jay asked.

Devilosa rolled her eyes.

She never had to explain herself before, let alone reveal herself to any one single being but God or Satan. She'd be nervous if it wasn't for her own impatience with the mounting situation before her. Now that the situation had gotten this far, she thought she'd nip it in the bud while she had the chance. After all, her magic was responsible for the soul displacement event that took place in the Aspire.

"I was supposed to take you up to heaven on God's orders," the angel explained. "But you up and took your own life, and I wasn't told that was going to happen."

"I don't know what came over me," Jay pleaded. "So this *was* a test, wasn't it? None of this is real, just a post-suicide evaluation of whether I'm worthy of heaven?"

"Quite the contrary," Devilosa replied. "You're *already* worthy of heaven. That's why God wanted you in the first place. There's many souls who live earthly lives a thousand times more deserving than you, and yet He chose you, and you bailed. What matters now is what happened *after* you bailed, how you were concerned for the soul of the boy, how you wanted to see the one you loved if it was the last thing you'd do. And you still managed to bring her flowers. What I'm trying to say is I'm obliged to take a soul from this world, but, in light of everything, I'm taking Ray's instead of yours. And you know where *he's* going."

The boy's eyes widened with panic.

"Ultimately," the spirit angel continued, "I get to keep my job and you get to stay here with the one you love, and because *I'm her* you'll always have me with you, however way you assemble the letters of my name, and I'll say hello in your dreams often. You two need each other now, need to support each other, and you'll both awaken in a few moments under very different circumstances. Happy Valentine's Day, and may you and yours have many more happy ones afterwards."

***

Suicide was *still* the word of the day, no doubt about that.

A SWAT team entered Lisa Dove's apartment after firing teargas into it, rescued Lisa and the boy, and found Ray Man's body sprawled across the livingroom carpet, dead due to an extreme loss of blood. Jay Heigh was taken from atop the Aspire's windshield to the UC Davis Medical Center where, as soon as his condition was proclaimed stable, already had a dozen county-employed shrinks and social services stewards scrambling to decide what to do with him.

By the time Lisa came to visit him with an armful of flowers and chocolates and a dancing plush animatronic rooster singing *You Sexy Thang* when you depressed its right feather with your thumb and forefinger, Jay was already a media celebrity.

"Hey, Jay," she'd said to him, her first words upon seeing him, her first words upon always seeing him prior to this, because, given his Christian name, it was always amusing. "I love you."

His suicidal freeway plunge had inadvertently brought eternal justice to a rampaging serial killer, and he lived to tell the tale. The whole world was talking about it. The only thing was, he never remembered a thing about what had happened. All he knew was Lisa, and his yearning to get to her that Valentine's Day. Everything else was just a blur in his memory, almost like dreaming of being someone else after having fallen into a deep sleep.

Although the boy's mother died as a direct result of Jay's actions, the boy, after some intensive care, awoke completely and miraculously free from his autism. After awhile longer, when Jay and Lisa were pronounced bride and groom, they adopted him and established a center for autism research in his mother's name. And they all lived....

....happily.....

....ever....

.......bewildered, as was the rest of the world, as to what the hell exactly happened to Jay Heigh's AMC Gremlin which mysteriously vanished in the middle of bumper-to-bumper traffic on the freeway that day.....

.....and completely oblivious to the fact that sometimes, when there's no apparent reason for traffic to slow, there's likely an angel who's been summoned to stand upon the freeway and single you out, to whisk you away, to your destiny.

LOOKS LIKE a RAT TO ME

I never liked rats much. They scare the bejesus out of me. It's a fact some folks are frightened by even the smallest, seemingly least imposing creatures on this planet. Mosquitoes, bugs, bees, spiders.

Themselves.

Sometimes it's so senseless it must be hereditary, or perhaps the syndrome hails from some otherwise inconsiderable traumatic episode straight from childhood. Me, I can't figure it out.

All I know is I hate rats.

But I love dogs.

I love *my* dog.

At least, I *did*

My name is Jeremy Sytes. I'm a middle-aged, run-of-the-mill average Joe Family Guy, so to speak. During the day I'm an assistant sales manager for the retail giant Kempco, and every night I return to the suburban home life I share with my wife Helen, toddler Terrance, and infant Jody. I recently self-published a collection of my own anecdotes for weary travelers, *Sytes for Sore Eyes*. Might as well mention it whenever I can, and it's doing well at online book stores.

Now, onto Viceroy.....

Viceroy was our Border terrier. He was a scruffy, spunky little canine with a face like Benji and a bluish wiry double coat that thinned down to tan-colored "socks" at his thighs and feet.

Viceroy hated rats, too.

We all did.

I'd stretched myself out over the blue fescue of the backyard lawn, around 11:30 p.m., gazing up at the stars and wispy rogue clouds and the quintuplet of spot lights from the Lakefest Auto Mall's Midnight Madness sale dancing like a major Hollywood movie premiere's in the southern sky.

A half-empty bottle of Bud stood on a bald spot of the lawn and within comfortable reach of me. My kids were in their beds, Helen reading a paperback in the den, Viceroy likely lounging at her bunny-slippered feet with his snout buried into his paws.

I was alone.

I was loving every minute of it.

I was surrounded by a peaceful quiet but for the sickly hum of the weathered Jacuzzi at the corner of the patio. I was used to that hum, didn't mind it a bit. The Jacuzzi had cost me only a couple hundred bucks. It was previously owned by a succession of heavy partiers and building contractor acquaintances of mine, who'd convinced me the tub's appearance was only a result of moving it from points A to B, C, D, and E. But they were right, it operated with rarely a tick. Yeah, it wasn't supposed to hum the way it did, but Helen and I'd enjoyed a good few months of otherwise unaffordable recreational relaxation in spite of that. It was a four- person tub held upright by a weary wooden frame encased by cobwebs and redwood-stained plywood along its four sides. The patio had no shelter, and the sauna's thick foam/cloth cover was green with algae from the rain and riddled with splotches of brown stains from my using it as a tabletop when I barbecue. And I 'que quite often.

It didn't matter to us that it was such an eyesore. What mattered to us was that it worked.

We were nearly into the first week of enjoying the tub when the yellow jacket wasp population in our yard grew to nightmarish proportions and I discovered they'd made a sizeable nest of the Jacuzzi's wooden innards. I took care of that, but it was a pain in the ass.

The other week I spotted a small rodent scurry across the patio's cement floor and squeeze itself into a hole in the wood of the hot tub's casing.

My god, it was attracting pests.

"That must've been a vole," Helen had told me. "An above-ground mole. I hear we have 'em up here."

"Looks like a rat to me," I'd told her. "So.....you're fine with it living inside our Jacuzzi?"

"We can phone the exterminators."

"We have exterminators? We can sick Viceroy on it....."

"Don't let our dog near that thing, it might have rabies," was Helen's final word, and the matter hadn't been brought up since, for we hadn't seen the damn rat in the stretch of time afterwards.

But lying there on the grass that night below the stars, I saw it again, the little prick.

I turned my gaze to one side, reaching, my beer bottle in my visual foreground and at my fingertips, the rat darting across the landscape no more than a few feet beyond. I could've sworn I heard children's laughter coming from the other side of the fence, the neighbor's kids, but I paid it no mind to their business. I had my own.

"Godammit!"

I rolled onto my belly, alert with adrenaline. Damn vermin could've been right there with me the entire hour or so that *I'd* been, foraging in the grass inches away from my head, and me blissfully unaware. I watched it as it went up to the patio, sniffed the air, made a leisurely promenade across the cement until it crept into the same crack of plywood it had the last time I'd seen it, into the recesses of the Jacuzzi structure's dank interior.

41

Nicholas Grabowsky

The rat had been utterly oblivious to my presence, or downright just didn't care, and this discernment upset me further.

I thought to get up, get Viceroy after its ass, and I did just that. I crept carefully across the patio, slid open the glass door, called inside with a voice soft but firm my dog's name.

Viceroy came running. He leapt over the sofa, into the air and in graceful avoidance of the living room's glass coffee table, ran out to me in the patio and humped my leg.

"Good dog," I told him, pulling him from me, patting him on the head and moving us both away from the door. "Now. *Go get the rat!*"

Viceroy spun around a few times in a chasing-his-tail kind of fashion, stood on his hind legs with paws in the air like a gallant steed, and bolted for the Jacuzzi. He knew *exactly* what I meant.

He went to sniffing around the parameter of red-stained plywood; thrust his black nose into the abysmal hole of the rodent's lair.

"That's it, Viceroy, go get it," I cheered, and while the dog was preoccupied, I crossed the yard to retrieve my beer.

I stopped cold for the brief distraction of a rustling in the bushes at the fence to my left. Something the size of my dog disappeared into that fat bulk of foliage the second I'd laid eyes on it, and I looked over my shoulder at Viceroy. He was exactly where I'd left him, now barking into the rat's hole. I would have instantly hushed him for fear he'd awaken the kids or alert Helen to our antics, but what I'd seen steal away into the bush concerned me a bit more.

As I began to doubt I'd seen anything at all, my interests fell momentarily beer-ward. I looked, but I could not for the life of me locate my bottle of Bud.

It had been right there, on the bald spot in the middle of the grass.....

But no; another quick look behind me and there was my beer bottle, resting safely atop the Jacuzzi's foam covering. Like I'd put it there myself.

A bit disoriented from the apparent brain fart of not remembering placing it there, I went to it, downed the remainder of it in jealous abandon, craving another immediately. I withdrew inside and into the kitchen, then emerged into the patio with fresh beer in hand to find no sign of Viceroy.

But I saw the rat scurry away from its Jacuzzi refuge, then out again onto the grass; this time, a family of more than a handful of the buggars in various sizes followed suit from out of the hole in one mass exodus. I was dumbfounded. Acting upon absolute frustration and in a bit of a panic, I threw my beer bottle at the last rodent to reach the grass. The bottle missed, the bursting of broken glass echoing into the late night, the foot-long tail of the last rat declining into the thickness of grass blades like a wiggle-worm toy pulled along by a string.

And that was my last beer.

I whistled, called out for my dog.

"Viceroy, come here, boy!"

I sojourned into the dark of the yard, suddenly finding myself overcome by a hell of a dizzy spell which brought me to my knees despite the fear of my knowledge of rats wandering through the grass.

There I met my Viceroy, his body limp and motionless and utterly pulverized. It took me several minutes to realize his true condition I could see him clearly before me, sprawled out across the grass, and the bulbous black trail which extended from his belly and down over the lawn into the bushes, I found to my horrified observation, was likely an intestine.

As well, it took me awhile to become aware of the movement all about me.

Something stirred from within the bushes before me.

I looked up at them, then drew my gaze higher.

Black shadows of at least a half dozen dog-sized rodent beasts shot across the electric power cables and phone lines above me, past the tree branches of the rear neighbor's yard that extended over my property. I couldn't believe what I saw. One two three four five six, and they each disappeared down a utilities pole, down into the dark brush of the corner of my yard.

I bolted to my feet, found myself out of breath as though I'd jogged all the way to the Lakefest Auto Mall and back, and I hadn't exerted myself but to stand.

Nicholas Grabowsky

Another rustling of the bushes before me doubled me back in surprise towards the house in several steps, and I could not take my eyes off my beloved Viceroy as I went. Then there came a moment within the bushes of furious commotion, until a black rodent head the size and shape of a two-gallon funnel poked itself out from the bush, seized my Viceroy between incisors long enough to resemble two scythes, and dragged his body into the obscurity of branches and heavy leaves.

Backing towards the patio had at this point been a series of reflexes in my favor, but my feet could only propel me as fast as my disbelief could give way to the certain urgency it would've taken for me to escape.

I finally turned, and already one of these creatures was making its way inside the house, through the inviting entrance of opened sliding glass doors I'd neglected to shut. The sight of this gave me the urgent strength I needed to pick up speed and run for those doors.

I entered the house, saw the vermin avoid the coffee table and scale over the sofa to the hallway like Viceroy had done in backwards fashion coming out to my summons not long before.

I kept running. In my inept clumsiness, I couldn't avoid the glass coffee table. I fell upon it, its foundation crumpled under my weight, and the glass shattered like a hundred beer bottles had been thrown with great force around and beneath me. I caught sight of my own blood escaping from a multitude of areas on my person and saturating my clothing as I pushed myself up, determined to continue pursuit rather than inspect my wounds.

By the time I'd reached the den, my foremost destination of concern, five of these vile and monstrous things had already begun their bloodthirsty assault on my wife....

.......tearing her to shreds against her struggles and screams right there on her recliner chair deathbed and to the point where she already resembled a grisly pile of blood-soaked beef having gone through a tremendous delicatessen cold cut shaver before I could even *hope* to save her.....

The window behind her was slid open, and another two or three dog-sized rats made their ways through the gaping screen

44

and into the room, unconcerned with my standing there baring mute witness to this unspeakable calamity.

One rat was fiendishly chewing on something red and glistening and an obvious appendage of Helen's, all by itself in the opposite corner of the room like a squirrel happily laboring over a morsel of nut it scored, turning it about in its hands, and I observed from my petrified stance in the doorway that Helen's head had been stolen away too rapidly for me to have seen it happen. The invaders permeated the air with the sounds of feasting, gnawing. It echoed throughout the house.

I believe I'd been standing there unable to move for quite a good deal of time. I was like a ghost to these damnable beasts, a distant spectator, and I regarded this as I became able to more and more think clearly. As I captured my senses, I remembered my children.....

I turned about in mad abandon, furiously animate, leapt up the flight of stairs to the kids' rooms in record time, came upon my three-year-old's room first.

Kicked open the door.

Flicked on the light switch.

There were no rats.

And yet, Terrance was awake and wide-eyed, and he was staring straight at me.

"Daddy, *no!*"

"Come on, Terry," I said, racing for his bed, but the closer I got to him the more frightened he became, and his eyes never left me.

My eyes likewise never left him but for a moment when I chanced to look down on my way to his bed and I noticed my tennis shoes were absent from my feet, as were my socks. My trousers were suddenly nonexistent and my lower torso had been stripped of all clothing. The exposed vastness of hair on my legs stood on end as if responding to electric static in the air.

I was stricken with a single thought, a rational supposition, a powerfully sane element of enlightenment in all this madness: *this can't be real. Either I'm seriously hallucinating, or I passed out, and I'm actually physically catching some zzz 's out back on the lawn.*

But there was no time to entertain this thought.

Any thoughts…..no, no time for a single goddamn one of them.

I snatched Terry into my arms as he kicked and flailed against me as though *I* was the threat and not the onslaught of rats. Fast as lightning I carried him from his bedroom, across the upstairs hallway, and into baby Jody's room.

I switched on the light.

I fell to my knees yet again, as I had a couple times already that night, and for the final time.

In the room there was a chest of drawers, the drawers of clothes having slid fully out and thrown on top of one another over the carpet. The large rats were climbing out of the gaping space where the drawers had been, probably having chewed through the wall behind the furniture piece in no more time than it took me to fetch Terrance.

That sight alone wasn't what brought me to my knees.

One of the rats was perched with his hind feet atop the curved metal frame at the foot-end of Jody' s crib, its body elongated and flexing over her, front paws limp and against its body, whiskered snout nostrils collapsing then expanding like two respirator bags.

That nose was black.

Its ears were not like the other rats'; they were more folded over their front and drooping. The tar black hair of its body thinned into a noticeable tan color around attenuated legs and feet that receded into dog-like paws the next second, and the thing that before was a rat took a swan dive right into my baby's cradle. Jody wailed.

And what emerged from the cradle with my daughter's neck clenched tightly between its jaws was no rat, but Viceroy. It took Jody with it into the doorway to hell that became of the section of dresser that once harbored drawers, into the wall.

I wanted to follow after him. Then I did not know *what* to do.

Again I noticed the rats were oblivious to my presence, for they still could've attacked me, as vulnerable as I was, at any time. For a mere mortal, fragile man engaged in a foiled and useless attempt to rescue his wife and children, I knew I was as easy a prey as any of them. It was as if my house was on fire, and the flames overtook everyone else yet did not harm *me*.

I began to hallucinate again, as I can describe it, if that was indeed what I was doing.

I was somehow, suddenly, out of place. I was oddly overwhelmed with hunger. I couldn't see at first, like I'd blacked out and had come to in a heartbeat, and I experienced the sensation of biting down on something writhing and struggling in my mouth between my jaws, keeping what ever it was forcefully at bay as it fought to live, tearing away at it as ravenously as I would the barbequed ribs of an all-you-can-eat restaurant parlor after getting stoned out of my mind.

But as I returned to the immediate events surrounding me, my vision focused onto the sight of my poor son Terrance, sprawled out before me with his midsection imploded like he'd swallowed a hand grenade which detonated from his insides out, blood and carnage like an animal carcass freshly slaughtered and split from throat to groin spilled over and about me, and I realized that I myself had been feeding on him.

Possibly for quite some time.....

I lost consciousness after this, not long after, and I knew this for certain as well as everything else I'd experienced that night, that I succumbed to a deep sleep, and that was it for me.

Except.....

I distinctly remember in the midst of that void of tranquil black a young police cadet returning his perplexed gaze down upon me and replying to someone else, as if there were others around him I did not see. And he said to this unseen person, "I dunno. Looks like a rat to me."

***

Here I am, several weeks or months later I do not know, describing my account to you in detail, halfway across the country away from what was once my home. You won't believe what I've been through since.....the men in white coats, the men in blue coats, the men in suit coats endlessly questioning me and clicking their ball-point pens, keeping me contained in this twelve-by-twelve metal cell most of the hours of each day until they come to a decision they all can agree upon as to what to do with me.

You won't believe *this*, either:

You remember the incident in California where that average Joe Family Guy went suddenly psycho and ripped his family to shreds with his bare hands?

It was in all the papers. The media lapped it up.

That was *me.*

And I know clear as day there was a cover-up, on the part of the police, the government, the Great Institution responsible for regulating everything we know, a sensational exchange of misinformation to rival even the Roswell alien aftermath, executed somewhere between the time I'd eaten my son and the time of my writing this confession of sorts.

On one hand, *Dateline*'s now-famous television segment brought up strong arguments but shaky evidence regarding their story about the growing myth of a colony of wererats wandering from house to house in west coast United States suburbia, increasing their number and leaving numerous families dead and dying and devastated in their wake. Their case in point was my own infamous tragedy.

But if you ask me, my personal opinion of this entire ordeal is that the neighbors' kids had spiked my beer.

THE FESTIVAL OF FALLEN SOULS

(Originally written for Johnny Martin Walters'
graphic novel series American Carnevil. The
characters of Sam Cross and Curtains are conceived
and owned by Johnny Martin Walters.)

Part one

JaMaican Prologue

I'll never forget looking down upon my own abdomen and seeing wrinkled portions of actual intestine sticking out of a yawning crevice a couple of inches above my naval. It was like I was holding an imploded bag of steaming chow mien with a hole ripped open in the middle and the fleshy noodles were hanging out.

And I was losing blood fast. It flowed over my hands as I cradled the wound, spilling across my belly, soaking into my jeans like I'd wet myself something fierce, and I was getting alarmingly light-headed.

I was hoping whoever found me that way didn't associate me with the smoking .44 Anaconda double action revolver a few feet away across the floor, the severed thumb and index finger of a local ganja guru at the foot of the toilet in a nearby stall like a discarded half-eaten chicken wing, the anti-Jamaican parliament slogans graffiti-strewn across the wall in fecal matter facing me below the window of the opposing wall.

I had nothing to do with the slogan shit.

Around here, and in my predicament, I'd have been fucked.

Maybe I was fucked already.

Nicholas Grabowsky

My U.S. Federal Marshal badge had escaped my person just the other day, as well as anything else I carried with me that I could use to identify myself.

I wasn't supposed to be here, in a shit portion of briar patch backcountry up Jamaica's great Black River, wasn't supposed to have ventured my dumb ass so far off my jurisdictional beaten path, in the cockroach- infested public restroom of an outdoor farmer's shopping district, dying there on the crusty tile beside a urinal rank with an acidy stench. If I was turned over to Jamaican officials, I'd be as good as dead, and then......

I started figuring I *should* die there, and save everyone a lot of trouble.

Especially me.

In hindsight I would've been better off.

Me and my bloody stomach noodles.

The restroom door opened, and I harkened to a male scream which escalated into a chorus of females doing the same thing and much louder. When I'd gathered strength enough to lift my head, I caught sight of two armed and uniformed Jamaican policemen barging through the entrance. Neither one looked directly at me, which struck me as peculiar. Instead, they parted at the door, one holding it open, and they faced each other at attention.

Entering next and from between them was an elderly-type man dressed like he was on his way to a Sear's portrait studio with a half-price coupon in hand, sporting a Southern gentleman's summer suit coat, trousers, and fedora, all in white like a Burl Ives/Colonel Sanders hybrid. A little over-the-top for me without a doubt; I'm just one of the wretchedly simple lost souls unconcerned with attire or even personal hygiene. But he had cold piercing eyes that shot straight into your soul when he gazed into yours, or so it always seemed, and when that happened, you knew he was for real. He could be wearing a bikini bathing suit, but, *those eyes*

They were *also* the eyes of my boss.

I know him as Mr. Curtains.

Just.....Mr. Curtains, as plain as he kept his clothes so flawlessly bleached and clean.

He was the *last* person I'd expected to see step out of the shadows of my predicament, and he became my savior that day. I mean, his presence alone meant there'd be no investigation regarding what I'd gotten myself into, no red tape or lengthy incarceration while governments bickered over what to do with me, and maybe even no *dying*, for that matter.

Curtains couldn't afford to see me dead.

He stepped up to me, knelt beside me, caught a whiff of the urinal and retreated a bit, and told me, plainly, "We're going to get you some help."

And he was.

You can bet your left ass cheek on that.

***

I'd closed my eyes to him just afterwards, as my alertness slipped down a rabbit hole and into a disturbing dream of a beautiful dark princess surrounded by forest animals and cloaked men made up of earthworms and soil all around her, devouring the animals to get to her.

And she was screaming......

THE JET RIDE UP

My name is Sam Cross. I am one in a secret "club" of government misfit puppets known as the OAC, or Operation American Carnevil, deeply embedded within the United States National Security Agency. We investigate supernatural/paranormal cases that even other government agencies which do this sort of thing won't have anything to do with, and our forte centers on illegal alien trafficking and traveling carnival/gypsy types. Put us in black suits with laser blasters or store us in files under "X" and we're all the same, only place my sort of career under the category of "*Asswipe*" and that's exactly what *I* do. When the U.S. Government shoots an abnormality out its rectum, I'm there to wipe it off. It's like society ate bad food that didn't agree with it, and here is Sam Cross, *Uncle Sam* Cross, the Tidy Bowl man, here to clean up all their diarrhea splatter before it attracts flies.

I'd recently steered way out of my jurisdiction, pursuing a case involving a legendary flesh-eating "organic ghost,"

51

released by traveling carnies I came across in Utah a few months prior to all this.

The Tunambra.

El Fantasma Orgánico.

Nasty prick.

Tunambra's reputation is that it looks human, a handsome youthful African male, except when he touches you, flesh to flesh, skin to skin, he goes right through you. But he can materialize at any time, so he can run a hand right into you, wrap his fingers around your heart, and materialize to squeeze it like a ripe tomato. I'm sure he's done that before and many times, but what he's known for is his hunger, and he likes to gnaw on muscle tissue and slurp up fatty build-up below the skin like stale grease.

He likes 'em plump or pumped up.

I read a classified forensics report that put it just that way.

I pursued *El Fantasma Orgánico* down to New Orleans and, in a decisive and emotional move, into Central America and beyond where I threw my Marshal badge out the window, literally, and the whole thing became personal.

It was in that Jamaican restroom where we met, Tunambra and I, face-to-face, and the bullets I plugged into him affected him so little he had no problem taking me against the wall with the strength of a big rig and driving his fingers into me. When he pulled out, he nearly took my intestines with him.

***

When I awoke again I was at first convinced I was still bleeding and dying and hadn't been moved an inch because Curtains was still staring at me with those soul- piercing eyes of his.

My abdomen still hurt like a sonofabitch, like I'd swallowed a switch blade that flicked open all by itself in my belly.

I sensed I was drugged thoroughly, because although I was in tremendous pain, I didn't *give a shit* that I was in pain.

I know a dose or two of happy juice when I feel it.

I lazily lifted my shirt; the carnage of my own abdomen I'd been inspecting last I knew had been tucked back in and stitched up rather nicely, so Curtains was explaining as he found me awake. A sticky gauge the size of a legal pad of paper over my lower rib cage and belly was covered securely in a white bandage wound several times around my body.

"Tunambra killed you, son," was what Curtains told me next. "You've been unconscious for several days. It deposited something inside you, something not unlike a tumor the size of a plastic egg of silly putty, and despite the efforts of the best medical practitioners in the world, it's something that cannot be removed or destroyed."

I sat there feeling stoned and relaxed and listening to his banter, slowly realizing I was seated beside the circular window of a private jet, and from what I further gathered from him I was on my way back to the States, to the Rocky Mountains of Northwestern Colorado, and more specifically to an annual festival held within the ghost town of Animas Forks where there abides a certain holistic healer who is guaranteed to rid me of the tumor and put me back into action and as good as goddamn new.

This was by no means an assignment. It was like my dying body was being flown forthwith to a special hidden medical facility only the government knew of, and those wealthy enough to be privy to it, where I had the only hope for life and from what Curtains said this healer was the motherfucking *fountain of youth,* whose existence was known only to a few hundred people in the entire expanse of the globe, no more.

She was a secret kept from the whole world.

She could cure Cancer, prolong life, restore health. Just like Jesus.

And yet, it was like something out of an infomercial. She'd cured Curtains once, of something he won't say.

He said he owed her a debt.

After all, like I'd said, Curtains couldn't afford to see me dead…….

I was wearing new clothes, black oversized shirt and thick sweat pants, and a black hooded jacket lined with a warm wool and an expensive feel, which I was advised would be taken out of my salary for my fuck-up in Jamaica.

Figures.

Out the window, it was dark.

Nicholas Grabowsky
It felt like morning to me, very early morning.

Touchdown

Our Learjet 31 touched down upon a private runway in Ironton, east of Interstate 550. I'd passed Ironton more than a few times traveling down that freeway. Looking down upon an aerial map of where I was, you might say we landed at a tiny zit on the face of the Continental Divide.

We rolled to a halt and the startlingly deep male baritone of the captain came up over the intercom like Worf's in *Star Trek*: "Okay sirs, weather here is thirty- four degrees, but will lead into a fairly sunny Spring day. Thank you for flying, gentlemen."
Courteous fucker.

Wished his private service could've thanked me more while we were flying, preferably in the form of a hot private stewardess with a landslide of cleavage, a three-course dinner and Early Times on the rocks. I love to wake up early with the Times, as the promotional slogan went.

Whiskey and a good hunkin' slab o' ribeye with green beans.

Fuck ....

I was on a liquid diet for at least a few days, doctor's orders so I learned, what with my guts being put back together and all.

Curtains unbuckled his seat belt and rose before I did, coughed, stretched, repositioned his fedora atop his equally white short head of hair. He grabbed a white overcoat thrown across the seat beside him and wriggled into it.

"It's time," he said. "And we're right on it."

I stood carefully and feebly upon my feet like an old man but found my footing despite my sudden dizziness. When I faced Curtains, the corners of his mouth almost appeared to raise in a half smile as a hand went into his coat, withdrew a semi-transparent amber prescription bottle of white pills and placed it in the palm of my hand. It was a bottle so big my hand wrapped around it and I could still see it.

"An OAC secret:" he confided, "we take care of our own."

No shit.

Label up in open palm, I briefly inspected—

PATIENT: 6AF7BC789

Hydrocodone, 500mg

Delta-9-Tetrahydrocannabinol, 500mg

500 capsules

refills expected

Great goddamn.

Despite the fact that Curtains was taking me to some Rocky Mountain enchantress as a last-ditch effort to save my life because I was supposedly *dying*, I was content to know I was going to be well-medicated constantly throughout this experience.

I'd been in deeper shit sober as cornflakes in milk, wishing I was frosted.

I looked up.

Curtains had already about-faced, making his way out of the plane.

I zipped my jacket halfway and followed, and as I did so I made it a point to grab an Aquafina from Captain James Earl Jones on the way out.

I had a few concentrated dewdrops from heaven to swallow....

THE BROWN COATS

I met up with Curtains outside the jet in the chilly dark early morning mountain air, and we sojourned across a cement stretch of roadway narrowing into a walkway towards an awaiting white limousine. The heavens were cloudless and filled with a vastness of stars, though as I looked I noticed there was no moon.

We were surrounded by grassy hills and a forest beyond to the east, a quiet cottage on the outskirts of the lighted runway to my right, and a garage-sized office building closer to where the limo waited at a driveway yawning open to a cul-de-sac street beneath a duo of overhanging street lights.

A mild icy breeze made me zip my jacket up to my neck, pull my hood over my head, dig my hands into my front jacket pockets. Clenching a prescription bottle the size of a can of party cashews, I appeared pregnant to myself as I peered down while we walked.

And I noticed as we went that we were far from alone.

To my left and right were a total of about two and a half dozen equally tall, equally gaunt figures, each holding black opened umbrellas above themselves in an almost *Mary Poppins* kind of way, all silent and still and watching us.

They were scattered here and there across the landscape everywhere I looked, some closer and more visible in the light to see clearly than the others in the distance, and one was standing at the opened side passenger door of our limo, our evident chauffeur.

Each of these umbrella figures appeared to be wearing the same thing ---ankle-length rusty brown overcoats buttoned to the neck with long opened tan woolly collars spilling down about their chests in upside-down V's.

Each must've towered over my 5'9" stature by a couple inches at least.

And their brown earthy hair was a mutual trait shared by each as well.....dripping down to the shoulders, flailed and matted like they were Geico cavemen all just risen from bed. There was a faint coat of crumpled grey/brown powder on sections of hair as if they had engaged in a great climactic dirt clod fight before we'd arrived.

Their faces of ghostly-pale skin, tiny noses and chalky plump rust-colored lips were predominantly hidden behind thick black sunglasses as oversized as a Roswell alien's eyes, but I detected a boyish youthfulness from behind them when I confronted the limo man that made me question whether he was even old enough to buy alcohol.

I thought to ask Curtains who the hell they were, but trying to read him while keeping up with his long hurried strides I detected he'd either been in their company before, or just didn't give a shit.

I think between the two of us, we'd already seen just about everything.

But if you'd have asked me, this welcoming committee was a local bunch. And this area had to be entirely secure because of the nature of our presence here as well as where we were going. Perhaps *they* were the security, yeah, and maybe this was Halloween.

Maybe it was the drugs kicking in.

"Good morning, sirs," the one at the limo greeted us in a voice almost monotone and much more mature than I'd expected, offered his umbrella over us as though to protect us from unseen pouring rain. "I am Adam. Welcome to Colorado."

We entered the vehicle and Adam followed, and I supposed to myself he wasn't the driver after all. Forthwith the limo took off at the slam of the door.

The Limo Ride

I took a rear window seat facing forward, curtains on the same rear seat at the other window. The sky window above us ensured the stars would be a constant surveyor on our road trip to Animas Forks, as well as our tall and enigmatic escort, who never seemed to withdraw his gaze of gleaming black plastic from my direction. He sat hunched at our end of a stretch of white leather seating along the inner side wall, his stick-like legs pulled towards his body so his knee caps were in line with his chin.

Across from him were two gentlemen eager for an introduction, so eager we'd already shaken hands before we were seated, and it was Curtain's duty to oblige.

"Federal Marshal Sam Cross," he said, both to me and for the sake of announcing who I was to all, "this is Mister Clive Cunning, and beside him is the distinguished Reverend Larry Farewell...."

"And I know you both met Adam, Chief of Private Security for the festival," added Mister Cunning.

Adam smiled but did not move otherwise. He gripped the closed umbrella across his lap rather tensely. I returned the smile with a spark of sarcasm against his strangeness.

"So how old are you?" I found myself asking him outright. I mean.....I could almost be his dad, I assumed. Almost. *Security Chief my ass*

"He's older than you are, Mr. Cross," said Cunning. Curtains cleared his throat.

"Sam, Clive Cunning is part of the Legislative Council of the Colorado General Assembly, among other things. You recall my mentioning you had fans in Washington, in high places, pulling for you *

(*And pulling the strings, was my thought.....*)

"Well, he's one of 'em."

This time when Cunning and I shook hands, I had to wrench myself free. He was as enthusiastic as a jackhammer and that seriously disturbed my blissfully mellow high.

Clive Cunning must've been around Curtain's age, an obvious head of toupee on his head of a graying blue/black and so loosely fastened I kept my eye on it to see if it would slide off. His eerily cheerful grin and lively glare was not unlike *Poltergeist II*'s maniacal ghostly preacher. He wore thermal blue sweats top to bottom covered in a jogger's light jacket and an American-flag-colored scarf wrapped around his neck almost as thick as a tire around a hubcap.

He held a glass of dark alcohol of some sort swimming in ice in the hand opposite the one which shook mine, and it sloshed about and splashed over his fingers.

Maybe he was tanked, and the more he spoke the more I was certain of it.

Curtains continued. "Larry Farewell is one of the nation's top evangelicals, founder of Christroads University and President of the Christroads Satellite Network."

Instinctively I extended my hand, but this time the reverend didn't.

"He's not, however, one of those Washington fans," Curtains explained, and it figured. Farewell had been around for a long time both as an influential political figure, Christian rights activist, and a television hell-fire Southern Baptist fundamentalist preacher whose viewers were well in the millions and not merely in numbers, but in dollars.

If I were him, I wouldn't approve of me, either. But to each his own.....

Someone of his persuasion didn't seem to fit in with everything, and I found myself asking, "This is supposed to be a pagan/goth-type holistic/herbal tree- hugging earth/moon goddess-worshipping kinda gig, isn't it, so I'm told? What's a dude like you...."

58

"The Lord healeth," said the reverend sternly to me, "but He's given us a source of healing as rapid and complete as if she were Christ Himself still walking in the flesh on this earth. Salonica is chosen of God. She just doesn't know it yet. And I have a terminal illness I'll deny if word gets out. I understand you have a certain dreadful affliction as well......"

"Word gets around," I said, casting a gaze towards Curtains, who shrugged his shoulders.

"You must," continued Farewell, "or you wouldn't be here."

"Correction," Cunning interjected. "There's nothing w r o n g with me, I'm just getting old, and Salonica......well, with her, I'll still be around for a long- ass time. Between you and me, I'll take the White House when I'm eighty and they'll all be saying I look half my age....."

"Salonica?" I repeated in question. "That's the name of this healer chick?"

Curtains nodded, then he said, "When we get to where we're headed, in and around the festival, you'll find two categories of people: the ones you'd expect to find at an event like this, folks of that type who come here year after year... .the witches, the herbalists, Goths, folklorists, vegans, a veritable backwoods open swap meet for those inclined to get together at a real life ghost town and spiritual hotbed for a nice celebration away from it all, to meet up, mingle, take part in religious ceremonies. And then there's.....well, folks like us. The few hundred or so elite ones, and I'm talking little over three hundred on the face of this planet, the rich, the politically powerful, a small mixture of celebrity and royalty we all come together under the cover of this festival, you see, because of the hands-down ultimate supernatural healer alive, the better half of the two owners of this needle prick in the Rocky Mountain landscape. And Salonica is only available to us once a year. Hell.....rich political figures frequent these parts by the thousands annually for the scenic vacation getaways, the high- profile fishing, the low-profile resorts. But when we're drawn here like this, all at once like this, we need a good cover to ensure nothing here is really going on outside of an event the rest of the conservative world turns a blind eye to."

Cunning added, "And if word got out about what's really going on here.....well, you understand. After all, knowing this little lady is like knowing everything about the lost continent of Atlantis, or having physical proof there's an afterlife, and being obligated to keep her existence under our hats because no one who values the healing power she grants can afford to exploit her....."

".....and then the whole world will know, and she'll die, basically, a slow death under exploitation, tabloid and otherwise," concluded Farewell. "And there would be no hope for her ultimate inclusion into the cause of the Lord Jesus."

"That's *your* agenda," Cunning rebuked him, bit his lip.

"We all have our own," said Curtains to me.

"The better half of two owners of the land the festival is on," I repeated, for I was still wondering about that part. "Who's the *other* half?"

"Thaddeus," Curtains said plainly. "You're destined to make his acquaintance at some point during your experience here."

"He's a minus to Salonica's plus, son," Farewell said to me. "Her hands heal, his hands kill."

"At one touch," Cunning added. "His is the touch of death. Two polar opposites, both ill-fated lovers. Some say it's a curse, and that I believe. How could it not be? But Thad's aware of all that, and our government has a special relationship with him. Mutual trust, I might say."

"Rumor has it they've both been here since before we were a country," said Curtains, then chuckled. "If you dig deep, there's a lot of superstition that you're gonna hear from this point forward. And if I were you, I'd believe most of it. What with all you're going to see...."

Adam continued to look uncomfortable, made me *feel* uncomfortable. I did so want to rip off those goddamn specks of his.

And then I noticed the bar at the opposite end. Cunning's drink had to come from *somewhere*.....

But I was fine. I wrenched my bottle of pills from my front jacket pocket.

"Hey now, Timothy Leary," Curtains stopped me. "That may be the Mother Lode of happy pills to ever grace those anxious hands of yours, but it ain't candy. Now I hate to be your *daddy* an' all...."

"*My own* dad hated to be my daddy," I replied, then sighed. He was right. I was feeling pretty baked about then, and thought a short snooze would do me good. I spotted a curious rectangular gizmo tucked away at a corner of the bar beside a wound-up roll of black wiring. I motioned to Adam, who was either staring straight at me throughout the conversation or fast asleep, towards that portion of the limo. "Could you get me that small square thing sitting in the corner over there, Lurch?"

He stirred, gazed in the direction I was pointing, fetched the iPod and earphones, thanked Adam with a nod. That was enough conversation for awhile, enough information for this weary lad. I placed the phones in my ears, gave Curtains the sort of wink to let him know I was out to lunch for awhile, and flipped on the first tune on the list.

Pink Floyd.

Comfortably Numb.

Perfect.

My mind tried to rest as I closed my eyes.

Salonica.

Private Security Chief Adam and his horde of look- alike wacky secret agent Brown Coats.

The Reverend Larry Farewell right there with me within arm's reach, and he wasn't in a TV set.

Thaddeus, the incarnate Grim Reaper, who'll reap what he sows if he ever gets the fuck within several yards of me, if it's true he can off me just by his skin touching mine.

The Tunambra, whom I cursed to hell way before he even put me here.

A tumor inside me the size of a silly putty egg.

I swear to Christ if that goddamn thing is successfully extracted from me rather than vanishing miraculously, I'll break it apart and press it against a Sunday Morning newspaper comic strip, preferably Berkley Breathed's *Opus* and press into it hard, and preserve it for a keepsake I'll shove up Tunambra's ass some day.

Hello......is there anybody in there?

Just nod if you can hear me.......

And I nodded, and drifted off.........

***

(When the limo ride ended, unbeknownst to me at the time, Clive Cunning snuck away into the night and into a large tented structure near the outskirts of the festival grounds. The one he went to meet rebuked him for talking too much, and Clive's habit of being annoying would have cost him his life if his black-robed superior hadn't thought to put on a glove before losing his temper and striking him with a clenched fist, afterwards sending him cowering away with a seriously broken nose and laughing about the incident to himself.....)

MOTEL

I awoke from the middle of a nightmare and into another one and then another, like I had snuck into a mental Cineplex and was theater swapping, and then into another nightmare that was about to begin. I found myself on a twin-sized bed in a motel room the size of *four* twin-sized beds and with a door leading to a bathroom. I didn't remember anything since I'd drifted off in the limo, how I got from there to here.

But I knew I was naked, and that didn't sit with me too well.

There was an open duffle bag on the dresser top beside the bed where I found a pile of various articles of clothing —some were mine and some weren't familiar at all—a three-pack of store-bought boxers, toiletries, my wallet and five hundred cash in twenties and fifties, an American Express card in my name, a Browning .22 rimfire semi-automatic, my prescription bottle, and.....

....and, my Federal Marshal badge.

My *badge*.

I'd be goddamned.

Same one I'd tossed away in Central America —you know your own badge when you see it. OAC never ceases to amaze me.

I gazed into the rectangular looking glass wall-mounted above the dresser, and my up-close-and-personal mirrored reflection returned my gaze with the same set of weary eyes. I inspected the uncomfortable bandages and gauze wrapped about my midsection, and there was so much of it, that to me I looked like a lucky survivor of a swallowed hand grenade accident.

Something stirred in the mirror-reflected bottom corner of the room, and I instinctively swirled to face it, snatching the pistol from the dresser clothes pile fast as light speed.

Light speed wasn't fast enough.

What was fast enough was the insanely intense euphoric vision of the thing that knocked the gun from my hand, the Tunambra, *El Fantasma Orgánico* itself, right in the room with me, and I was overswept by an intense numbness and suspension of belief, and of a feeling that I'd somehow returned to that Jamaican men's room where it all started, all over again.....

Part Two
IT WAS ONLY CLIVE, THE DRUNK BASTARD

"Whoa there, gunslinger," Clive Cunning was now suddenly telling me.

When reality snapped back into place for me, I realized my gun remained in my grip and had never left it, and I'd pulled the trigger of an unloaded weapon straight into Cunning's left eye.

If I were him I would've pissed my pants.

"The hell are you doing.....!?" I shouted, and I *had* no pants, so I was close to pissing all over *him*.

The Tunambra he wasn't. Must've been the drugs, the dreams, the fact that I was dying.

He retreated away from me, cowering.

"I... I didn't want to startle you."

"Well you fell on your face with that one, didn't you," I told him, adding, "dumb ass freaky fuck. Where's Curtains?"

I lowered my weapon.

63

Nicholas Grabowsky

He didn't answer. Instead, growing balls, he bitched at how I made him spill half the contents of the cocktail glass he was holding.

And I was suddenly offended, being alone with him sans clothing, and he had been silently watching me crouched in the corner of the room like a perverted Gollum the whole damn time up until now, however long that'd been.

He was wearing the same thermal blue sweats, all- American double-thick neck scarf and disheveled toupee as I'd seen him in last. Sticking out of one swollen purple nostril was a bloody crumpled tissue, as if somebody very recently got pissed off and broke his nose.

He returned to the corner of the room between the drooping window curtains and the air conditioner as if nothing between us happened at all, said he'd wait there for me to get my shit together, that he'd been asked personally by Thaddeus to escort me through the festival and directly to him, then proceeded to sip the remainder of his drink and look away as if the conversation was over.

Oh.

Kay..........

I regarded him for a moment. Take away the toupee and pull his ears out, and he looked like Bat Boy all grown up.

I didn't shave, freshen up, shower, not with Freaky Fuck in my room. I dressed hurryingly, jeans, black long-sleeve shirt, tennis shoes and the new jacket. I tucked in my semi-automatic, fully loaded this time, behind my belt buckle.

The wound in my abdomen throbbed from the inside out.

I swallowed a good two, three.....five prescription pills, perhaps. I guess I figured I'd *pass* out before I'd ever *wig* out from an unintended overdose, and if I *passed* out, I wouldn't have to go through this entire goddamn ordeal conscious.

My new Timex read 4:34 pm.

I opened the motel room door to the bright sunshine and cool clean unpolluted air, and a rocky mountain high that would've knocked John Denver on his ass had he been me.

I felt like Dorothy opening her front door to Munchkin Land, though from where I stood it was still a black and white world as much on the outside as it was in the room and with this new world I suspected there were secrets hidden

64

beneath every stone just the same, within the eyes of many a lost soul, behind the sunglasses of every Brown Coat and under the hats of society's elite, revealed to me slowly with every step I took towards destiny.

The Festival

I followed Cunning out of the motel room and the entire festival presented itself to me, filling my eyes with such unexpected establishing-shot spectacle that I had to stand there for a moment to soak it all in.

We were in an enclosed valley the size of over two football fields. Mountainous terrain trailed five hundred meters up along the borders on all sides, with dense clusters of Douglas Firs scaling towards snow-capped mountain peaks, thinning the further down into the valley they reached and making way for a rugged white rocky landscape and the open grassland carpeting the expanse of the festival grounds. In the farthest distance from me I spied waterfalls streaming downwards from sloping cliffs.

One of the Brown Coats that I recognized as Adam joined us in our sojourn with opened umbrella strategically tilted to shade us from the mild sun for a moment long enough to trade Cunning's empty glass for a full one, and then he left us alone.

I was met with a sizeable crowd, a good four, five thousand attendees I estimated, maybe more, enough to fill a southern Baptist megachurch on Easter morning.

And it was indeed festive.

I looked behind me.

The motel I'd emerged from resembled a modest California mission with wooden planks for outside walkways and a gravel path which wound around the building to a paved road leading through a backyard of forest. Judging by its size, it couldn't have catered to more than a few dozen guests. It made me feel special, having been checked into a room this close rather than a Ramada miles down the road, and I likely shared that motel with men far more important or powerful than I. A small souvenir store at my far left reflected the motel's same design, flooded with all manners of patronage.

The ticket lines were '80's blockbuster movie line long, and the only ticket booth I spotted resembled a fold-down plywood July Fourth fireworks stand, the sort a boy scout troupe would rent from Red Devil, situated there like a couple of kids built it in their backyard, painted it black with white stenciled peace signs, and had it hauled out tied atop a long-bed truck.

The prospect of standing in line to was about to test my patience, or lack of. This was no county fair la-laland recreational getaway, when all was said and done and drugs aside. I wanted no delays. And if I ever longed for a vacation I'd take a one-way ticket to the moon, if that were ever possible, because there weren't any people on the moon.

"Now don't mind the lines none," Cunning said reassuringly. "We're special. Well, *I'm* special and *you're* a victim of circumstance. I'd like to think of myself as Thad's right-hand when I'm here, for Thaddeus and I are like *that*."

He thrust two fingers upwards and invadingly close to my nostrils, snapped them together like a cool crooner.

"But Thad requests your presence, so we'll hurry you right along. We can march right up here to the front....."

The festival main entrance beside us extending from the end of the ticket booth to the beginning of a long weathered wooden fence had a cloth banner stretching twenty-or-so feet wide above the in-and-out flow of public beneath, and Cunning caught my gaze and read the banner's words for me, as if I couldn't read.

"THE FESTIVAL OF FALLEN SOULS. Don't know why it's called that, but sure is catchy. Used to be the *Animas Forks Folk Festival*, and if you say it several times fast you can't help saying the word 'fuck.' I think that's why they changed it. Funny Shit. Wait here."

"Yes, 'mam."

And I waited, the wire mesh window of the fireworks stand ticket booth less than a yard in front of me. I leaned forward nonchalantly, stealing a few steps for a bolder view, I saw through the mesh a brow-raising state-of-the-art high-tech control room like I was peering into the innards of a CIA surveillance van.

Whoa.

I took a step back.

I marveled how I couldn't see it inside unless I positioned myself close and peered through the wire mesh at a certain angle.

There was something odd about its material....

The service window I was closest to took the next in line, two blue-haired post-teen Goth girls each as long and tall as Popeye's Olive Oyl with black dresses down to their black and white striped stockings.

Two adults," I heard one say, and the other echoed her words.

"Thirty *even*," said the woman at the booth, drenched in beaded necklaces and Tammy Faye makeup who accepted their debit card, returned it the next instant with two tickets as robot-like as an animatronic carnival fortune teller selling astrology cards out of a windowed machine.

Next in line, three stoner dudes.

"Forty-five *even*," and the gypsy lady took the cash and passed out tickets.

Next, a middle-aged politician. The haircut gave it away.

"One admission ticket, first-class." He handed her a card and what looked like a coupon torn out of a newspaper.

She took the coupon, put it in her mouth. Looked like she fucking ate it.

She swiped the man's card, gave it back to him. Swallowed hard. "Twenty-three thousand, five-fifty, *even*. Thank you. She's in the ghost town this year, sir. All the way past the petting zoo towards the back. *Next, please.....*"

Cunning returned.

"Right this way, Quickdraw. I bought you a drink. Follow me. Post-haste!"

He placed in my hands a cocktail glass full of presumably his concoction of choice.

Thank God.

I'd been dry since Jamaica.

He grabbed my wrist for a second to haul me in his direction, and what with as admittedly homophobic as I am I'd be damned if he led me into the crowd, beneath the festival banner, holding hands like a couple of Laura Ingalls types merrily traipsing down a hillfull of prairie grass.

Nobody touches me.

But he let go of me the next instant and I almost wished he hadn't, because we merged into a thick flow of people and he was so animate and hurried it was difficult keeping up with him, the crowd as condensed as a can of beef potato hash and slow like a herd of corralling steers.

"Moo," I said aloud.

"Say what?" Cunning halted and turned towards me. He sneezed onto his sleeve, wiped his nose across the length of it leaving a snail trail and his one nostril's bloody tissue, partially spilled his own drink and cursed.

I dismissed him as the pause in our journey gave me opportunity enough to sip the one he'd given me, which I hadn't yet, and then the silver-spooned bastard suddenly snatched it away.

"Holy shit, man, you can't drink in your condition," he exclaimed, and he placed my drink into the hands of one of those Brown Coat pricks who took it like a surreal butler with a shiny silver tray, retracted his umbrella with the flick of a thumb and proceeded to sink away into the sea of earth-hugging hippies and spiritualists and Goth people.

"Hey," I called after him, and persisted. "*Hey.....*"

I wrenched my other hand free of Cunning's, dismissing the thought of my ever allowing him to take it. My free hand immediately went for the Brown Coat's shoulder. The anomalous security official seemed to have shrunk two feet in stature the further I reached for him through the crowd until I nabbed him. And then he turned, more precisely *twisted* to me like emerging upwards atop a rotating pedestal, rose up to meet me, to stare me down from behind his black plastic veil, umbrella opening like an inverted satellite dish summoned into position toward the heavens.

It was Adam, again.

Fucker gets around.

He seemed to have arranged his composure for a confrontation as though I'd done something to disturb the peace, and I could see he no longer held my drink. Don't know how the hell it disappeared so quickly, but I wasn't about to start anything, so.....

.....and then Cunning fell into me.

Honestly, I don't know what happened with that, whether some rowdy asshole knocked him into me, or what, but the force of his weight knocked me over as well, right the fuck onto the cold hard ground. I didn't like him anyway, and I was suddenly and thoroughly pissed off. I grabbed at the bastard with both hands curled into his sweatshirt below his All-American scarf, wrenched him up and off me, lifted myself from off the ground, thrust him with all my might against a mule-driven wooden cart passing us by peddling organic candied apples and pears.

A beer-bellied bearded man in green leotards rounded the cart and approached me like a character in pro-wrestling would to an opponent. Splashed across his leotards and spandex suit were the words ALL ORGANIC in white and various font sizes.

Adam drew closer behind me.

Cunning conjured up a loogey and hocked it right into my face, then hissed at me that I made him spill his drink for the last time, that I would pay, that my federal agent days were over, that sort of crap.

Sounded like threats to me.

I could do with one less political fan pulling for me in Washington.......

I wasted no time drawing out my weapon, first extending it point-blankly at the all-organic fat fuck to make him back off.

Then I stuck it up Cunning's bloated nostril.

I had an explosive display of emotion to convey to him, right then and there, but I couldn't think of a goddamn word to say. Cunning grinned at me, gritted his teeth as the sun above us both was eclipsed by more than one black umbrella, and I could hear the saliva bubbling up from behind his tonsils as though he thought I'd allow him another mucous projectile to match the one dripping down my brow.

So I blew that bloated nostril away, the bullet blazing upwards to high heaven, snotty red gore covering the bastard's face. And mine. It felt good. And Cunning wasn't grinning anymore.

"Don't worry," I spoke into his ear, "this Salonica chick will make it all better. Heal you right up, and then all's you've learned here is a *lesson*.... "

I had no time to experience his reaction to my words, for Adam was upon me next, shot his hand out over my shoulder to seize my wrist and wrestle the gun from me without so much as a pause for negotiation.

I had time enough to barely blink before that happened, and my then-itchy trigger finger went balls- out ballistic amidst an adrenaline-rushed struggle against Adam for my weapon.

I abandoned Cunning, spun around into a *kaleidoscope* of Adams.

Holy *shit.*

I'd never seen more than one up close at the same time.

Each one of the several around us looked like spitting images of the other. Their opened umbrellas fell collectively over us like a giant black tarp over a house readying to be fumigated, but just before that....

In my panic and struggle, I pulled several rounds out into the open air in all directions, and I thought I'd caught sight of a small individual in a furry bear-type character costume fall into a school of children, of much of the crowd pulling back into a semi-circle around us, of a single black balloon being let loose from a young boy's hand and sailing into the white clouds above.....

I suddenly found myself seriously screwed.

But what the hell? The government sends me here, gives me *drugs*, hands me a *gun*.....

Before I was overtaken, I dropped the Adam I struggled with to the ground, wrenched off those bulbous ebony oversized specs of his, and I really wished I hadn't done that, and in retrospect I guess I *deserved* to see the rude awakening of horror I saw next, simply because I'd been *asking for it* two eye sockets, hollow and vacuous and eyeless like a duo of ditches dug into a soil-ridden face.....and that face came alive, its pasty lips parting and its skin crumbling into a dirt-like sundry substance, like fertilizer

70

sifting, like vibrating raw earth, and the heads and bodies of earthworms pushed upwards from beneath its matted hair and deteriorating human flesh, like pinkish-brown twisting animals forced through the heads of plastic people in a play dough barber shop.

My dad used to shove my face into a bucket half filled with nightcrawlers and damp shoveled soil before we'd go fishing to rid me of my fear of them.

It never did.

I pushed him away from me, fell on my back, dropped my gun and surrendered, palms up and opened, and I found I had to catch my breath before a single darkened figure cloaked in flowing black came upon me and lifted me up, brought me to my feet, and for a moment I saw nothing but blackness.

"I've been waiting for you," it whispered. *"Come with me....."*

A hand grabbed my wrist again, harder this time, *his* hand, black-gloved, insistent and strong as a bungee backlash, and it pulled me suddenly through the opposing flow of fair-goers like *Gone With the Wind*, like a music video on fast forward with no audio. My eyes were exposed to a thousand faces, an endless succession of peddlers' booths, gypsy trailer yard sales and organic farmer's market stands, t-shirt racks, folk singers with guitar cases open for chunk change, a multitude of body piercing opportunities, cultists pimping their many gospels.

An End Times preacher silently pushed his self-published books at a fold-down table, very intimidated by his environment.

A roach coach served sushi and vegan food. Greenpeace passed out buttons and flyers.

Krishnas chanted, tamborined to Lennon's *Give Peace A Chance.*

And everywhere I looked, a sunglassed, openedumbrella-clad Adam seemed to play duck-and-cover amongst the crowd, popping up here and disappearing there. I caught sight of them tending to people's needs, pausing to pet a wandering dog or goat. Watching me.

An oxygen bar was set up in a revival-sized tent that also housed stalls for horses readying for horseback rides, crystal displays and tarot readings to their far opposite, fitness and fortune-teller celebrities signing their books and photos, and after that I was led past the outside corral of a petting zoo, and an assortment of picnickers and children of all ages running amok this way and that.

I lost consciousness.

Thaddeus Proves Points

I woke up like a vagrant from his nap in a community park, face down in slender grass and wet sand. I lifted myself up into a knee fold, sat my ass atop the heels of my shoes, realizing I was getting pretty goddamn sick of waking up from something and not knowing where I was.

Man, what a nightmare.

I'd never been so stoned in all my life.

I instinctively reached for my weapon and didn't find it. What I *did* find was *myself* questioning if I ever had one at all, if that whole episode I awoke from hadn't been merely in my head, something I dreamt.

Ahhh, but there was my prescription bottle. Disregarding the tendency to look around me I was actually *afraid to,* at first.....I regarded the label on the container for a moment or two:

Hmmm, 'Patient 6AF7BC789, 'is what they call me.

Wait a minute.

6AF7BC789 ....

6 is AFraid of 7BeCause 789........

I think I might've killed somebody.

Maybe somebody's child, and all over the matter of my drink being denied me, a drunken fool knocking me over and talking down to me, my own accursed anger.

But those Brown Coat bastards.....

........*Adam*, collectively......

I guess you could call them *all* Adam.....Adam One, Adam Two, Three, Fifty-three, like Thing One and Thing Two in Seuss' *Cat In the Hat* only Adam goes on and on like the progeny of horny energizer bunnies. And their true faces could scare the diarrhea out of children come trick-or-treat time.

I returned the pills to my pocket, distracted myself from my thoughts by daring to look around.

I was in the center of an acre or so of territory isolated from the rest of the festival grounds, shrouded on all sides by sloping woodland.

I'd been tossed onto an embankment like a duffle bag of dirty laundry, alongside a rolling stream several meters wide and shallow enough to expose countless rounded moss-covered stones, waters knee-deep to an average adult and clear as well, as a mountain spring. A waterfall the width of a one-way street descended from an overhanging cliff, down a hundred feet of sloping smooth straight rock before free falling into the wading waters below and curtaining a dark cavern yawning insidiously from out of the mountainside.

Bathing in the stream and beneath the waterfall were at least a couple dozen people of both sexes and varying adult ages, from young to very old, wading, showering, splashing water over their bodies with their hands, naked but for tight black netting wrapped around their bodies and over their heads that clung to their skin like wet t- shirts, revealing all or nothing depending on the angle each stood in the sunlight, looking at them from my direction .reminded me of the same peculiar mesh- like material I'd noticed back at the ticket booth. The way they behaved was slow-moving and serene, almost erotic, not one less than a few yards away from the other. They moved like their bathing experience was a personal thing, an intoxicating self-baptism, like the waters were sacred, like strangers pleasuring themselves in a public shower and unconcerned with the others nearby. Hell, they could have been under the effects of some indigenous psilocybin.

Fucking hippies.

Roosted in a crouched, vulture-like squat on top of the largest boulder along my side of the stream to the left of the falls, overlooking the bathers like a black-clad heavy metal lifeguard, was Thaddeus.

I assumed it was him.

After all, I knew he wanted to see me pronto, he was the central figure in this setting that stuck out like an erect penis through a hole in a wall, and he turned and looked directly at me like he wasn't surprised I was there.

As soon as our eyes met, he rose from his perch upon the great stone, hopped off and onto the sandy turf beside the stream with black boots laced up to the knees, as suave as Errol Flynn and with hands in black leather gloves upon his hips like a superhero landing from flight and damn proud of himself.

He wore several layers of black clothing, shirts, pants, all tattered and mangled as if pulled through a shredder, held together by a silver-buckled thick black belt and what looked like bare bicycle chains slung over one shoulder like ammunition belts, a multitude of silver trinkets and cross-like pendants about his neck and fastened all about him, flowing layers of shredded cape that cascaded past his boots and dragged across the grass as he approached me.

What he wore couldn't have been the extent of his wardrobe, so I assumed for the festival's sake his attire was entirely for dramatic purposes and he was really a tshirt-and-jeans kinda guy. God knows.

Long dark curls of full hair cascaded below his shoulders, his face full-bearded and making it difficult to for me to determine what age he'd be under normal conditions, perhaps middle-aged, glare both calculating and subtly tyrannical.

His hands left his waist and he halted a few feet away, stared me down.

I noticed the son of a bitch had taken my Federal Marshal's badge, for he wore it over the breast of his shirt like it was his.

"I am Thaddeus," he announced, wasting no further time, "and you are Detective Sam Cross, currently on the payroll of the American Government's ultra top secret Operation American Carnevil branch. I've heard so much about you. I pity your condition. Then again, if you've heard of me you know you've never been so close to death in all your relatively young life."

"I've been closer," I told him, and I believed I had. I mean, *look* at me.

He was large, overwhelming, his countenance eclipsed the sun like a medieval black knight of heavy metal doom.

Nevertheless, he really didn't intimidate me. The way I see it, anyone that seems larger than life is usually all theatrics on the outside with a chewy tootsie roll center full of deeply personal issues.

With a flick of a gloved hand, he summoned a band of Brown Coats, some of which rose all about me like they'd been camouflaged within the grass and been there all along, one rose out from within the stream, a few from behind the nearby trees. They immediately encircled the two of us in a very wide football huddle, umbrellas opened, and if they all sat down, I imagined we could play a very crazy game of duck duck goose altogether.

Thaddeus then chuckled to himself and knelt down towards me, extended a thick black leather gloved hand with its index finger straight out as if to touch the tip of my nose.

All the Adams stood still, like human flies with coats, umbrellas blocking the sun from our inner circle.

"I'm aware of the nature of your condition," Thaddeus said to me. "But something about you leaves me suspect to the true reason you're here, detective. That's why I had to meet you. To inspect you. To prove a few points before I decide whether or not I should send you on your way, let you see my dear sweet Sal so she could rid you of that unfortunate tumor of yours. Here's my first point...."

He revealed my semi-automatic from beneath his cape, tucked under his belt. He withdrew it, eyes never leaving mine as if to read any possible reaction I had to this, and my instincts told me he was about to make his point with my own gun to my head and a mob boss interrogation.

He motioned to a Brown Coat. "Bring me that reverend son of a bitch while I'm doing this, dude. You know who. Might as well prove all my points here at once."

Adam nodded, departed into the trees, and the others closed the gap he'd left in our circle.

"I love these fuckers," Thad said to me. "I conjure them up from the soil, out of the dust of the ground, breath into their nostrils the breath of life like the god I am to help me out this time of year when you sickly little pricks come around. But I guess with the soil around here, there aren't enough early birds to catch all the *worms*..... "

He continued, "Plus I get to make use of an old vaudevillian wardrobe collection willed to me by a

Broadway producer friend who died a half century before you were born. And check this out....."

He knelt to the ground, picked up a stone the size of a golf ball, aimed, and flung it into the underside of one of their umbrellas. The Adams jumped all in unison, not in surprise, but chain-reacting like the vibrations of a stricken gong.

"Now ain't that the shit, every time I do it," he said. "The umbrellas are transmitters, from one to another, how they communicate amongst themselves. And then this is how *you and I* communicate....."

He brought the gun up to the side of his head and immediately pounded a few rounds into it, held his other gloved hand up to catch the bullets out the other side like tiny baseballs to a catcher's mitt. He shook the bullets away and they dropped into the grass. White smoke arose from beneath his hair.

I cleared my throat.

"I can't be killed," he said, passed my gun on to an Adam who took it and went away, tightening our circle, "case you were wondering. Case you're wondering also, your gun and badge will be returned to you, just not presently. Your party foul back there cost you points. But you'll be glad to know you didn't kill anyone."

He pushed aside his cape and sat cross-legged before me on the embankment.

"I can't physically die, hurt, touch skin to skin with my dearest love. Whenever we try to touch each other, our skin evaporates into spirit and we pass through one another, and when that happens I can't even feel her soul. The most success we've had being intimate is when we're fully clothed, gloved, ski masks, like teenagers on a snow trip, plastic wrap over our lips so we can press them together and actually feel ourselves kissing. It's like we're fucking invisible to each other, but we can see each other just fine. It's embarrassing to admit that. And it sucks hog balls. But two hundred years ago, she and I were starving and alone in several feet of snow storm and separated from our caravan in our journey westward .our son and baby daughter died in our arms and we'd eaten what was left of the horse that just the month prior bared the burden of carrying our supplies and then there comes this ghostly apparition into our shelter one night and makes this deal with us, guaranteeing our eternal survival if we'd mutually agree to the curse you see in effect before you all these many years since. Ah, but allow me to drive my point home. Company's here."

The Brown Coat circle broke again, and in sauntered the distinguished Reverend Larry Farewell. He was dressed in tan suit coat and yellow tie, dress pants, same stuff I was used to seeing him in on television whenever I channel surfed. "Thaddeus, my friend. So good to see you."

"Hi Larry, how's the Lord doing these days?"

"The same as yesterday, today, and forever," replied Farewell to Thad with a jovial grin. Then he noticed me there, knelt before Thaddeus on the ground, and I was certain he didn't know what to think of it.

I'm not actually kneeling before him, was what I was about to say, *I just woke up from a nap, and, well.......*

Thad motioned to the Adams. "Okay, boys, you know what to do. Hold 'im, strip 'im, tape his mouth shut. We don't want to disturb the bathers. And bring me the blood."

As soon as the Brown Coats set to work, Farewell turned ghostly pale, panicked, tried to wrench free for a moment but fell limp and distraught the next as if accepting fate. They forced him to his knees, peeled off his clothes, and while one of them pulled out a roll of gray duct tape and ripped free a fat several inches for that pudgy sniveling grimace of his, he shouted, "*You won't get away with this! The Lord Jesus Christ has my soul!!!!*"

He proceeded to pull off his own black leather gloves, dropping them to the ground, rolling up his sleeves.

"And He *has*," Thad told him, calmly nonchalant over the whole ordeal. "Good Lord decides what to do with souls, no one else does, but down here on God's green Earth, your body's just a vessel made from the dust of the ground, quite like these Adam bastards but *they're* fresh. I just need to prove a point to the detective here, and you have been *very* naughty."

"Blood!" he then cried to the Adams, quite cross with them. "Don't make me ask you thrice....."

While the one Adam wasted no time taping his mouth, another came forward and brought before Thad a black porcelain vase decorated with same white peace signs I'd seen splashed all over the ticket booth. Thad dipped his hand inside the vase, drew forth a handful of wet thick liquid, reddish black. He splashed it across Farewell's chest, and the reverend painfully flinched like from a lashing by a whip.

Thad turned to me. "That was *my* blood. Seals the fate between him and I. You see, though he's alive, he's already dead now. And he knows it, too. Just *look at him.....*"

I looked.

Farewell was as frightened as any man I'd ever seen. I felt sorry for him. Either this was going to turn into another parlor trick as it could have been with the gun to the head routine, or the man was about to die. I changed my sitting position to where I could sit my butt firmly in the sandy grass and more comfortably, but the trick was to sit a bit further away without revealing I was preparing to witness anything horrid.

Thaddeus approached the trembling reverend and knelt down before him. He placed one single bare hand over the man's forehead and whispered to him a gentle command: *"Feel no pain."*

Thad took Farewell's rigid left arm, raised it, palm out, wrist up. As he did so, it went limp. Holding it up that way, Thad brought a thumb and forefinger from his own hand, fingernails manicured into ivory-white vampiric pointed talons, and proceeded to dig into the skin of Farewell's wrist.

"Ahhhhh," he said, then, to Farewell, "feel no pain?" Farewell shook his head feverishly, sweating something fierce.

And then Thad said in reply, almost rapturously, "Greeeeeeeeeeeeat, man, lovin' it," feeling, digging, beginning to pull on something tenuous out from the skin that resembled a guitar string, "I think we're good to go....."

Then, to me, "Watch *this*......"

What little blood at first escaped the reverend's wrist now came out suddenly like a severed hose gushing fluid from beneath a hood of a car, spraying everyone inside the circle of Adams with gore, including my face and hair and the new jacket I wasn't sure I'd really paid for yet.

Thaddeus dug and pulled on veins and arteries from out of the wrist forcefully and then with both hands, which in the process tore open a wide crevice across the underside of Farewell's arm up to the shoulder with all the force of pulling electrical wiring from out the length of a wall of thin sheet rock. The reverend tightened his eyes shut, tears flowing down his face across clenched teeth.

Im-fucking-possible.

Thad caught a snag at the shoulder. Determined, he pushed Farewell backwards onto the ground, cast aside the stringy carnage, made for the poor man's chest. With both hands, nails-first, he dug into Farewell's rib cage, past a wall of yellow fat which burst outwards like stove-top popcorn through foil, and pulled apart the man's bones into a gaping cavity that burst forth an upsurge of blood like lava flowing from broken volcanic rock that gathered into a pool I had to move to avoid.

Farewell still clenched his teeth. Poor fucker was still *alive*.

Thaddeus reached into the man's chest, pushed aside his lungs, gripped his beating heart and wrenched it out forcefully but with seasoned surgical care.

As he scooped it up with both hands and brought it upwards, he took the heel of one black boot and sunk it deep inside his victim's chest, stepping through the right lung for a firm foothold and squashing it like a plump London Broil which splattered out the sides like one stepping on a liver-colored balloon filled with duck pâté.....he continued with certain restraint so that a great bulk of Larry's circulatory system extended and pulled and was yanked out as intact as possible while remaining attached to the heart like a squid head with yards of tentacles holding onto something fast because it did not want to be captured, like a stubborn weed being pulled from out of the ground with all its roots until whatever dark magic which kept the tissue in a stronghold exhausted and the stringy mass snapped apart from every crevice of the body they were extracted from, like beet-red wet noodles, like a spoonful of thick spaghetti with a gelatinous meatball of writhing black muscle on top, being lifted to feed the mouth of a hungry giant....

The reverend lay across the grassy embankment lifeless, eyes wide and bulging, body contorted on its back in such a way it reminded me of John Belushi's Joe Cocker imitation. Blood emptied into the stream, dripped from each blood-sprayed Adam, from the hand I wiped my face with. Everywhere I *looked* there was blood.

Thaddeus cradled the heart and fleshy carnage, rocked it like a baby to sleep, began to sing softly to it.....

"*Away in a manger.....................*"

And then he arose and said, "*Farewell*, Larry.....say hi to the Good Lord for me."

With no further thought, he discarded the armful of gore to the ground.

He took a few steps away from the body, knelt down to me so that our faces were no further than a foot in length apart.

"You fuck with me, you get what *he* got.

Sonofabitch had plans to make my lover *public*, thinks

she belongs to the Lord. She belongs to *ME!!!!*" And I believed it.

I agreed with him.

He proved his point, that he was badass, and that I shouldn't fuck with him.

I was convinced he could read my thoughts, and, as my face graced his cold and calculating scrutiny, he knew I had nothing to hide.

He released me into the hands of Clive Cunning, who, wearing a large cotton gauge over the center of his face, started bitching to me rather nasally about how I blew his nose clean off. Sad sucker even lost his toupee.

The circle of Adams separated as Cunning led me away, and I could hear Thad's voice behind me, telling me, "You best respect my Salonica, you hear, Federal Marshal Sam Cross of the *OAC*......"

ROOM OF THE NEXT ONES

"Shit here with me and wait," Cunning instructed, pressing a blood-and-puss-filled cloth into a portion of where his nose had been, under a section of gauze that started to bleed down his upper lip.

"*Shit* here with you?"

"Funny, wise-ash. *You* try talking with no goddamn *nosesh......*"

"You first."

"We're in the sacred Room of the Next Onesh."

"The Next Ones?"

"Yesh."

"And what the hell is *that*, half camel half sheep? Tell it to stop looking at me."

"It'sh a llama."

Indeed, a llama was looking at me with lazy eyes from three feet away, over a conventional hinged wooden door with the top half missing, the bottom half shut. Losing its curiosity toward me, it backed off and disappeared beyond the doorway. I lifted myself from my chair to catch a better look at where it went. All I could see were trees and the tops of tall bushes, and the outside night.

Night had fallen quickly. When I'd followed Cunning to this place, it was already past eight thirty. He'd led me past tall trees, behind tents, avoiding crowds, into a grass clearing where a petting zoo rose up to my right and dispersed wooden houses to my left, *Little House on the Prairie*-type old western one-room homesteads, large tiki-like torches burning around each house and helping to illuminate the dusk-ridden area. Animals, mostly farm-type, ran rampant here and there over the landscape. Ducks, goats, chickens, peacocks, a few deer that showed no apparent fear of being there. A hundred or so people lounged out along the grassland in distinct clusters of twelve, each group circling its own small campfire. Large tiki- like torches burned around each house.

"*They're all waiting to go where we're going,*" Cunning had told me.

I popped another couple of my meds.

And where we went was towards and into the wooden dwelling at the center of this livened ghost town, the largest one, with an enclosed rear yard of trees and bushes and fencing. Four to six Brown Coats with opened umbrellas kept watch over the front entrance as we passed them to enter. Half of them had blood stains on their coats.

And so there we were.

Chairs like mine of hand-crafted antique dark wood with ruby red cushions and backing lined the inner windowless walls of what I now learned was the Room of the Next Ones, every seat filled with a man or woman I could only guess were society's elite waiting for a miracle cure from Thaddeus' one and only. I recognized some of them, couldn't place where I saw them from. Wait. One dude was a news anchorman. One an Arab prince I saw on CNN. A Vegas casino owner. A senator. A rap star. European royalty. Some faces I've seen in movies. An old wealthy man outfitted with a portable respirator. A South American dictator. Japanese billionaires. And... .could that be *Cher*?

Well I'd be damned.

I was in the waiting room of a doctor's office for the rich and famous, or infamous. Most all of them were even reading magazines, crossing their legs, biding their time.

Besides myself, the room full of "next ones" and the chairs upon which we all sat, were two overhanging crystal chandeliers and what appeared to be a large birdbath situated in the center of the room like a font for holy water which we all, upon entering the room, were required to wash our faces and hands in.

I thought to ask Cunning what that was.

"Oh, that's Shalonica'sh urine," he replied.

After all I'd seen so far, it was only this bit of news that could make me puke.

And I almost did.

"Detective Sam Cross," a Brown Coat appeared at the door beside me where the llama had been only a minute ago, and announced my name like a nurse for the next patient, "and Mister Cunning."

"Shee?" Cunning said to me. "I told you. *We're the next onesh*........."

SaLoNiCa

We followed the Brown Coat for only a couple of feet until he abruptly stepped off to one side, turned, stood at attention. I cast my gaze downwards and right up to me walked a wee man, no more than a yard in height, which took his place, greeted me. He wore identical clothing to the Adams', same hair, same dirt- smudged complexion and pudgy lips but no sunglasses so there was more of him to see. This time, that was a good thing. He had full, beaming eyes and lacked of the bothersome cosmetic complication of earthworms burrowing in and out of his skin.

And he had a very warm personality.

The little fellow shook my hand.

"Hello Mister Cross, my name is Adam," he said. "*The* Adam.......n o   n o,   n o t   t h e   *A d a m   a n d E v e* .....Adam.....but among the ones here created by Thad, I was the first. I was the perfect one, and the others after me came out all malformed, much taller. But I hear that's the case with Adam and Eve as well. Maybe they were *my* size, and the majority of the rest of the human race came out taller and they weren't supposed to be that way. All of us my size, you see, we're *the right size*, have been all along. It's the rest of you buggars came out giants. Follow me, please...."

We followed him into a cobblestone courtyard situated out back enclosed by dense shrubbery and tall trees, plants and flowing colors of flowers of every sort both in the landscape and bursting forth out of multitudes of all variations of hand-crafted pottery, climbing vines overtaking marble statues of men, women and animals set on stone pillars. There was a small fish pond in the corner surrounded by striking birds of paradise in full bloom, and flamingos rested single-legged in the gentle currents of water pouring over some rocks into the pond from what looked like a silver gravy server the size of a wheelbarrow. Victorian era street lamps dispersed throughout the yard illuminated the setting. It was lush, atmospheric, full of nature and art, meditatively quiet but for the songs of nightbirds in the trees above and the music of frogs and crickets, and two voices conversing together ahead of us.

I spotted my llama, making its way along the side of the house through a parting of hedges, towards an astonishing congregation of various other animals spread over and around the expanse of an elevated wooden backyard patio pool deck at the yard's side opposite me.

The deck was sizeable enough to be a stage where I'd imagined a rock band could perform and with plenty of space should the festival program directors decide to throw a new year's bash.

Maybe they do that sort of thing here off-season.

An adult male lion rested on the stage with an immense mane, sharing its space with an assortment of goats, a tan-colored mare, a Great Dane and several other canines, cats, a Galapagos tortoise, a couples of camels, ostriches each remarkably unopposed to the presence of its companions and quite sedately composed.

What looked like a Black Mamba coiled itself around one of the street lamps as my gaze wandered, watching me. A horde of rodent-sized animals seemed to move about in the darkness beneath the wooden deck. A full-sized black-stained gazebo shelter looming above the deck in a full circle mimicked the Adams' black umbrellas, its inner ceiling held up by diagonal beams bolted into a single wooden pillar coming out of the center of the stage. It seemed home to a number of birds, which chirped and hopped two and fro among the beams, their nests twisted in the dull light like cocoons in thick cobwebs.

I noticed an above-ground Jacuzzi to the right of the deck, large enough to fill it with a dozen people, and a woman in a suit dress and coat was standing before it and speaking to a black hooded figure bathing in the waters. At the far end of the sauna, I saw a Brown Coat dipping what appeared to be a five-gallon wooden bucket into the hot tub's water, disappearing into the dark, being replaced by another one who'd dump water into the hot tub, and this cycle was repeated often.

Adam looked up at me briefly, as if reading my thoughts, and quietly fed me a dose of narrative. "Ah, some of my tall brothers.....their job over there is to fetch some of the water Sal bathes in to dump into the mountain stream that falls over Thaddeus' cave. Then they replace it. You see, the bathers you saw know that, that's why they bathe there."

As we approached, I found us passing twelve people, six off to my left and six to my right, all sitting cross- legged upon very large bean-bag-like chairs, all garbed in black robes with little unveilings of street clothing beneath, all with black wool gaucho hats like Zorro's bolero, which effectively kept their faces in shadow when they chose to look up.

Adam halted, and so did we. He turned, motioned for two of his taller siblings, ordered them to take Cunning aside for now, that Sal needed to see me alone. I was relieved when they took Freaky Fuck away, and, though with respectful restraint and whispers, he protested and sniffled all the way.

"Hold on," Adam said to me, "she's still with her last client. In the meantime, these twelve people here are the Approbation Officers. They're anonymous clients that volunteer to be here and rotate every four hours from a large waiting list of them. Salonica refuses to heal without them. She believes every human being needs a satisfying degree of support and praise after experiencing a personal miracle, and the release found in sharing the moment with others frees them of the need to tell anyone else of their experience here. That, and the fact that there'd be no more healing if word gets out. The exploitation will kill her. And you and I both know, Thad will deal with whoever attempts to fuck it all up if he has to. Ain't nobody fucked it up yet. We're sittin' pretty, what with all the money we rake in off our clientele."

"About time somebody mentioned money," I said below a whisper. "I noticed that back at the ticket booth."

Adam turned away, and we both waited.

The black hooded figure raised herself halfway out of the Jacuzzi and I saw a black hand fall over the suit lady's forehead and

.......and she was healed.

And oh, the suit chick was elated.

The Approbation Officers broke out in a round of applause.

The black hooded figure sunk back into the spa and faced away.

The lady about-faced and stepped away from the Jacuzzi, high heels championing the rounded cobblestones of the yard floor, making her way towards us. One of her hands clenched her chest as she released an exclamation of rapturous joy to us that her arthritis was completely gone and that she felt ten years younger, and she could breath better. She enthusiastically shook the hands of

85

each Approbation Officer, and they congratulated her, were all very happy to hear that she was happy.

She then went away, disappearing down a walkway around the side of the house.

"Okay now, time for you," said Adam to me, "just walk over there, sit on that stone directly in front of the steps, and she'll come out to meet you. Good luck, man."

"Thanks," I told him, and he watched me go. I didn't think luck applied.

I went, sat myself atop a solitary stone that seemed to fit comfortably with the conformities of my ass.

The figure bathing in the Jacuzzi lifted herself completely out of the waters, rising to a stand upon the deck. She wore an outfit identical to the bathers that covered her skin and conformed to her body, though slit down the sides at the legs and into shredded lengths all the way down the arms from the shoulders, exposing bare, smooth black skin of a voluptuous, trim, bare- footed body beneath. She was dripping wet, and her attire clung to her like that of a sea witch cast ashore. She pushed off the material which cloaked her head and it fell down her back, exposing long tar-black hair braided in several places interwoven with metallic silver strands of beads. A cape shredded in several layers followed her tall and beautiful majesty across the deck as, step by step, she distanced herself from her emergence out of the tub.

Truly, from the theatrical attire alone, this was Thaddeus' babe.

And she was hands down the most gorgeous black woman I'd ever seen.

She eyeballed me with a curious gaze, turned to the animals resting placid upon the stage and paused to caress the heads of a few of them. After a moment, she returned her gaze to me, stern yet empathetic, reading me, made her way to the top of the steps, eyes never leaving mine, sat herself down and gave me her full attention.

I found myself suddenly awestruck, overwhelmed by the sheer reality of the vision I was now facing, of where I was, my surroundings, my circumstances, what I had seen. Even on the jet ride up, if Curtains had explained all of what I'd be facing all up through now, I'd have laughed my ass off as if it was all a joke.

Maybe my medication was meant for far more than just pain.

I *do* have anger issues, and for awhile there I *did* freak out halfway through the festival grounds with a gun in my hands. But I can't imagine where this whole experience would have gone if I'd been *sober* throughout, but I believe it would've gone south and rather quick-like. If you knew me, you'd think I'd have been as relatively placid as the animals in this here backyard Garden of Eden the whole damn time.....

And nothing had prepared me for the fact that Salonica was black.

She was quick to read my surprise concerning that, but said nothing. I bet she got that kind of reaction frequently, anyway.

A couple of hundred years of it.

Certainly all those years back, it was unheard of for white folk to take an African slave girl for his own with eternal love and for raising a proper family....with.....a hefty *fuck you* to the rest of the world.....and it occurred to me that perhaps in the tale Thaddeus told me, his family was separated from their westward caravan for a reason, and *that* was the reason. A moment of silence passed between her and I, and in afterthought I believe she actually fed me that insight without saying one word.

And then she spoke.

"Welcome, Sam. I've been waiting for you."

I was overwhelmed, but not intimidated. "So you're the big dog upon which all this hype is centered, the great secret goddess everyone wants to see. Honestly, I don't wish to sound disrespectful, and from what they say I'm indeed dying, so if you can just get on with this I'll be on my way. I feel like I'm wearing a bodice with these bandages, and, despite the outright pathetic life I endure from day to day, I'd rather not die just yet. I don't know. I've seen more than your average television-fed American can spit at, had countless opportunities to die at the hands of, well, carny freaks and fuckin' sideshow hippies, but all I want to do is relax somewhere with a cigarette and have the world leave me the fuck alone for awhile. Please. Heal me."

That was a mouthful.

Salonica regarded me for a moment, then lifted herself off the steps and proceeded down them, straight up to me, set herself down on relaxed bended knees and faced me for a more intimate conversation, close-up, one on one. Her candor was relaxing, graceful, set me at ease like a famous celebrity who moved into the house next door to mine and was now at my doorstep to break the ice.

"Sam," she said to me calmly. "You don't have to explain yourself. I know everything about you. That being so, you are the most unique among any who have come before me, and I embrace you in spirit like no other."

That went above my head.

"So.....you've said this thousands of times, I take it, like a faith healer about to administer the power of God."

"I say this only to you," said Salonica. "Now, take off your jacket, your shirt. Just throw them out of the way for now."

I did just as she requested. My exposed bandages felt like someone had saran-wrapped a welcome mat to my lower chest and belly.

Her glare turned fanciful, as though I was a male stripper having bared my chest to her, and she was feeling frisky. She crept up to me, wrapped her arms around me loosely, invading the parameter of my own personal space and making me feel uncomfortable despite my medicated high.

Her fingers slid across the surface of my bandages, the dressing of my Tanumbra-inflicted wound, found an end to the white gauze tape and proceeded to peel it off my body, layer after layer, round and round my upper torso as I raised my arms to allow her room, and in no time she was down to pulling off the square bandage like ticky-tape from over the exit wound of my abdomen just below my rib cage. The sight of it made me feel like going after Tanumbra all over again, the abominable sonofabitch. It was like looking down at a blotchy red sewn-up section of myself that had been impaled with the lance of a jousting knight. Salonica cast aside my dressing to the cobblestone floor, looked at me, wrapped both arms over my shoulders and brought our faces together as though she intended to kiss my lips passionately.

I would have let her.

"My dear Marshal Sam Cross," she whispered to me seductively, "I bet if you knew why you're really here, you would have come before me anyway, risked everything. Have you yet wondered why only the elite come to see me? Why, with all my power, I have seen none of the poor and helpless, none of the needy and truly sick and dying who frequent this world by the billions. For far too long have I been kept hidden by the wealthy in order to suit their needs, and for an equal length of time I've grown weary of this unfulfilling gig. I've come to the conclusion I'd be better off assisting the sick and needy without my powers rather than being stuck here within these mountains forever, living as I do. Since I can't physically touch another human being, only but to heal them, I have my animals, other beings to actually feel and touch and hold, and everything nature has to offer is drawn to me, becomes tranquil and healthy in my presence. My lover is jaded by all of this, but you can't blame him in his situation. I mean, with what he can do, he could've asserted himself and become the anti-Christ almost by definition, ruled the world, what with his disregard for mortals. We could have gone off into all sorts of directions in our situation, what with we can both do. We have powers that can turn the world on its head, beyond science, beyond reason. But it's what we *can't* do that vexes us, and, now that all's virtually said and done, I can admit that it's a real delight in seeing you. You see, we're cursed, him and I, and with every curse, there's a way to reverse it. Thank you Sam, and I'll always remember you."

I didn't understand one word of what she said, but as I cast my gaze down between us, I could tell the fingers of one hand had already disappeared into my wound, and I felt no pain, just a slight tingling below my ribs.

Out from my abdomen, she withdrew what looked like a large black prune, which she placed between her breasts, and it absorbed into the skin of her breast plate.

She then brought her lips to mine, kissed me sincerely, before I knew what the hell was going on.

Nicholas Grabowsky

And then she said to me, "The curse has now been broken. I'm sorry you didn't know, but no one could have accomplished the deed unless they had no idea what they were really here for. Run. Run, before they all discover what has taken place here, and that you're the one who at last brought freedom to us."

Suddenly something was wrong with the animals on and around the stage behind her. They became restless, getting up and moving about like they'd woken from sleep and didn't know where they were, like they'd been sitting around forever patiently posing for a portrait and the artist just announced that he was done. Rats and mice scurried from under the cage, immediately besieged by cats. The great lion sat up, winced, then swiped at the camel closest to him and, without warning, erupted in a roar that ripped through the air like thunder and shook the ground. Flocks of birds by the thousands took to the air from out of every crevice and tree and from beneath the umbrella-like deck shelter, and the sky turned black with them like an Egyptian plague. Pandemonium ensued, animals scattering, tumbling into one another, the neck of the camel now crushed between the lion's jaws. A few wolves ran rabid after the goats, bringing them down. The Black Mamba had vanished.

Salonica kept us there for moments during this, unmoving, her eyes never leaving mine. "Run," she said to me, more urgently. *"They're already here....."*

I don't think it was the medication which made me slow to respond, don't think it had anything to do with what tranquilizing power she had over me. I think it's simply because I couldn't believe what was going on around me. My eyes leaving hers, I found that my wound had healed up, good as new. And I suddenly was as sober as a little Mormon girl.

Salonica kept her cool. Her gaze left me and I followed it, turned around, rose at the sight of Thaddeus himself marching right up to me, pulling off and tossing aside his black leather gloves, exposing his bare hands. He brought with him Brown Coats by the dozens, approaching me from every direction, from behind him, at his sides, from around the stage.

I was a dead man.

If I wasn't so distracted by this certain doom, I would have caught sight of Curtains looking up from beneath his

90

own Approbation Officer bolero hat to inspect what was happening to me, before he exited somewhere with the other eleven of them that had been seated with him, all of them panicked but he.

I couldn't react quickly enough. Thad thrust one hand into my neck, gripping, lifting me up, his other hand spread open against the side of my head like a Vulcan mind meld. He brought me close and into his glare.

"Detective Cross!" he screamed. *"You deceived me!"*

He was touching me, as much as I could allow any man, and I wasn't dying. He was thoroughly dismayed. He set me down, released me.

Behind him and all around, the Brown Coats, every last one of them, fell to the ground all at once like sacks of garden soil ripped open at the bottom and all the dirt spilled out below them, with everything they wore, their coats, sunglasses, black umbrellas resting like garnishes beside each resulting mound of earth and clothing accessories. Their remains were everywhere.

Thaddeus looked down upon his hands in astonishment, at the utter chaos all around him, at his vanquished minions. He then looked upon me, and I readied myself for a fight, man to man. Instead, he sighed, and I saw within his features an almost immediate resignation to what he once was, a sense of relief from a seriously heavy burden, but then the fucker pushed me to one side and out of his way like a rude prick trying to fetch his girl inside a nightclub.

Salonica was quick to receive him into her arms, and despite the utter havoc around us I risked a remaining quick moment with them. It was a touching scene, the two lovers touching skin to skin, checking themselves out, like they couldn't believe the miracle, and they were swept up in the realization. Apparently that's what they've been wanting all along, and nothing else mattered to them just yet.

"Ahem," a voice addressed me off to the side. I looked, then looked down. Why, the little Adam was alive and well, for some reason, and I was glad to see him. He handed me my shirt and jacket, and put them on hurryingly. "Thanks for that, sorry certain decision- makers had to use you and all, but Tanumbra *did* put the damn thing in you. They say Tanumbra

was released by his captors, a traveling carnival side show group of fellows you were going to be assigned to investigate, and he stole from them what he eventually gave to you. It's a long story. The thing is we have a happily ever after with these two, who must get going themselves if they're ever to escape unnoticed, and if you know what's best you'd better get the fuck outta here now because when everyone here knows it's you who did this, all these people are going to be crying out for your b l o o d .... "

"That's just fucking *great*," I said. "Hold on."

I wasn't about to flee yet. I tapped Thaddeus on the shoulder, who broke from his embrace with Sal long enough to hand me over my Federal Marshal badge without looking at me.

I took it, then got the hell out of there, and already the little Adam was making for the house's back door where people in the Room of the Next Ones were already poking their heads out. As I passed the door, making my way for the side walkway around the house, I heard Adam announce to the room:

"Okay folks, the curse is broken. You can all go home now....."

I saw Cunning clenching his blood-soaked nose bandages, having a full-on fit.

I ran.

I followed the side walkway, out a back gate, onto a grove of grassland into the night. Behind me I heard screams, wails, sounds of panic. I turned to look back. The people encircling the campfires were standing, running about. People flooded out the front door of the house of the Next Ones, some were pointing in my direction, some held torches. Animals ran amok. It was utterly surreal, and I desperately had to escape it for fear of my life.

The festival was still going on, and people were everywhere. I circumvented the grounds, ducking behind shadows, running, trying not to be seen and very successful in doing so. From what I saw, nothing I was fleeing from affected the rest of the festival grounds, and everyone seemed to be enjoying themselves.

I went straight for the motel. My door was unlocked. I found my bags already packed, but I went through them anyway, as quickly as I could. I hoisted them out of the room, and a limo was outside waiting for me with an opened door and no one around. I made for it, with my luggage, closed the door, and the limo took off.

As soon as I realized I was headed in the direction out of there, and then towards the private runway I'd arrived at in Ironton, I knew exactly where I wanted to go from there.

I didn't bother to see who it was that drove me there, but the Learjet was ready for me when we arrived, and the James Earl Jones-sounding pilot was there to greet me.

"Where to, Detective, and in a hurry, I presume?"

"Take me to Jamaica," I told him. "Refuel where you don't normally. We need to get there pronto and in one piece."

All I wanted now was to make Tunambra pay for this whole godforsaken shit-hole I was in. Everyone with power and money will surely be after my ass from now on, and I knew I could never be safe.

Ah, but I still had my medication, and Salonica's power couldn't have possibly affected *that*.....

TunaMBRa

I arrived in Jamaica without incident. Through my connections there, I was able to acquire weapons and lay low, gained information and indeed, evidence told me without a doubt Tunambra was still somewhere within the country.

I found my way back to the market place up the great Black River's backcountry, to the public men's restroom where my whole story *began*.....and was about to *end*, because Tunambra was waiting for me there.

Just like old times, as they say.

It was more than just pure luck or mere coincidence. The sonofabitch had been waiting for me all along.

I noticed the illicit anti-government graffiti on the walls had all been painted over, replaced with new illicit anti-government graffiti.

He was crouching there in the corner, in the very same place he'd previously left me for dead, between the first toilet stall and the urinal. I pulled out my semiautomatic from my drawers, approached him with extreme caution.

And then the fucker actually *spoke* to me, for the very first time.

"You think there's a reason some joker with the American Federal Government spelled your particular branch Operation American Carnevil with an e-v-i-l at the end?"

I didn't know. I didn't care. I just wanted to plug the bastard with bullets right through his brain and heart and every which way so that he was *dead*.

Gone.

And good fucking riddance.....

He knew I wasn't going to give him a chance for shit, and without further ado I blew him the hell away until my weapon was spent, and I could swear the fucker tried to fight back, his hair turned wild, his eyes yellow, his teeth lengthening into a hideous mouthful of frightening, widened snarl.

In afterthought, considering all that time I'd spent in pursuit of him, not to mention considering what I'd been through *because* of him, I almost wish I would have given him time to talk to me more. I mean, it was obvious he wanted me to kill him in the end. And had it not been for my relentless addictive pursuit and bloodthirst for his ass, I may have come up with a few pieces consequently absent from this whole ordeal, questions that could have otherwise been answered.

But Tunambra was now deader than shit, and the restroom door burst open suddenly to Jamaican policemen summoned by my not having the hindsight to equip my gun with a silencer, and there was no Curtains to save me now, apparently....

Curtains Closed

I was arrested, frisked, disarmed, dismantled, dis - everythinged. I had no rights. Tossed into a Jamaican prison, with no idea of the outcome.

But I was allowed cigarettes, and when the jail bars slammed into place I resolved to lay down comfortably on the lower bunker with a bed above me, lit my smoke from a matchbook the guards most graciously had provided, and, for once, everything was quiet and serene around me. I sucked in the smoke, exhaled.

I had gotten the wish I'd said to Salonica, that all I wanted was to get the hell away, relax, and enjoy a smoke.

I didn't know what to do about my situation, and I didn't at the moment care.

"Well Sam, whaddya think, all said and done?" came a familiar voice from the bunker above me.

I sat up, got off my bed, stood up, and none other than Curtains rolled over on the top bunk and faced me, head propped up with one hand.

I couldn't believe he was there.

"We're better off in here," he told me. "They'll come looking for us, and when things die down, you'll be off and about your duties in no time. That is, unless you want out, then we have a nice comfy spot for you somewhere secret, where you can't get hurt. But you don't rightly want that, do you. You're a whore for adventure, Sam, and you know it well as I. That's why I chose you for OAC. You can't get enough of it. There are a hell of a lot of evil bastards out there among them carnies. Evil as in e-v-i-l."

I thought about it for a minute, what he said. Then, reverting back to my bed below his, I took a few drags from my smoke, and replied to my boss, "Yeah. I guess you're right, sir. I guess I live for this kinda shit........"

And I knew I did.

There was a lot more ahead for this ol' boy.......

The Father Keeper

(Author's note: this story came to me like a dream, so I wrote it like one. The ancient Minoan city of Knossos is fictitious here, as is its king, though I did do plenty of research to do history a degree of justice.)

1.
The Startling, Televised Introduction in the Minoan Ruins

It's been said some people have to die before they become famous.....

I cannot reveal the story behind my death, and my determination to overcome it, without revealing who I am, who I was, back when I was physically alive more than a few thousand years before any of your father's fathers coughed up phlegm from their groins and into the mothers of present civilization. It seemed personally to me that I'd been entombed beneath hundreds of feet of volcanic ash for *countless* thousands of years, instead of just a few.

As a mortal, I found myself often yearning to fly right straight into the heavens, to see what the heavens were all about, and then back again to my family so I could continue on with my life but with the knowledge acquired from having gone there and back. I know it sounds cliché, but perhaps I could have known beforehand what was to become of myself and my family, to my once grand city of Knossos and to the entire world I knew, had I been able to fly to the Great Flip-side of the Sky and retrieve information that could have saved us all, back then.

I could've made a difference, you bet your ass. Maybe the unseen millions of you who are hearing this could've been affected, if say, the life I knew continued on, and my home town in now-

96

ancient Crete was cataclysm-free from the get-go. No earthquakes, no tsunamis, no angry fiery earth to spew up and bury a thriving society no better or worse than any of those having risen from rich histories all over *today's* globe.

Long after my death, my spirit *did* learn to fly .really *soar* the way I would in my dreams, but away from my devastated homeland and from the undead pestilence which threatened my city in the months just before its fatal demise. We humans *do* have souls, and after the earth consumed me, it took my soul what seemed like forever to break free from all that volcanic ash which buried me, to rise high enough to reach sunlight, and, walking the earth essentially as a ghost, my soul has learned to pull itself into the air and literally fly around the world, kind of like the way Superman does in the movies only not nearly as quickly. I've passed through your towns and cities, walked your streets, glided across vast oceans. I've observed the world unnoticed over the last fifty years or so, to my estimation, and it was a sweet gig for awhile until I was summoned back here for the ultimate televised séance to let you all know I exist and to tell you the story of my death. What luck that a landslide of volcano spew preserved the moment of my final breath as perfectly as a three-dimensional snapshot for you, when all your chisels and brushes were finally retired, so your media can have an iconic image to flaunt that's no more or less handsome than your average Greek or Roman god statue, as far as I'm concerned.

I think what I'm meant to do is ultimately tell this story in a way you can understand, to warn you, I suppose, of imminent peril. The very fact that I am talking through a medium standing beside my remains with a dozen archeologists and a Rediscovery Channel camera crew tells me you may be on the brink of apocalypse. I mean, a mankind eager enough to dig up the past would've found my remains sooner or later, but if you found *me*, you've most certainly found *them*, the undead ones which surrounded me minutes before my civilization's sudden Pompeii-like catastrophe.

Throughout your history, from what I can tell, there's been no evidence of the cursed undead wreaking havoc among you, except to say in popular folklore. I thank the Snake Goddess for that, because the undead are nasty fuckers. They are physical embodiments of a plague for which there will *never* be a cure, and if ever they should exist again, Goddess forbid, it's going to take another volcano eruption equivalent to a 600 kiloton atomic bomb to stifle their rampage.

Believe me, I *know.*

Let me introduce you to them, and you to me, to my life as it was in the Aegean Palace Civilization of Minoa on ancient Crete, before Christ around about 1300 years, when one of those wretched undead washed up along the ancient shores of my own backyard in an event that marked the beginning of our end.....

2.
The Man from the Sea
Who Eats Lungs

Those who lived along our coastal shores back in the day were most familiar with the children's bedtime story of Meytani, a literal translation of the name being "man from the sea who eats lungs." It was a story often told to me as well, and to my siblings, and both my parents and their parents down through the generations. It was said that there lived a man in the ocean depths who'd now and again emerge from the waves when the ocean was restless at night and walk upon our beaches. He would seek out victims, particularly children whose innocent curiosities and propensity for mischief made them easy to catch, and when he did, he'd tear open their rib cages and devour their meaty lungs down to where each poor child had but one air sack left to utter a prayer or final breath before it popped. Meytani supposed that by eating human lungflesh, he'd develop the ability to breath air as we do and walk among us, as one of us.....

***

The Undead Man was discovered face-down upon a raft of tree branches and hemp rope upon a beach a mile or so north of my home city of Knossos, at a time when Knossos representatives and port slaves were anticipating the arrival of Egyptian trade ships, and the trade ships never came.

Instead, there was this lonely humanoid skin and bones carcass of a man washed up with that raft, and when the men hired to keep watch upon the beach first spotted him, they fretted and fussed among themselves as to whether they should immediately inform their superiors, or to send one of themselves out to see first if the man on the raft was alive and carried any valuables.

It was my uncle who elected to investigate, to venture out to the raft while his peers watched from a comfortable distance. According to their accounts, they witnessed my uncle approach the raft, lean over to inspect the man, then rise to indicate to them that all was clear, the man seemed to be dead, that they'd all best hurry up and report this.

And then suddenly, the dead man came to life, seized my uncle, brought him down. By the time the others had finished scratching their heads and wondering what to do before running to his aid, the raft man had eaten through my uncle's chest and entire side of his body, had pulled open the rib cage bones past the point of snapping them, torn out a lung and was feasting on it like a raw beef brisket.

They say his blood tainted the ocean waters permanently red on that shore.

My uncle's fellow watch-keepers were all utterly horrified.

"*Meytani*," one uttered.

Then it registered with the rest of them, the bedtime tale.

Meytani........

It was also a profound superstition among my people that death surrounded the *discoverers* of death washed up along the ocean shores of the North. When this particular brand of death washed up to their eventual scrutiny, they realized the extent of just how badly their fates were ultimately screwed, and they started to run.

They went straight to summoning the aid of more men, and, with swords drawn and hatchets raised, their accumulated two dozen or so in number severed the limbs and head from Meytani's body but Meytani would not die. The fingers of its hands still flexed and reached, its dismembered legs kicked and toes extended, and its head rolled across the raft on its own accord to where its mouth could position itself for another bite of my uncle's lung. After much effort, the men gathered up the pieces of Meytani and uncle into sacks of heavy cloth and brought everything they found before Knossos' supreme regional CEO (or *king* as we'll call him here), including the raft, so he could decide what to make of it all, how to go about dealing with the situation.

At first, Knossos' King Anpor was extremely irate that the men did not bring word of the matter prior to bringing the matter itself in the flesh before him. He could have been afraid of the curse the initial party of men brought with them, but his allegiance to the Snake Goddess, our Supreme Goddess, cemented a spiritual pact that nullified the threat of curses on palace grounds. Truly, the entire palace, its square footage equal to a medium-sized shopping mall of present day, was showered with blessings and prosperity, a nice place to be, and most of it was open for all us citizens to come and go as we pleased, with plenty to do there. Anpor was simply pissed off because it was Bath Day when his servants notified him there were men with a raft and squirming cloth bags awaiting his presence in the Throne Room chambers. His anger fell to the wind when those bags were opened, and it took no time at all for him to realize what luck, ironically, had befallen him.

In Anpor's eyes, our prison system was highly flawed. It never used to be that way, but, let me explain: We had a relatively free society where everyone knew their roles, tended to their families and responsibilities, and we as a society were run as a business to which Anpor was more or less our community manager, and our prosperity rested on his authority. He answered only to his peers, a bureaucracy of Minoan kings who all networked together for the greater prosperity of our nation. The secret to our success was that most everyone among us created something to trade and export to overseas countries as far away as Greece, Egypt, and the Far East, in return for other resources that kept us going. There was no real currency, for we traded even amongst ourselves and that was sufficient for us. The majority of the citizens in our city contributed to the creation and exportation of ceramics, pottery, sculptures, mostly vases and jugs, when they weren't fulfilling their obligations of maintaining their homes and neighborhoods in some other way beneficial to the community, such as sewage detail or crop raising.

There were no homeless save for nomadic vagabonds that chose to live in wilderness regions and were just passing through, though beggars nonetheless showed up at the marketplace every day asking for valuables to trade, without any degree of pride or manners, the slothful ones or the drunkards, but no one had a reason to steal, to go hungry, to not be a productive member of society. When there were misunderstandings or domestic violence, the sort of criminal activity brought about by any society with human problems, and it became a great issue, a group of elders who lived in Knossos Palace would decide over those matters and in some cases would condemn convicted criminals to life as a slave or to death if they were deemed intolerable and unbeneficial if they were otherwise allowed to live.

In those latter days of our beloved Minoa, there existed among all of us a fear of the imminent collapse of our culture. Earthquakes were commonplace throughout the prior year. Strongphyle, a Minoan island consisting entirely of one volcano that was long taken for granted to be dormant, became suddenly active, and the citizens of the nearby island city of Akrotiri were forced to evacuate because the ground there became too hot to walk upon and devastated the land with spontaneous wildfires. Most of us kept our cool, but our climate of doom and mostly suppressed hysteria spawned a rampant criminal element that led to an overflow of prisoners, hence a problem for Anpor, hence a solution for our king in the form of Meytani.

You see, Meytani's disembodied head was allowed to consume the rest of my uncle for the purposes of observation, and despite the macabre fascination it invoked, Anpor became keen on the fact that not a shred of consumed flesh emerged in turn from out the bottom of its neck. As it ate, my uncle simply disappeared. It was said Anpor's initial reaction to witnessing this was "*Holy crap. I guess lungs aren't the only thing this fucker eats.*" But before Uncle disappeared completely, all who watched could almost swear that what remained of him started to twitch a little on its own, to come to life itself.

He ordered the creature to be sewn up, back together and as good as possibly new, by expert seamstresses aided by the strongest of men, and be placed into the public execution arena located in the judicial building at the palace's western side. It was a popular arena, where a convict was simply hog-tied and placed in the center of the pit and upon a marble platform, and an appointed magistrate wearing a mask of the Great Mother Serpent would emerge from out of a wooden door and slit the condemned's throat, and empty the blood into a receptacle where it was taken to be used as a main ingredient for a popular skin care cream my mother sometimes used.

The next in line on our ever-expanding prison death row was thrown into the arena with Meytani almost immediately, and it instantly became less remarkable that it was undead and more

101

impressive that despite the amount of living flesh it consumed, it never gave out any bodily waste or fluids like the living did. The living in our city seemed to produce more waste than anyone in modern civilization could ever conceive, what with your luxury of toilets where there's a dump and a flush and you never have to deal with your shit again, and our below-ground mass public graves were growing even more crowded than the condemn prisoners waiting to take residence there.

Our king had found for himself the ultimate human garbage disposal.

It had a voracious appetite, and in the next three months it fully consumed 248 prisoners, some from surrounding cities in dire need of a black hole into which they could dump bucketsful of undesirable others with a bare minimum result of leftovers to deal with.

All remaining bones were broken and placed into hand-held rock grinders to fertilize Anpor's gardens.

Clothing of the condemned was salvaged and traded away as collector's items. It was quite like being able to purchase BTK's prison jumpsuit for the price of a very fine ceramic vase that you yourself made, and people thrilled upon that sort of thing in my culture.

You know.....throughout all of this, nobody ever bothered to pay respects to my uncle, nor to mourn him, with the exception of my immediate family, the loss of uncle's life eclipsed by the sensational eating stamina of the undead raft man Meytani.

Anpor, from the very beginning, realized he needed to appoint a keeper of this zombie, someone to maintain the sacrificial pit and fetch the skeletons and clothing of its victims, someone to essentially mop the floors, sweep up the bones and do the paperwork. By cultural law, my father was obligated to take over his brother's responsibilities until another could be selected, and that often took a very long time to do. Since it was my uncle who first discovered Meytani, whom Anpor would have normally appointed its caretaker as a result, the king figured my father was bound to fill the role instead.

Dad was a jewelry-smith-turned pottery craftsman by trade, our entire family worked for him, and you can imagine the impact it had on us when he was suddenly ordered away for a full four or five hours each day. It was a bum deal, a hardship for everyone, and now that everyone's dead and this happened a few thousand years ago I can proclaim without fear of consequence that King Anpor can lick my asshole.

But then one day, resulting from some careless action, my father was bitten by the undead raft man and escaped with his life, thinking nothing of it at first as though he was bitten by a stray dog, tending to his wounds with proper cleansing and offering up healing prayers to the Lady of the Beasts, a goddess of the land that helped us battle everything from stuffy noses to issues of the blood to tapeworms in domesticated animals.

Somehow, though, my father didn't seem to be getting any better since the day of the bite. We began to fear he was dying.

I soon found myself with the responsibility of taking care of him, and I found it ironic that just as my father was the zombie's keeper, I was to become my father's.

3.
Lato's Way of Life, Back Then

I suppose I should introduce you to who I was, and am.

My birth name is Lato Merna. Literally translated from Minoan into English, you would call me Lain Artsandcrafts, but, I beg you, please don't. *Lato* literally means *to have lain*, or *having lain*, as in just having been aroused from slumber and is now fully alert and walking about. *Merna* is actually two words combined, *mer* meaning *The Arts* and *na* meaning *engaged in domestic crafts*, particularly beaded adornments (compared to *ne* which specifies drawing or painting), though in time pottery became our specialty.

My family consisted of myself, only sixteen at the time, my father Darik and mother Sephra. There was Hin, my younger brother by about two years, blind in one eye from a birth defect. Then there was Stiru and Bamu, my sisters of eight and ten. We lived in what can be compared nowadays to a three-room condominium in a "condominium housing district," that always seemed like an immense labyrinth to get out of into open terrain. Our living structures of rounded stone and cement were built together in single-storied units of ten dwellings each, the size and number of rooms in each individual dwelling varied. We were middle-class and proud, had an enclosed exterior rear patio and inside ladder to an opening in the ceiling that led to a rooftop lounge with a grass canopy where we could relax on sunny days and watch the birds take flight from the rooftops of our neighbors. Our one wooden window frame, in our main room, actually sported a glass pane an inch and a half thick, something that took us seven months of labor to own, though we had no front door. At night, we covered our doorways with thin grass mesh to keep out flying insects.

The front room, our main room, served as our primary living space where we slept and ate, cooked meals at the fire pit below a chimney structure escalating through the roof at the room's center.

We prayed there also, mostly to the Snake Goddess, the Mountain Mother, Lady of the Beasts, and Rain Goat, and our shrine took up enough space to park a Volkswagen Bug into, and scaled the wall up almost to the ceiling. It was more than a shrine, though. It was there where we displayed statues of religious and traditional importance and figurines of wildlife adorned with flower petals and sweet-smelling herbs which made up the most of it, clay handprints of all of us and items us kids had made in day school. Everything we collected for fancy was displayed there, and like trading cards we collected "trading stones" with hundreds of different deities and likenesses of popular athletes we'd often swap with neighbors depending on how each stone's magical powers affected our moods at any given day. If on a given day one of us was depressed, it was probably due to he or she possessing a Hawk God trading stone somewhere on their shrine at the wrong time of year, and you'd have to find someone willing to trade it with you for something more cheerful, like the childish Spirit of Happy Pigeon who lives in our diaphragms and gives us the ability to laugh.

(When we *do* laugh, it means Happy Pigeon has found a morsel of tape worm or cancer and is gulping it down, causing a tickle below our lungs which tells us something not right is being dealt with and that everything's going to be okay. In other words, when we laugh, we're in the process of healing. Such is the logic of one example of our deities.)

Every household had a shrine similar to ours.

You know, come to think of it, none of us ever really congregated in churches as a tradition. Religious ceremonies took place on a regular basis in the palace and even around town, but we rarely were required to attend, save for religious holidays. Most ceremonies

104

simply went on, regardless, and acquired spectators who chose to stop and observe from time to time. Mostly, our church was in our own private home.

Now, onto snakes.....

Each family cared for several, usually garden snake sized, for it was damn good luck to have them. In the marketplace, it was to a trader's benefit that he carry a stock of mice to feed our snakes, because Goddess forbid they went hungry before any of us humans did. Snakes, in our city, were like sacred cows. To kill one openly, where there were witnesses... ....well, it soon became said that you could meet the undead raft man, face to face, as a consequence for *that*. As far as I knew, none of them were poisonous or so big as to threaten to eat our children or animals, we kept the eggs of captive fowl away from them if we wanted to, and crushing one beneath the wheels of our carts was often unavoidable and overlooked in a *see no evil* kind of way by most. There was this old hag the next condominium district over who raised hell whenever she witnessed the accidental death of a snake, and she really needed to do something better with her time.

Snakes, to us, dwelt at the core of our way of life, and their numbers and alliance and very presence among us *alone* were responsible for our national security, which is why we never had the need for any real form of a military establishment. We were indebted to them for having never been attacked by an invading army, and for being at peace with the outside world. At the core of it, though, aside from superstition, snake worship was essential in keeping the rodent population below the bare minimum and, consequently, disease. Looking back, having snakes everywhere prevented disease spread by vermin, for they *ate* vermin, and nobody's ever heard of *snakes* spreading disease. We even collected snake waste for use in houseplant fertilizers. We had to do something with all that shit, and when every season they all shed their skins we had ourselves everything from snake scale soup to paper-like headdresses we'd all design ourselves to wear while rooting for our favorite athletes at bull-jumping events.

Snakes were our way of life.

Arts and crafts were our way of life.

Family was our way of life.

And, to me, Father *was* my life, at least the most important figure in it, the one I looked up to the most. In my society, the emotional bond between a father and his first son was considered the closest any two human beings could have.......

4.
The Night of Father's Undeath

I remember the day palace messengers arrived with the news of my uncle and of my father's unwanted part- time job, as clearly as the night Father came home from the palace with a piece of flesh torn from out of the ball of his right shoulder. In both instances, my mother and siblings were hard at work out back creating ceramic pottery and I had just arrived pulling a cart of pitchers filled with water from the public well, wooden boxes of iced meat and vegetables I'd gained through trading on my cross-town journey, a handful of trading stones I'd swapped with friends, and a sack of pink newborn mice.

"Lato," he'd said to me when he was first taken away to report to palace authorities, "tell everyone I'll be all right, they'll employ a more suitable replacement in no time and we'll be back to normal days. Tell Mother I'll be fine."

"Lato," he'd said to me again just the same when I arrived home the night of his injury, and he pulled me aside, "don't tell anyone about my little accident. People will talk. Mother will worry. Let it heal."

The flesh of Father's right breast had been torn, and by the time he gave in to my persistence in taking a look it had ceased bleeding, was a wet red gory patch that tapered into his arm pit and extended from a deep and nasty crevice where the nipple was supposed to still be. Father insisted only a small chunk of flesh was missing and the rest was surface skin that would likely heal, and at worst he'd ultimately be scarred for life. But Father knew the ways of Meytani, and for many reasons had more cause to be afraid of it than any of us. To alleviate our concerns he'd always keep the details of his job to himself, and any time we'd pester him he'd respond with superficial banter.

Like he was doing regarding the wound.

Many of our relatives, neighbors and peers had visited the palace at a time when the new form of public executions were taking place, told us all about it, but we had no time on our hands to see

Meytani publicly eat anyone, or to even visit the palace at all, because we were spending so much time making up for his absence in the way we made our living. Father and Meytani were practically bedfellows, though we knew very little of the creature.

And father was not compensated for his time there, except for meals, exclusive passes for sports events such as bull-jumping which we were often too busy to attend in those latter days, and he had first dibs on the hand- me-down clothing collected from the deceased in the pit before it was auctioned off as souvenirs. The night my father came home from the assault, I was actually wearing a nice deep brown wrap-around robe from someone convicted of stabbing his pregnant wife several times with a tiger tooth dagger and was as a result one of the growing numbers doomed to be eaten by Father's undead raft man.

The night of the bite, Father grew very ill and feverish. It was physically impossible for him to report to his palace duties the next day. We were all overcome with worry and an anxiety which slowed that day's productivity to a halt by late morning, when a messenger sent by Anpor himself stepped through our doorway, unrolled a scroll, and while reading proclaimed that if the Keeper of Meytani was unable to fulfill his duties by sunrise the following day, I was to take his place until he sufficiently recovered from his illness, or until someone else should be appointed Keeper in his stead. Like *that* was ever going to happen. Furthermore, I was to take *Father* with me, by whatever means necessary, regardless of his condition.

That following night, I spent a great deal of time with my father, taking care of him, tending to his needs, constantly by his side. The Lady of the Beasts would not answer our prayers, though apparently without hesitation she'd minimized Ghira's menstrual cramps....Ghira, a neighbor a few families down and a self-proclaimed healer, brought Father a Healing Salad composed of various nutritious wild weeds, and told us all about it. Mother swapped a few trading stones with her in hopes a few of Ghira's would do the trick for Dad.

I took a more hands-on approach. I fed him, washed him, kept cool his head with palm ice wrapped in palm leaves wiped his ass for him in the wet room with a sponge attached to the end of a stick and had to wring his diarrhea out of it with my own hands to make it sanitary enough that the rest of us could continue using it. I was always on the alert should any lengthy period of time elapse without Father having a bowel movement. Since Meytani could not defecate or produce any form of waste, I looked to this aspect as an indicator that Father had become undead, too.

And then an alarming length of time passed without him in need of the wet room.

The tone of Father's skin, I noticed also, was beginning to change.

His wound was worsening to an alarming degree, excreting brown puss out the area of his nipple that I had to wipe away whenever I needed to change the dressing cloths and by late night was four times its original size.

We kept the fire pit burning for him with the rest of the week's timber rations to keep him warm because he was oh, so cold, and he was begging us constantly to turn up the heat because he wasn't warm enough. We all slept together.

He was terribly parched and demanded water constantly, though when we gave it to him, he would not drink. To keep him nourished, I found that chunks of watermelon rather than liquids were more to his liking, as he preferred rather to bite at something... .oftentimes snapping into the air like a dog.....and I would simply hold the chunks out in front of him and he'd devour them bite after bite in what appeared to be an automated, unconscious reflex.

Soon, around three hours after summer sundown, he wasn't able to talk at all.

And then he stopped breathing.

I didn't notice it at first.....

It was in the middle of the night when I awoke to a mild rumbling of the earth which shook our home and everything in it for a period long enough to make me realize I wasn't dreaming, then the rumbling ceased without having caused any evident damage. Everyone else was fast asleep, including Father, so it seemed, and I decided to step outside and gaze at the moon to see what time it was, to see if anyone in our immediate community felt the quake and was up and about. I couldn't find the moon, and all was quiet. We had a public timepiece run by water droplets and marbles in the town center square but I had no desire to walk that far to know it was still around about early morning, with at least a few hours to spare before daybreak.

I returned to our floorbed of cloth-covered sheep's wool tied together over cushions of hay and to my place beside Father, tried to stir him, felt for his heartbeat, placed my ear against his nostrils. Panicked, I gripped his good shoulder, shook him, pushed him away, brought him back to me and forced open his eyelids with my fingers.

And they stayed open, stared directly back at me.

It immediately seemed to me, for a fleeting moment, that Father was alive again. We were there together for what seemed like quite some time, staring into each other's tearful eyes, myself wondering if his were *dead* eyes and fearful of making any move to find out for sure. But he raised his hand up to my face, his initial movement startling me, placed a loving palm up to embrace the side of my cheek. He smiled. I didn't think to smile back. I didn't know what to think of it I mean, was this a *farewell* smile or an *I'll be okay* s m i l e . . . . .

His fingers felt the side of my face, began to fumble forwards over my hair and past my ear, drawing himself closer to me, and I realized he was making an attempt to feel for Hin, my younger brother who rested on my opposite side as comfortably as if Father was well and everything was fine. He reached over, felt and felt, then he seized my brother as instantly as a cobra strike and brought him over me by his throat. Hin's one seeing eye was widened. Gasping for air, he looked down upon me, his good eye a trading stone's length away, then gazed at Father in horror. My father reached over with his other hand, rubbed his thumb into Hin's blind eye as though he were curious about it, feeling it, like a blind man running his hands over another man's face to gain a mental picture.

In the next instant, Father opened his mouth wide, pulled my brother all the way to him, and bit into Hin's head from the side so that the pressure from his lower teeth popped my brother's good eye into a fluid that hit my lips like someone cracked a quail egg over my mouth.

I screamed.

My brother screamed, and Father held him firmly over me as his teeth scraped and dug into my brother's face, tearing out flesh and hair, stripping off Hin's entire eyebrow and slurping it down, blood spilling upon me while my sisters and mother awoke and began to scream as well after realizing the hell that had befallen us.

Their screams distracted Father away from Hin, and he tossed my limp brother towards the fire as he gazed their way. He began to rise. The skin of his unclothed body was entirely the color of various shades of sewage or like that of an apricot left to dry out in the hot sun, abhorrently wrinkled, shrunken, his eyes wild when he focused in on my oldest sister Bamu. We all stood there together, looking at him, when he threw himself over me and took her. She ran instantly in Mother's direction, but Father gained a hold of Bamu's left leg and brought her down, pulled her to him as she struggled to crawl away, bit down into her exposed ankle before any of us could pry her free. When we did, Father lunged out and seized *Mother* by the wrist, thrust her up to him, tore a chunk of muscle from her arm the size of a double portion of lamb chops, before I kicked him away.

He fell backwards, onto the bed, and it took no time at all for him to get back up again and stare us down like he was sizing us up for another attack.

I stood up to him. The more I stood up to him, the more he backed down, I noticed, and he would not attack me. Instead, he leaned over, rummaged over the bed a bit, then retrieved Mother's arm muscles he'd lost his grip on when I kicked him and began to chew on them. Mother was in severe pain, sobbing on her knees behind me.

Father looked up at me, calm and innocent and docile, cast a gaze past me at Mother almost as if he was concerned, then offered me a piece of Mother's armflesh he'd been chewing on.

I knew not what to do, hadn't a clue.

Mother then became extremely vocal.

"My Darik's become the same as that which washed upon the shores!" she cried out. "Cursed be Anpor to have made the father of my children keep watch over such an abomination!"

Her outburst was like nothing I've ever heard come from her lips and could have led to all our arrests for disturbing the peace and open disrespect for the king. We all knew that, and Mother crying out like that only meant that she was so suddenly devastated she was ready to die.

I hurried over to her, quieted her down, grabbed a cloth and wrapped it around her very open wound as best I could, which was bleeding profusely and I swore I saw bone. I tied another cloth around her arm just below her shoulder and above the wound as tight as I could. My younger sister Stiru helped keep Bamu calm by holding her, and I told her to find a cloth for Bamu's wound as well. Hin remained unmoving and sprawled across the floor, and I went to tend to him next until Father started up again, following me.

He wanted to tend to Hin, too.

I stood in between him and my brother, ordered my father back.

And Father retreated, took enough steps backwards to knock himself into the wall of stones in the corner of our hay mattress floorbed, eyes darting from me to the others and back to me again as if not knowing what else to do but obey. He lowered himself into a crouch and perched himself there, alertly watching all of us, and it occurred to me then that there was no way our family would ever recover from this that, just like the cataclysmic rumors of the end of our civilization, this proud and prosperous family was altogether doomed.

Neighbors flooded in, having awakened to Mother's cries and the prior commotion and came running. There must've been a couple dozen of them, all ages, and they panicked when they beheld Father and the aftermath of bloodshed he'd unleashed on our family.

It was decided that my family members be taken away and into the care of those skilled in healing and medicine, not the Ghira types but the ones who actually knew what they were doing, and most of them returned to their homes to begin a mourning ritual over the death of Father. We all agreed Father was dead, though he still walked about. But even if there remained any life within him, we'd still have to put him down. He was a diseased version of my father, his skin and features were sucked into himself like he'd been vacuum-packed, his hair was falling out, his genitalia wasn't even there, like he'd torn it off, and I actually found my eyes roaming the ground for any discarded trace of it.

He kept staring at me, and my presence there kept him at bay.

So I was entrusted to look after him alone, and I was to take him away with me to the raft man's sacrificial pit at Anpor's palace come morning as planned.

When everything had settled down in our home, and all was finally quiet, I kept watch over Father until the first moment of sunrise.

And sunrise arrived not at all too soon.

111

5.
Leading Father to Work

It was time to take Father on the morning trek to report to his duties.

Well......*our* duties. *My* duties, I supposed.

He was able to walk and to follow me, but leading him through town, past spectators, up the great hill and into the colossal stone Snake Goddess mouth of the Knossos Palace entrance was going to be a sonofabitch and a long, laborious chore.

And it was.

I tried to be smart about it. I covered Father's head in a thick burlap sack to keep anyone from seeing his face and to keep him from seeing them and attacking. I figured he didn't *breathe* anyway, so I wasn't smothering him. I tied a very thick rope around his neck like a collar and utilized the remaining six or so feet of it as a leash. He fought against my first attempts to clothe him, but I managed to secure any of his remaining dignity with a loincloth I salvaged from the unwashed laundry pile in the wet room. It wasn't like Father didn't already reek of a repugnant stench all *on his own* ... .

I made a conscious attempt to avert down roads and pathways where we'd be least observed by onlookers, and it was evident by the crowds we attracted that word was spreading about us. We could not avoid the marketplace, and when we went through everyone ceased what they were doing, all stopped and stared. Some, as we went, volunteered to clean our paths of snakes beforehand lest we should tread upon them, which was a great show of respect and compassion to us. One woman ran to me and offered me up some bread dipped into salty fish oil and goat's cheese, Goddess bless her, for I hadn't eaten since yesterday. I was very surprised. I thought Father and I would be the object of some degree of ridicule. I think the town at first only wanted to hurry us along without incident. It took no great wise man to figure out once Father was inside the palace, he'd never be allowed to leave. Realizing that, I began to worry about my fate as well, and about whether the remainder of my family would survive.

Walking my dad was like helping an old lady across three miles of street to the other side. He was slow and careful in his steps, like he was still alive and walking in his sleep. Just outside of the marketplace, an infant cradled in a straw-filled basket just outside the doorway of its home screamed and wailed with no one immediately at its care to silence it, and its cries distracted Father from my constant beckoning to move forward in my direction. He livened, made a desperate sprint in the direction of the sound, swept up the infant by one foot. Onlookers shrieked. I tried keeping Father at bay with the rope, but he was too strong for me to contain. A woman emerged from the doorway just as Father was biting and gnawing on the writhing, terrified child like a mantis eating its prey alive, turning it over to attempt bites off the plumpest areas something he just couldn't succeed doing with his entire head in a sack the way it was, though try he did. The woman wrestled her infant away, Father's inability to see being in her favor, and the baby was physically unharmed. People urged us along more vocally after that, and some of what they shouted didn't sound like we'd ever be welcomed among them again once they were rid of us. A hell of an opposite reaction from when we first set out.

I was beginning to feel by then that the Snake Goddess was imposing upon me increasingly potent doses of dread throughout my entire ordeal thus far, just to see what I would do, to get a rise out of me. I cursed her name. I became very conscious of the fact I was leaving behind all that I knew of my home life as I reached the town outskirts and proceeded up the ascending dirt road to the hilltop on which Knossos Palace rested and overlooked us all. That was the latest dose of dread, the dehumanizing and anti-climactic feeling I experienced when I realized everything I cared about and loved had turned to shit, irreparably.

Father's languid, limping baby steps confounded my impatience to reach the palace, and I didn't wish to hurry him lest I upset him. But after the previous upset regarding the infant all I wanted to do was get the hell to my destination. The uphill climb gave no regard to my impatience, neither did Father, neither did the Snake Goddess, apparently. Getting to the palace was no small journey at this pace. It gave me time to reflect, to further curse, to mumble aloud my very worrisome concerns over Mom and Hin, Stiru and Bamu, my fate within the palace walls, what was to become of Father.

"Come on, Dad, move your ass, it's getting too goddamn hot for this," I shrieked at him before I could stop myself, but Father didn't care. He took his own sweet time.

I became aware of the fact that I hadn't seen a single soul since I left town, and this brought to me another dose of dread.

Typically, at this time of morning, there'd be carts and pedestrian traffic flowing this way and that, and we'd have to constantly get out of rude people's way. This morning, the road was barren, and I hadn't seen so much as a stray animal.

Oddly enough, not even a snake.

6.
The Palace, Meytani, and King Anpor

Knossos Palace was the size of a present-day suburban shopping mall, with a colossal face of stone looking down upon the town in the shape of a female serpentine/human hybrid with an obscenely wide rectangular mouth held open by six pillars three stories high and each as wide in diameter as monster truck tires. A stone forked tongue descended from between the centermost two pillars and down the landscape of the hill several meters, its opposite end extending deep into the "throat" of the grand entrance hall and narrowing into a long bed of flowering plants, ferns and dwarf fruit and nut trees. The promenade could accommodate several hundred citizens and bureaucrats simply standing in social clusters conversing comfortably and drinking wine as it had seen more times than I've scratched my ass. The interior ceiling was littered with colorfully painted depictions of notables and goddesses and bull jumping events, and coated with a material which glowed brilliantly at night during a storm, whenever lightning struck two copper poles rising into the heavens from the highest points of the palace structure. Very large flat stones flanking the entrance and outer sides reflected sunlight onto the ceiling during the day, which nurtured the interior garden, and which at night also caused the ceiling to glow to almost the degree of splendor as from lightning but lasted much longer. It was always quite a marvelous wonder when it glowed, from the perspective of the town and particularly of those strolling and engaged in social banter beneath.

Father and I worked our ways up the steps alongside the stone tongue and made our way past the promenade garden. Our footsteps echoed. To my left and right and all around me, still no single human being was in sight. No guards, no servants or workers or messengers or meandering holy men. We arrived at the point where the great ceiling sloped in a descending angle and into an overhang twelve feet from the marble flooring held by several vine-covered pillars, and we made our ways beneath it until we fully entered the base court area of the palace itself. It was an open concourse an acre wide with the sky as its canopy and a multitude of winding brick walkways, stone benches and elaborate marble statues, small streams and falls of running recycled water, tropical flora and fauna.....fauna being snakes, of course, and there was an subterranean snake chamber just below this base court where most of the serpents on palace property nested.

I halted, gazed about in every direction, threw my hands in the air in an exhausted surrender to fate. Honestly, I did not know what to do at this point, where to go from there. Father pressed on, bumping into me. Startled, I jumped, shrieked, thought he was attacking me. It was all good.....he just didn't know any better, and I placed my hands upon him to let him know we've ceased walking for now.

I let the rope leash fall free from my hands. I decided it was no longer necessary for Father to have that grim burlap sack over his head, and removed it from him. He blinked, looked around, looked at me. He appeared much the same as when I'd covered him, his hair matted, his face discolored to ghastly proportions like he'd been both green with a terrible illness and beaten black and blue to near death.

Near death.

What returned my stare were eyes that had been swept way *past* that point, vacant, lifeless, glossy, as though Father was in a deep trance and some minute form of self-awareness stirred behind those eyes still, as if his frustrated spirit existed light years away contending with his body's malfunctioning remote controls.

In an instant and without provocation nor with any warning, Father lunged himself forward and seized me. Both his strength and sudden burst of vitality had me at a disadvantage, but to devour me was not his intent and I found myself thrown with great force to one side. I hit the ground hard, tumbled onto my back, my head making contact with the stone bare feet of an ironically naked

Goddess of Adornment statue built to human scale. This shattered my senses for a moment or two. When I was able to discern what had just taken place and where I was in relation to it, and I was able to look up at my father and see him clearly, I saw what I thought was at first two of him.

Father was the one standing at my left, that much became clear. He was facing the figure at my right, staring it down, and it in turn stared right down upon *me*. I did not move, stunned by either the blow of the fall or my mounting recognition of whom Father had just saved me from, what it was that kept Father poised to my defense should it decide to make another attempt to eat me.

Meytani's facial features constricted and relaxed as it exchanged gazes between the both of us, as if desperate and at odds in deciding what to do. A snake slithered past its feet, distracting the creature, and then it returned its gaze to mine and cautiously proceeded to narrow the gap between us with a few passive, hobbling steps for a closer inspection.

Father, though remaining attentive, allowed it to do so.

Meytani's appearance was frightening to behold, perhaps less frightening if I were able to run from it and wasn't feeling so damnably helpless. It was like a hairless, wizened elderly man suffering from severe malnutrition, skin a dry sandpapery black and littered with scabby tissue that glistened like oily opened wounds, clinging tight to its bones as if vacuum- wrapped to them and actually holding its skeleton intact. I could plainly see the accumulation of black threading interwoven about its joints and limbs where it'd been sewn together by Anpor's seamstresses. Its chest was stained with dried gore, the result of using it as a surface to wipe its hands on when it fed. The way it walked was impossibly awkward, as though its weight was not fully succumbed to gravitational pull but orchestrated lazily by invisible marionette strings. Its sunken eyes shook with each step like gelatinous black olives with tiny pupils for pits surrounded by craterous sockets.

It reached out to me, crept close enough to touch me. As I found myself able to panic, I looked toward Father for help.

It extended its skeletal fingers further.

Father looked on, this time with less concern. He could've started whistling a tune and he'd be more engrossed in my situation.

Meytani's fingertips met the trembling skin of my ankle, slid downwards across it to the ball of my foot at the sandal. Its touch was remarkably wet and cold, like an ice cube. It then retreated in backwards steps away from me, sparing me, and I could've pissed myself a pond.

It was like Father had *taught* it something provided it with some insight uniquely pertaining to *me*.....and '*don't harm him, that's my son*,' though reasonably obvious, didn't seem to be what it was.....

Before I had the slightest chance to reflect on any of this, a larger figure eclipsed my vision without introduction, a muscle-bound behemoth of a man garbed in animal fur and brandishing a body-length metal shield. With all the momentum of a football quarterback, he plowed himself shield-first into Meytani, and the zombie raft man fell hard. Another figure of like description appeared, again from out of nowhere, knocking Father to the ground.

The two new figures, whom I began to recognize as two of Anpor's prized athletes that often took positions as keepers of the peace, took positions in front of me, their backs facing me in guarded attention against the sudden commotion of many people flooding urgently from out of hiding to where we were. As a crowd gathered, the two musclemen stepped aside for three palace servants to rush to my aide. Together, they lifted me up, set my ass down upon the nearest stone bench. A maidservant rushed towards me, offering me a dipper of water to drink.

And goddammit, I drank.

But that was nothing compared to when another offered me white wine. I finished off what they gave me, deliriously demanded more, until the next dipper I drank from was held steady by the hands of King Anpor himself, standing suddenly before me, and in realization to this a bit of wine found its way down my Sunday throat which sent me into a migraine-inducing coughing fit.

As long as I sat there, Anpor was my height. If I rose erect, the top of his sleek bald head would only come up just below five feet to my nipples. Sixty-eight years old (it was said), he sported a full white beard spilling across his portly belly and wide as ear was to ear, the lobes of each ear sporting a series of wrist-sized golden rings descending in links down to his plump shoulders and wrap-around red robe. The robe was held together by snakeskin straps around his waist, wrists, ankles, down his butt crack and cupping his groin like a playground rubber swing seat.

This was as close as I'd ever been to our Great King.

I mean, the sight of him was very commonplace as he was a public man, a social man, and he even made it a point to parade down our streets with a colorful accompanying entourage twice a month to let us know all was good and festive and prosperous in these here parts and that he was happy to be our king. Sure, his height got in the way of being seen, but he enlisted dozens of aides whose job it was to lift him above crowds, carry around wooden pedestals and steps of varying sizes should he feel the need to stand taller, fetch things for him that were beyond his reach, that sort of thing. He used to insist on walking wherever he went and was by no means slothful, but he lately often seemed deliberately over-pampered on palace grounds, so I'd heard, as a way to deal with the mounting stress of the times and the threat of the earth caving in on us at any moment, and always had ready a young maiden by his side to feed him portions of finger foods at his beckoned call, because he *could*. She was with us, standing nearby with a cluster of red grapes and a *happy-to-serve-you* grocery store free sample lady smile.

Over Anpor's shoulder I could see two separate flurries of white-robed palace guards working with ropes and multi-roped throwing nets to subdue both Father and Meytani, the two animal skin clad gargantuans directing the affair and barking orders. Under their command, they were tended to with determined swiftness, hog-tied and taken away before the zombies could truly begin to fight back.

"Best way to demobilize them is to ram them with momentous force when they're not looking, knock 'em down, overtake them, make it impossible for them to move," said the king to me in a rough baritone which echoed above the pandemonium behind him. "I speak like I've handled this before, but really it sounded like a good idea when I thought of it and apparently is. We might have to use this wisdom if their population grows. Hand me another grape, will you please, babe....."

The servant readily popped a grape into Anpor's mouth, and he chewed, his warm congeniality a stark contrast to the attentive eyes which studied me, made me want to puke my intimidated guts right up and onto his royal sandals. It took a moment for it to dawn on me that he'd plainly just said '*if their population grows*,' and I realized another dose of dread was about to strike.

"*Population*, my King?"

"Shit, son," he told me, "can you not see there are two of them now? And that's only two *in our presence*, for there are *more*..... "

Anpor then shrunk down to the point of where he was looking up at me. A servant scurried to a kneeling position directly behind him, tending to some sort of affair at the floor and beyond my line of sight. The King crept up close to me, whispered, "News of the condition of your family has spread even now throughout Knossos, reached my ears, and I'm sorry to say they must be destroyed. All save for Stiru, your sister, who hasn't yet suffered the bite of death. They have become Meytani, just as your father Darik, just as the others in the city who *they* have bitten, just as the ones who have been bitten within the palace since early this very morning when inexperienced caretakers fell victim to Meytani's sudden rage and caused its escape. This undead pestilence is growing, Meytani is increasing its number and more rapidly as time passes. *My Goddess*, Lato.......you know not the extent of what has transpired merely in this day alone, and the day is not yet at an end......."

My king broke eye contact for a moment enough to turn and squint away in a curious fashion, his expression turning next into a candid grimace, then into a burst of satisfaction which he immediately disregarded a half second later to return to the business at hand. The servant behind him after a few seconds arose from her position at Anpor's posterior not a moment too soon with a shallow copper pan of wet brown sausage-sized coiled feces and soiled rags, dismissed herself with a curtsey and went away. Anpor straightened himself to again face me eye-to-eye, and he received another grape into his mouth and chewed, studied me.

"Meytani's morning rampage invoked an immediate evacuation of most of the palace grounds and resulted in a few grisly casualties," the king further explained. "I've ordered every citizen who has suffered the bite of death to be rounded up and contained within Meytani's grand public execution arena, where Meytani and your father will both join them. It will do your king a great service to understand, my dear Lato, and to take your father's place as the keeper of Meytani. They are *all* Meytani now, and can continue to be a tremendous asset to us once we further understand them,

119

whether they're truly dead and what makes them that way, how they do not shit that which they consume, that sort of thing. All we have to do is keep these bastards confined and properly tended to, constantly, and once that's taken care of everything else will be gravy. You are clearly the one most suited to bear the responsibility of overseeing these matters. You seem curiously immune to Meytani's desire to eat you or, for that matter, do you any harm at all.....and by observing this remarkable ability of yours I must say my heart is moved by your power over the undead, they react to you as though you hold in your possession many good trading stones "

Speaking before deciding whether or not I should mention it, I conveyed to him a sudden insight and resolve. "I take it you ordered everyone into hiding as my father and I approached the palace, knowing the man from the sea who eats lungs was running rampant within these walls and knowing we were bound to run into it, wanting to see if it had the same reaction to me as Father without anyone else's intervention. It worked. I don't blame you. I nearly gave up the ghost when your ghastly executioner went to touch me and I lay helpless, and although I'm mortified and astonished at the outcome and I weep over tremendous loss, I understand, Your Worship, and I am your servant."

Anpor regarded me for just a moment, smiled, placed the wooden wine dipper into my hand.

"Smart lad," he remarked. Then, withdrawing from me, he said, "I have very little time. No time to waste, to eat, to shit, no time to wait for *you*. Very little time I have. But I must tend to matters with greater urgency than you, for I am your king. You can tarry, I must go."

His turn toward one of the servants served as a silent signal for that servant to immediately rise to attention, about-face, and cry aloud *'Tow heeeek-AH'* which echoed through the hallways. The cry summoned a bean bag-like carriage made from hide and fine horsehair and stuffed fat with something comfortable, supported by a wooden platform attached to two poles at either side and brought by a running quintuplet of male slaves which held the carriage up to knee-height until they arrived and halted, lowered it for the king to board. Anpor seized the cluster of grapes from the finger food maiden, plopped onto the carriage, signaled with the wave of his hand another maiden standing alertly by with a handful of umbrella-sized peacock feathers to fan him.

"My servants will take you directly to the public execution arena where you will meet with me, and I'll show you the ropes. Forgive me for not walking with you, I must hurry ahead, no time to lose these serious perilous times require my full mental attention, not to be distracted by everyday inconveniences. Now *bust a nut, people, let's move it........*"

The four slaves heaved and lifted, and off they went with Anpor down the hallway in a rapid hustle, the maid with the peacock feathers laboring to keep up with them.

I arose from the stone bench as his remaining entourage gathered themselves ready to lead me, but only before I could swallow another dipper full of that damn fine white wine.

7.
To the Arena and Good Night

The three servants who tended to me, along with a small assemblage of guards (I felt they were there to ensure I didn't freak out and flee) escorted me across a brick pathway through a stunning section of the base court gardens and out its west side, past an array of phallic ivory statues rising up from various locations within a shallow bathing pool, out the mouth of a wide exit, through a smaller garden of bamboo and stunted bonsai-type trees, across the stone concourse of an exterior promenade and arriving at the steps of the building which housed the great public execution arena of Meytani. It was a stone domed building the size of, say, Disneyland's Space Mountain, and resembled a colossal slow cooker, the kind rounded at the top that housewives bring to church banquets, with protruding devil-goddess mouths coming out on two sides like handles.

As I approached the steps those accompanying me abandoned me, and while I ascended I became aware of clamor and commotion coming from below my feet. Descending steps flanked the ascending ones upon which I was treading, and with curious eyes I noticed that these led down to a sub level. I dared not stray to satisfy my impulse to pry, walked right up to the top entrance and made my way inside the structure to meet again with the king in a respectfully timely manner. I stepped into an interior, torch-lit hallway, its walls displaying sculpted and chiseled artistic depictions of various forms of execution administered over the years, until it yawned open onto the first observer's level of the arena itself.

I found myself standing at a wooden railing overlooking a round pit the size of an eight car garage, a single story below me, illuminated by both the fires of many torches and window-sized openings within the walls for ventilation and sunlight during the day. The arena held many wooden seats and benches on a series of four levels that interconnected and spiraled upwards into a mezzanine and two balconies reaching towards the top of the dome, all situated so where, looking down, every spectator was afforded a good view regardless of where he sat.

I began to feel a bit dizzy, my buzz from the white wine gnawing away at my willingness to stand.

Below me, in the arena, there moved about many nude and misshapen figures from out of its dark parameters. They were human, or once recently were, twisting and contorting their wounded discolored bodies into the firelight with each deliberation to step forward and see what was going on around them, as if my very presence triggered an alarm in their otherwise mosque- silent environment and stirred them into revealing themselves. Snakes of various ordinary sizes uncoiled and languidly fled from their slumbering positions in the squares of sunlight streaming downwards upon the dirt arena floor from the dome windows, to make way for a gathering of roughly two dozen of Meytani's undead progeny at the arena's centermost point, where there stood a single round platform of marble about a meter in diameter and rising two feet above the ground. Short of stepping onto the platform itself, the array of undead cast their gazes upwards and about, then were suddenly distracted by a flood of light emitted from the opening of a large door on the level below me through which Meytani itself and my father were thrown into the arena to join them. The door closed. I noticed the presence of a large stack of hay directly below me that I otherwise would not have seen if the door hadn't opened.

"Ah, there you are, my boy....."

King Anpor startled me, placed a hand upon the small of my back and joined me at my side, and I sensed during the silent momentary pause between us that he was making an attempt to convey to me a subtle sort of comfort only a surrogate father can provide.

"Ever been here before, son?"

"I've never witnessed an execution here," I replied.

"Oh, you *will*," he said to me. "I've arranged for several to take place first thing in the morning, the first event of its kind here in Knossos what with there being way more than just one Meytani and all. Word is being spread right now. We'll hopefully attract a large crowd."

I couldn't help but keep my eyes on the poor cursed ones in the arena below. They were the spawn of the underworld, and I was to take care of them.

"Look at them," Anpor continued. "They can't wait. My goddess, they're going to rip the condemned right the fuck apart. But to other matters, I don't require you to prepare for it. Relax tonight, take it easy. I've prepared for you living quarters around back. How's that wine treating you......

The wine was treating me just fine. But before I could respond, I slipped into an overwhelming episode of vertigo just as Anpor's comforting hand gave me a forceful nudge and sent me over the railing.

I fell into the arena, straight down onto the haystack below. The fall didn't hurt, but rendered me stunned. I caught the attentions of all Meytani, who abandoned their gathering at the marble platform and began to move towards me. I saw Father and the original raft man, who gave me no attention at all but instead withdrew into the shadows to sit this one out. My gaze drifted in horror from one creature to another as they all listlessly approached. I dreaded the possible outcome, though at the same time found myself searching the ghoulish faces of each for signs of someone I once knew, of Mother or Hin or Bamu. It took no time for the assemblage of Meytani to lose interest in me, and after encircling the haystack for a ghastly orgy of roaming hollow eyes upon my person they did not touch me, nor did any make an attempt to do so. Needless to say, I was extremely relieved.

I looked up at my king. He smiled from above at the railing, shrugged his shoulders and cast me a wave.

"Sorry about that, just checking," he called down to me, chuckling, as if my plight amused him. "Yes, you're indeed a well-qualified keeper. Would you have so easily come here if you knew I was going to fill you full of wine and push you into an arena full of flesh eaters? I think *not*..... "

He then raised his voice much higher, "Okay folks, we found ourselves a keeper. Take him out of there, bathe him, bless him, feed him, get him laid, show him to bed. With this divine fortune, perhaps the Great Goddess is as pleased as I am at this moment, and the Earth will no longer be an angry one, threatening to consume us all like those Meytani down there. I conclude there will be no further worries no further worries *from now on*....."

Servants rushed from the inner hallways to join him at the railing in looking down upon me. The finger food maiden was one of them, and I swore she winked at me. The arena door opened and two palace guards hurried to retrieve me, lifted me from the hay and carried me away before the walking corpses could react to their intrusion.

For the next couple of hours or so, I felt certain the king was right, that there would be no further worries, that all would be gravy.

But he was wrong.

8.
From Bliss into the Darkness Beyond

In fact, what Anpor declared couldn't have been farther from the truth.

Nobody would realize this for another few hours or so, certainly not me. I was taken into the custody of four beautiful young maidens into the water pond of carved ivory phallic symbols I'd earlier passed by in the base court gardens, who each took turns cuddling and fondling and blowing me while they sponged me down and I was blessed by a high priest. After this, I feasted on grilled veal and lamb shanks, potatoes, yams and whole wheat leavened bread. My quarters was the equivalent of a small wooden shed in the corner of a courtyard to the right of the execution arena building, nestled beneath the branches of a healthy group of fig trees. It was a bit rickety, weather-worn and battered by age, with no door at its entrance and no rear wall at all but sported a private patio in the back enclosed by a circular fence thick with trailing ivy. Upon a bed-length slab of stone situated just beneath the ceiling of the shed, surrounded by flickering candles, lay for me a nest of hay and knitted quilts and the king's own finger food maiden waiting and winking and telling me to come, although, in the words of AC/DC, I was already t h e r e .

***

The events of the evening were to me a blissful distraction of my own woes, and gave me no time to process my new reality or contemplate what was in store, to mourn the loss of my old life and of my family, to long for a reunion with my surviving sister.

When I finally fell asleep that night, I fell into a deep sleep, and I had a frightening series of dreams......

I dreamt I was Death, set upon a raft at sea to drift utterly alone through immeasurable time, waiting to be found by Man. The blazing sun brought with it long uninterrupted hours of intense agony during the day, but its merciful absence at night only made me realize just how hungry I was.

And I wasn't hungry in a conventional sense.

I was hungry to devour all of mankind and end their rein on this world.

Yes, I wanted to eat them, eat them all, both figuratively and literally.

I knew that once I was found by man, I would.

I would spread myself out like a plague, and those whom I could not consume fully would *become* me, and I would increase my number.

I didn't know from where it was that I came, but I felt I was born of fire, because fire was all I could remember, yet somehow I knew my body had once been the home of a human soul.

I dreamt I was myself on a night ten years prior to all of this, Mother sitting with the family in our home with Stiru, Bamu, Hin, and Father, telling us the story of *the man from the sea who eats lungs* by firelight at our beds. She came to a part of the story no one typically remembers, a part towards the end, when the flesh-eating man from the sea was finally able to walk among us. It consumed every living person in the land with the exception of one lowly young soul, the son of a pottery maker, whom it would not touch.

I asked Mother, "Why was *he* saved?"

And she told me, "Well, he *was* saved, I suppose......saved for *last*."

I dreamt I was suddenly swept far, far away, into another land, another time, perhaps, where my soul was able to fly.

I dreamt I was standing before an audience of countless millions of people at once, yet I could see only a few dozen, surrounding me, with bright lights and instruments and wearing peculiar attire, all their attentions upon me. I'd staged myself upon the marble platform at the center of Meytani's great public execution arena, my hands held upwards and readying for my soul to fly into a blinding radiance that was suddenly smothered by an avalanche of pitch black darkness.

And the earth trembled with me in fear.

It was still trembling as I opened my eyes.

I bolted out of bed and into immediate attention, panicked and not yet able to process the fact that I was genuinely awake and not still dreaming. I stole a thin quilt from my bed of hay and wrapped it about me, backing away into the outside private patio, fighting against the tumultuous rolling of the ground beneath my feet which threatened to buckle me over. The heavens were polluted from horizon to horizon by a torrid of intense smoky blackness so condensed I could actually reach out and touch it from where I was, the sky itself disintegrating and falling upon me like sooty gray snow which already blanketed everything.

The quake subsided, and I turned to find my shed occupied by three figures congregated into a shadowy corner.

"Hello?" I cried.

Two of them stirred, raised their positions out of the darkness just enough to where they could see me, and I could see them. They lifted their haglike, gore-smeared faces further into my view, saw who I was, and with slackened interest returned to the bloody feast they'd made of the poor young girl who'd hours before made me a man. Her body was cradled between the undead creatures, her bowels spilt forth from a hollow stomach cavity and pooled into her lap. I saw mangled fingerless hands drooping over her thighs, and it appeared as if the two undead things were dipping her severed fingers into the bowel spillage before gobbling them up like shrimp with cocktail sauce.

The earth again rumbled with confounding fury and toppled me backwards onto the ground. As I fought to regain my footing to retreat into the shed for a hastened escape out the front entranceway, its walls disintegrated and the roof came crashing down, burying my new home under a cloud of black dust. I grabbed hold of the edge of the roof to brace myself upright against the violent tremors, and that was when I became aware of the palace hill shifting below me, tilting at an angle, like a great goddess had inserted a shovel into the hill and began lifting. The shed no longer an obstruction to my view of the mayhem around me, I beheld with astonishment the dome of the great execution arena collapse inwards on itself, the entire stone building teetering to the right, cracks like veins ripping across its outer walls from its foundation. I hopped onto my roof and scurried across it, jumped off at the opposite end and lost my footing once again. When I managed to stand, I noticed the entire west side of the palace had been leveled, and a radiating orange hue rising up from the distant outskirts of the palace grounds told me Knossos was ablaze. All about me people fled wildly, stricken mindless by sheer terror, stumbling into one another, not knowing where to go for escape, their panicked confusion making them easy prey for the outpouring of Meytani set free from their broken prison.

I made my way onto a grassy clearing, avoiding a legless corpse as it bolted from my right to take down an approaching elderly woman in mid-flee, and it was joined by another of its kind in pinning her down, burrowing its teeth into her throat to make her stop shrieking and flailing about while they fed together. I backed into another Meytani, who was missing its lower jaw. It pushed me aside and lumbered away into the raining black ash.

I retreated down a garden path to my left which wound into the direction of the execution arena, bare feet tripping as I went over the outstretched legs of a body sprawled along the soot-covered foliage below a woman with a child arched over it and weeping. The path opened into a small scenic clearing that I avoided should the hillside crumble loose and spill down the slope, which it did a moment later, but I could not avoid catching sight of the billowing clouds of gray smoke and a vast flood of burning earth along the vista in the direction of Strongphyle at the Northern coast, the flames sweeping across the land atop a molten sea rolling towards Knossos from out of the horizon.

The falling ash grew heavier then, obscuring my view, blinding my eyes. I pulled the bed sheet wrapped about me over my head, held it up with my arms like a tent in an effort to see where I was going as I pushed myself further along the path, running virtually buck naked towards the region where instinct told me stood the remnants of the arena.

The volcanic North had unleashed its wrath, just as the people and its leaders and all-seeing soothsayers feared it would. When the Strongphyle region became active, talk of the world's end increased, and we all knew it was only a matter of time before it actually happened. It was also evident to me that the story of Meytani was more of a *prophecy* than merely something spooky to entertain children at bedtime. Kudos to whoever was responsible for the tradition of telling the story, though its advent was of no consequence in itself regarding our civilization's demise. We were all of us doomed together in destruction, both my people and Meytani's invasive plague. I wondered if Meytani itself was capable of foresight, if it knew of the coming apocalypse even as its raft washed ashore on our beaches, whether it ultimately decided, *fuck it, I'll try and eat them all anyway.*

As I pressed onwards, the tumultuous rumbling of the restless terrain subsided, granting me enough time to safely reach the destination near delirium steered me towards without having to champion each step like a tightrope artist or someone having to scale a rapidly descending escalator. I circumvented the execution arena ruins until I found what remained of its front entrance. The way it looked, the whole of the frontal structure had caved in on itself and slid forward, leaving in its wake a colossal pile of boulder-sized broken rock and debris and pulverized stone. There were no intact remains of the ascending steps that had earlier taken me to the inner arena's first level, let alone an entrance to the first level at all.

Shit.

I needed to get *inside*.

The rational part of me, or whatever remained of it, knew under these conditions that anyone determined to survive would be inclined to stay away from crumbling buildings or other large things that can fall on them. I honestly didn't know where it was I should logically take refuge, what area I could run to where the odds of survival would be more in my favor. But that was just the thing. Survival wasn't an issue. The issue was, I was damn well certain where I wanted to be when the angry earth took me, and I would give it my last dying effort to get there.

I was inexplicably drawn to the marble platform I'd seen at the center of Meytani's arena during my encounter with the king. I remembered my ensuing dream, how I stood at that very spot before millions of enigmatic spectators, gaining the attentions of a world beyond the one so very violently coming to an end all around me.

I discovered an opening beneath the rubble wide enough to draw my curiosity and deep enough to suggest a way in, and I went for it. As I went, I rid myself of the ash accumulated over my head and resituated the bed sheet about my naked person for clothing and to free my hands. I found myself descending into a tunnel which I hoped was taking me directly into the below-ground chambers surrounding the arena itself, a treacherous gravel-swept landscape devoid of light that narrowed and wound to the right and then left, until I felt my way through a crevice large enough to squeeze through, emerging into an open cavity still illuminated by torchlight out the other side.

I looked all around me.

I'd made it to the arena.

To my assessment, it was as if the walls of the grand structure were the first to have given way under the tension of the quakes, and the domed ceiling's own dislocated weight had sent it crashing straight downwards through the spiraling levels of balcony and mezzanine until the earth swayed towards the direction of the main entrance and changed its course. The earth had so far miraculously spared the arena pit itself. The ceiling, two-thirds intact, had aborted its descent just short of the first level, leaving heaping mounds of broken stone and debris littering the arena floor and the level above.

Hundreds of people lay wounded, dead, or dying, and there was no where I could thwart my vision so the sight of death could not fill it. I beheld pulverized bodies and parts of bodies protruding from between layers of boulder-sized horizontal slabs like human sandwiches prepared for a post apocalyptic lunch retreat for giant underworld lords. Blood cascaded from the carnage like spring water trickling down mountains of melting snow, collecting onto the first level walkway before spilling over the sides like a curtain of raindrops around the entire circumference of the arena pit. The air was thick with the moans of the dying and the distant commotion of the city's destruction outside, and a flurry of volcanic ash drifting down from the ceiling's opened wound.

I remembered Anpor's words before our last parting announcing a grand Meytani execution event taking place this morning certain to attract a multitude of spectators. Meytani likely had no idea how festive for them this execution would turn out to be. I spied some of these wretched undead crawling about beyond what remained of the wooden railing on the first level, some scaling the piles of rocks like spiders, seizing and feasting on the easy pickings of those still living but pinned and helpless.

From among the rubble where I was, I located the marble platform and my imminent place of death. I had no time to lose. I hiked up my bedsheet and hurried my way over, braving the debris-ridden obstacle course, avoiding the mutilated carcasses of the condemned left over from the morning's event intermingled with the bodies of spectators thrown to their deaths to join them.

Suddenly, there came a loud and rebellious cry from among them. It was from King Anpor himself, not far away from me on the arena floor. I'd made it to the marble platform, but when I turned and saw him, I abandoned it for a moment to step over to him. He lay upon his side, one shoulder buried into the ground and the other dislocated to the extent it protruded fully over his head like a fender around an automobile tire and locked his free arm straight up into the air. A stone slab the size of a royal banquet table had fallen upon him at such an angle that it buried itself into the king's midsection above the pelvis and forced out an area of ribcage exposed like a sliver of wood bending upwards from the strain of a chisel. He was able to kick and flail his legs in a lethargic tantrum like a round June beetle pinned into a bug specimen display case as he cried in agony and defiance, *"You sons of bitches! It's the Sacred Goddesses that have chosen to end our world, not you! The Great Snake Goddess Herself will take me into her bosom before the unholy likes of any of you bastards can get to me! Your bite cannot claim me, nor can it the world! You hear me?!!"*

And they heard him.

His cries caught the attentions of every Meytani within the ruins, distracting them from their ravenous preoccupations with the dying, and more poured into the first level from large cavities within the walls that likely gave them access to and from the outside grounds. They accumulated along the railing, encircling us within the arena from above as the king egged them on with insults and curses, until, one by one and then a few at a time, they flung themselves into the pit, gathered themselves each to their feet and collectively began to close in around us. I elected not to make Anpor aware of my presence as soon as I gathered the impression he was blind, and there was nothing I could say to comfort him anyway. The crowd of the undead pushed into us, nudging me aside and smothering the king with a tidal wave of ash and gore-swept hands reaching for him from all directions, finding him, tearing him apart to where all I could see of him was his one arm reaching above their heads, and the middle-most finger of his oblige them without further distraction. I lifted myself up onto it, managed to balance myself long enough to stand. The building shook as the weight of the palace hill shifted once more, and I could have witnessed the remainder of the great dome crumbling and burying everything around me, but my attentions were drawn to this brilliant white light spilling down from above, so blinding was it that I raised my hands to shield my eyes.

I plunged into the depths of death without being afforded so much as a rat's chance in Knossos to plug my nose and hold my breath.

I fell into a deep sleep for awhile, and when I awoke from it, I began to realize where I was.....

......and what I wanted to do.

I wanted to set myself free, to fly away from this abysmal wasteland.

After awhile and through great effort, I did just that, and I'd been so engrossed in my phantasmal escapades as a roaming voyeur over the last handful of decades I'd forgotten how at any moment my spirit would be summoned back to Knossos once the Knossos I grew up and died in had been recovered, that is .back to my body still standing upon that marble platform with my hands against the bright light and forever frozen that way by volcanic earth spew, to fulfill my ultimate destiny.

An Epilogue, or, A Return to Present Times

The power of the medium I'm speaking through is very strong, suggesting to me she's one of the most gifted among you. Planting her bare hands directly upon my remains helped lock onto my spirit, had me kicking and screaming through space like I was being sucked through a straw extending all the way from the other side of the globe. I'd been observing former Chilean dictator Augusto Pinochet's limo driver undergoing the surgical removal of his testicles in an effort to become a woman. Just prior to that, I'd been in a Peruvian village enjoying a saxophone serenade from a young local who thought he was alone, and not long before that I had a hell of a hoot impersonating Jesus through a Ouija board for roommates in a Brazilian flat.

My soul would be content simply spending its days 'til kingdom come continuing to soar around the earth among you, watching your history pass, witnessing the inevitable results of all of you taking the time to pay so much special attention to me after this momentous broadcast event wraps. Fate has clearly groomed me for the very act of telling my story, but now, having told it, I cannot remain here, neither within this medium nor in this world any longer. A formidable spirit has awakened within this ancient land, for one thing, and it won't permit me to stay for any Q & A. Regretfully, the heart of the medium I'm speaking through will stop beating just as soon as I leave, so no Q & A for her either, I'm afraid.

Should the undead you've discovered preserved here with me awaken and resume their assault on this world, well......I don't think they need to be here at all to accomplish that, which is why I was spared, made to get up here on this platform to ultimately tell my tale. I suspect Meytani was privy to the impending fate it shared with Minoa all along and took advantage of my destiny, because civilized modern society has been eating *itself* alive from the inside out for the longest time now, from what *I've* witnessed, and tonight's show is going to play a major role in a media feeding frenzy which will achieve the same result as a horde of undead gradually consuming the world anyway. If I'd been bitten, my soul would have left this earth like the rest of the victims of their onslaught, never to return for my moment in the spotlight that in itself can trigger eventual apocalypse.

It's been said some people have to die before they become famous......

Nicholas Grabowsky

RED AFTERWORLD

"Symbolism is only potent when it is
given meaning."
---NG

Part One:

BEFORE THE END

1.

PREACHERS, MESSIAHS, AND VAMPIRE BOYS

My name it is Sam Hall, Sam Hall.

Not too long ago I popped a CD into my player and Johnny Cash sung back to me those very words, and I went all *I'll be damned* over that song, because the Man in Black was singing about *me*.   It was the first time I'd heard it, and I could find nothing on the CD booklet as to who wrote it or where it came from and I assume it's old, *public domain* old, as I was later told a traditional version existed where Sam Hall was a chimney sweep who went a-swingin' for burglary.   But when I heard Cash's rendition and then played it over and over again, it was like my own personal prophecy come alive.

You see, I've had a recurring nightmare all my life where I killed a man, smashed into his head several times an object which, from dream to dream, is sometimes a hefty mallet, sometimes my own fists, but usually the head of a statue of some Greek goddess unknown to me that fell from its stone body during a life-or-death struggle between myself and the man I ultimately killed.   The climax of the dream, unless someone awoke me just short of it, would always be my own public hanging, a gloomy event to say the least, Old West style and in 1857 to be exact, from the lowest branch of a leafless tree which only had four branches to it, and my branch was just high enough so when the horse beneath me was swatted on her be-hind to skid addle, my feet couldn't touch the ground.   Didn't matter anyways, because the horse---my *own* frickin' horse---went off like a thoroughbred in the Kentucky Derby so fast the noose snapped my neck on the way down to a limp and raggedy swinging yours truly where, before my vision reverted to the kind of static fizz you used to get on your television late at night when the channel you were watching switched to an Indian head before going off the air, I saw her ride off into the last

135

sunrise I would ever see before I woke up beneath the quilts of a bed in another life. Each time when I awoke after having this dream, I'd be pissed off to the extent I'd scream and lash out at anyone close to me. I lost many a woman that way.

I visited a palm reader before I became an end-times preacher. She told me that my nightmares indicated a past life experience, and I thought, no shit, I didn't need to pay anyone a double sawbuck to tell me something I didn't already figure. What she said next was how I'd eventually be heralded by some as a messiah at the end of the world, and how it would lead to great things.

Great things.

Oh....and I would eventually meet a vampire.

That, to me, was a heaping pile of bullshit, for awhile. At the time of the reading I was homeless, a personality staple at a shelter in downtown Los Angeles, and my begging for that money with a cardboard sign on a concrete island where people made a left-hand turn in their vehicles at a busy intersection collectively made that reading possible. I sacrificed a meal of ninety-nine-cent gas station hot dogs and a twelver of Old Milwaukee for that piece of crap insight.

Never considered there'd be any truth to it.

In my sixties, years after the reading, the end of the world *did* happen, in the kind of fashion many had long anticipated and would deem Biblically apocalyptic, and by then I had joined a Christian sect that favored my then-fervent opinions on the current conditions of the world and what we all must do about it. People really dug what I had to say, and I was very opinionated. Public and private donations from abroad led to the ownership of my own AM radio station, and an hour per week for my own show on public broadcasting across America. On the television show as well as radio, people would call in live and ask me questions about the Bible and my personal views on the state of the world, and I would sit in an expensive leather recliner chair cross-legged in a suit and tie with a Bible in my lap and shelves of related books behind me for atmosphere. The money coming in to maintain my ministry was enough to not only keep me off the streets but provided for me a modest three-bedroom home in Southern California, in the city of Brea, and I met a woman in her forties who married me and gave me a son by the time I was 69. Oddly enough, the features of the woman I married, Janis, resembled the Greek goddess statue whose stone head I often used in killing the faceless man in my dreams, though I never let Janis in on that.

I never told anyone about the palm reader, or how I was supposed to eventually meet a real vampire. These renegade Christians would've hung me by the neck all over again with that confession.

Just months before the end of the world as everyone knew it, I had enough of a following and influence that I was able to purchase thirty-two-hundred spotlights from a manufacturer in Sarasota Florida, wholesale, the kind automotive dealers would rent to flash against a backdrop of sky to the masses announcing a New Year's Eve close-out sale or for Hollywood studios to utilize for a red carpet premiere, for a police commissioner to call forth a bat man for that matter, and I distributed these costly things all over North America to flash messages of peace across the sky simultaneously, after given my word to do so, when it was evident the end of the world was nigh; for instance, as soon as I knew Americans were about to be overcome by mushrooms, not the botanical kind but the cloud sort. My reasoning was, if governments were going to press little red nuke buttons, I would press buttons of my own. That way, should people see my messages and survive catastrophe, they would have hope.

When the time *did* come, my image was the last most people on my continent ever saw.......coming down, as it seemed, from the clouds.

***

Fifteen, sixteen years prior to the end of the world, there was once a boy who tried to make himself and others believe he was a vampire.

The early stages of this delusion developed in his kindergarten days, lying in bed late at night fully alert and coming down off an imagination high instilled from an overexposure to Dracula flics on the Sci-fi Channel. October thirty-first Halloween traditions had already indoctrinated him with the basics of vampire lore. What really got him started was the Dracula from Rankin/Bass' *Mad Monster Party*, however. Far less creepy, but so utterly cool. The kid even memorized the words to *It's Our Time to Shine* from that film, where Francesca sings and Dracula does a tap dance routine, and he would often sing it to himself in moments alone.

He formulated an alter-ego-sort-of fantasy life from then, where he chose to envision himself not as Dracula, but someone he felt could be superior and boss an imaginary Dracula around. His late-night bedroom antics involved sitting atop his pillow while loyal subjects of his Monster Kingdom would step from out of the walls and do his bidding.

Most of the time, his bidding was to sit and discuss issues of the day, such as how he was forced to eat peas at dinnertime but, under the scrutiny of Mom and Dad, he would pretend to eat them, put a spoonful of the green round gopher turds into his mouth and spit them into his glass of milk while pretending to drink it. The milk was thick enough to conceal the deed, and when his parents weren't paying attention he'd get up and rinse out his glass, get more milk until he was all the fuck done with his peas.

Dracula and the monsters would just laugh and laugh, and the boy always had a good time with them. As this ritual progressed, Wile E. Coyote joined the post-bed-time clan, if only for the fact that as many times as he'd watched the poor damn coyot chase the Roadrunner, he wanted him to catch and eat his ass. The boy figured, with his vast resources, he could rescue this dog family outcast from that confounding situation. That gave his kingdom something to do. There were many nights where Dracula and his henchmen actually caught the Roadrunner, would bring the struggling fowl straight to the boy's room, and the boy would insist on driving his fangs straight into its abdomen and sucking out most of the blood before breaking its neck and handing the dead thing over to an appreciative Wile E. It was so fun to play, once was never enough.

He brought his fantasy to school with him every day, though much like his lunch he would keep it contained until the proper time arrived to make use of it. In this case, the proper time was when the teachers set the children loose for outside play. While the other kids engaged in tag or jump-rope or games of like-kind, in frolic and folly and dangling from jungle gyms like monkeys, this boy would run around the play yard, flapping his jacket like he was flying, and bite girls on the arms. One boy who dared defy him had his fingers pried from the monkey bars and broke his arm as a result of the fall, an incident in which Vampire Boy denied being a part of. His teachers grew worried, not knowing what to do, and so did his parents.

He was raised an only child until years later when his parents gave him a baby sister, Kira, and that didn't happen until he was fourteen.

But by then, he'd found Jesus.

He was fresh out of elementary school when the Good Lord changed his ways and worldviews, and another phase in life where the opportunity to be somebody arose in a way far more substantial than the false feelings of self-importance Vampire Boy brought with him. His family became members of a local evangelical Protestant church prominent enough to boast a congregation of 2600, and from puberty through high school graduation the boy's days were filled with holy rollers and intense efforts to convert people into holy rollers. He was branded a nerd in school because of it, was serious enough in his commitment to even be branded a nerd by those his age at church......most of which were jocks and kids in higher income brackets who ignored him, until opportunities arose by enthusiastic votes from the clergy to let him preach at youth services and lead Sunday schools. After that, he became a popular guy. Debbie Von Wald, a bubblegum blonde older than he by a year and one of the adult choir's most showcased talents, actually came on to him.

Into his life about nineteen years, was when Debbie proclaimed she was pregnant. First, she found out by pissing onto a test strip, then her parents coerced her out of the bathroom and into admitting why she was so upset, which led to an emergency meeting with the church youth pastor, and so forth. By the time word fell upon the ears of our dear boy, a scandal had already been created. This sparked a *sequence* of scandals as soon as gossip spread, where prominent male clergy began to resign and abandon their marriages because they confessed proudly to be gay, where the Music Minister was revealed to have been diverting church funding into his personal checking account, that sort of finger-pointing, gossipy bullshit.

Turned out also, Debbie's twins weren't our boy's at all. Belonged to Ron Rickles, a sophomore with a twitchy hand problem he preferred Jesus to heal rather than modern medicine, but secretly *didn't* want Jesus' intervention because his affliction served as an asset during lonely bathroom times with proper lubrication and a magazine. He was also Pastor Rickles' youngest son.

The boy's hands were still dirty in admitting to screwing Debbie in the first place, in everyone's eyes. In the end, both he and his family lost interest in organized religion, because of all its bullshit. His emergence into young adulthood had suffered by then from a lack of stimulus from the outside world, walking the line of being *in* the world and not *of* it, as was always a church motto, so when he entered into the second decade of his life he was more naive than most, was still living with his parents, had so much to discover about the ways of the world.......

.......and then the world began to end.

***

It was on an early Sunday morning where Kira was restless and our boy was jobless with hair that hadn't endured much grooming since he dropped out of church, the two of them together enjoying a three a.m. living room channel surf and leftover pizza feast, when KLGQ announced that New York had been nuked from a bomb planted inside a subway. CNN was reporting on Chicago in past tense. An airborne virus had been unleashed into the heart of Vegas that was invoking violent pandemonium from the sudden heavy acid trips of scores of Sin City citizens. We were under terrorist attack, and the President was preparing a speech to tell us all about it within the hour.

When later that same week two nearby amusement parks suffered the same fate as Vegas, the boy's family decided it was time to put the house up for sale and move the hell away from *any* major city.

They settled into the neighborhood of a small town in southwestern Arizona.

And, as it so happened, across the street from a *real* vampire.........

2.

TOAD AND DAYTON MONDAY

Sam Hall here has to scoot out of the picture for awhile, now that we're on a roll with our main man, the ex-Vampire Boy/ex-holy roller.

His name was Dayton Monday.

Nineteen months had passed since the Mondays moved from out of the smack-dab center of Southern California and into a modern but isolated adobe-themed tract home neighborhood in Coolidge, Arizona, southeast of Phoenix, 744 Refuge Drive just before Refuge ended into a cul-de-sac. Dayton was about twenty-two at the time, been through two gal-pal relationships and currently lamenting over the last one (who found him in a motel room with the first); was of late discharged from his job flipping burgers for Sonic at the rest stop off Interstate 10 for his fifth no-call/no-show in two months.

It was no big deal to anyone that he was still living with Mom, Dad and little sis Kira, hadn't made more of an effort to break out on his own. These days, having family members left in the world was sacred, and to be living with them under the same roof was increasingly common, the more the merrier, in a time where the word *merry* was hardly even associated with Christmas anymore.

If I were to place you on the street in front of Dayton's parents' house right at that time, and directed your gaze straight up, you wouldn't believe the state of the night sky. It was as if the stars had fallen, but fallen short, like luminous ping pong balls upon Captain Kangaroo and Mister Moose that did not reach them this time but hung there, just above their heads, leaving the producers of that now-ancient children's television show scratching *theirs*.......or like spilt billions of luminous cordless white Christmas tree lights upon a vast plate of spotless glass under which existed our world.

Our world likely hadn't witnessed so many stars all at once from a terrestrial point of view, even from upon the highest

141

mountaintops on the clearest of nights, for millions of years. Even so, the constellations seemed to be in an impossible state of disarray. There was no Sagittarius, no Capricorn. No Big or Little Dipper. No North Star, as far as anyone could tell.

They all looked the same from down below, and they were so unusually numerous and scattered about that it was impossible to connect the dots one to another astrologically anymore.

Horoscopes were *all* fucked up, but, then again, so was the world.

Under this particular canopy of midsummer night sky stood a 54-year-old biker roughneck upon the driveway of his home smoking a cigarette from between the fingers of one hand while clutching the end of a garden hose in the other, watering his front lawn. His thumb against the hose mouth regulated the spray more expertly than any nozzle, and with a learned precision and determined aim he hit a squirrel dead on and off its sojourn across the wooden side fence in a jet stream of H2O.

Bobby Lee Horton had been a resident of the Arizona desert all his civilian life, and since his years serving his country as a United States Marine on the Iraqi/Afghanistan front lines he returned home fully intact and reclaimed his life.....found the wife who divorced him before he enlisted and wooed her back to him, reunited with their war-protesting vagabond son (who was dodging the recent mandatory draft) before a drunk driver plowed a Thunderbird into him just off Cirby Road last November, cut him in half against an oak tree with a yellow ribbon wrapped around it for the troops. Any remnants of relatives to ol' Bob had perished in the many world cities bombed in nuclear fashion since New York and Chicago, eight in all so far, and all that remained of known significant others to Bobby was his wife, who lived with him there on Refuge Drive, and a second cousin with three children in the Florida Straits.

He had an extended family, of course. His reputation within the community was upstanding and he was not only popular around that region but oftentimes newsworthy. He'd been financially responsible for five years' worth of July Fourth parades and fireworks shows at Pavilion Park, wore a Santa suit in front of his driveway every night in December before a symphony of lights decorating his home for the season and gave away free toys, contracted a crew each year for Phoenix' ultimate Halloween haunted house. Home gardening became his habitual passion, and his vegetable and annual floral gardens around the back of his property were highlighted in a *Better Homes & Gardens* issue the same year global *warming* and *going green* concerns shifted to global *warring* and *going red* (as in country-wide anger and a resulting genuine slogan), and it was rare that anyone bothered about the earth itself anymore, what it could provide versus what we could take from it. For those living around him, Bobby was commendable.

Most notably, he was also a full-fledged senior member of the Brotherhood of the Black Heroes. We'll get to that later.

And then there was Dayton, the younger dude from across the street. In the days to follow Bobby's son's passing, Bobby Lee and Dayton developed a friendship and a blossoming bond.

A bit of Bob's gardening rubbed off on Dayton, and our boy began spending more time as a result taking an active interest in doing up his parents' property all nice and pretty with a wide rectangular section of thriving veggies where there once was a corner lawn, flower beds out back surrounding the patio just outside an awning of hanging potted vines. He built a sixty-gallon above-ground pond upon the sheltered concrete just outside the sliding glass doors, made from the wood of wine barrels sealed together, with a pump and a statue of a little boy peeing into it he bought at the Wal-mart in Florence.

Dayton also developed a curiosity about this whole Brotherhood of the Black Heroes thing Bobby was into.

A *deep* curiosity.

Bobby Lee was about to oblige him.

***

Now prior to tonight, Dayton and Bobby had their discussions about it, the Black Heroes, trading whiskey shots and sipping beer in Bobby's garage with Bob's 2008 Harley-Davidson Softail FXSTC off to one side, forever in spare parts limbo since the day he dismantled it for one minor forgotten repair and then kept doing so when he came across a rare meth acquisition and stayed awake with the garage door down for six days. Sometimes, a straggler friend or two would come knocking and hang out with the two, looking to borrow some money or get connected with a bag of

143

purple buds, but some were neighbors wanting nothing more than good company while sharing a twelve-pack and weeping over humanity's current state. And then, a couple specific others would be Black Heroes members, biker-looking dudes, who only dropped by after the sky grew dark.

Bobby's name as a Black Heroes' Brother was Toad, a name he chose for himself during his own initiation into the fraternity's five hundred or so members back in the day. Since then, in the U.S. alone, the Brotherhood grew to 9,700 strong, and the Brotherhood were picky-choosey about who joined them. But *back in the day* was several centuries ago, around abouts, nearly as long as Toad had been alive and not counting the 54 years he's had a social security number applied to him.

Looking at him, even knowing him the way Dayton did, there was nothing to indicate that Bobby was any different than most anyone else, when it comes to human beings. He ate, he drank, he came out in daylight, held steady jobs, had a wife and son, drank some more and had health problems.

But everything about Bobby was Black Heroes. Bobby's garage was decked out with their paraphernalia.....Black Heroes stickers in both English and Latin on the walls and cabinets, on his Harley, on his pick-up truck's window and bumper, he drank from Black Heroes mugs and wore Black Heroes black t-shirts, probably wore Black Heroes pajamas to bed for all Dayton knew. Bob attended Black Heroes' annual Bean Feeds and other gatherings somewhere deep in the Tonto National Forest, helped organize their local summer parades and Toys 4 Kidz drive around Christmastime. Some members were influential in both the film industry, politics, Wall Street, and I hear say two were past U.S. Presidents. Each of the fifty states had their own Black Heroes chapter, as it turned out. They were, on the surface, a men's fraternity that were highly charitable and loved to party.

Dayton found himself drawn into wanting to know more about them, and for some time this was all Bobby would tell him.

After awhile, Bobby found himself dropping hints, trying to get a feel for how deep Dayton's interests really flowed.

"So, uh, buddy.....what you think about vampires?" he'd say.

Dayton would laugh. "If they were real, God bless 'em."

"No, really. If the Brotherhood of the Black Heroes were vampires, would you still want to join them?"

"If they could help save the world, and I could still live my life, not have to sleep in some coffin or be afraid of crosses and garlic, I think I would be okay."

"Well," Bobby would say, "we're immortal, and we can do everything I can do. But crosses are out of the question."

Dayton always chuckled away these hints.

Bobby assumed Dayton chuckled more out of nervousness than drink the times they together flew around the subject like mosquitoes outside a screen door. He was intrigued by the accounts of those pre-teen, vampire wannabe years Day so often openly reflected on when he was drunk. And then there was Dayton's more recent past, the entire church life ordeal, altogether making Bobby realize that this friend of his from across the street had actively been searching for meaning and respect all of his life.

At some point between them there developed the chemistry of a fundamental misunderstanding, for when Dayton persisted at becoming a Brother himself, Bobby was certain he had made himself clear about the nature of what he was asking, was sure Day was a ripe candidate for initiation with bells and whistles. Bobby also figured, what he didn't tell Dayton, the boy would endure regardless and make him proud.

If Dayton Monday knew what he was getting himself into with Toad and the Black Heroes, he would have thought better and joined the military, the Red Cross, even Greanpeace......hell, *anyone* else, if he wanted to be somebody and hold for himself any hope in making a difference in regards to the state the world was in lately, somehow. Honestly, when Bobby Lee dropped obvious clues as to the true nature of his fraternity, Dayton assumed it was all a smoke screen with shits and giggles, because it was obvious the Black Heroes had secrets known only to themselves, and *vampires* weren't *real*.........

***

Purposely oblivious to all the hoopla concerning the world's current climate, aware yet decidedly distant, Bobby continued to water his front lawn.

Every newscast on TV reported nothing but what was going on globally, as if local murders and robberies and rampant pedophiles

145

and school shooters were as much second-hand news as pit bull bite cases on Judge Judy.

The surrounding neighborhood seemed to noticeably be in denial, or otherwise unaffected, with the exception of a certain pandemonium in the atmosphere of daylight hours to which Bob, primarily a day sleeper these days, was unaware of until his wife filled him in with today's goings-on when he awoke from a deep sleep around dusk.

Everyone else in the neighborhood, tonight, seemed to be calmly sedated and dead to the world.

On the outside looking in, and looking in on Bobby Lee, one wouldn't suspect the Earth was experiencing the magnitude of chaos it was at the time. To Bob, for now, its impact seemed obliviously no more impersonal then how his vote mattered on any given political election the last few decades. His life and his personal goings-on, lately, remained the same, despite the recent loss of his son and how the rapid collapse of the ozone made his gardens fry in 125-degree heat during the summer days.

But tonight was special. Tonight was the third Friday in July, the beginning of Bean Feed Weekend for the Heroes, and Toad had committed another willing newcomer into the Brotherhood.

The thing that kind of worried him, however, was that if Dayton didn't work out, the boy would have to die, and then Toad would have to risk his own life if he were to step into that affair, if it became necessary, and at best he would be obliged to take Day's place for the remainder of the initiation.

And initiation was a bitch.

3.

ALIEN FACE PENDANT

That night, the third Friday of July that year, before Toad/Bobby Lee set out to water his lawn and spray a squirrel off his fence, Dayton's parents retired to their bed.....around 9:30 pm, I'd say, after a half hour of Super Satellite's commercial-free Jeopardy 3D and enough of the following evening news to avoid hearing how scientists were scratching their heads over how the earth's rotation has shifted and what politicians were pledging to do about it.

Kira, now eight years old, avoided the nightly news and felt safe in her room full of stuffed animals and comfort, playing Poofy Unicorns on her Playsphere Station IV, occasionally tiptoeing down the hallway to spy on her brother's doings. In a burgundy nightgown she crept, until she arrived at his door. His bedroom light was on. The door was ajar and with her index finger she pushed it carefully open about an inch and leaned over to take a peek inside. As soon as she did so, the door abruptly closed, right into her forehead. She tried the knob, which she found already locked. So she began to knock.

Dayton did his best to ignore her. He settled back into the swivel chair before his desk on the other side of the door. Thinking better of it, and of how advantageous it was for him to be certain his parents remained asleep, he leaned back over and unlocked it. Kira ceased knocking. After a pause, Dayton assumed she had went away.

He continued about his business, pen in hand and blank notebook pages in front of him. Tonight was *his* night, a damn special one, and before he went to bed he wanted to make sure his family would *understand* when they awoke in the morning to discover him missing.

His letter, after he finished composing it, read something like this:

147

Dear Mom, Dad, and Kira,

I'm going away for a little while, just for the weekend so I'll make up for the chores when I get back.

I know you think Bobby Lee is a good man on the surface, but on the other hand you don't like smelling alcohol and cigarettes on my breath after I've returned from hanging out with him sometimes. I can understand that, but all he wants to do is live his life peacefully with his wife, do his gardening, and help people in need. He did lose his son. And with the war going on, everyone's distressed and confused.

I know you're worried about me. We've been through hell recently, from the church ordeal with Debbie Von Wald to the move when the terrorist attacks got too close to home, to my losing my job, to the news about Grandma and Poppa and Aunt Georgina, and Jeff and Sue, how they're not around anymore, and I know you're concerned that any day Uncle Sam will come calling for me.

Sometimes I think if the draft did send me a notice I would disappear into Mexico. It's what everybody's doing. Border patrol used to be for the illegals getting into our own country, and now many families are fighting to get out. If I did that, I'd be on the run, and if I bit the bullet and joined the U.S. forces, I'd still be leaving my family and may not return, and the point is, I don't want to leave you.

So what I'm doing is going away for the weekend, joining the Brotherhood of the Black Heroes, the organization Bobby Lee's into. He's spending his own money, four hundred twenty-five dollars, to sponsor me through the initiation. Once I'm one of them, I can work my way up to really making a difference in our community, within our country, hopefully. Although until our move we've never heard of them, they've been around for hundreds of years and some were participants in the Boston Tea Party, (so they say of their brothers past), some are Freemasons as well, and all are committed to an undeclared civil war that can set America back in the right direction again and keep us safe.

'Nos es immortalis , nos mos increbresco , nos es ex nostrum mens.'

'We are immortal, we will prevail, we are out of our minds,' is their motto. I'll be wearing a black t-shirt which says that on the

148

front when I get back, probably Monday afternoon. At that time, I'll have a lot to tell you, I'm sure. But I'm going to be okay.

If around the time you read this you find a window broken, a window screen sliced up, any kind of evidence that an intruder invaded our house last night, it was only due to the rule that any potential initiate must first be abducted while sleeping in his bed by the Bretheren, taken out and into the night as they say, and into the trials to follow. It's a tradition hundreds of years old.

I'll work off any damages, and I'm sure you'll understand.

I love all of you, and when I see you next, I'll be a man.

***

When Kira had ceased knocking and Dayton ultimately unlocked the door for her, a hand seized her shoulder from behind. Startled, she quickly turned, expecting to see that it was either Mom or Dad or even both of them, staring her down with *you-should-be-in-bed*-looking eyes and with no reason for doing so....for one, there was nothing important to do tomorrow anyway, and for another, bedtimes were pointless where the end of the world was concerned.

But who she faced, who knelt down to her, pushed her against the hallway cabinets with a palm across her mouth to stifle her reaction to seeing him there......

.......*was Dayton.*

"Shhhh, Kira, it's me," he whispered. "We have to be quiet....."

He relaxed his hold with caution.

"I *am* quiet," she snapped, a little too loud for her brother's comfort until her voice softened. "It's you, the drama queen action hero who throws his sister against the wall who needs to be quiet. Who's in your room?"

Dayton was out of breath and shirtless, bare-footed, wearing only black jeans and a teardrop-shaped pendant dangling from his neck. He was soaking wet, like he'd emerged seconds ago from a backyard swimming pool and was in need of a towel from the cabinets behind Kira. But the Mondays didn't have a swimming pool. Water dripped from body to carpet, and his saturated jeans clung to his legs and waist. His black hair had been short since before bedtime, and there was no other explanation for its past-the-shoulders length other than it actually being a wig designed for a

149

heavy metal Halloween, or perhaps his head was sporting a mop dipped in tar.

He didn't at first answer Kira but rather removed his pendant from around his neck, up and over his head, lifted her hands together and placed it in them. Then he said, "Listen. Kira, I don't have much time. I need you to give this to the friend in my room. Tell him to put it on, to keep it on him at all times and never lose sight of it. Tell him.....tell him it's part of his initiation. He's joining Bobby Lee's Black Heroes tonight, and they have to come into the house and get him, like they're pretending to kidnap him, so keep the sliding glass door to the patio open for them after I leave, okay?"

"So it's a game?" Kira asked. Then, "Why are you all wet?"

Dayton eyed a wooden crucifix perched upon the hallway wall, stood erect and snatched it, knelt back down and handed it to her. Even after all he'd learned, he was surprised he was immune to its power. "And keep this out of sight, whatever you do. It'll offend the guys coming for my friend in there."

Kira opened a cabinet behind her, placed the crucifix upon a stack of linens, closed the door. "That good?"

"Good enough. God, I missed you so much."

"What are you talking about? You're acting all weird. Have you been smoking the bud or something?"

But Dayton meant every word that he missed her, and his eyes were holding back tears with each moment he looked upon her. That frightened Kira slightly, all the seriousness and urgency, but what scared her further were his last words before he gave her a heartfelt embrace, rose, and turned to leave. "Tell Mom and Dad I love them, and I love you too. Remember, do what I told you, but wait a couple minutes after I leave first. Yes, it's a game, and we're gonna win it. Right, Girly-girl?"

"Right, Dayton-ayton."

Dayton all but forgot those pet names they'd developed for each other. Saying goodbye to a past full of loved ones was no easy task, especially when that past was suddenly all around him and as real as it ever was, but he never thought to do so the first time aside from the letter his earlier self had just completed writing and cherished this mind-blowing golden opportunity to dig into his yesteryear, quite literally. He still couldn't believe he was there.

He was so thoroughly tempted to check in on his parents slumbering in their bed that he ached to give in, but to do so would be to risk everything if per chance they awoke and saw him. Besides, he was hungry, and he hadn't been around too many humans for quite some time. For him, the tantalizing smell of living blood permeated the house. If he could see the smell, the air would be glowing like radiation surrounding a mad scientist's test tube in a 1950's sci-fi flic.

He retreated into the living room darkness, leaving Kira alone in the hallway with a lingering question mark above her head should she be a character in a comic strip and this wasn't real life at all. After a brief hesitation, she followed after him, but when she emerged into the living room he was already gone, the patio sliding glass door open wide to the outside night, parted drapes rolling against the incoming warm summer breeze.

She gazed upon the pendant face-up within her hands, its string of black leather to which it was bound hanging between and beneath the digits of her fingers, held it at an angle against where a ray of moonlight filtered in from beyond the patio window glass so she could inspect it more clearly. A UFO alien face returned her gaze, only several millimeters thick and an inch and a half in diameter, with black oblong eyes slanting inwards at its center above a black horizontal slit of a mouth just above the teardrop pointy end below, surrounded by a shiny smooth deep red resin that incorporated the rest of its face, encompassed by a rim of the same tarnished gold-like metal as was entirely on its backside.

She figured after viewing it that more than a couple of minutes had already passed, and, wondering who it was she'd been instructed to deliver the pendant to, whatever friend it was who currently occupied Dayton's room, she carefully made her way to do the deed.

Without knocking this time, she turned the unlocked doorknob and entered to find her brother, short-haired and dry and ready for bed, rising from his swivel chair and switching off his desk lamp.

***

So it's a game?
Yes, it's a game, and we're gonna win it......
Kira played well.

151

She handed the alien pendant over to her brother and told him everything, and Dayton chuckled and figured it was a game, too. He figured the guys that would come to retrieve him for the initiation had already arrived, had encountered his sister outside his door, and he accepted the pendant before hurrying her out of the room so he could turn off his bedroom light and go to bed. Only after bed could they take him.

Kira's ceaseless questions frustrated him, and if he hadn't known any better he'd have sworn she was mesmerized over his presence there, how it almost seemed like when she invaded his privacy she didn't expect him to be there, but rather someone else in his stead.

She actually bet a full week's allowance that it was him all dripping wet in a wig outside his door, all part of the game, all along, and not a Black Hero Brother just messing with her, somehow incredibly well........

4.

ABDUCTION BY BLACK SHEETS

They came for Dayton sooner than he'd expected or hoped. As he remained beneath the covers of his bed, waiting for them to come and take him, he wished he could grasp the meaning of the alien face pendant he wore around his neck as much as he could take it physically into his palm and wrap his fingers about it......

***

"Gary, you bastard, slow down! It's gonna spill all over the place," Tendon snapped in a quirky sort of frustration. He was cutting two lines of Ajax cleanser across the backside of the open glove compartment in front of him and his friend was playing speed demon, the sudden left and right turns and vaults over curbs and sidewalks was just not cool at all, and Tendon was desperate to at least suck up one more nostril's worth of the household cleaner's bleach-laced easy rinse formula before they got to their destination.

"Goddammit," yelped the reckless driver right away in response, "Brotherhood names from now on, *Tendon*, and that there ain't no pristine and sparkly crystal meth ya got going on neither. If it spills, just shake out more from the can. We got plenty."

Gary's Black Heroes name was Wars. I hear say that most common fraternities force initiates into having to deal with names given to them, but in the Black Heroes, you get to choose your own name. The thing is, once you name yourself, you have to live with it forever. At least among the Brethren. *Tendon* was way better than *Harvey*, for example, but *Wars* to *Gary* was more befitting. For a myriad of reasons, other Brothers had to live with names like *Hot Showers* or *Dike* or *Toilet* or even *Penis Hole*, let alone *Betty Davis*, because they were drunk and loaded when they chose their names.

Wars, like Tendon, was punk ass white trailer trash to those who knew him both well and casually. They were hairless anarchist skinheads adorned with nose/ear/cheek/tongue piercings and fashionable adornments of the like with abounding body tattoos the both of them, drinking buddies and high school drop-outs around about 1999, both welcomed into the fold after a grueling three nights of unspeakable abuse by the Heroes just before the Millennium's End Celebration and Flesh Feast came to a halt at the stroke of midnight New Year's Day 2000, a couple or so decades ago. It was a Kodak Moment for each of them, and they were that particular initiation's sole survivors out of thirty-four potential vampires total. As far as vampires go, they were not only still young and feisty and inexperienced but looked the part, forever eighteen, forever punk ass white trailer trash.

Eighteen, and they liked it, as Alice Cooper sung, never to look a day older.

In the Coolidge, Arizona streets, and with the particular shape of current times, Wars' fervent driving endangered no one, for the streets that time of night were vacant. There was no reason for the hurry except to say at these hours Wars could get away with it, and he always tried to get away with anything he *could*. After all, he couldn't die. At least not from a car accident.

Still, it was enough to upset any shotgun passenger of like kind trying to snort lines of Ajax from the backside of a glove box.

***

Bobby Lee was still watering his lawn with a garden hose when an old and weathered black two-door Ford Focus ZX3 pulled up to the street curb and silenced, killed its lights. Both doors opened, and out stepped Wars and Tendon. They wore primarily black, from their snakeskin boots to jeans and t-shirts to the bed sheets wrapped about them like they were enroute to a Gothic toga party, to their silver belts and wristbands which held the sheets fashionably to them. Tendon waited for Wars to join him at the sidewalk, and then they together ventured over to Toad across his wet lawn, almost like Doublemint Gum twins of a dark sort, the way they did so.

Toad always intimidated them, not because he was biker-lookin', with his back-length head-full of split-end-chocked brown hair and an unkempt beard which covered half his face and fell down to his Adam's apple, but because compared to their own lives since human conception, he was hundreds of years old and once

154

even had his own kingdom back in the day, on the world's opposite side, long ago. They respected that.

Their arrival barely stirred Toad into raising an eyebrow to glance their way. He turned a quarter circle away to where perennial flowers arose from the well-tilled soil beneath the kitchen window to drench them, back facing his two guests.

"What's cooking there, buddies?" said he to the approaching duo.

"We are running late, Sire, and you don't appear to be ready yet," said Wars.

"I'll have my wife fetch my wardrobe accessories," Toad said, "but I ain't changing, 'cept for my sacred robes of course, on top of what I got on already." He was garbed in partially soiled work clothes, plain black t-shirt with a breast pocket and blue jeans.

He tipped a hand to his wife, a blonde knock-out sporting cosmetic-coated age beneath an over-stretched white wifebeater t-shirt poking her head out his house' front door. She blew him a weary kiss, drew herself back inside and shut the door.

"You go along without me, do your deed," said Toad to the guys. "I'll be waiting at the car soon as I finish up here. Be sure and tape his eyes real good, now."

"No problem, my Lord," came War's reply.

"Kiss me," Toad extended his free hand to them, palm down, fingers limp, like the Pope with a ring to smooch. Mind you, he didn't so much as lift his gaze to them once during this conversation, just focused on the simple nightly yard maintenance task at hand.

Wars and Tendon both looked at each other quizzically, then together moved to take their Lord's hand and, before they could bring it up to their lips, he slapped both their faces in a backhanded sort of Three Stooges way.

And Toad uttered, "Kiss me, and then kiss my ass. That's not what I mean...."

He turned his hand palm-up, made a *gimme* kind of motion with his fingers, and Tendon hurried to pull out a sandwich bag from a front pants pocket beneath his black toga and opened it to withdraw a mighty fat joint of good Hawaiian Indica, and from his shirt pocket a lighter. He took the first hit, then placed it between

Toad's fingers before Wars could exclaim a *hey* of protest from being left out.

Toad puffed on it for a couple of languid moments while the two impatiently waited, before saying to them like a Mafioso with a cigar, "Well, what are you waiting for? Go to it, boys......."

***

Tendon went around the right side yard of the Monday home, Wars around the left. Tendon had it easy; there was actually a gate to open and walk through. Wars climbed a tree and hopped the fence. When they met each other at the backyard patio, they caught sight of something submerging itself into an above-ground pond the size of a two-person sauna beneath the awning, something that was at least large enough to resemble a human in shadow, but by the time they finished a careful approach to inspect the situation the water left no signs of what they thought they saw. If Tendon had been alone, he'd swear the Ajax was screwing with his brain. But as for Wars......

"There was a presence here," he whispered. "One of us."

"Yeah," replied Tendon, "what's up with that?"

"Hellifien-o."

"What?"

"Hellifien-o."

"What's '*hellifien-o*?"

"Dude," said Wars, "you need to not be stupid right now....."

On the alert more than they anticipated, they found the sliding glass patio door to be unlocked. Wars slid it open quietly and one after the other they entered into the somber darkness of the house. Tendon buried a hand beneath his bed sheet robe and withdrew a roll of white duct tape thick enough to be as round and wide as a dinner plate and began to pull out a stretch of it. The sudden noise of him doing so pissed Wars off.

They'd been instructed as to which room to invade, which door of the three down the hallway to open where they'd find the one they came for. When they found the door, Wars turned the knob and entered first followed by Tendon, who, while closing it behind them, whistled softly the first few bars of *Strangers in the Night* in polite homage to Chris Sarandon's vampire Jerry Dandrige in *Fright Night*, who whistled the same tune under similar circumstances.

156

Dayton Monday didn't anticipate his abduction to be, say, the sort of ruthless endeavor a victim of a random house invasion by a couple of gang-bangers would experience, but he did, and it was brutal. No fun and games, no bullshit, nothing coming close to anyone saying *we're just going to rough you up a bit, tie you up, and ship you out to your destination for the evening, it's just tradition, just be submissive and play out your role.* In the process of taking Dayton by force, wrapping him in his own white bed sheets like a Caftan being forced upon a woman in Tehrān and binding his limbs in white duct tape, he was beaten and stricken about the head and below the rib cage and treated like a piece of shit mob hit.

Just after Wars took out a knife and slit the screen in the open bedroom window wide enough to throw the mummy-stiff body of Dayton in a heave-ho fashion into the outside, the voice of a little girl out of nowhere startled them to no end.

"Excuse me," said little Kira, standing in the shadows in the corner of the room behind the door. "You're going to take care of him after this, won't you?"

Neither one of them knew how long she'd been standing there, nor that she'd been standing there at all. Mutually, they felt like two Grinches upon discovery by Cindy Lou Who, just as they were shoving a Christmas tree up her fireplace.

Wars and Tendon exchanged glances, Dayton's screams stifled behind duct tape and layers of one hundred percent cotton linen, though his eyes, his only visible feature beneath everything, cried out to Kira in a manner more desperate than any attempt his vocal chords could summon as soon as he saw her. A swell of blood started seeping through his wrappings just over his brow and the ball of his left shoulder.

Wars chose to answer her, after a brief pause to decide what to say. "Why, dear missy, we have nothing but the finest in mind for this here noble man. We're taking him out for repairs and will bring him back a big bold man for you, better than new."

Then he nodded to Tendon, and together they tossed her protesting brother out his own window, taking no time at all to follow suit into the night without so much as a glance back to see the little girl's suspicious but otherwise stoic reaction to witnessing the occasion.

***

Wars' Ford Focus sped down a nearby highway not long afterwards, straight out of Coolidge, Wars driving, Tendon in the front passenger seat. Toad sat in the back seat behind Tendon, black jeans and t-shirt and black bed sheet wrapped around his attire and held together by silver belts and bracelets and buckles. Beside him was Dayton.

"My holy jeezus," remarked Toad at the sight of his friend, "you look like a giant spider spewed you into a cocoon for a late night snack."

"Mmmmmfffff," replied Dayton.

Toad leaned over and ripped the white tape off Dayton's mouth, then reclined back into his seat beside the window. "Hey buddy, howya like it so far?"

Dayton took no time at all to belt out a fervent protest after a few coughs and hacking a bloody spitwad onto the portion of seat between them.

"WHAT THE FUCK YOU PEOPLE THINK YOU'RE DOIN'?!"

"You *people*?" repeated Toad, a little offended, and yet, it was often difficult to tell whether ol' Bobby Lee was joking or not. At this point, the pain from the senseless beatings between his bed and War's vehicle was not a joke. "All us Black Sheets are called *you people* now and then, motherfucker, and we hate your goddamn prejudice.....!"

And with that, in a single fisted blow, Toad busted Dayton's nose something awful.

Tendon, after turning and seeing this, laughed his ass off until Toad silenced him with a thud from the same fist into the back of his seat. Toad then reverted his attentions to Dayton, who for the first time returned his gaze in utter fear.

Toad leaned toward Day, took out a switchblade knife from an unseen pocket and flicked it open, proceeded to cut a hole into the section of tape and material surrounding Dayton's left ear. As soon as he was through, he leaned further into that ear, and said to Dayton calmly, "Sorry buddy. But if you want to be one of us, you have to bear the cross......I don't mean literally, of course, in our

158

company, that just wouldn't be right….. but, to the point…..when Jesus was turned in, he went through all kinds of pain and emotional trauma, gut-wrenching persecution, the whole nine yards. And then, in the long run, he prevailed. We are the *Brotherhood of the Black Heroes* baby, and how much less should we have to suffer to become immortal?"

Wars, Tendon, and Toad then abruptly chanted with loud, frat-boy beer-drinker's voices, all in unison, "Nos es immortalis , nos mos increbresco , nos es ex nostrum mens!"

Tendon reverted to his kitchen cleanser addiction while Wars indulged in his tendency to play *Speed Racer* with the accelerator. Toad ripped off a piece of duct tape from Dayton's ankles and secured it over the initiate's mouth before he could think to answer.

Tendon spoke. "Heya, my Lord back there……I know Wars and I aren't allowed to speak until spoken to, but yesterday you told me as soon as we all got in the car to, uh, report on the status of our cargo of fun. Aside from your neighbor friend, of course."

Toad waited.

"We're *all* hooked up. Got our own portable bar in the trunk. Got snuff, sniff, a bag of green goodness and it's *medical*, Sire, got Drain-o, got ludes and those little plastic vials you squeeze onto the bait of yellow jacket traps, got a bottle of absinth hadn't been open since 1954, real nice, all the poison you want."

"Yeah, I'm buzzin'," said Toad, "but that's enough talk now. Hey Wars, just drive."

"Yes Lord."

Then, to Dayton, Toad said frankly but reassuringly, "Okay. Day, there's no turning back. I'm your sponsor. I'm paying lots for you, plus your meals and blackshirt once you're initiated. If you don't want to be one of the Brotherhood of the Black Heroes, it's too late to turn back. Or I'm out that money. And we kill you. You'd think the constellations getting all disorderly would doom us all, but lookee here: we're all right. And nobody's nuked *us* yet."

"I can't feel my hands," Dayton wanted to say.

"Oh, you're going to be less comfortable than that most of the night," said Toad to him, reading his thoughts clear as day. "Soon as we get there. But you'll be able to walk. I'll be with you to make sure nobody crosses the line, me or my boys here, and when

it's all over it'll be behind you. It's all worth it. To be one of us.
That's what you want, isn't it?"

Dayton didn't respond. He didn't want to be there, but he knew
becoming a Black Sheet wasn't going to be easy.

He, still, had no *idea*.......

"Okay buddy!"   And Toad slapped him on his knee,
enthusiastic with glee.

***

Conversation diminished into a silence which seemed the
length of hours to Dayton, all the while wrestling with inner
anticipation and anxiety and dreaded speculation suddenly
manifested into the words Toad uttered next.

"Okay buddy. We're here."

Dayton heard the sounds of gravel crackling beneath tires over
wheels turning at a snail's pace, slower and more methodically, and
he sensed that at last they were about to park.

Then they did.

And without to much as a pause to fart, as soon as the engine
was killed and the car doors both opened, Dayton was seized at
once by all the hell that had been expecting him......

5.

TRIAD

When the doors of the Ford Focus opened and Dayton sensed the immediate abandonment of his abductors as they vacated the vehicle, he became suddenly aware of loudspeaker-blared country music and of a deep penetrating chill before a multitude of hands fell upon him, lifting, pulling, gripping him then handing him over to other sets of hands like a rock star on a sea of fans.

"Prepare to live in the *now*, motherfucker," whispered a sinister voice into his left ear.

"And in the now, you belong to *us*," came a voice to his right.

As he was carried out into the night air and was positioned to stand upon his bare feet and backed against the car, as his duct tape was ripped from his ankles, wrists, his head and from over his eyes in that order, Johnny Cash was going down in a burning ring of fire all around him, musically, and the air was thick with that song. Only the spectacle of misplaced stars above was familiar to him when he opened his eyes, encompassed by desert wasteland and the commotion of distant festivities beyond where he could see. He could feel his hands again and found himself able to stand on his own. He hadn't had feeling in his hands and feet in what seemed like God knew how much time it took for Wars to drive him there.

He stood naked but for a moment while three black-cloaked individuals situated his sheet to the point that it appeared more fashionable to the occasion, wrapped more white duct tape around his waist for a makeshift belt and each wrist and ankle. In the process one of them stopped, stood very still, backed away from Dayton with his eyes fixed upon the alien face pendant still hanging from Dayton's neck. When the others took notice that their brother was acting strangely, they ceased what they were doing as well until he gained all their attention, and then *everyone* was staring at Dayton's pendant. There were ten fully cloaked figures in all, faces shrouded, surrounding him; Mars, Tendon, and Bobby Lee Horton/Toad directly beside the Focus, Toad the last to

161

take notice of what his buddy wore and the first to make his response vocal.

Softly he swore, as he approached Dayton for further inspection of it, bringing his hand closer to it but remaining careful not to touch it. "Well I'm be goddamn……"

Dayton's fears hadn't subsided since his close friend and sponsor had belted him one across the face, but his eyes darted from one to another of his captors, trying unsuccessfully to read them.

"He mustn't be wearing anything other than white for this," remarked a cloaked one.

"Take it off him, he can't do it himself," said another. "He's not allowed."

The first to have noticed the pendant asked, to no one in particular, "Isn't this a matter for Triad? Shouldn't *they* decide?"

Tendon took a few steps forward to inspect the pendant more closely, but Toad's raised arm barred him from proceeding further. Then Toad asked him directly, looking straight and sternly into his eyes to ensure full attention, "You didn't notice this when you first took him?"

"We were in a hurry….."

"Did you see anything unusual? Everything was completely normal, typical house break-in, kidnapping, know what I mean?"

"We thought we saw a figure go feet-first into an above-ground patio pond, and disappear with no trace, which was impossible, but, seeing things or not, we sensed one of us right afterwards," Wars volunteered nervously.

Toad lowered his arm from Tendon, casually relieved, resolute, yet still inquisitive.

"Can I ask what you're talking about?" Dayton forced himself to interrupt.

"Shut the fuck up and keep your eyes on the ground," one of the cloaks roared.

Dayton did as instructed, timidly, shaken.

"Well boys," Toad said to all a bit louder, ignoring his friend, "that explains it. This ain't no issue of appropriate color for him to being wearin', for those of us who can't sense it yet. It's not like it's a cross, crucifix or nothing Jesusy anyway, either, as you can

162

plainly see. What we got here is a case of *you fuck with it, you die.* All you boys hear me straight?"

Another of the cloaked ones put out the question, "With all respect, Sire, why are we reacting to it like it's a cross?"

"We're reacting to it because we sense its importance and some of us just don't know why," said Toad. "It might look like some bullshit piece of two-dollar street vendor trinket tomfoolery, but what we're sensing is that it's been passed through time."

"My roast beef sandwich was passed through time," responded another of the cloaks, "and I pinched it out three hours ago......"

That aroused a chuckle from some, especially Toad.

Toad lit up a Marlboro, took a drag. "Toilet here made a funny. Good one. Mind you all, touch that sonofabitch and ya'll are gonna create a paradox that can fuck everything up for all of us. Keep it on him, and put him through the unspeakable hell all us Heroes had to go through to become what we are now. Okay, boys?"

"He'll see Triad, then," asked Wars.

"Hell yeah he'll see Triad, and if they approve him, he's goin' through like a slow locomotive into a locomotive meat grinder."

"Could've been better said, Sire," Tendon told him honestly.

As the cloaked ones completed preparing Dayton's attire, gathered his reluctantly submissive self up and carried him away, Toad said to Tendon in confidence, blowing a stream of cigarette smoke into the air, "Works good for me as his sponsor. Can't very well take his place if he doesn't work out, 'cause he *has to* work out. So, what goodies ya got stashed in the car? Let's get ripped tonight......."

***

As Dayton was taken away, over a dune dotted by Joshua trees and then down the embankment on the opposite side, his unexpected environment overwhelmed him. His sense of dislocation was outright hallucinatory, his state of mind was post rape syndrome and he hadn't yet been raped. As he bade a silent farewell to his abductors at the Focus, it occurred to him that Toad's vow prior to all of this, of making sure no harm would come to him, was intentionally prefabricated bullshit.

The cloaked figures hastened him down a trodden path towards a vast ravine, where Johnny Cash's booming melody crescendoed into his view's establishing shot of the camp festival scene now set before him.

Trailers, motor homes, tents and makeshift canopies, campfires, bonfires filled the acres of desert canyon like a surreal Hell's Angels midnight outdoor swap meet in a half-mile-wide nest they'd made of the gully that the rest of the world would never see.

Most of what he was *able* to see, as far as he could tell, gave him the impression that his new captors were carrying him around the back of the camp. They took him not far from a long row of tented structures overflowing with the animate silhouettes of many figures whose talk and laughter drifted into the air with the smoke of their campfires, cigarettes, barbecues, and Johnny Cash. Motorcycles and pick-up trucks lined a dirt driveway to Dayton's left as he was taken, before the butterfingers carelessness of a few accidentally dropped his head onto a stone embedded in the trail as they went with him. He came to his senses, grunted, looked around again, caught sight of even more vehicles parked further down the way towards the scene as the pain of the impact subsided.

He turned his head upwards to steal a look at one of his captors.

One of them turned, faceless, whispered harshly down at him. "Did you just eye-fuck me, motherfucker?"

Over the course of the night, it would be a common phrase directed towards Mr. Monday, among many more designed specifically to make him feel like shit.

***

They took him to a beige and weathered 2007 Gulfstream Endura motor home with all four awnings drawn, just barely two dozen yards outside the perimeters of the camp, and its side door swung open to them as though their presence was detected by some infrared trigger that did so because there was no visible person that opened the door to greet them. They set Dayton on his bare feet and dispersed into the night in several directions casually, all but three of them.

They simply stood there in front of him, stared him down. There was a few seconds of silence between them, and Dayton decided after coming to terms with whether or not he should, to say something, all the while looking towards the ground so as not to gaze at the Brothers directly and be reprimanded.

"Excuse me, but, you guys have something to drink?"

"Yeah," replied one cloak, and all so eagerly, "*you.*"

By this point, regardless of what Dayton had been through so far, this talk about vampires was all still part of the initiation as far as he was concerned. The three took him inside. The door closed behind them. It was dark except for a mild light coming in through the windows and windshield up at the driver's area. It was quiet.

Dayton was placed in a corner at a square table and made to sit upon a cushioned bench in an area he was certain could transform into a bed.

The shades of the rectangular window to his right were suddenly widened, to reveal the three cloaked but otherwise invisible ones that brought him inside hovering before him at the table's opposite side.

He gazed at them.

My God, Dayton thought, they are cloaks, and nothing more, nothing but empty space within them, for as they moved within the streams of moonlight coming through the window he could not detect faces beyond the cloaks, only vacant nothingness.

They whispered amongst themselves for a brief moment.

Suddenly their hoods fell back, and out from within each twirled white spheres like the heads of torpedoes being locked and loaded, weathered and cracked and yellowing, and as they extended further, twisting, rotating like bony turbines, their cloaks dropped from them altogether, spilling over the tableside and onto the motor home floor.

What stood upon the tabletop surface and facing Dayton were now three naked and almost skeletal dwarves. They were a third less in size than how tall they'd been in black garb, under a yard apiece, until they simultaneously sat in different relaxed positions and became half that size as well.

They gazed upon Dayton through the eyeless sockets of their oversized skull-like heads until something awoke from within them and twisted outwards into red pupiless eyes.

The closest one to Dayton held a very large meat cleaver which it set down beside itself, its hand never leaving the handle, fingers fondling its leather tassel and several items attached to it on a ring which made the cleaver look like it was attached to a keychain. A thin layer of baby-pink skin stretched over their bodies like a cross between silly putty and Halloween cotton cobwebs had been pulled and tightened over each ligament to the extent that it was see-through, like the saran wrap transparent skin housing the abdominal cavity and many areas of bone, especially in the face. Their dinkies hung like wet pretzel sticks over marble-sized fleshy scrotums between their legs, which they had no problem exposing. Or scratching.

They each looked exactly the same, aside from distinguishing facial characteristics, spoke with the same whisper when they spoke. Something about them gave off a hunch to Dayton that they were once, perhaps, living children.

As for Dayton himself, at this point, one might as well say an instinct kicked in that made him numb to any panic such a profoundly evolving predicament he'd gotten himself into would be expected to unfold.

These three had suddenly ceased to be the human beings he'd taken them for, and now nothing seemed real but the necessity to maintain a composure for the sake of survival, to pay attention and respond correctly. Fear and comprehension were reserved for that hoped-for rest stop ahead, some period up the road where he would be alone and could soak it all in.

The one in the middle withdrew a cigarette and Bic lighter from a marsupial-like pocket of skin just above his groin and lit up.

"We're here to see if you'll be worth it," whispered one of them.

"If you're worth our time," said another.

"If *you're* worth *our* time," said the third.

"Why do you want to be one of us?"

"Word has it you always wanted to be, since way before puberty, bit girls on the arms just to prove a point."

"Heh, a point....." another chuckled.

Dayton realized his hands were clenching the table all too tightly. He backed away, realizing his grip and resting his arms over the cushions at his sides against the wall casually. That made him feel noticeably vulnerable, so he placed his hands on his knees and clenched his thighs.

"Bobby Lee Horton brought me. I'm here to join the Brotherhood of the Black Heroes."

"We're fucking geniuses, dude. We know that already. We want to know why."

"Oh, and Toad's his Black Sheep name," said another, "so remember that, and say it with reverence."

"The Black Heroes make a difference," Dayton replied in answer to their question. "They're charitable and give so much to the country and the community. I want to make a difference, too."

"Yes," said one, "our Christmas Toys for Girls and Boys did go over quite well last year, or was it the year before.....?"

"And we backed our senator all the way through last year's election, who's one of us."

"As were, what was it......two U.S. Presidents, I can't keep tract."

"Though we're largely Green Party."

"Tree huggers. We largely don't have the influence we'd like."

"You'd think by common lore we're all aristocrats or something."

"Um," Dayton leaned forward, his nervous hands upon the table once again. "Who.....I don't......understand......"

"We are Triad," explained one. "We are the oldest of the Brotherhood....."

"Well, the oldest *here*......"

".....and we've taken you away privately for a little chat, to see if you're fit for our organization."

"Or at least fit for feeding."

"Initiates always see us first."

"And we approve you."

"So now we must number you."

"You are Number 21."

"The last one tonight, in fact. This event is held, oh.....annually, sometimes skipping a year, and we don't consider many."

"Many considered don't survive. Some of the initiates just don't have it in them."

Dayton blinked, tried to shake off his misunderstanding with a quick couple of disconcerted head movements. His boldness, absent seconds ago as it was, was like helium jetting into a rubber balloon which burst too soon for him to prevent it from being so uninhibitedly explosive. "I was raised right. I'm part of a normal American family with down home American values. I believe in God, I wave our flag, I support our troops and our President despite his flaws. I love my parents and little sister. I get drunk some times, smoke pot, no real drug problems though, uplifting modern Country is my music of choice, that and old time rock n' roll, but my past church life has soured me towards conventional Christian religious persuasion."

"We love Johnny Cash," remarked one of them.

There was a short bit of uncomfortable silence between them.

Then, Dayton said, reluctantly but honestly, fearing he'd better agree, "Johnny Cash is cool......"

The three of them abruptly applauded him.

"That's all we needed to know," said one.

"Do you know what that is around your neck?" asked another.

Dayton didn't know what to say. Fearing for his life, he thought he'd better say something. "The guys back at the car said it's important......"

After Triad whispered one to another, one of them responded, "It is. But let's get to the matter at hand here....."

The one with the meat cleaver then seized his blade handle and struck down at the table like a little mad man, like an evil organic marionette sans strings, and after a few heartbeats Dayton found himself looking down at the table, on his severed thumb, at the leakage of blood pooling around it over the mock-mahogany fiberglass tabletop.

The pain proceeded the realization, but before that happened the cleaver-wielding creature produced a single unwrapped condom from his front flesh pouch, scooped up the thumb and inserted it inside, produced a thick tan rubber band from a bag full and wrapped it tight at its base around the thumb's bleeding stump.

"The rubber band helps to stop the flow of blood," said the smoking one. His smoke now filled the unventilated home-on-wheels, accumulating into a mild drifting fog.

Then the pain hit, and Dayton screamed, took his hand into his other, fell back and lifted it up for a clearer view in disbelief.

"Throughout the ordeal set before you," one told him, "to lose the condom is to lose your thumb, is to lose your life, and will result in absolute failure."

That one reached out, pulled the wrist of Dayton's other arm down to the table. It stuck out its pinky finger which displayed a three-inch-long cocaine nail of sorts, dug deeply into Dayton's exposed wrist palm-up, extracted and punctured a vein.

Dayton fought squirmishly, but the force which held him down was unfathomably strong.

"Relax," the one doing so said. With precision and all the calmness of one to whom this was an everyday thing, the creature severed the vein and pulled it out a good half-yard like a starter cord unreeled from a lawn mower.

Dayton was overcome with a cold chill which permeated his body.

"Relax," said Meat Cleaver, "at least it's a vein. Arteries carry all the nutrients." And with that, the vein was passed to him, and he placed it into his mouth like a bluish spaghetti strand, and he sucked in randomly Dayton's blood as if through a straw.

Dayton was paralyzed, stricken by a horror he could not suppress but mindful of his condom-thumb should it fall off.

"We are part of the Brotherhood of the Black Heroes," the one centered proclaimed candidly but with certain authority. "And we are vampires."

"We are all that remains of vampires," spoke another.

"Know this, for you will be tested," said the centered smoking one, who was then passed Dayton's vein and took blood from it like inhaling a doobie.

Meat Cleaver continued for him, as Dayton's nerves slowly gave way to a solemn weakness. "The Brotherhood of the Black Heroes was, contrary to what we've said in the media, founded in the late fifteenth century by the original Black Hero of Hungary, Count Ferency Nadasdy, who was wed to the teen Elizabeth Bathory in 1575. Nadasdy was always out on business trips, waging war and leading battles on horseback to opposing countries, while his young wife, confined in his castle, stooped to whoring around. She whored with a vampire, developed an obsession with maintaining eternal youth by bathing in the blood of her maidens. I mean, it did nourish her skin tone, but there was more to it than that."

"Our dear Hungarian Count," continued another, "regardless of what the history books say, returned and became a vampire himself at her hands, through her enticements, from her selfish bitterness against his staying away for so many months at a time."

"....with not so much as a letter, so the Countess complained, or so much as paying some messenger boy a forint to sprint across the countryside and deliver his bride a verbal telegram saying *I miss you babe, I'm thinking about you sugarlumpkins, anything......*"

".......and for a long time afterwards, female and male vampires separated, took sides, and rarely was one attracted to the other since," said another. "After all, we're undead, whatever's left of our hearts beats backwards and blood doesn't flow through our system when we drink it. When we drink, we *absorb*. It's very refreshing."

"Like we're doing with some of yours, now."

"We can be sexual. I mean, we have special pills for that."

"But as you'll see, we're hellraisers."

"We're still affected by the same drugs we were before we turned."

"As well as household cleaners, gasoline...."

"Rat poison, Draino...."

"Stuff gets us high."

"You're in for one hell of an awakening."

"This is what we are, and we're all that's left."

"Oh.......our females and us have reconciled since, somewhat, but none are allowed here."

"Except for food and sport. After all, we're a *brotherhood*."

"Of the Black Heroes."

"Welcome."

"I think we're done."

The one who extracted the vein in the first place pulled out a sharp metal scissors and snipped off Dayton's vein at the wrist. After one placed a bandage over the broken wound, Dayton finally fainted.

6.

ON TO THE BASICS

One of Triad knocked a knuckle to the motor home dining area window a good few times and loud enough to summon something waiting for Dayton outside.

As if living things themselves, their cloaks crept back up over the edge of the table and onto them and, together, Triad disappeared, swallowed up inside their cloaks in backwards rotation, like three human screws drilled into their wardrobe by giant invisible electric screwdrivers. They rose into the anonymous stature of what they were prior to the meeting, like grown up trick-or-treaters in cheap Grim Reaper costumes, when the motor home side door opened abruptly.

Triad then seized Dayton together and at once. They slid his unconscious face off the table and onto the floor with a thud that was something awful to have heard. They lifted him up, brought him to the doorway, through it, and with a heave-ho tossed Number 21 like a sack of manure off the back of a farm truck, onto the dry-dusty yellow-grassed sand of the ground.

***

Basics sat waiting in the same frame of mind as a lady on a park bench filing her nails, just outside the motor home, seated atop a rock the size of a Pinto. A chorus line of yawning and stretching Joshua trees behind him were tall enough to dwarf him despite his size and the fact that he was sitting that high up. He wondered why Triad felt it a necessity to take a few knuckle-raps on the kitchen window to summon him. He caught on early that he was only needed when Triad tossed another vampire wanna-be out the door, and, between the window tapping and the tossing out, sometimes it took awhile.

So Basics, having heard the tapping and not so readily responding this time, waited for 21 while singing a simple, off-key tune to himself while taking hefty sips from a fourteen-ounce Coors during pauses to do so between the lyric lines:

Sometimes I want a can a Coke,
(sip)
iced tea or beer like this,
(sip)
but sometimes all I really want
(sip)
is just a can-na-bis.

He was garbed in several layers of black bed sheet. His skin was of darkest Africa both in heritage and color, and although he couldn't carry a tune, nor even dance for that matter, he was a heavy influence in the world of Wall Street trading and an agent for chart-topping Hip-hop artists as well as making the Guinness Book of World Records for the man with the largest hand for the past twelve years. That right hand just kept getting bigger, to the point where Basics, in his life outside the whole Black Heroes/vampire thing with a normal name, resorted to an entirely private life behind a computer. They called it a form of Proteus syndrome, his condition, same as described for *Elephant Man* John Merrick, though entirely contained within his right hand. It was a powerful hand, strength-wise, and Basics often lamented if only it was that way in Poker. He didn't get out much, because of the fact that people stared; he often joked that it was because he was black.

As soon as Triad kicked Dayton out a yard or so outside the motor home door and then closed it, poor soul lying on the ground face-down and unconsciously oblivious to where he was, Basics tossed his beer, slid from off the rock and sauntered over to a five-gallon Rubbermaid tub of water. He took it, lifted it with ease, dowsed Dayton with its contents. He was remarkably able to grasp a single beer keg and chug it like a twelve-ounce can. The muscles in his left arm bulged to a believable support of the hand, but unbelievable in regards to the rest of him.

Basics, towering over Dayton with empty tub in hand, *the* hand, was the first sight that Dayton awoke to, and it wasn't any less distressing as the last sight he'd seen before he lost himself to his moment of alertness power failure.

Awake now he was, drenched, the single white bed sheet draped around himself almost as transparent and clinging as the skins of Triad in their true form, like the embodiment of a wet t-shirt contest with no women beneath, just one waterlogged puppy of a guy.

"I have you for three minutes," Basics told him. "And don't you fucking look at me."

Number 21 obeyed, cast his gaze to the damp soil below him.

With his colossal right hand alone, Basics carried Dayton over a short terrain of desert underbrush pathway into camp with no more effort than a bouncer carrying a women's purse to Lost and Found in a nightclub.

Dayton hadn't fully snapped out of the echoes of delirium that assaulted his mind since the get-go of Basic's wet howdoyado. His body remained limp like a fainted Fay Wray in the grip of Kong. When Basics brought him to his destination, setting him down upon his feet, he found himself with no recollection of the time between the motorhome oust and the *now*.

(*Except that it burns……that ring of fire burns, yes indeedy……*)

"It's time to live *in* the now, Number Twenty-one," announced Basics to Dayton, as automated as if Basics had said something similar twenty times before. "Welcome to the Brotherhood of the Black Heroes' Annual Camp Meetin' and Bean Feed."

As soon as he was certain Dayton could stand on his own, he released his grip and went away.

(*…..and it burns, burns burns and burns……….*)

***

Just a little dizzy spell on Dayton's part, was all, a little light-headedness, and then…….

***

Vampires.

The Brotherhood of the Black Heroes were *vampires*.

Wake-up call to Dayton Monday:

Vampires were real, and they weren't like he imagined when he was a kid, or pretended to have been way back when, or even heard of.

Apparently, you have to sever your thumb to become one, or at least to start the process.

Goddamn that shit hurt, and Dayton found himself scrutinizing his condom-full-of-thumb, fingering around with it, hesitantly

173

squeezing in careful inspection like Jeff Goldblum's *The Fly* inspecting diseased fingernails, so that the blood and air inside the prophylactic bloated into a miniature lava lamp with only a fraction of light to reveal its contents but just enough to repulse him into looking away.

Perhaps, all said and done tonight, there were surgeons waiting to stitch thumbs right back up after passing all the tests or trials, and at worst he'd have to wear a hand cast for a year and then he and his thumb would be whole again, no problem.......

His heart had drawn him far away from the darker fancies and flirtations of his youth, from the macabre curiosities that draw a good number of us towards the flesh and to the night. Vampires were all around him and every which way, and in the process of recruiting him into their fold. There was nothing he could do to explain to them that this was all a mistake, this was not what he thought he was getting into.

He feared for his life.

Dayton's only comfort was in the likelihood that when Basics relieved him of his custody, he left him standing at the end of a long row of twenty other men in white bed sheets who felt almost exactly the way he did.

He looked to his left, down the row.

His companions were all of diverse adult ages and stature, cold and shivering and intellectually docile, a few on the verge of tears, all gazing directly on the ground below them towards their bare feet. They could've been nude beneath those sheets, probably were. It was clear that initiates were only permitted to wear white, as in contrast black was the dominant permissible color for the Black Hero Brothers to wear, during these sorts of fraternity functions. How bed sheets played into everything was anyone's guess, but they were dirt cheap when ordered direct from the manufacturer and distributed in mass quantities. There was a trendy myth going around for decades that you can tell you're bedfellows with a vampire when black sheets adorn his bed.

Standing in line side by side as they were, waiting for their hazing to continue, Dayton and the other initiates looked like they were auditioning for *Jesus Christ Superstar.*

Johnny Cash belted out from every direction *sugar in the mornin', sugar in the evenin', sugar in the suppertime* with no care in the world, because he was only a recording.......

7.

THE FLYING SISTERS AND
THE BRIGHT LIGHT

Way beyond the outskirts of the Black Heroes' camp but within enough proximity to get a good view of a portion of it with Zhumell 20x80 SuperGiant binoculars on a tripod half buried in the desert soil, festivities of a similar sort but on a smaller scale were going down.

Blamia Kiss was a metal/folk band that had cut three commercial albums over the last eight years and had two Billboard top-twenty songs to their credit halfway through their career that eventually became karaoke favorites, though afterwards their audience and record sales waned to the point they empathized with Spinal Tap playing second billing to a puppet show at an amusement park. This particular gig was of a personal nature, and didn't require roadies or sound tests nor equipment set-up beyond a few tent pitches and getting a campfire going, although two of the five of them had brought acoustic guitars, and the drummer a tambourine and drumsticks to keep up the time on rocks or empty soup cans should any of them break out in song for lack of anything better to do during their desert wilderness stakeout of their male vampire adversaries' big night out.

Whenever the Black Heroes staged a camp meeting, a bean feed, a get-together of this magnitude, there was always a cluster of vampires of the female variety off in the outskirts somewhere with binoculars or radar devices, with covert pawns sent as spies to infiltrate the camp as mortal girl meat, anything that could provide to them insight as to what all the male Nosferatu were up to. Their presence was never unbeknownst to the males, but no one took the females as a threat and their scrutiny from afar remained largely ignored.

Women vampires, over the centuries and despite their best intentions, had never been able to institute an order amongst themselves or to come together in a universal sisterhood. Whenever they attempted to do so, one of them would end up backstabbing the other over reasons involving a breach of trust or gossip, and their drama would escalate to the point it caused a domino effect that toppled over the best efforts of those who didn't wish to be involved or suggested sound solutions. Male vampires, in contrast, developed a camaraderie that remained steadfast since their origins that the women could not quite comprehend and were always curious to understand. Really, when it all came down to it, the secret to the men's success in maintaining a strong sociality for hundreds of years was no secret at all, for they wore it on their sleeves: they loved to party. It's not that vampire women didn't, it's just that with the women it was a more complicated affair. Some bitch with an attitude would always ruin it for everyone. With the males, should a Brother become grossly insubordinate, he was hung by his toes upside-down over hot coals with no further thought to him, until he got his shit together and was ready to come back down and party with some respect.

Escarlata hated men, especially vampire men.

She was no different in that respect than the majority of her kind throughout the ages, for she was a vampire woman, and the sad truth between the sexes was that they despised each other, the men and the women. It was a resentment originated from the Count Ferency Nadasdy and Elizabeth Bathory situation centuries ago, and it was accepted that their bitterness and unresolved discourse between the two of them was inherited through their bloodline to all modern vampires. It could be construed as a curse, but vampires never looked at it that way. They were extremely adamant in their feelings against the other, like two ex-lovers eternally vindictive over a bad episode or nasty argument who spend the rest of their existence fucking everyone else just to spite their ex and never again experiencing the love they once knew. This comparison is an accurate one more than you'd think. No one was ever lacking in companionship of the opposite sex, because there were always humans to fuck around with, to do things for you, to eat.

Escarlata abandoned her set-up of binoculars and shuffled her body down the dusty embankment, righted herself and went to join the other four. She was dressed to kill, and killing wasn't too far from the truth. While her companions settled more for comfort on this wilderness night out with t-shirts and cut-off jeans, Lata wore a tight-fitting black leather bikini with a hip-hugging utility belt which sported little spy devices and odds and ends and something that almost resembled a light saber. She needed to feel important and sexy that way.

The four were seated around a modest campfire flickering light across a one-person trailer home that more resembled an outhouse with a kitchen window, hitched to a hybrid Chevy 4x4 pick-up with a crew cab. A keg of home-brewed ale sat on a wooden stand beside a fold-out card table of empty cups and appetizers, condiments, and silverware rolled up nicely in paper napkins. Three tents were set up around them, though sleeping bags were arranged immediately around the fire, and various meats were sizzling on a round barbeque charcoal grill near the bassist, who'd occasionally poke at the food with a fork and scratch at the swirling tattoos of her hairless head.

There was a man with them, albeit in a couple dozen pieces. Most of him was in three five-gallon buckets or a hefty bag with a Manbeef.com bumper sticker slapped on it discarded in the truck's flatbed, and some good hand-sized rib and arm muscle pieces weren't very hard to distinguish between the chicken and ground buffalo burgers on the grill.

Bald Bassist saw Escarlata approaching. Lata had her eyes glued to the Black Heroes' camp for a good two hours now, and the girls were beginning to grow weary of her taking so long, especially BB.

"Here comes Catwoman," she said, and the other girls glanced that way before they returned their eyes to the fire or, in the tall blonde drummer's case, her Electric People Magazine, where it wasn't just about people anymore, but *electric* people.

"Any of you wanna fly over and take a closer look at them?" Lata dropped onto a fold-out beach chair and stretched out her legs.

"Meat's almost done," replied Bald Bassist, "but nothing like goin' back out again to work up an appetite, breasts to the wind."

The other two emitted enthusiastic *hell-yeahs* of approval spontaneity, then they drew their eyes right back to the campfire flames to watch them dance. Before Escarlata's binocular escapade, these two had flown off a quarter mile away to share a joint and talk and were at present very content and willing to fly about again, if not for spying on the Brotherhood, then just for fun. They sat side by side each other sharing a picnic blanket, Suzuki and Molly, Japanese Lead Guitarist/Julliard Graduate and rhythm guitar/keyboardist/pale-skinned black-haired Robert Smith from *The Cure* wannabe, respectively.

They were all quiet for a moment, Lata reflective and more anxious to talk than the rest of *Blamia Kiss*, who were more inclined to simply enjoy themselves rather than pay any mind to what the Black Heroes were doing. Escarlata was not only their charismatic lead singer and chief song lyricist, but the one who brought them together to the Great Outdoors for the weekend because, as vampire females, somebody had to carry on the tradition of keeping tract of the men's doings on occasions like this while utilizing the best methods of surveillance they could afford.

Nobody else seemed to want to. Last time, it was another small group of girls who camped out to spy on the men. The times before that, the vampire women came in greater numbers where one or two of the older ones, sisters who were actually bitten by *Countess Bathory* herself over half a century ago, hung out. And you should've seen New Year's Eve 2000, the last year to date the sisters had their own initiates to haze, several canopies set up to sell and trade homemade trinkets, a man-roast and murder ball tournament. This year, Escarlata maintained that the tradition could not be broken and at least got her band to participate, though she was a bit more militant when it came to the spying aspects of the endeavor where the rest reflected the attitudes of most of their kind, they'd become complacent or could care less what the men were doing. After all, the women had their own annual shindig in coastal North Carolina that was quite the bomb, every February 14th. If a girl turned a guy down for a Valentine's Day date, especially in pre-apocalyptic years, it became commonplace for one to joke that the girl was a vampire.

"Hey, does anyone want to know what I saw?" asked Lata to her peers. "Or am I the last one who cares anymore?"

Bald Bassist gnawed on a teriyaki beef stick and swatted a fly with a roll of paper towels. Since they were vampires, they had no problems with mosquitoes, though flies were attracted a little more to the undead than they were the living, and just as much to

179

barbequed food. "I figured you'd say even before sitting down, if it was anything exciting," she said.

"*Was* it anything exciting?" asked Molly, not withdrawing her eyes from the fire.

Escarlata motioned for some of what BB was chewing on, and the bassist tossed her the package. "The audio mic raises Johnny Cash from the dead, and sitting there watching the Black Zeroes it was cool to have that to listen to while watching……"

"I miss Johnny and June," commented Drummer remorsefully.

"But you should've seen it," continued Lata, "they had four burning inverted wooden crosses, like Satanist wannabes, and this one dude did cartwheels in front of all of them, probably drunk on anti-freeze or whatever, and he burnt right the fuck up into ashes as soon as he saw the crosses right-side-up when dude was upside-down. Hella funny shit……."

All the girls lit up, straightened up, livened up, bellowed with laughter.

"Holy shit, and we missed it," remarked a solemn Drummer with an *awe shucks* and a finger snap, though she was just as amused as anyone else.

Lata was proud of herself that she could convey this bit of info. "You missed it, I saw it. The camcorder couldn't focus in enough, so if I popped the tape into the monitor in the Chevy the replay probably looks like a flea circus. However……."

"Yeah," replied Molly, "*however,* if we really want to see anything….."

"We gotta fly," they all agreed in unison.

"So fly then," said Lata, and the others looked at each other to acknowledge who was going.

Suzuki glanced at Molly for an affirmation. "We'll go."

Drummer began tapping at her kneecaps in rhythm, "But when ya get back, we got meat, daddum daddum da dump dump dump-a bam, and we can jam a little while, break out some strings and do our things. Fuck the guys, let's enjoy ourselves."

And Molly gave a thumb's up to that.

When it came to flying, the women rarely had a problem with it. It was a supernatural gift passed down to all vampires, the ability to defy gravity and jump off the ground after a good running leap like George Reeve's Superman to the skies whenever they had a mind to, but as soon as they were airborne it was a slow process, kind of like diving into very deep water and then having to swim about to get anywhere, only inverted, where one had to dive *up* rather than dive *down*. Nobody sprouted wings, that concept was ridiculous, as was the assumption that they could simply take off without giving Mother Nature her due and shoot off into the heavens. It took more of an effort than that.

For vampires, it was exactly like swimming, of manipulating the molecules around themselves with arm and leg movements that propelled them up and away, with as much leg muscle momentum as to push them off to a good launching, and hefty arm strokes to keep them going to their destination. After lift-off, one could freestyle, backstroke, sink, elevate, do everything in the air as mortals do under water, difference is when you actually swim in your clothes, your clothes get wet, and you have to hold breaths of air. But when you're flying like vampires, you're *flying*, baby, swimming through the air, and the only thing that weighs you down is what you wear.

Thing is, the males didn't prefer to, made them queasy, gave them migraines. For most of them, to so much as jump high enough was to instigate the worst hangover in a matter of seconds. The men, knowing how enjoyable flying was for the females, always attempted to justify things by announcing that they were the ones centered enough to keep their feet on the ground and the women were, for lack of a better word, more *flighty*.

Whatever the case.....

Escarlata bit off a chunk of jerky and stood, Suzuki and Molly rising with her.

Lata flung her long black hair over one shoulder like a *Charlie's* angel and, before she headed back up the slope to her surveillance gear, said to the others, "Okay girls, let get to it."

As soon as she'd climbed up enough away to not hear them, the others made fun of her last words between themselves before the two volunteers sauntered off outside the grounds, made a running start, and swam up to the deep dark constellationally challenged skies.

Both Molly and Suzuki reached about two hundred feet above their camp before the duo began circling around each other, spinning in mock ballet, laughing and frolicking and angling their flight patterns towards the Black Heroes' camp but not with any determined sense of urgency.

On ground, Escarlata positioned herself behind her series of state-of-the-art binoculars, a camcorder, a long-distance audio boom, a high-tech Viewmaster-kind-of-apparatus which compared what the binoculars could see with an internet-wired database of images of male vampires, and a bag of sea salt/vinegar Potato Chimps.

Soon as Lata got comfy, depressed the *up* volume on the remote of an external speaker to capture the Brothers' latest Johnny Cash tune, placed her eye sockets liberally against the rubber eye socket rests of her binocular spy gadget, something catastrophic happened.

The entire sky lit up something fierce, like God had walked in and turned on the lights to a pajama party of the damned in a bedroom with the name *Arizona* on the door.

The images of a man who almost resembled Willie Nelson without the locks filled the vastness of sky in a kaleidoscope of swirling spotlit images, and this man began to talk, almost sing, and his voice thundered as like the deep baritone voice of God throughout the heavens:

"My name is Samuel, and I'll see you all in hell, damn your eyes!"

It was the next moment after Lata heard these words that the stars fell, when the sky burned and collapsed like a rooftop all aflame over our world and left it barren and desolate and, all said and done and a small number of years into the future, was rendered into the exact same state as this region has ever been, with miles of desert and rocks and Joshua trees......

........and a handful of the only surviving vampires, not to mention possibly the last shards of humanity remaining on the planet, wandering about the wastelands struggling to survive while at the same time trying with intense effort just to figure things out.

Part Two:

AFTER

THE END

8.

DESERT YEARS, LATER

The sun set slowly over the vast desolation of southwestern United States desert. It took the most time on this particular day setting than on any of the other three hundred seventy-two days to a year now, as was Dayton Monday's understanding, and he'd indeed heard his share of rumors and proclamations about the state of Mother Earth after her divorce from physics finalized a handful of years ago. *Awake after dusk* was always the rule for him, the rule for any vampire remaining since the bright lights raped the land. Dayton remembered how just before his mortal death vampires could actually walk about in daylight if they had to, no problem. Bull*shit*, nowadays.

For Mr. Monday, this offset in the balance of Earth's nature was not only merely a consequence of its last and most devastating global war but a chance to sleep in awhile longer, like on any good Sunday morning when you've partied your ass off the night prior.

The preceding darkness of dusk swept the remnants of day into a corner of the sky and under the rug of the world's opposite side, and the accompanying red apocryphal rain arrived as though God had squeezed a ruby red grapefruit into a great heavenly juicer and the juicer went crazy.

As soon as eventide and its soft crimson sky splatter summoned his nocturnal consciousness into awakening, Dayton yawned within a full-body sleeping bag completely zipped up and buried beneath three feet of dirt. His left hand fumbled fiercely near his waist for a chain latched to an interior zipper, found it, unzipped it into an avalanche of muddy grainy blackness. He fought upwards to emerge into the red rain and the belated night like he was fighting against the weight of the world, wrestling from the restraints of his sleeping bag and the soil he'd buried himself so easily in that morning before daybreak, but which all day hardened in the sun and was now heavy as sin to navigate out of.

Dayton picked himself up, found his footing as he exhumed himself fully and stood, stretched, brushed the caked earth from off of him. As he did often, he made sure his alien face pendant still hung from his neck over his chest, and as always, there it was. It was the only material object he ever truly owned for as long as he'd been living this life, left over from the last. It reminded him of the family he'd lost, of initiation night with Toad and the Black Heroes, the night his existence in this world split into two parts: *before the end* and *after the end*, and how the physical act of having it on his person was responsible for his survival throughout that transition. Most of all, it reminded him of his sister, and he missed Kira the most. He perambulated around for a moment to liven his leg muscles, kicking some rocks while amusing himself with the way his sleeping bag resembled a deep green carnivorous flower that had just burrowed out of the ground, spit him out, and died.

The red rain which blanketed the wilderness about him subsided to a welcomed light drizzle. He turned his attentions toward the old Widow Hamlin's estate, just a mile and a half to the North, across the interstate highway past where another vampire same age as Dayton rested, the Vampire Wayne.

He gazed out in that direction, wondering if Wayne was up yet, and several minutes went by before he began his sojourn to meet up with Wayne, as he did most every night these days, to spy on the estate together, which housed the only human being around for hundreds (if not thousands) of miles. And it wasn't merely the object of Dayton and Wayne's scrutiny, but Hamlin and her solar-powered, fully-functioning self-sufficient home attracted other renegade vampires as well, may even attract surviving humans in the long run. It certainly attracted desert wildlife from miles around searching for food. Vampires had to search for food also, and for lack of anything better, desert varmints and their blood were common cuisine, so even though Widow Hamlin's estate itself was protected against intruders both living and undead, for vampires as well as other predators, the area was a food magnet. Coyotes, gophers, rattlers, grey or brown hares the size of easy chair recliners (some of them), bobcats, even possums and raccoons, birds, a zoo full of these things, wild and free and abundant.

Tumbleweeds rolled rampant along the highway as Dayton approached, like the black asphalt was a magnet to them. The four lanes of paved road rarely had seen any vehicular passers-by in Dayton's entire vampire lifetime. His blue jeans were soiled and weathered many times over. He was shirtless, borderline scrawny at his limbs and ribcage with a slight belly he blamed not on lack of exercise but how he gorged on food right before burying himself, which was never a healthy practice. He was heavily bearded like Jim Morrison in his latter days. His thick black head of hair fell down his back into a bushel of curls over his rear jeans pockets, much like Wayne's blonde unkempt locks or any other surviving vampire's in this region, because a vampire's hair grows, and pocketknives and arrowheads are a pain in the ass for keeping things trim. Besides, when you fan it out with your hands it makes you look larger than other predators in a confrontation. Wayne often kept it tucked under his multi-pocketed armless fisherman's vest in a loosely-tied ponytail which poked out the bottom just over his torn black Levi's. He preferred to wear it that way because it exposed the depiction of a cock and balls he sprayed onto the back of the vest last winter with a can of long-lasting red waterproof paint like graffiti, a thick uneven vertical line flanked by two half circles. It was no work of art, but it sure as hell made a statement.

Dayton met up with Wayne at the other side of the empty highway, sat down with him along the roadside embankment, and together they gazed towards the lone homestead of the deceased Tom Hamlin's wife, thinking about how Tricks Matrix and her girls must've had themselves a bloody fine meaty fiesta the night Tricks snatched ol' *Tom* away.

Tricks and her clan dwelt several miles to the West, a handful of vampire women, in the same canyon terrain as where the Black Heroes held the Bean Feed of their lives before their camp was incinerated by the bright lights that ended things for everybody everywhere. Three of them were *there* when it happened. Because of the women's ages-long resentment for the Heroes, building a settlement right at ground zero of the vampire devastation as soon as the area became inhabitable again was like dancing on all their graves. And they *did* dance.

***

"Hey Dayton."

"Hey Wayne. You know, one of these days I'm going to get myself empty pages of paper, a notebook or something, and stuff to write with."

"Yeah? What'll you write about, Day?"

"How I became a vampire, survived the end of the world. Always wanted to write, but never gave it much thought before then, never seemed to have the time. Now, we have all the time in the world....."

"Or what we have left of it. And who do you suppose will read it?"

Dayton sighed. "Nobody, I suppose. But if I buried it, put it in a cave somewhere...."

"Like the Dead Sea Scrolls."

"......like the Dead Sea Scrolls, someone might find it later, I don't know. It's something to do."

"Something to do," Wayne trailed off into a reminiscing whisper. "I'm so sick of eating prairie meat, so tired of....."

"Of wanting the Widow Hamlin?"

"God, yes," said Wayne. I want to *eat* her." He scratched at his thick blonde beard.

"And *drink* her, from a straw out the neck of her disembodied inverted head."

"Well, yes....." Wayne snatched a cricket in mid-jump, devoured it like the last potato chip in a bag. "The problem is the *tree......*"

Yes, that great old oak tree protruding from the rear yard of the widow's two-bedroom home in the middle of absolutely nowhere, providing ample shade for over a quarter of her property, which doubled mid-day, its topmost branches reaching the height of three stories into the sky.

"Messiahs," remarked Wayne. "Screw things up, don't they?"

Day exclaimed. "Why can't we go back to the days we missed out on, before the Heroes' camp meeting where Toad made me immortal, and live to enjoy an afternoon stroll again, where we could eat our ex girlfriends and good old vampire kinship was as common as a gas station on a street corner."

"You remember *gas stations*?" Wayne said in jest.

"Sort of....."

"Before....."

"Before the world went to shit….."
"When crosses really mattered."

When Earth's Messiah made his second coming, the heavens opened, and He turned out to be *Sam Hall,* a man hung by the neck from a rope slung around the branch of a tree in this very same region of the world, mid-1800's. As a result, crosses, particularly for vampires, turned out to be nothing but God's sick sacred practical joke of the damned.

Trees.

Vampires, all along, were supposed to be afraid of *trees.*

Of any sort.

Samuel, the true savior, died on a *tree.*

That confirmed, Day and Wayne figured their nocturnal ancestors had it wrong all those centuries past. You can read it in Vampire Psychology 101, if there was such a thing. Go figure. Crosses, not really a threat at all, it turns out. But trees, yes. All of them. Vampire flesh dissolves to the touch. Supposedly. Especially trees with nooses hanging from them. None of them wanted to find out for certain, and they believed all the nasty rumors.

And that luscious plump human marshmallow of blood-flowing goodness was nestled in these apocalyptic times of new awareness beneath the branches of a big ass tree.

"Wait. Look," exclaimed Wayne.

Day waited, looked.

The widow Hamlin was out and about, as would be expected during the day, spritzing her summer yellow pear tomatoes with an insecticide mixture, keeping careful watch over potential nighttime predators on the prowl but whistling a tune as if to purposely tempt them because she was bored and needed to attract attention and potential excitement. Bloodsucking mosquitoes were the greatest nuisance for sure, for as tiny as they were they were consistently ongoing in their assault after the temperature dropped and the night fell, but as a target for vampires or wildlife desperate to intrude upon her business Hamlin was constantly, usually, on the alert. And wise.

She knew they were watching, and she spritzed her tomatoes in utter contempt. After her husband, she was alone now, and feeling a little depressed and reckless……

Dayton and Wayne silently watched the widow, watched her house, her tree, the Frankenstein sky and the rare sight of a distant crescent moon hanging in their midst like a disembodied McDonald's *Mac Tonight* head, sans Vegas sunglasses, gleaming down upon them from behind a red transparent tapestry blanketing the sky of doom's afterworld and parting the clouds of red rain.

They sat for, say, at least a couple of hours without saying a further word to each other, without looking behind them or about, feeling more undead than they'd felt the night before. And the night before that.

The widow had been outside the whole time thus far, tending to her garden, trimming, plucking, picking and spritzing, with the exception of a few moments of brief withdrawal into the house.

She was on hands and knees beneath the brightest point of her front property where sun-powered light stakes went poking from out of the ground at random locations, each one slanted like six-foot-tall spears purposely chucked there from a distance. She'd been burrowing into a dense cluster of eggplant a moment ago.

"She's mocking us isn't she, Wayne? Goddamn tease," Dayton complained, but his counterpart didn't respond. In spite of his hunger, Wayne was still content with carrying on tonight's marathon of silence, hoping maybe to break a record. But Dayton insisted. "Why else would she wait 'til we're afoot before she does her yardwork?"

Still silence from Wayne. Then he blinked, thought to do something and moved, stopped, then went ahead to do what he'd thought of doing anyway.

He retrieved a small silver scalpel from the breast pocket of his shirt and, without so much as a flinch, cut off his entire left ear lobe. Then he cut off his right. He flung the scalpel into the dirt and proceeded to suck on one of them, not too eagerly, like sucking on an orange slice.

As Dayton watched him, half surprised and half not, Wayne offered him the other lobe. It suddenly became an odd temptation, but he shook his head against the donation.

Wayne placed it into his shirt pocket and broke his own silence. "We'll keep it for later."

"Why'd you do that for?"

189

"I want something that tastes even remotely human."

"Do you think this is hell, eternal hell, and we're damned to live this way forever?" Dayton asked with existential sentiment.

"It may be more hell for *her* than it is for us," Wayne supposed. "We *are* eternal, and this is our hell. For a time. But look at the old woman......"

Dayton looked. The Mac Tonight moon looked. The widow Hamlin gardened.

"She's lost her god. In all her days, her idea of God was one thing, but it must've blown her mortal-ass mind when it turned out a bitter old murderer hung from a tree by an Old West lynch mob was the Messiah."

"Sam Hall."

"That blew all our minds."

"Yes, all our convictions were misconceptions."

"Goddamn trees. Didn't Johnny Cash sing about this?"

"Yes. And we never listened."

Wayne grabbed his scalpel and rose to his shoeless feet.

Dayton followed suit. "What?"

"Either our next meal is her, or my balls are coming off. Good blood stored in scrotum sacks and we don't need 'em except for the little fleshy canteens that they are."

"I'm not sucking on your balls, Wayne....."

"So let's go get her." And Wayne started off for the widow Hamlin's house, tree or no tree. He readied himself to leap into the air, but Dayton held him quick and grounded: the last male vampire to attempt flight was seized away by a very large bird of prey the instant he did, they heard tell, but even if that didn't happen, he was certain to find himself with a very sour stomach.

So Dayton followed Wayne against his better instincts and trekked across the stretch of wasteland one step at a time to take part in whatever Wayne's scheme was to get the widow and avoid the traps and solar lighting and anti-vampire energies of the big oak tree.

***

With the hot afternoon sun making it almost unbearable for any mammal to tread outside during daylight hours, Hamlin's widow found the cool night air very refreshing. But she had a multitude of other comforts and that cool night air's only difference from air conditioning was that it was natural. Her home had the luxury of electricity and hot and cold running water, partly due to an abundance of solar power collected by the panels atop the house during the day. *All* cities, she figured, had been reduced to rubble and if anyone in the world was still broadcasting radio or television she wouldn't know; all communication had died too long ago for her to know for certain what was going on in the world, if anything. But she sensed that somebody out there was running the show.

Hell, though dialing numbers only resulted in distant static, her telephone still had a dial tone. Damn desert vampires had made no effort to take that away from her, the hope that someone someday would ring her, her internet connection may some day spring to life, a face may appear on the television screen that wasn't prerecorded and popped into a player.

Her late husband had foolishly wheel-barrowed garbage to their own private dump site over the hill way too close to dusk, and he never returned. She went looking for him immediately after daybreak the following morning, and after very little time she found his wheelbarrow, garbage scattered abroad, half way between the waste site and the home. Upon a nearby rock was a ceramic dinner plate, and upon that was a finger of Tom's with no Tom attached to it, still wearing his wedding ring. There was a toothpick sticking out of the finger with a rectangular piece of paper reading *bon appétit*.

"Excuse me, ma'am, might we have a word with you?"

The sight of the two undead males only several yards away caught her so off guard that she fell to her side and onto basket full of tomatoes, spilling its contents, pulverizing the fruit in an effort to stand. Footing gained, she scrambled immediately into the house, returning moments later holding in one hand the small whittled wooden sculpture of a tree with a little string noose slung about a tiny extending branch. She raised it up to them.

"In the name of Sam Hall, be gone, foul blood feeders," the widow bellowed like a Christian preacher of olden days.

Wayne, who'd been daring enough to call out to her, stood his ground while Dayton flinched back, repelled. He cried back to her, "Not working! And we're not the ones who took your husband. We just want to talk."

The widow listened, likely not expecting something so civilized as diplomacy coming out from the night...

....though Dayton nearly ruined it all: "You have any chickens? Perhaps a house cat or caged bird you wouldn't mind getting rid of?"

"What my companion is trying to say," Wayne hushed him down, "is that we're trying to survive in this screwed up environment as much as you are, and, well......you may have some luxuries we don't......and we wish to negotiate a compromise to our mutual benefits......"

"We want better living."

"What you have to negotiate, you can do it right where you are, don't come any closer," the woman said. "But hear ye, I have nothing but ill will towards your kind, or anyone else who wishes to eat me."

"Oh....*my maker be damned,*" Wayne cursed impatiently, and proceeded to march forward. "Let's take her."

This unanticipated move sent Dayton into a panic. "No......no, Wayne! The solar lights, the traps, the *tree*! You're doomed, you'll melt away *screaming*.....!"

Rather than remaining a spectator, Dayton followed close behind as his vampire friend advanced.

Truth was, he'd never gone anywhere close enough to that great oak tree to ever feel anything except fear. He'd never actually seen any traps in action for a vampire, but there were cages of various sizes with spring door mechanisms which captured a wandering prairie varmint who'd stray too close to the vegetable garden and was consequentially served up for evening dinner. As for the light stakes, their rays did sting, but they were no where near as excruciating as direct sunlight.

Truth was also, trees never harmed a vampire before the Messiah's second coming, before the apocalyptical shit hit the celestial fan, and the fear of crosses had been nothing but a psychological mind-fuck for vampires all along. If Wayne had been as much of a talker as Dayton, he'd have expressed his reasoning a lot sooner, for he'd been harboring this conviction for quite some time, apparently, that trees were as much bullshit as crosses.

So.......

Wayne marched right up, past the young corn rows, the mustard/spinach and rampant potato vines, straight past the narrowing parameter of glowing, sun-powered lamp stakes. Dayton stopped walking altogether in disbelief as Wayne overtook the widow, knocked the sacred hanging tree dissuasion out of her hand, grabbed hold of her, sunk his teeth deep into her neck like a cheetah to a gazelle on *National Geographic.*

Dayton stood there, watching him feed, for a moment oblivious to the fact that he himself was starving and Wayne had just scored a prime flesh buffet, but all he could think about was the alien face pendant around his neck, and the possibility that its power could be playing a factor in their ability to defy the forces which kept them a comfortable distance from the Hamlin property, and any other vampire, for so very long.

9.

TRICKS MATRIX

Tricks Matrix had been watching the Hamlin homestead for a little under an hour now. The night vision in her binoculars had been acting up something awful and whenever the settings would abruptly switch to daylight mode it would piss her off to no end until the night vision kicked in again and she could see. Though they were several miles away, she could view the goings-on at the homestead and even hear sounds, not conversations but loud noises only, likes screams or a lawn mower running, and the surveillance equipment around her was end-times state-of-the-art, as much as was left over and could be gathered abroad after the nukes came and this Sam Hall character declared himself God, and some of her girls......the surviving ones who actually witnessed the Black Heroes' demise....had some of these devices left over from their stakeout that eventful night.

Women.

If they weren't spying on hundreds of men, they were spying on two.

These particular two had now, under her scrutiny, accomplished something she and her clan hadn't been able to. They had simply sauntered onto the property, killed the Misses, and were making themselves comfortable on her land. One of them actually went inside the house.

The oak tree had no power over them, nor the light stakes, nor nothing.

Tricks had herself flown near the house several times, and the tree indeed seemed to hold a definite power over her and her kind. The whole tree thing wasn't just superstition, but the whole mythology seemed to have kind of shifted from crosses to trees after the world's end. The way she understood it, crosses truly worked against vampires in their golden age. Now, she had one around her neck to spite the revelation that they no longer had any meaning, except that many people once died on them. All her clan wore crosses in defiance of what they once represented, because they could, though every once in a blue moon they would fall asleep fearing that they would wake up and the whole cross thing would be reinstated, and they would no longer be survivors of anything, just ash.

Tricks was wearing some of the singed black bed sheets she'd found amongst the aftermath of devastation in the Black Heroes' camp, looking quite like a biblical leper, though beneath all of that she hadn't lost the slim and trim physique she'd maintained without Jenny Craig since well before her metabolism was raped into this vampire state. Most of surveillance equipment had the same stuff draped over it, for protection against the red rain, same reason she wore it, though it also turned her on to wear the fraternal adornments of deceased males. She'd allowed her sleek dark auburn hair to grow down the length of her back to her waste, even though she had the resources to cut and shape it into something sexy as she used to, but as far as she was concerned there was really nothing in this red afterworld to look sexy for, no one, for no reason. Besides, the hair made her look larger to other predators. And it felt good to fly with it.

Lying across the outer banks of the rim of the small canyon where her clan roosted, watching the homestead and the goings-on thereabouts, gave Tricks a good session of much-wanted peace, beneath a little rain, listening to desert crickets and admiring a moon that hadn't made an appearance in God-knows-how-long, albeit a half of one, passing the time keeping up with the Joneses, or Hamlins in this case, a handful of miles away, and gnawing on Tom Hamlin's dismembered hand from a plastic container when she got the munchies, which was minus a ring finger.

Tricks wasn't the oldest of her companions, and she was always of the opinion Escarlata would have been the better leader. But Tricks had her shit together, brought the clan through some tough times, and Lata had issues and a pocketful of ill-conceived plans, and really didn't want the job, anyway. Tricks was bitten at ground zero before ground zero became that way, was one of the line-up of fine human women taken from their families against their will so that the bastard Black Heroes initiates could have something to sink their teeth into after someone sunk his teeth into *them*. A sacrifice, essentially, was what she was meant to be. But the guy who was made a vampire that night made her one as well, instead of just killing her, and he did it somehow to save her from the end of the world.

And so he did.

And then the bright lights came, and he died. She didn't.

That instant before she was taken away from him, before the shit hit the fan, marked the only moment in her existence that she ever felt true love toward anyone, even the mortal family she would never see again.

Now, as a vampire she-person of the night, she shared her resentment of the males through the inherent resentment of the bloodline, but also for the Heroes taking her from her mortal life and placing her in the position that they did. That, and the fact the whole nightmare was still fresh in her mind, made her strong-willed and gave her a mental clarity the others didn't seem to possess, though their traumas still lingered fresh in *their* minds. She didn't witness her sisters burn to cinders in mid-air the way Escarlata, BB and Drummer had, the day everyone's lives were forever changed. Those girls were downtrodden and had never been the same since, and were always complaining about it. Tricks felt they had no more of a cause to complain than she did, but yesteryear laments didn't hold a candle to a willingness to stay alive in present times, and the yearning to strive for a better way of living, the way Tricks wanted and wished for all of them. The foremost obstacle which kept the rest of them from coming to their senses, achieving their full potentials, aside from Tricks, was that they thought about the past too goddamn much.

"Hey Tricks, seen anything unusual tonight?" asked Escarlata as she landed from the short flight to get there, feet on the ground and stepping up the embankment a few yards behind.

"Matter of fact yes," Tricks told her, eyes still focused into a duo of ultra-long-distance lenses nestled into the soil with a tripod. "Wanna take a look?"

"Not any time soon, thanks, and fuck you." The last time Lata had gazed through binoculars, the rubber eye pieces melted around her eyes and the equipment she held dissolved in her hands, and all the skin from her shoulders on up became a glistening deep red before it healed over the years to a dark sun-tanned Chestnut brown that kept peeling off like a skin disease. Her exposed shoulders resembled a jigsaw puzzle where the missing pieces where designated by large crimson splotches. Around both eyes were circular scars, as pronounced as a practical joke, and although she'd managed over the years to have tweezersed-out the little foreign objects from her skin that were once a part of a pair of binoculars, the area around both eyeballs resembled something a Batman character had to go through to become a villain. Needless to say, she'd never been able to cast her gaze through lenses of any sort since, not even through empty toilet tissue rolls.

"No, really," said Tricks, turning to look upon Lata directly, "you can't cower away from an idea. That's what I've been saying, that fear is an idea. What are the chances that if you should look into a pair of one of these puppies once more the whole world will be fried again? Some times, you just have to get over it and *look*."

Lata stood silent for a few seconds, her long black hair tied together in one butt-long weave of ponytail, thick as an anaconda, dropped her ass to the ground and crossed her legs Indian-style, settling in all nice and comfy to converse with the Chief. She was clad in a flamingoes-pink padded underwire bikini top with a scoop neckline and over-the-shoulder straps with frilly torn black jeans that were a bit too tight to be comfortable, no shoes. She contemplated responding, thought for a moment, and then, in sudden realization, "You saw something *new*! What happened? Was it the two bastard males? What'd they do? Are they *dead* yet?"

"Lata, vampires are immortal."

"Tell that to Suzuki and Molly....."

"Yes, and to the hundreds who fell victim to the bright lights here, I hope their immortality sent them to a place that matches where they deserve to be. But we're getting way off the point here."

Escarlata waited.

"The two remaining vampires that have been living on the outskirts of the Hamlin estate just killed the widow and overtook the property, and neither the great oak tree nor anything else stood in their way. They strolled up, took the bitch, and now it looks like they own the goddamn place. How the hell did *they* do that and we couldn't, after all this time? I mean, you know how *long* we've been watching them?"

"Yeah sweety," said Lata, "but we *got* the *man*. It was only a matter of time before someone, if not us, got to his wifey-wifey, with *him* no longer around."

"It wasn't a question of waiting for the right moment, like *we* did with ol' Tom," insisted Tricks, holding the man's grossly chewed up hand as testament. "I saw it, I heard it best I could. Pricks just waltzed on over and seized it, the whole two acres, like they owned the place already and showed her the deed."

Escarlata dropped to her knees and crawled towards the equipment, overwhelmingly curious. Tricks rolled out of her way. For the first time since the last time, Lata positioned her eyes into the lenses of the binoculars to check out what was going on from afar, and the rubber eye pieces matched almost perfectly to her scars.

"You gotta be shittin'me," she said to Tricks. "When did *this* happen?"

"Just the last hour, while I was watching."

"Bullshit, Tricks," Lata exclaimed after a moment of observation. "Unless she's a walking corpse, the Widow Hamlin's right there, alive and well, tending to her garden, as usual. What the hell are you on, girl? Ajax? Or was this just your way of making me see through these goddamn things again....."

10.

THE HOMESTEAD

After all this time of contemplation and silence and rarely hinting of his developing scheme while gazing off towards the Hamlin property with Dayton, Wayne really had it all worked out. Taking the widow's life was just the beginning. The way Wayne orchestrated it, he had potential observers in mind, other vampires mostly, or possibly even humans, mutants, aliens, the Road Warrior, who knew anymore. When the two had their fill of her, there was no time to lose.....

......and the widow Hamlin had returned to tending her garden in no time at all, as if the whole violent vampiric encounter never even occurred.

An elaborate maze of fishing line with a gauge heavy enough to pull in a marlin extended throughout the front garden like tough strands of spider webbing connected to an elaborate assemblage of pulleys fixed into every towering sun-powered light in the garden, wooden stakes, fence posts, anything sturdy enough to do the job. Four rope-thick strands went into the house, straight through the lower portion of the front livingroom window screen, two through the kitchen window, making it impossible to close those windows fully but they closed well enough. Fat straps of leather were tied about the ends of each wire drooping below the windows inside the house.

From behind those windows Dayton and Wayne could act as puppeteers.......at the other ends of the lines were very nasty fishing hooks the size of silver dollars attached to strategic parts of the misses beneath her garments. She was hunched over among the dozens of full-sized tomato plants, an unseen block of firewood against her belly keeping her a couple feet above the ground, and equally unseen were the vampire duo, manipulating her arms, legs, and head from time to time throughout the night. The Hamlins already had the line strung out there to alert those inside the house of any trespasser who happened to trip them while wandering about; Wayne simply predetermined how to reroute them and knew just where to find the tools to do so way before-hand, so with a little hustle they made it happen lickety-split.

Problem was, it was a lamentable waste of good meat, human meat. Aside from the blood feast they'd ingested, and what little of it they managed to catch in little Tupperware containers for later, her remaining blood emptied slowly throughout the night like a car engine into the drip pan of the soil below her. The vampires had prepared one of the three chest freezers they found in the garage for storing her remains come morning, and for during each day afterwards, as long as they could keep her from rotting and falling apart. Her exposure to the nighttime elements imposed a shelf life of possibly several nights tops, which would buy them time enough to construct another scarecrow-like monstrosity from materials in the home.

The Widow Hamlin was a write-off, food-wise, and, though a rare delicacy lately, one human was an intelligible sacrifice for securing a house like this, with freezers-full of meats of all sorts and all its modern luxuries. Besides, vampires' metabolisms were funky compared to those of myth, and vegetables could and were consumed by them, but human blood was preferred against Miracle-Gro ten to one for fertilizer. To that regard, and of the fact that you are what you eat, eating Hamlin-fed tomatoes were the next best thing to drinking the widow's blood straight-up.

That night, Dayton and Wayne canvassed the house and its rear yard, the garage and two large sheds, while synchronizing new-found wristwatches to beep every half hour so they could return to the windows and move the widow around a bit. For a couple of guys that for the longest time barely owned three or four pieces of clothing between them, a couple of sleeping bags, and a few sacks of belongings buried like lost treasure in the surrounding desert, it was like a mega-jackpot lottery won, seizing the place for their own. Through their hour-long scramble to set up the body among the tomato plants and get all the puppeteering mechanisms situated, neither one had time to stop and smell the roses, especially Dayton, who had to constantly pay attention to Wayne's instructions and adhere to them while trying to figure out just what the hell it was they were doing.

But now that they'd settled, come across the wristwatches on a table beside an empty hallway coat rack and split into two for a property-wide walkabout, Dayton was anxious to be the one trolling around outside and in the sheds. After all, the tree was out there, and he wanted to touch it. Wayne, although the proven bold one, preferred to be the one *not* out there directly with the tree, and Dayton didn't blame him. There was a lot of cool shit inside.

The great oak tree towered above Dayton as he approached it, lifted open the palm of his hand and placed it upon its haggard bark. Hearsay and fear repelled him and other vampires from this place because of this tree, and for so long. It seemed, like crosses, that the whole tree/vampire thing was merely a myth, too, but then again he knew he had something special hanging from around his neck.

"Hallelujah," he said, quietly, and gripped his alien-face pendant, believing its power responsible for all this, and if not totally, he was persuaded towards this line of thinking.

He went about inspecting the sheds first, discovered power tools, power generators, a hardware store's-worth of hand and garden tools, fertilizers and insecticides, trimmers, gasoline containers, chainsaws. A nice circular flower garden faced the sheds with a kiddie-pool-sized empty bird bath dead center of it, dwarf fruit and nut trees. A two-by-four lacquered wooden cross with the words NO MORE YESTERDAY hand-engraved upon the horizontal beam poked out from the ground about a dwarf's height past the sheds, near an empty chicken coop and a cage beside it containing three spooked adult desert hares. Beyond that were a couple dozen potted purple Indica marijuana specimens, almost fully mature.

Wayne rushed out the back door of the kitchen and hurried over to Dayton, holding a flat square object above his head and waving it around enthusiastically like a prize.

"Dayton," he exclaimed, "dude, I found a special edition of Cornell Wilde's *The Naked Prey* on DVD! Man, they got *everything* in there….."

Just before Dayton went into the house with him, Wayne turned. He stood still for a moment, eyes gazing up at the tree reverently.

"I told myself that after we got everything done, got settled, I would come out here and face the tree, give it the kind of bird I got on the back of my vest," he said.

Dayton told him, "But now, you kinda feel like thanking it. You have to thank *something*. And I sure as hell ain't gonna thank Sam Hall. More importantly, I sure as hell need a shave."

"And a haircut."

"Shampoo."

"Dadump dump......."

***

The boys situated themselves real good by morning.

The faucets in the bathrooms and kitchen gave crystal clear filtered water, hot and cold, and the electricity generated from the solar panels on the roof made the house fully functional without having to deal with the bills, if there were any utilities representatives around anymore to demand them or postal people to deliver them, which there never was. The phone lines were active, but there was nobody on the receiving end, cell phones, dial-up, every which way. You could dial any number you liked but it would either ring endlessly or an automated voice told you the number was no longer in service before it sent a sequence of very annoying beeps, no matter who you were calling......Verizon, the New York Times, the White House, Cousin Memford. The internet remained in existence, you could visit any website still out there to be seen, but none had been modified for over three years and no attempts to communicate were responded to. There were no television or cable channels, everything was all static. Nothing on the radio, am, fm, satellite, broadband, short band, what have you. It was like a Romero zombie film, where you find yourself in a self-sufficient outpost somewhere in a desolate world with no communication and there's eminent peril closing in on you and you don't have a clue regarding how much time you have to enjoy things while they lasted.

Dayton and Wayne enjoyed things.

You bet they did, got themselves all cleaned up, wearing clothes from Tom's wardrobe, hair cut to the shoulders, beards down to goatees and stubble, smelling like Irish Spring. There was a bounty of food in the fridge and canned goods, a good lot of it containing meat, and freezers-full of parts of dead animals that, when thawed, would get bloody. Yummy yummy.

There was also a 2016 Ford Hydro-Mustang convertible in the garage that must not have been taken out for a ride since before the bright lights came, because it was otherwise known the Hamlins had no method of transportation, not so much as a bicycle, let alone a vehicle fueled only by water. It was now Wayne and Dayton's little secret, an escape pod should their ship go down, which was probably how the Hamlins intended it to be.

But the CD/DVD collection was impressive. In their free time outside of maintaining the place, it was good for them to know they had state-of-the-art entertainment, always, to pass the time. Damn good. The Hamlins even had a 3D projection unit for the post-Blue Ray generation. The first thing they saw together, however, was *Naked Prey*, Wayne's all-time favorite, on the flat panel HD. Before Dayton got itchy to spend time by himself, after a next few days and nights of no worries, he'd already seen *A Clockwork Orange*, *Revenge of the Pink Panther*, a season of Judge Judy episodes, and watched the *Naked Prey* movie three times.

During daylight hours, in fear of the sun, they rested inside the walk-in closet of the Hamlin's master bedroom, a series of surveillance monitors on wall shelving, and alarms to go off upon the detection of any movement in the immediate area.

Only perhaps Sam Hall knew what would happen should someone straggle onto the estate mid-day, as vampires who couldn't expose themselves fully to the post-apocalyptic sun would think, but Wayne had figured with enough layers of clothing and head protection, anything was possible. He had an assemblage of what he thought they should wear, including motorcycle helmets, hanging upon hooks like Firefighter's gear on the inside wall next to the closet door, just in case, so he could defend the home during the day if need be, or escape in the Ford, looking like Darkman.

After the first few nights, Dayton made his way up via extendable aluminum ladder to the rooftop, to sit between the solar panels alone, watch the vastness of the nighttime desert plains, and write with a handful of pens on a yellow notepad about his experience with the Black Heroes and how he became a vampire himself. For once in a long time, there was no red rain, not even a drizzle, though he did bring a small black pop-out umbrella in case wetness happened and he didn't want to go anywhere just yet because he was on a roll.

Before he set pen to paper, he relaxed a bit, let his mind wander, and his gaze began drifting into the night sky. All he surveyed was silent, still, except for an occasional bird or stirring about at the outskirts of a small wild animal, but from the sky he began to notice three human female-like figures almost swimming through the air a distance enough away for Dayton to squish them between his fingers like gnats if he held his hand up to them from his point of view.

Trick's girls.

After a short while, they got smaller and smaller until he could no longer see them and was able to fully concentrate on his memoirs again.

After some intense meditation, Dayton was able to pull from his memory the last hours of the world's climactic end, the way he lived it, how he became what he was, and how he survived what was to likely be the last Black Heroes' Annual Camp Meetin' and Bean Feed the world would ever see.

And the last time he'd ever held a woman.

Let's see, Dayton thought to himself, *what got me through the Black Heroes initiation process in the first place? What was going on in my head at the time? Let's go from there. Matter of fact, let's start just after Basics left me with the other White Sheets, after my encounter with Triad in the motor home. I have a long night ahead if I'm gonna relive this, and thank God I got a few good reefers from those prime plants out back. Three cheers for the Hamlins.......*

11.

Becoming Like Toad
By Dayton Monday

I think what got me through the initiation process and into becoming a fully functioning corpse of a man that needs blood and meat to stay immortal, was a combination of fear and damn good Oscar-worthy acting. In my years as a regular guy I'd never come face to face with the threat of death. So, previous to Toad's abduction of my person I never knew how I'd react to a situation where I was convinced my life was at stake.

Now I know.

Whether I was drugged and hallucinating or my experience at the *Black Heroes' Annual Camp Meetin' and Bean Feed* was soberly genuine, I gave an amazing performance in the starring role as *"Number Twenty-one"* in my own conversion into living death.

Little did anyone know, including myself, that the rest of the world was about to change as drastically as I was to be.

I was standing, the last in an assembled line of twenty-one initiates, all individually garbed in white bed sheets and little else, each with their left hand's severed thumb wrapped in a bloody condom with a rubber band around the stub, like mine, and aware of the dire necessity to keep them there. I remember developing this vague idea that when all of this was over, they had surgeons waiting to sew our thumbs back on.

Surrounding us were tents and open shelters with crowded tables and outdoor kitchens, grills blazing and barbequing foods in rows of canopied booths like a midnight marketplace, where things were sold and bartered and marveled at and eaten.

Our row of guys stood alongside a cleared dirt path which stretched into the night both to my right and left like a temporary avenue. Mini camp sites and tented structures lined both sides, to my rear and front, and as I became caught up in the act of viewing my surroundings a man approached who barked to me the command of keeping my eyes on my feet at all times lest I be caught eye-fucking someone.

When I found myself able to look up at anything without being caught in the act of eye-fucking, I saw men of various statures and builds and ages above legal drinking, most sporting variations of facial hair like biker dudes, and in contrast to us initiates they were all without exception dressed in various dark shades of black and wrapped in oversized black bed sheets, silver trinkets, belts, wrist bands and jewelry adorning their majority.

Directly ahead of me was a tented structure larger than most beneath which squabbled a half dozen patrons over something to do with the full-bodied swordfish, hammerhead sharks, marlin and tuna hanging tail-down on meat hooks from steel overhead beams. I was momentarily awestruck at the sight, for I wasn't used to seeing large ocean fish that size outside the Discovery Channel and I understood that lately all but tuna were declared endangered species. A good five-foot-long swordfish was beheaded over a chopping block by a Brother wielding a butcher knife and wearing a body-length bloodied black apron. He then handed the head across the counter in exchange for currency from a fat-armed man who, when taking it away, stuck his hand into it and proceeded into a series of fencing gestures which amused those around him into laughter.

Many men were clearly drinking or intoxicated from one substance or another; almost all carried a glass, cup, or drinking container, and I noticed a Bud truck not far down the opposing side of the dirt avenue with a line of Brothers waiting for one of several tabs to fill empty receptacles. Two Brothers fell into the dirt several feet in front of me, each hoisting the other up and then falling again, chuckling heartily after managing to maintain their balance long enough to resume their casual journey to nowhere.

A moment after I became aware again that Johnny Cash was always with us in song, Number Twenty expressed to me how he longed for a bit of green bud. Then he began to talk and talk as if he'd had some, in what little time we had for a moment's peace. He remarked at how vampires were like nothing he'd heard about, but for the undead/bloodsucking factors. True, there were no aristocratic Draculas here, but as it turned out neither one of us had yet seen *From Dusk 'Til Dawn,* and had we, we'd swear the ones in that film were Brothers, too. Twenty remarked how he never believed vampires existed in real life, and how, now proven wrong, he was beginning to question his lifelong disbelief in everything from zombies and ghosts down to the Jersey Devil. He talked of his reasoning that vampires got themselves so intensely loaded with drugs and drink because they were technically dead already and could reap all the intoxicating benefits of recreational what-nots with none of the repercussions. Vampires could party for weeks, he surmised, probably needed to overindulge to keep them going, especially on weekends like these when the whole fraternity gets together. It seemed like they had a distinctive grudge against women, although devout womanizers, as I came to notice, and they despised traditional crosses though throughout camp there were many of them, albeit upside down and burning.

"What the are *you* lookin' at, punkmaster?" It was Toad, and he was suddenly right in front of me. "You ready to be washed in the blood? To eat my friggin' heart?"

"Sorry," I said, and cast my gaze down at my muddy bare feet.

"That's not an answer, you piece of shit!"

"Sorry, I mean yes, I'm ready!" I responded with a shout like a recruit to a drill sergeant, and I thought to myself, *all this time I'd been worried about dodging the draft, and I've wound up in a boot camp anyway.*

A Niagara Falls of gushing freezing Nestea Plunge ice water overtook me from head to feet, and I realized a figure was standing behind me with a wooden tub at the same moment I looked down and saw the liquid I was dowsed with was black and gelatinous and pouring down my legs to pool around where I stood. My white garb was now, in the light, a very deep red. The same thing happened to the guy on my left, like in the climax of Brian DePalma's *Carrie* to the title prom queen, and so forth, down the line, as Toad stepped before each and shouted the same thing he shouted at me.

Another man with a long beard and a tall top hat replaced him before me, flanked by a duo of men only half his height, baring blackface and shaven heads. Mister Tophat presented a thick kitchen counter corkboard from out behind him and raised it flat, and a dwarf sidekick in turn placed upon it a living toad the size of a boxing glove which thrashed about until the bearded man

207

revealed a large Boa knife and plunged it into its head while the dwarves helped hold it down. In a matter of seconds, Tophat flayed and filleted the toad like a sushi chef until he presented me between two fingers its beating heart, which I had to eat. He proceeded on to the next guy, and the next, with the same amphibious sacrifice for all.

We were forced to move away after that, altogether, and we rarely separated. Mutually, we witnessed and were forced to participate in the same things: for instance, these drunken bastards, I noticed, made it a point to urinate in a 6 by 6 hard plastic kiddy pool that filled up with enough pee for one to fully immerse in lying down. I was baptized by an elected Brother with a generic beach bucket of the rancid acidy yellow stuff, standing in the pool's center and taking it over the head like that first immersion of blood in the line Basics left me at, and then I found myself dowsing every other initiate with a bucket of Brother pee like a John the Baptist of liquid body waste. Afterwards, I had to race against my fellow "White Sheets" through a thirty-foot-long trench of human remains, a milky substance and a mixture of popular toasted oat cereals.

On occasion, I was ordered to step aside by one or more Brothers I wasn't allowed to eye-fuck, and they would command me to perform demeaning tricks like stuffing pork entrails up my ass, Fecal Matter Casserole down my throat, and holding spiny cactus in my underarms. Someone spread red lipstick across my lips and nose and eyebrows. I was made to tap dance and sing songs with words such as *I like it, I love it, I want some more of it* over and over again.

Constantly, it seemed, I was inspected to see how I was holding up, with particular attention paid to my condom-wrapped severed thumb and the alien face pendant which remained around my neck. I noticed I was tended to a bit more regularly than the others. I was grateful for that. Once, I thought I overheard a Brother say to another, *dude, we have to make sure this one goes through……*

Folsom Prison Blues started on the loud speakers about the time we were made to jog in formation around the entire camp grounds naked, fearing we'd be killed if the donuts inserted over our flimsy erections fell to the ground. All this, while Brothers stood on the sidelines spitting on us and throwing insults and entrails and empty beer cans.   Most of us got through the humiliating exercise by holding our penis tips up with one hand, except for Number Fourteen, who was a strange one, and had no problem keeping it up at all.

As the night progressed, there was no telling how long the hazing would last.   Every fifteen minutes or so, a voice would shout out loud above Mister Cash's tunes FIFTEEN MINUTES TO GO, MORTAL RUNTS, but fifteen minutes came and went more often than their proclamations remained bearable.

I saw Brothers drinking straight from other Brothers' wrists and then spitting the blood out of their mouths and into the drinks in their hands, swishing it around with fingers or Halloween party toothpick umbrellas, and reverting back to casual conversation.   I saw garage-sized shade canopies harboring Black Heroes-related merchandise including hats, visors, caps, vests, bling-bling, hand-carved wooden plaques and surf boards, motorcycle parts and accessories, bumper stickers reading SUPPORT YOUR LOCAL BLACK HEROES or BLACK HEROES MAKE A BRIGHTER DAY, or WE ARE IMMORTAL, WE WILL PREVAIL, WE ARE OUT OF OUR MINDS.

At one point, Number Six went into a spasmodic fit of convulsions and contortions after being forced to eat what looked like a hand-sized mushroom and was the only one singled out to do so.   He seemed the weakest and the one who straggled behind the most, and after the incident I never saw him again.

At one point, we passed a sloped clearing where several yards-long plastic sheets of slip n' slide surface descended down from atop the landscape like a backyard summer block party for children to have fun and cool down.   I saw four guillotines situated up at the top of the slip n' slide and a screaming, nude woman struggling and squirming helplessly beneath each one, necks extended, and then the blades fell and all four heads tumbled downwards.   Their black blood flowed down the yellow rows of plastic sheeting like water gushing out four fire hydrants as several Brothers stretched out on their backs readying to make blood angels.   Other Brothers waited by the dozens down below where the plastic sheet canvass narrowed into a long metal trowel where any could dip their plastic cups and glassware and Black Heroes mugs into the red syrupy

209

goodness that accumulated there while four of them won prizes for catching the women's heads after they came down the slope.

Death was a very real presence throughout the camp, in some ways no more or less a festive presence like a Death Metal Halloween gathering or Day of the Dead celebration, but since the sobering confrontation with Triad I was made aware of death as if he was a celebrity icon making an appearance there and of whom I was destined to meet, shake hands with, and obtain an autographed personalized glossy photo of before I'd be sent my way. Perhaps death was imminent in the knowledge that before the night was up, I'd become a Brother myself. But this was the first time I actually witnessed death, with the execution of the women, death of any sort in real time right before my eyes.

I bore witness to more bloodlust and bloodshed as the night progressed, with every *"fifteen minutes"* ambiguous voice announcement and each new loudspeaker Cash tune. One young woman was killed and cut into pieces behind a pop-up carport for a flesh fiesta of smokehouse *girl-in-grillin'* (was what they called it) waiting for her the next tent over, and a few minutes later I saw a round weeble-looking dude strolling proudly around with a wooden walking stick sporting a female rib cage with its breasts and flesh sewn back impaled through its top end like he was carrying around a banner.

Overall, in regards to women, the *Black Heroes' Annual Camp Meetin' and Bean Feed* was a no-women-or-children-or-pets-allowed social gathering, and, vampires or not, it seemed evident that most of the Brothers had wives waiting for them in a normal suburban home, though clearly these men despised women openly here. I saw females slaughtered and sold, cooked and eaten, and if there was sex involved it was an aspect I hadn't yet seen. I was aware, through overheard conversation, that there was a pill quite like Viagra which enabled vampires to engage in sex. But in my opinion, there was no interest in sex among these creatures, just a balls-to-the-wall testosterone frenzy of male mayhem and earthy drunken debauchery with no respect for life or the living and a general superiority complex that made them all, in their own eyes, above the law and the social status quo.

At one point I witnessed the demise of a Brother which seemed like a sort of justice for at least one of the lives they'd taken, albeit accidental. He'd been doing summer salts and cartwheels before a series of inverted burning crosses and must've come into visual contact with a cross during a moment he was upside down in mid-cartwheel, causing him to spontaneously combust while on-lookers pointed and laughed at his stupidity as the flames consumed him in his black fraternity bed sheet. Curiously, in the end, the bed sheet was all that remained of him.

Hours into the night and all us White Sheets were granted ten minutes of rest, on a trailside near an open bar set-up where Brothers flocked and mingled and went this way and that past us. None were allowed during this time to haggle or abuse us in some humiliating way, but they were all permitted to afford us drinks. Harsh, rancid, potent alcoholic beverages. Some offered us water so we wouldn't dehydrate, which was wise and welcomed being how by that time we were all drunk as skunks. We were also wide awake and alert, though inwardly tremendously weary. In a brief exchange of words with a fellow White Sheet, I learned that whereas I was fearful of losing my life, the consensus was the others wanted to get it all over with so they could relax and party with the rest of the camp.

Their accumulative anxiousness to become vampires grew even more fervid after we were all each given a ceramic bowl full of piping hot blood beans, fresh from one of a half dozen cauldrons bubbling and brewing and suspended above roaring fires throughout the festival. The event wasn't called a bean feed for not, you know. The ingredients in the bean mixture were a mystery to me except for the red chili beans themselves, as it was explained to us that these particular beans were not only common red ones but grown by Brothers with "red thumbs," so they said, which boiled down to the fact they were nurtured with human blood moreso than with your average all-purpose 6-10-10 plant food. What kicked our asses was the ample sprinkling of cocaine on the top, or a similar white powdery intoxicating substance, like parmesan cheese through small hand-held metal sifters.

We sat there during our short break, rarely at first talking amongst ourselves, and Johnny Cash's *When the Man Comes Around* issued forth into the grand hellish firelit desert world of ultimate inhuman abandon, the unholy souls of the damned living it up as if damnation itself had granted them amnesty and they'd be like this forever.

I found myself with time enough to think, to absorb it all, for the experience and its realities to sink in a bit, and at first all I could do was catch my breath, eat my beans and drink, listen to the Man in Black. What remained of us by that time was what we started with minus four. Whatever happened to those four was likely a shared fate with Number Six, and all in an orderly row as we were, I now sat beside Number Nineteen. I didn't even realize that Number 20, who'd been right behind me or at my side until this point, was gone.

"My name's Wayne," Nineteen said to me out of the blue.

"Dayton Monday."

"Pleasure."

"At least we can say the word. This whole predicament gives me the feeling I'll never know what it's like again."

"What, pleasure?"

"Yes."

"All the Black Sheets seem to be having a good enough time of it, and we'll be joining them before the night's through."

"That's what I'm afraid of."

"What did you think you were getting into here? Oh yes, you're Twenty-one. I heard some words about you, that you had no idea about the vampire angle with the Brothers. But you wanted to be one when you were a kid, flapping your jacket around at recess time and biting girls and all."

"How'd you know about that?" I asked, somewhat embarrassed, but he ignored me.

"It seems your sponsor brought you in for other reasons. Maybe because you wanted to be a part of something so badly, we all want to be a part of something, but he had to be convinced you have what it takes to make him proud. I mean.....the four who didn't make it this far, their sponsors are unceremoniously stripped of their Brotherhood and have to go through a harsher initiation all over again next time. I hear Toad's yours. He ruled an entire country once. Hey....they all seem to ooh and ahh over that pendant of yours, think it's something special. I mean, it's even got a little black in it......White Sheets can't wear black, it's sacrilege. How's your thumb doing? I don't know about you, but I am *flying* right now….."

"Haven't you heard?" I responded, "Male vampires don't like to fly."

"Yeah, I heard," said Wayne. "But apparently they find other ways to."

"Fuckin' White Sheets, let's MOVE!" came the call which disrupted the silence following Wayne's remark.

Then, "FIFTEEN MINUTES, HOT SHOWERS……"

"PARTY TIME, MORTAL DEATH, DRINK UP, PEOPLE……."

And with that, we drank up indeed, rising to our feet and, single-file, we shuffled away to our destinies.

***

Our stinking, filthy, rancid selves were caked with blood and excrement, our white bed sheets clinging to us like extra skins with all the detestable elements of what we'd been through so far, and I had the distinct feeling we were headed for the final round. It had to end, for all of us, sooner or later.

Multitudes are marching to that big kettle drum……..

And we soon found ourselves led to the extreme rear of the camp, where a majority of the Brothers were likewise congregating into a large circle surrounding a massive and vibrant bonfire fueled by wood and debris.

We were all stripped naked again, and it felt liberating to be released from burdens of our filthy attire. One Brother hosed us off; the stream of water was liberating as it was welcomed and indescribably refreshing, not hot as was promised, but for a few moments, all us remaining White Sheets were in a certain state of ecstasy……

……for a few moments……

The intense bonfire heat dried us almost instantly as we were led, remaining in single-file, onto the three steps of a wooden stage with enough square feet of floor to accommodate three times as many of us. I recalled during the duration of my time there having been led through here before, where a Black Heroes metal band called *Two Fetus Snow* was rocking the large crowd with a cover of *Ring of Fire*. Now us White Sheets took the stage and stood there all in a row, nude, before a raging blaze half the size of my parents'

213

home, with a roller-rink-sized clearing. We stood mute and more vulnerable than we'd ever been thus far to hundreds of jubilant and cheering Black Heroes fuckers like we were to be auctioned off for prostitution, or like we were rock stars. You pick.

Up until this moment I'd never established the feeling of a sense of leadership directed towards a single Black Sheep among them. They all displayed on the surface a status of mutual equality, with no one introduced to us as someone in charge or referred to as such since Triad.

I stole a gaze down the row of us to my left and saw young naked women, late teen to twenty-something, beautiful, lean, accompanied by a nude man of equal age range and an adult German Shepherd. The same as we did, they shuffled single-file until each one found their place before each one of us. The naked young man took a stance facing Number Fourteen, whilst the women took their places likewise before the other White Sheets, directly facing them as well and only several inches nose-to-nose.

And before me......*I* had the *German Shepherd.*

The multitude of Black Sheets roared, as did the firelight, as did my accumulating assessment of what we were in for next, particularly me.

And then, to my amusement, a leader figure actually emerged from along them, carrying in one hand a burning torch like a triumphant medieval crusader before pitching it into the bonfire, drank what was likely blood from a wine glass in the other hand, and then another Brother raced from the crowd to hand him a cordless microphone.

I looked out at the crowd, the fire, the fucked-up stars above, the chorus line of nudie girls standing before most of us, the German Shepherd before me, and I thought......

....you can *imagine* what I thought......

***

"My fellow fuckers, damn wretched souls, all thee cursed with the blood we all mutually share and which through this bloodline gave us life after the deaths of the far less meaningful mortal ones we had before this one, I bid you welcome."

These were the first words proclaimed into the microphone by their apparent leader, who proceeded then to proclaim himself such by stating he was one of the oldest among them, along with the handful of those who had no desire to be leaders and Triad, the "Beloved Three." That leader was none other than His Royal Highness, Sire Toad.

The crowd roared gloriously in his honor, their roars directed as much to him as towards what was about to happen to us White Sheets. Their credo chants of *Nos es immortalis , nos mos increbresco , nos es ex nostrum mens* were followed by *we are immortal, we will prevail, we are out of our minds,* and these chants then crescendoed into *WHITE SHEETS, WHITE SHEETS, WHITE SHEETS............*

"All right," Toad hushed them. "We all encourage the growth of the population of our sacred fraternity to the extent we are tonight, so I know you're all anxious for the show to begin. Those who you see before you on this stage are about to transform into our fold, and you all know what that's like. It's a bitch, ain't it?"

The volume meter of the crowd, if there had been one, would've gone off the charts and imploded, metal springs leaping free, in applaused agreement with Sire Toad.

I noticed the girls inching closer to their men, the male, erection and all, inching ever closer to his White Sheet who likewise had a woody thrice as long......the pooch before me about-facing at the command of a faceless voice and raising its hind quarters to me, exposing dangling doggy balls and an anus with swirling creases like the part of a pink balloon you put your mouth over to blow into.

There arose within me a sort of panic which for the sake of my life I suppressed, but I was *not* about to screw a German Shepherd and I feared after all the night's trials I was ultimately doomed to let my sponsor down.

Hell, I was ultimately *doomed*, anyway, at this point.

"Since we're technically undead," resumed Toad's address to all, "and we can't give in to the lust of the flesh the way that living men do, at least not without these red babies....." and with that, he withdrew from a pocket beneath his black bed sheet a tiny pill which he raised in his hand to show all......

".......so," he continued, "we're gonna give these initiates an opportunity a lot of us weren't granted before we became what we are. A good, ball-busting, hell of a last get-down-on-it downhome fuckfest. And each to his own preference. Ain't that right, buddy, Number Twenty-one over there?"

The Black Heroes, as one, chanted ODD ONE, ODD ONE, ODD ONE......

The other White Sheets, I saw, were already against their pre-chosen partners and all over them, desperately, passionately, the guy next to me already dropping his blonde to the stage spread-eagled and penetrating her.

I looked at the German Shepherd, then at the row of Black Sheets lining up behind every initiate but me.

Toad then whistled into his microphone while looking straight towards me, and my canine sex toy suddenly made a mad dash off the stage in a heartbeat, as if it too was relieved the joke was finally over, and Toad laughed and laughed into the mic about how he had Dayton Monday going there for awhile.

Then, a naked young woman with emerald eyes and neck-length brown hair which curved upwards like a '60's beach flic chick eclipsed my view and held her hands to my waist.

I was so relieved I found myself embracing the girl with which I was to abandon my remaining dignity and copulate with in an orgy on a stage before hundreds of vampires cheering me on. Embracing, as in *hugging*. Thank *God* for her. Thank *God*.

"Name's Dayton," I said into her ear, then I asked, "are you real?"

We separated, and then she looked into my eyes. She seemed troubled after I asked that, as if my words had made her lose character in the night's performance, and she was almost suddenly tearful.

"Maybe the only thing real in this goddamn circus," she told me. "I just want to go home. Can you promise me when all this is over that I can go home? I'll promise with my life that I won't say a word about any of this, I swear to God......"

I was taken aback by her sobering plea, her desperation, her innocence. She was the only purely human element I would encounter that night, and perhaps in my asking her if she was real she wondered the same thing about me.

I looked around us. Toad was lecturing into his mic about Bathgory and the Black Hero of Hungary, and I caught a brief allusion to how Triad themselves were partially responsible for all of this, as though vampires would not exist in their contemporary state without them. I caught wind of a sense of resentment through Toad's speech towards this Countess Bathgory, of whose head and body, he claimed, were currently separated by a distance of hundreds of thousands of miles, as East was to West, so she could never resurrect herself and bother any of them ever again......

.......it was she who turned the original Black Hero into a creature of the night, and the Black Heroes fraternity owed their existence to that happening, but this crowd, as festive as they may seem......well, I got the feeling that they weren't all too thrilled with what they were when it all came down to it. And I think they resented the entire opposite sex, not just the Countess, because of it.

I gazed into the anguished features of the girl before me, and my inability to respond to her plea made her noticeably lose interest, perhaps hope, but I was plagued by an onslaught of distraction and wouldn't have known how to reply had I time to think.

I couldn't talk, least of all have sex with her under these conditions. I couldn't make myself no more aroused than I would have with the dog. By that time, and by the look of my fellow White Sheets spent and standing exhausted and fulfilled with what could have been the best sexual encounter of their lives, I had missed my chance to indulge as well.

How could I screw *anything*, I mean, even with the cocaine-laced bowl of blood beans coursing through my system as well as the whiskey and the all-consuming situation itself.......even regardless of that, there was the helpless victim of a poor young woman here, expecting sex but praying to live through all of this as much as *I* secretly was.......

Then the Black Sheets behind us pressed ever closer, and when I turned to the presence now breathing down my neck I saw that it was Toad himself. I hadn't noticed when he'd abandoned the mic and the center of attention to take a position behind me, and I was extremely startled.

"Don't worry buddy," he said into my ear, "it's almost over now. And don't worry about the damsel in distress. I am the key to your imminent immortality, but she is the door. After I take you, you will die. But after you take her, you will live forever."

A nude elderly woman emerged from out of the crowd, fleeing, and cast herself screaming into the bonfire.

"Dammit," cursed Toad, "they aren't supposed to start yet."

Then, after a brief pause: *"Now* they can start......."

12.

CHAINSAWS AND
BLOOD TOMATOES

Dayton paused from his writing to recline in thought no sooner than his note tablet was snatched out of his hand.

The last half hour of scribbling down his initiation account made him aware that he'd been taking too long upon the roof without checking in on Wayne, and for an instant he thought his friend had ventured up to him thoroughly pissed off because he hadn't done so. Dayton had prepared the argument that he'd at least served a purpose in keeping watch over the property while he'd been writing and basking in the quiet, but it wasn't Wayne up there on the roof with him, it was Tricks, and that argument was suddenly shot all to shit.

All her long auburn hair rained down upon him and he scrambled backwards up the roof towards the crest. Tricks Matrix was suspended upside-down in the air just a couple of feet above where he'd been sitting, holding the tablet as far away from him as possible, cackling softly to herself. Wearing the scorched black sheets of vampire Brothers, she looked like an inverted assemblage of withering black rose petals without a stem, her hair fluid and spread wide as a peacock's hind feathers until she jerked her head to one side to make the hair come together so she could look at me without letting it get in the way. She floated there, waving his notepad around like a prize.

"Hey, Shakespeare," came out her words in verbal cursive doodles of glee, "you supposed to be on the lookout or something? I'd give a garden snail that responsibility before I volunteered *you*......."

Dayton found his footing and slowly rose. He could think of a thousand things to say to her, but what he chose to say was "Give me my notepad, I was writing something important!"

Tricks pushed herself backwards a couple of feet away from him, still hovering and upside-down, holding out the notepad to tease him like a schoolgirl bully who'd just stolen his homework. "What, this? You want it??? If these papers are so all-important to you, don'tcha think you would've guarded them more carefully? Or this house, for that matter? You men are all *bullshit!*"

She gave a single-fingered motion with her free hand to someone other than the two of them that Dayton hadn't noticed yet, and suddenly something behind him struck the side of his head with such physical force that it catapulted him three yards away into the nearby red brick chimney and, though the impact left the chimney intact, Dayton fell onto a solar panel and cracked it, rolled onto his chest, and cracked it some more. A light from below in the direction of the kitchen shorted out.

Escarlata set foot upon the roof and began to step towards him, and Tricks did a back flip forward to where she was right-side-up again and submitted to gravity as well. As they approached, Dayton lifted himself by the palms of his hands to face them. As he did so, he noticed the third vampire landing into the tomato garden, wrestling the meat puppet he and Wayne had made of the Widow Hamlin from out of her hooks and fishing line restraints.

Dayton never before had a close confrontation with the females from the West, but had always figured one was inevitable, if they and he and Wayne and a few strangers just passing through were all that was left of the world, it would happen sooner or later. The only dealings he'd had with them were from a distance, a *fuck you guys* message dropped from a rock from the nighttime sky, sightings of them soaring about in the heavens but never getting too close, and hearsay from the occasional wanderer, the same ones who'd subjected both he and Wayne to Sam Hall mythology and the post-war state of the earth and all the apparent nonsense about trees.

His first instinct was to get off the roof, and swiftly, forsaking his notepad and his eagerness to at least take one of the girls down with him in hopes to impart some pain right the hell back, and preferably to the one that hit him first. He wondered where Wayne was, and he wanted desperately to prevent the other female from taking the widow.

But Tricks was already upon him. With one hand outstretched to hold the notepad just short of his reach and the other gripping the collar of his silky black loosely-buttoned dress shirt as she crawled up onto him, straddling him, she began talking matter-of-factly, "Where's the power of the great tree now? Maybe it had no power to begin with, though it certainly seemed that way until you and your friend downstairs asserted yourselves so. Always repelled us or any other vampire I've observed, that tree. Until now. What, did God turn off the switch again on our set of rules, like he did with crosses? Or has it always been just a matter of mindset and will?"

"It's a matter of *something*," answered Dayton, "and if you were privy enough to understand it all, unlike me, I would hope you'd be good enough to share your knowledge so we *all* could survive without having to look over our shoulders or watch for enemies flying out from the horizon."

"Look here, we're still standing," Tricks told Lata, dismissing what Dayton said. "I could have taken this place long ago. These men aren't special, because there never *was* any power here against us, just in our minds."

"Apparently," said Lata, "or maybe the tree's dying. It does look a little weathered."

Tricks pulled Dayton up to her, sneering down at him in contempt, and in doing so, the top four or five buttons of his shirt popped off and the silky material began to rip and tear, and he fell backwards against the solar paneling with Tricks still holding a piece of collar attached to the garment above the belly.

"Damn," she cursed, "just when I was about to tell him something climactic and witty while figuring out how I should kill him, and we have a wardrobe malfunction....."

Lata marched forward. "Allow *me*, let me throw him over a sharp fence post or do something equally lethal....."

Tricks was abruptly taken aback the moment Dayton's pendant came dangling and protruding out from between the torn seams over his bare chest. Upon seeing it, she freaked out, stumbled backwards and away, falling on her ass and still scooting down the roof shingles desperately, not in fear, but in complete disbelief. She dropped Dayton's notepad, momentarily, before she had mind to collect it up again, its importance to her increasing ten-fold from the status of something meaningless that she kept from the male to tease him.

Lata was spooked. "What? What's wrong? What do you see? Holy crap, Tricks….."

"My God," exclaimed Tricks to Dayton, her demeanor softening to an almost apologetic reverence. "I……I'm so sorry."

Escarlata was puzzled. "What are you doing???"

Dayton was equally puzzled, until he realized Tricks was transfixed by his alien pendant.

"Nothing," Tricks instructed, coming to her senses, pushing herself off the roof into the air, "just leave him alone. The plans still goes, just spare *him*. I'll figure things out later."

Lata took to the air as well, her, Tricks, and the notepad.

The third female was still struggling to pull the Widow Hamlin off the ground, and Dayton asserted his attentions towards the attempted theft, rolled himself completely off the roof and landed straight upon his feet into a fervent sprint.

"Wayne!" he cried out. "Wayne, you sonofabitch, get your ass out here, we have guests, and they *got our woman*….!"

Dayton raced across the small rectangular front grass lawn, leapt over a wheelbarrow and dashed through the vegetable garden, fishing line snapping against his weight and speed and making things easier for BB to carry away the widow's carcass like a vulture making a mad getaway with a large morsel of food. Lady Hamlin's body split in the process from the top to the bottom of her spine, down the seams as it was, in the same fashion as Dayton's shirt was torn, like a whole cooked fryer hen abandoned on the kitchen counter for a hot summertime seven days falling apart when you try to pick it up. Her clothing barely held her intact, ripping against the stubborn steal fish hooks, and some of her spilled out the sleeves and pant legs the way an exorbitant accumulation of shit in an infant's diaper would seep out and drop everywhere when you opened it.

Dayton nearly reached her when Wayne's voice shouted out from behind him, halting Day in his tracks, and he turned to see him, rushing out the front doorway.

"Dayton……shit, we're under attack!"

"Where were you, you prick?" Dayton yelled in response.

But before Wayne had a chance to respond, a figure came up from behind him out of the house, and with a swift kick pushed an unwary Wayne onto his belly and the square section of patio cementway.

It was Tom Hamlin, alive and walking, who stepped from out of the house and placed a thick alligator boot between Wayne's shoulder blades before raising a wooden cross half his height and plunging its pencil-sharpened bottom end straight into Wayne's upper back, all the way through until it was out the other side.

Wayne didn't move. Tom raised a hand to wave at Dayton, smiling with sarcasm, to indicate he didn't have a hand on that wrist, just a heavily bandaged stump.

"Made a deal with the girls," he cried out. "The price of my hand for the well-being of my wife and myself and my home, if I gave them food and resources, and helped 'em get rid of you two. That was before you killed my wife and disgraced my home, started playin' my DVDs and smokin' my weed. One down, one to go....."

Ol' Tom started for Dayton, and before Day turned away he noticed that the cross Wayne was impaled with must've been uprooted from the rear yard, its horizontal beam reading NO MORE YESTERDAY in carved lettering that shined beneath the front porch light. By the time he saw the bald-headed she-thing reach far away into the sky with her half of Tom's wife, meeting up with the other two females that assaulted him upon the rooftop, they were too far away to pursue.

But Dayton was relentless. He pushed himself away from the ground, spread his arms, and swam through the air in their direction several yards before he plummeted to the dry dirt ground, rolled over onto his stomach and puked half a bucket of red disgusting partially digested slop. When he pulled himself away from his puke, he cast his gaze in the direction of Tom Hamlin, who was as ever-approaching as a killer in a slasher film. Dayton fumbled to his feet to prepare himself for a fight, and it was a fight he was hungry for, never mind the girls, for this bastard had murdered his friend right before his eyes, mercy not a factor.

As soon as he stood upright, his left heel sunk into a muddy slope his regurgitation was partially responsible for, and he fell over face-first, slid limply down a sloped embankment away from the garden until he found himself chin-deep in a pool of water accumulated from the tiny rapids that cascaded over the soil from the tomato area and into the patch of tall grass that now surrounded him. He jolted up again, to his knees, wiped the muck from his face. Tom was stepping over the remains of his wife through the tomato patch while pulling a solar torch from out of the ground to position it over his shoulder like one of the African natives with a spear in *The Naked Prey,* about to chuck one into a nude but ever-evasive Cornell Wilde as they hunted him across the savanna.

But then Dayton slipped once more as he tried to rise, and his entire head fell into the shallow pool. He was never this clumsy, but he was feverishly irate and fearing for his own supposedly immortal life, and not thinking too clearly at all. Besides, it wasn't supposed to be wet anywhere here outside the vegetable area, unless the sprinklers had gone awry when he'd been rooftop writing and not paying attention to anything else. His head beneath the soil like an ostrich , his attentions riveted to what he saw out the other end, like he'd found himself gone right clear through to China.

There was a spacious vacuum of air on the opposite side, and darkness......an awning ceiling, the sounds of flowing water, the sliding glass doors of a patio leading into a house very familiar to him, a suburban backyard, a glimmer of yesteryear. A vision, perhaps, and nothing more, but for a fleeting moment it was as tangible as the real thing.

Thing was, Dayton's ass was still sticking out into the world above, where a good friend had just been impaled by a man who was coming after him to do the same thing because he helped kill his wife.

Those bitches, he thought as he pulled himself out of the red wet dirt, thoroughly enraged. He rose to find Tom Hamlin directly behind him. Because he only had one hand, he found it difficult to keep as good of a grip upon the solar light rod as he did the cross, mostly because the rod was thicker than he could wrap one hand around, and it was six feet long. Dayton tore the rod away from him with no problem and beat the old man back with it, striking first his head, then his side, then his head again. The man fell to the ground and cowered from the blows, crawling up the embankment in a fevered attempt to get away.

Dayton wouldn't allow him that. He continued to pound and pulverize the living fuck out of the man before he was barely recognizable as human, drove the sharp end of the rod into his abdomen until he became nothing more than a morbid tiki torch stand when he died.

Dayton then sprinted toward the house, rushed to his friend's side on the cement before the front door, pulled the cross from his chest and heaved it out of the way. He turned Wayne over onto his back, ever so carefully, set him down and remained there on his knees, not knowing what else to do. There was now a gaping hole in Wayne's rib cage, bones cracked and bent away from each other like prison bars after a world's strongest man demonstration, blood pooling into the cavity and trickling out from between Wayne's lips and streaming over the cement underneath the both of them. Wayne's eyes fluttered open. He was alive, but he was dying.

"I got the bastard," Dayton said to him, extremely distraught. "It was Tricks Matrix and two of her girls. I wasn't looking out for us as good as I should have. I'm sorry......"

Wayne was about to say something, cleared his throat, spit a blood clot from his mouth that trailed down his cheek and cleared his throat again. "Didn't see that one coming, bro. I mean, *I* didn't either. It wasn't just you. I was caught up in the house discovering new things. Found some bottles of cheap rum and bourbon whiskey."

"Wayne, what can I do?"

"We are immortal, we will prevail, we are out of our minds......"

"But we're not immortal, are we?" Dayton questioned.

"Not when shit happens," Wayne forced a reply, "but we are certainly out of our minds....."

"Wayne...."

"Dayton," he said, "you take care of the house as best you can, damn those bitches. You know what? The coupla chainsaws in the sheds out back? You wanna know what you can do?"

"Tell me....."

"Go up in that old oak tree, trim it, cut it, make it look like Sam Hall's hangin' tree. If there's any power left in it, turning it into a replica should intensify that power, don'tcha think? Maybe it'll ward off the girls, buy you time. Worse comes to worst, load up that Mustang in the garage and get away from here. I knew our oasis here would change hands again, it was just a matter of time."

Taking a chainsaw to the tree sounded like a crazy waste of time.

"Wayne, I think this thing I got around my neck is responsible for our surviving the blast which killed most of the rest of us, because you were near me when it happened, and I think it has a power, too, and that may be why we were able to......."

"What?" Wayne tried to chuckle, but coughed out a seepage of black blood in the process. "That alien face? I'm not surviving *now*, am I? I'm dying here."

Dayton had expected Wayne to be dead already, by the time he'd finished off ol' Tom and rushed to his aide, so there was no time to lose in talking things out. "I saw a vision, out past the garden. I think it was the patio of my parents' house. Wayne, I was *there*! What does that *mean*?"

"You wanna know why I wanted to be a Black Hero?" Wayne asked, not fully comprehending what Dayton was trying to tell him. "It was because I wanted to live forever. Unlike you, who had no idea what the hell you were getting into, because you wanted to be a goody-good and do things for the community. Isn't that funny? There's no fucking *community* left, and *I* wanted to live *forever*......"

"Yeah," Dayton said, and sighed. "That's funny, Wayne. That's funny."

***

Dayton had no time to lose after Wayne ceased talking and his eyes turned glossy. He wasn't sure what to expect from his friend throughout the next few hours until morning. Vampires didn't die easily, so was the way he understood things, and in light of the fact that any supposed mortal impaled through the chest with a sharpened two-by-four would have been dead instantly without the opportunity to say dying words, Dayton had held a vague hope that throughout the course of time Wayne would eventually heal up good as new, but that never happened.

Day brought Wayne's body into the house, set him down upon the livingroom sofa, and popped in *Naked Prey* on the television DVD player if for no other reason but to honor him. He gathered the remains of ol' Tom, placed his remains in the same garage freezer chest as they'd been keeping the widow during the day, tidied up as best as he could outside, all the while tempted to place his head into the red wet dirt down the embankment beyond the tomato patch. There was simply no time for that. The sun was coming up soon, and he had a last dying wish to fulfill for his friend, no matter how ridiculous it seemed.

He went into one of the backyard sheds soon as he could, powered up one of them chainsaws, and went to work shaping the great oak tree into what best resembled the notorious Sam Hall hangin' tree, after locating and confiscating the widow's hand-held chiseled wooden image of the one she'd tried to use against Wayne that fell from her grip to the garden soil when it didn't quite work for her, and he set it upon a rollaway stool out back to use for a model as he worked.

Come sunrise, Dayton had situated himself into his resting place inside the Hamlin's master bedroom's walk-in closet, switched on the surveillance monitors and intrusion alarms, forsook Wayne's remains upon the sofa which by then had decimated to a grey dust by the time he was through with everything, and had himself a most unusual-looking tree overseeing the property, with a hanging rope to boot slung over one branch strung up at one end into a noose.

***

The following evening found Dayton sobbing, just before sunset, upon his makeshift bed besides racks of shoes and surrounded by the dresses and slacks and sport coats still hanging on closet rods, facing the door and the monitors surrounding it. When he opened his eyes he ceased crying, wiping the tears away, checked the monitors and the red and green lights and glowing digital readouts of the security system, and the alarm on the bedside plastic clock which was set to go off at a certain time but never did.

He wasn't sure why he woke up crying. Must've been something he was dreaming about that affected him so, but he didn't think he *had* dreams as a vampire because he never remembered any of them. And he never cried since, either. Not even for his family. It gave him an eerie feeling.

As he rested there for just a few lingering lazy moments longer, all the monitors at once turned to static, which immediately

227

jolted Dayton into the world of the living, wide awake and alert. An image began to form within the realm of static on each television of a single face, a man's face beset with age, with shoulder-length hair parted to one side and a matching beard that swallowed the lower half of his face a couple inches out, except for his lips which parted and spoke to him in surround sound. And there weren't any surround sound speakers in the closet.

"Dayton," it said to him, stern and resolute but forced, like a father's last words to his son. "There is no more yesterday. No more yesterday, but for *you*."

The monitors receded into full screen static again, before flipping back into their regular modes and settings.

Dayton sat straight up. He wore the kind of shorts that reminded him of his high school gym class and a white triple-x-large t-shirt which drooped over them to the extent that it looked like the shirt was all he was wearing, exhibiting the words *you get 'em, we spread 'em (back to nature)* in an advert for Phoenix Recycling. He bent over and crouched in front of the screens, did a quick inspection of the equipment, then leaned backwards and fumbled for a two-liter bottle of unopened ginger ale standing upright on Wayne's small cot. He unscrewed the cap, fell backwards, and dowsed his face with its contents until it was depleted.

"God," Dayton said aloud, "I thought by now I'd be saving the world, or helping *someone* who was going to. But this *is* the world, where I *am right now*, isn't it? Is this how it ends for me? Alone? Surrounded by creature comforts that only matter if I can enjoy them? And for how long will this last? Forever? Am I becoming delusional and afraid that I could die at any time just like Wayne?"

What a hearty hello to the evening.

And then he remembered the patch of grass beyond the tomato garden, and everything he wanted to do that couldn't get done that prior morning.

***

A distance away, someone else awoke crying, and she too hadn't let out a single teardrop since she was made a vampire, nor since could she dream dreams.

"Trisha, wake up, you've made yourself upset," said Drummer, who'd only stirred from slumber five minutes ago to her friend's distressing sobbing.

Tricks stirred into consciousness, rolled to her side and opened her eyes wearily. "Um....did you just call me what I think you called me?"

Drummer pulled her hair to one side, matted from deep sleep like she'd been submerged into a pillow for weeks. "Sorry. But only humans cry, at least more often than us. Thought you'd respond better if I used the name you've had all your life before *we* came along.........."

"And all my death, I'm another thing entirely."

"So true," said Escarlata, stepping into view from behind, wearing what Drummer wore, what everyone in their camp wore when they slept lately.....sweat shorts and t-shirts. "But now that you're awake, we must figure out just what happened between you and the male last night, and since you read his memoirs, certainly you must share."

Drummer reached for a book of matches and proceeded to light candles within the small cave they all shared. The other girls, seven adult vampires in all besides Tricks and Latta and Drummer, were at work just outside the cave setting up camp with tents and a small fire and weathered wooden beams that provided shelters from the red rain when they were set up proper with plastic sheeting. It was a nightly ritual, for none of them dared leave any clues to their presence during daylight hours should human survivors venture into the canyon and discover a settlement of vulnerable voluptuous women, vampire or not. At night, they had no worries of that sort, only worries of another nuclear bomb being dropped upon *them*, this time.

Tricks, like the rest of her sisters during the day, had been resting upon an old comforter and several blankets within the deepest reaches of the cave, which was a good thirty meters in. Around them were stacks of canned meats, hands guns and rifles and a litter of old stuffed animals both of toy store and taxidermy origin, three motorized wheelbarrows and several opened umbrellas fixed upon the cave ceiling with spikes used for mountain climbing, or crampons as they were called, for decoration and in defiance of indoor umbrella superstition, and the wordplay between crampons and tampons sparked a daily ritual of jest directed towards it.

"Lata," Tricks told her, "I read the male's memoirs on that tablet I stole from him, and I saw what he had around his neck. I know who he is, and I thought he was dead. Tonight, I'm going back to the Hamlin house. *Alone*."

Not far away from them, at the northern mouth of the canyon where the girls had settled, there stood a lone man in shadow, both him and his horse, behind a cover of Joshua trees, and he would remain there in careful watch for a few hours longer before he'd decide to head out in the direction of the homestead once more so he, from a distance, could watch that too.

***

Dayton dressed himself in nothing more than black jeans for the evening, set right to work taking care of matters that were on his mental agenda. Firstly, he cased the property, finding all was quiet and determining there was nothing yet that required his concern approaching his desert sanctuary.

He then tended to Wayne's remains, carefully gathering the grey dust upon the livingroom sofa where he'd placed him early that morning with a hand broom into a metal dustpan, then dropped into a shallow hole in the soil below the kitchen window between a half dozen rosemary plants, after which he inserted the very NO MORE YESTERDAY cross which Tom Hamlin had driven through his back.

He found the alcohol stash Wayne told him he discovered before all hell had come down on them, and the cheap generic liquor store rum went down smooth half a fifth's worth by the time he decided to venture into the tomato area of the garden and pick some of the softball-sized red beefsteak ones hoping they tasted like the widow Hamlin's blood. And that they did. They were delicious, and he gathered a basketful, buried what was left of Tom's wife right there so more of her tasty goodness would seep up into another juicy crop.

Of course, he was extremely curious about that section of grass and mud just past the garden over the embankment, and since he awoke earlier, he'd been drawn to it. Truth is, he was also afraid of it, and he'd been taking his time getting around to checking it out once again, delving into more concrete matters like burying his friend and picking tomatoes before he built up the nerve to venture in that direction. Given time to ponder, he was also beginning to suspect that perhaps, if he wasn't truly out of his mind and what he experienced in that area just before he beat Tom Hamlin to death was real, it was some sort of trap or trick. If it was, then who on this godforsaken earth was capable of such hocus pocus?

If that wasn't the case, and all he had to do to was to submerge himself into the wet soil to escape this world and return to his parents' house or to even see his family again, as remarkable as it seemed, what would he find there? And what would be the repercussions, the consequences of going back, if indeed it was some sort of time porthole he discovered that could be utilized to *save* his family?

He set the basket of tomatoes down for a sec, decided to step over a handful of yards. Ol' Tom was there on the slope, solar stake having fallen into the dirt over the course of the day, the extreme heat of daylight hour sun having done seemingly more damage to him than Dayton had done himself, and more than likely a few predators had made parts of him an afternoon snack, so it appeared.

The ground seemed very dry, the weather having sucked up the moisture while he'd been sleeping. He slid himself down past Tom's carcass, set foot on the area which had swallowed the upper half of his body when he fell after trying to chase down the vampire bitch who tore apart and stole away their scarecrow widow. He brushed his bare feet upon the ground, stomped around a bit and, growing even more stubborn and disappointed, hopped around and danced a triple two-step. Nothing happened, and he sauntered over to Ol' Tom and kicked him upside the head for it, as if Tom was the perpetrator of this frustrating farce. Tom's head broke away from his mangled corpse, tumbled down the slope and rolled onto the dirt area as if to say *hey stupid, even I can prove there's nothing here.*

Dayton resolved himself to tend to other affairs, abandoning the area and sojourning back to the house, eyes canvassing the skies and surrounding terrain for signs of eminent danger. He decided to continue with his writing from last night, even though what he accomplished so far had been taken from him. He almost wanted to do so in spite of everything, though somehow he felt he had to, and, boldly, he situated himself upon the rooftop between the solar panels with a pen and new notepad and a fifth of cheap rum, and continued with his account of how he became a vampire at the end of the world.

This time, however, he would try to keep watch more carefully......

13.

BECOMING LIKE TOAD, CONTINUED
By Dayton Monday

The Brotherhood of the Black Heroes' Annual Camp Meetin' and Bean Feed, for us initiates, had proven to be a living hell thus far until we were brought up onto that stage to have sex for the last time as full-fledged human beings before our transition into the fold of vampires was a done deal. The colossal bonfire in our midst was raging, its smoke blanketing the night sky, Brothers shouting their *we are immortal* credo and singing aloud yet another rendition of Cash's *Ring of Fire* while some even formed a mosh pit of sorts which took on a life of its own, Brothers dancing and slamming into other Brothers, chucking beer mugs into the flames before laughing and falling over or rushing to the stage to taunt the initiates into fucking their partners faster. These were hellraisers, that was for damn sure, but during the climax of our hazing I never thought that term would turn out to be a literal one.

Released from whatever restraints had held them in the camp outskirts came dozens of unclad women and men, rushing past the multitude of Black Sheets after emerging from among them, all of them varying adult ages. One older man, like the woman before him, made a mad dash towards the bonfire and dove head-first into it. Another gave her life the same way, but most simply stopped short of the flames, appearing confused, wandering and spinning about like the wound-up toys of a shopping mall store front display table. One woman caught my eye as she about-faced in an unbridled attempt to flee, only to be held fast and tossed backwards into several others, causing a dozen of them to stumble forward like dominoes onto the ground and perilously close to being burned alive themselves. It was obvious to me that not one of them had come here willingly, and knowing they were all about to die or were dying already made me nauseous. The poor souls, it seemed, were resolved to their awful fate, and it soon became apparent to me that the ones with any sense of a premeditated plan of what to

233

do with their circumstances were the ones to immediately rush into the flames to get their deaths over with; the ones who remained were very soon to become food. But not for the Brothers.

As I gazed upwards, I caught sight of many bat-like shapes hovering and flying from out of the towering black smoke. The air became thick with them.....sickly, human/mammalian dwarfed deformities, the abominations of a netherworld no longer nether but right before my eyes, the illustrations in a demonology encyclopedia come to life with full HD clarity. One by one, the humans scurrying about futilely to save themselves were attacked, some tackled to the ground, torn apart and immediately feasted upon with ravenous abandon. Others were seized, taken up and carried away like helpless vermin, their struggles unavailing and their eyes wide and petrified like rabbits in the talons of hungry falcons.

I found myself staring down at the young woman I held, her flesh pressed against mine, sweat upon sweat, soul against soul, and she held onto me for comfort as for any degree of comfort in return I was holding onto her. Sex with her was by far out of the question. Only a maniac would indulge under these conditions, and I knew deep down I wasn't like anyone present. It was too late for sex anyway.

"Please save me," the girl pleaded.

Toad, directly behind me, apparently heard her, mocked her.

"Oh Dayton, oh my darling please save me," he mimicked in a high squeaky voice. Then, he remarked with awestruck glee, "A sight to see, ain't it, buddy? Look at 'em all, having fun like that. Those ugly fuckers that came down, they've existed since way before Ferency Nadasdy was swimmin' around in his old man's semen and before all that bullshit happened with his wife the Countess. They're our guests, they've come a long way to get here and don't visit very often. Yep, it's a special night, for damn sure."

My ability to communicate vocally had exited stage right, and before I could summon the will and the courage to beg him to spare my eternal soul and return me to my precious home and family, to weep and beseech him for humanity's sake like a little boy stripped of all inhibition and laden with the sort of remorse and humility any true neighbor and friend *had* to take pity on, he took me.

He took me, and in doing so, he took me away, not away from our places on the stage, not out from the arms of the woman I embraced nor from such madness as no greater scene in hell could portray, but from the mortal life I knew. When he came down upon me it was like I'd been stabbed in the side of my neck with a fork, the pain excruciating, and he held me fast. My heart pounded. My body lapsed into the sort of seizure I can only describe as a vicious leg muscle cramp I could not massage into docility which overcame the whole of my physical structure until it subsided and my body stiffened, paralyzed.

Vampire venom was nasty, and I experienced that fact firsthand before I succumbed to that state of rag doll submissiveness enough for Toad to drain me and rob my bodily functions of the life which had kept them going strong for twenty-two years. I felt my organs shut down like the lights of an office building switched off a section at a time by a custodian having mopped his last restroom floor going home for the night. Something snapped from within my gut, like a wire spring popping loose within a mechanical clock. My ears crackled like radio airwave static that switched off into silence. My heart spasmed and flipped as though it had been tossed into a tumble dryer before I felt it turn inside-out as it seemed, before it stopped beating altogether. My bowels churned, and whatever they held emptied with an accompanying sensation not unlike a soft serve machine actively soft-serving. I stopped breathing. I lost my vision.

The next sensation I encountered was Toad's grip upon my shoulders loosening, relaxing, scissors-sharp teeth retreating out of my lower neck, and my vision was suddenly restored to find the up-close-and-personal sight of his arm torn open at the wrist before he thrust the wound against my mouth, arteries and veins erupting into an orgasm of blood which brought my lips to life, then my jaw muscles, my tongue, my throat. I absorbed the bloodflow rather than drank, and my swallowing was just a reflex and nothing more, for I felt the blood invade and reanimate every cell of my body from that point on like a firecracker string ignited by the intake. My heart stirred, however faintly, then switched gears the way a computer printer would turn on and warm up and slide its ink cartridges into place.

Toad yanked his wrist free. I was energized, though oblivious to everything around me at first but Toad, myself, the girl, and Johnny Cash.

"Hey Dayton, buddy," said Toad to me, "what a rush, huh?"

My eyes focused upon the girl who still clung to me for dear life, fearing she would at any moment be facing certain death. She was trembling, and I continued to hold her, not knowing what to do next.

"Take her now," Toad persuaded, "Go ahead.....lean forward and bite into her like bobbing for that apple you just know you could have if you submerged yourself and struck down hard enough. You need to take her life. It's almost over now, all this.....it's almost over...."

"Fifteen minutes, hot showers," I managed to say, recounting what I'd been hearing all night. "I don't want to kill her."

"She's yours. You must. Then it'll be over and we can both of us have some drinks and laugh about it and grill up something meaty."

"Please....." the girl cried out to me, her head slouched forward onto my shoulder and buried there, her embrace solid and tightening like a scared child.

By the time I took notice of the other initiates, each one of them had been converted and had already gorged themselves upon the blood of their human partners, discarding the lifeless bodies across the stage as easily as slamming down the last set of chicken bones in a hot wings-eating contest at the state fair after time was called, and a handful of Brothers emerged from the festal crowd, dragging the carcasses off to pitch them into the bonfire. Eyes were drawn towards me, and I was beginning to get the feeling I was becoming an embarrassment to my sponsor.

"Don't you see why I brought you're here?" Toad implored. "Man, you can't say what I did for you wasn't worth it. Didn't that just give you a sense of profound liberation from the shackles of your daily trivial existence, after wanting more but constantly finding yourself trapped within the confines of the waking world where you're constantly questioning the meaning of your life in the warm sunshine when all the while the night was calling, like death, which is really where all the fun begins? You know, Mankind is inherently drawn towards nightlife, where they can't wait to break free from their daily routines and bust-a-move soon as the sun goes down."

I responded, "I've seen you walk about in the daytime as regular as any human being. You were my friend. Why did you bring me into this?"

"Why," answered Toad, "so we can be buddies *forever*. And yes, over the course of time we've learned to live and work in daylight hours, we've become highly adaptive, you know, but night is our bliss. Matter of fact, there ain't no light bright enough to harm us anymore, and maybe, someday, we'll even get beyond this thing about crosses....."

"I still won't kill her."

Toad had enough of me. Enraged, he tore the girl off of me, pushed me to one side.

"Awe, fuck you, ya panty-waste" he spat, extremely disappointed, and he took my girl, sunk his protruding fangs deep into her neck, and she screamed out to me with a single hand extended in a desperate effort to summon my aide. I tried to tear them apart, but Toad backhanded me with such a force it sent me flying onto my ass and into the new vampire right next to me, toppling him down as well.

***

In the next instant, distracting everyone within the camp, the sky split in two as though God Himself opened the bedroom door to our surreal slumber party, catching us all at an awkward moment as if we were doing things we weren't supposed to be doing, like we should have known better, shame on us, and we were going to pay dearly for it without milk and cookies.

Night turned to day with a flick of that heavenly switch, the same moment as the loudspeaker Johnny Cash music morphed into yet another song, even more boisterous, ringing through my ears to the point that it hurt.

My name it is Sam Hall, it is Sam Hall......

Across the night sky there came a series of images as though projected from the spotlights of a premier car dealership, which even the bonfire smoke could not conceal from those below. The face of a man times two dozen cascaded across the stratosphere, white-bearded, white-haired, swirling about and then standing still, then swirling about again, his lips moving, talking, but no one could hear what he was saying for the music.

Toad separated from the girl for a moment long enough for me to take the opportunity to push her off the stage, and I fell along with her, grabbed her, held onto her, took her with me beneath the stage's wooden platform for shelter, my used-to-be friend as distracted as anyone else by what was going on above.

"It's okay, I got you," I told her in an attempt to comfort her, "you're going to be safe...."

She was shivering, near death, and I was beside myself with trying to figure out what I should do. All around us, the Brothers and flying wizened creatures and what remained of their prey that was still alive were all in a chaotic frenzy, and Toad was calling out to me.

"Goddammit, Dayton, we're not done with you!" cried Toad. "You nor the rest of your lineup have chosen your Black Sheet names, and what the fuck is going on???!!"

Suddenly there came another voice from directly behind me. "Dude, she's dying. If you're gonna save her, give her your blood....."

I looked, and the guy that had been beside me on the stage was lying with us, cowering, and because we were all naked I wouldn't let him get any closer. I felt funny that way. I thought for a moment, trying to comprehend what he was saying, then as I realized what I should do I immediately brought my mouth to my left wrist and tore it open in desperate abandon with my newfound sharp incisors, forced it into the mouth of the girl. At first, she pushed it away. But I insisted, and in no time she fed from my veins hungrily.

One of the winged ancient ones fluttered to our whereabouts and landed less than a yard away, set its knuckles down upon the dirt, sniffed the air, its eyes scanning the three of us. In many ways, it resembled Triad.....same height, same features, but hairy and rodent-like, baring a rat-long tail like a nightcrawler earthworm, with human-like fingers and toes sporting sharp extensions that would come close to the Guinness record for longest nails, and a set of leathery wings that were almost as short as Daniel Cupid's. When it realized the girl was feeding on me, it shook a single finger my way like a high school principle catching a couple students having sex beneath the gym bleachers but letting it go because he was way too embarrassed to say anything.

But then it stopped, suddenly curious about me in particular, and while my wrist remained fixed against the girl's lips it approached me. I followed its gaze towards my chest and realized it was fascinated with my red alien face pendant. It let out a squawk of disapproval and fluttered away into the mayhem of the camp.

Outside of us, I could hear the music, the words echoing forth and encompassing all of us……

"My name is Samuel, and I'll see you all in hell, damn your eyes!"

A second later was when the bright lights came. The stage above us melted against their intense heat, and every single thing which moved was incinerated as though the bonfire itself burst into a supernova, though I knew what hit us fell straight out of the sky. I held tight to the girl, and the vampire beside us held onto me as well, frightened and blinded and thinking he was about to die. But he didn't.

Neither did I, nor the girl.

After the blast, I was alone, and there was nothing left around me but scorched earth and charred fragments of material things. Likely, I'd been out for hours, even days, and after I was able to stand I found myself wandering around in circles across a barren desert beneath a crimson nighttime sky, unable to withstand the intense red rays of a new sun enough to bury myself deep in the soil to escape from it, until nighttime fell again and I learned, eventually, to survive and make good of everything despite the often relentless downpour of harsh red rain.

A short while further I came across a few other survivors who filled my ears with information concerning the current state of the world, and soon afterwards my own world developed into what it came to be.

14.

TRICKS, SAM HALL, AND THE RED WET DIRT

Dayton set down his pen and notepad, took a swig of rum, sighed. There was more to write about, that much was certain, but it only concerned his doldrum exploits in the endless desert wasteland and the few souls he'd encountered there, the myths he'd learned about crosses and trees and Sam Hall, how he and Wayne crossed paths after the end of the world, bits and pieces that were only relevant in an appendix if indeed he was writing a book, which he wasn't. Really, the reason for his writing anything in the first place was to get his mind together, his thoughts on paper, to help him figure things out, and then there was the slight chance that should he die someone else eventually would come across what he wrote and understand at least a piece of his existence's pie, if they ever cared to.

Besides, tonight he'd been paying attention to more than just writing and drinking and doing some thinking. Tonight, unlike last night, he'd been actively keeping an eye out for potential visitors. He spotted a solitary female figure approaching in the night sky coming from the direction of Trick's clan, her hair so thick and long it doubled her size, and she made no effort not to be seen. Since she truly appeared to be alone, Dayton wasn't extremely alarmed. He at first figured it was a messenger. She wore a black sleeveless tank top and black faded jeans torn every which way, and seemed to be carrying something in one hand......pages of paper......a very familiar-looking notepad which flapped and fluttered in the gusts of breeze she created with every determined armstroke forward beneath the canvass of stars.......

Dayton pretended not to notice her, made himself appear to be preoccupied with writing and took another swig of rum, hoping that perhaps *he* could catch *her* off guard this time if his obliviousness ploy was convincing enough. She arrived upon the roof, bare feet landing a couple of long solar panels to his right, past the brick chimney he'd been thrown into around this time the night prior by one of her binocular-eyed vixens.

"Dayton," she said as she approached, halting just a few yards away. She sounded deliberately reserved, she knew his name, she wanted to talk, and he raised his head to look directly at her. She held out to him the very notepad she'd laughed over and stolen from him. She seemed apologetic, even remorseful, and it appeared as if she didn't know what to say to him before she spoke again more confidently. "I'm the one you held in your arms at the end of the world, up there on that stage for everyone to watch you rape and kill me. Remember? You risked your own life to refuse to do anything but hold me, to keep me safe. You stood up against a centuries-old vampire king for *me*. You tore out your wrist and gave me life again after he took mine, without a single selfish thought, and you sheltered me when the lights came that destroyed all the civilization I ever knew. How I got there in your arms and the creature I became afterwards wasn't your fault. You saved me. With all my soul, I am indebted to you, Dayton, and I'll gladly give you my life in return for what happened last night. I thought you were dead until then, I'm sorry, I didn't know. But I must humble myself even further than that. I love you."

She knelt as one would to show respect for a lord, setting the notepad at her side, head down, and Dayton found himself utterly speechless for almost a good hour's time.

Tricks had already said enough after her first couple of sentences for recognition to strike him silly, and she was so servile and sorrowful that he was sure he could maintain the silence between them clear through until sunrise. The length of her silence gave him time to ponder, but also provided further evidence that she was dead serious of her intentions, because nobody except for maybe *Ghandi* would attempt to remain still for so long just to prove a point to one person.

During that time, and after swallowing many more swigs of that good ol' amber toxin-in-a-bottle that had been his best friend since he'd brought it up there with him, Dayton found his attentions drifting from Tricks to that damnably curious patch of soil and grass beyond the tomatoes that seemed to have dried up earlier. He would study Tricks for a few moments, revert his gaze towards that patch, then he'd take the alien face pendant that forever dangled from his neck as if to ask whether *it* had any bright ideas, until Dayton came up with a bright idea of his own.

He rose with his rum and notepad, and said to Tricks after an exhausted sigh, "I take it the tree thing didn't fend you off."

Tricks cast a glance to the great oak tree, or what remained of it after its chainsaw encounter with Dayton. "I noticed it. Nice work. I think what really kept us from encountering each other up close and personal was all that goddamn red rain we'd been having. And other factors. But it's obvious this tree thing isn't working. I'm beginning to think it was just a myth from the beginning."

"What I want to know is," Dayton asked after a pause for reflection, "what did you think?"

She looked up at him, not knowing what he meant. "I'm sorry?"

"What I wrote. What did you think?" He motioned a finger to the notepad beside her.

"It made me understand you, what you went through and why."

"So instead of, like, pissing on it, you chose to read it and *that* clued you in?"

"No. What clued me in was what you wear around your neck, because with all that beard and hippy hairstyle and how I thought you were dead, go figure……"

"Yeah," Dayton said, "this thing around my neck. "It's about time I get to the bottom of what it means, maybe put it to use. Meet me down below. I gotta get myself a shovel."

He slid off the roof, landing with both feet firmly on the ground like a kid jumping off a playground slide, and raced into the house. Tricks followed suit, waited for him just outside. He re-emerged with his rum in one hand and a heavy duty shovel in the other. He sauntered past her, and, having no idea what he had in mind, trailed along behind him. Together, they ventured past the garden and down the dirt embankment where Ol' Tom still lay.

When Dayton found the right spot, he set down his booze and began to dig.

***

"What's out here?" Tricks found herself asking.

By the time she spoke, Day had already dug himself a hole a couple feet deep, until red watery liquid sprung out from the

242

bottom like the black oil of a Jed Clampett-wanna-be's wet dream. Dayton relinquished his shovel and began to dig into the muddy red dirt with his hands.

"Destiny, I hope," he replied. "Or at least answers….."

With one hand, he reached deep into the ground, and the further he lowered himself, the more easily his hand and arm slid through into a void filled with a substance as fluid as pure water…….and then he felt his hand slip into a pocket of nothingness as though it had submerged from an inverted swimming pool into air.

Tricks tried to get his attention, distracted by something approaching them. "Dayton….."

"Okay beautiful," Dayton told her, ready to plunge into his own personal time portal face-first, confident and even jubilant that he found what he was looking for and that it was indeed real, "I trust you. Wait for me. This is going to seem very weird to you, but I'll be back in a heartbeat."

He raised his head, took a deep breath.

"Whatever you're going to do," Tricks told him plainly, "well……we have *company*."

***

Dayton pulled himself up to attention, grabbing the shovel, following her gaze into the open prairie outside the property. Not far away, a horse was approaching, the semblance of a man walking beside it, leading it along by its bridle in a casual pace. When he came into view, he looked very familiar; an older man, white beard and hair, and from his free hand dangled a necklace which he lifted in front of him.

"This is an age of miracles and mayhem," he announced to the both of them. "A hole in the ground that can take you back a buncha years ain't nothing compared to some of the shit *I've* seen lately. But truth be told, the Lord sent me here. He said I must go hereabouts and search the desert for an undead soul, to whom love was proclaimed and a door has been opened. When I find him I'm supposed to give him something that I see you already have."

He lifted the necklace into view, stopping just short of several feet away, cautious of Dayton's shovel raised to strike should he come any closer.

Dayton immediately knew what it was, composed himself, pitched the shovel into the ground, straightened his pants and wiped away most of the mud from his hands and arms. Everything was suddenly quite clear to him, as though he'd dreamt of this moment a long time ago, or like déjà vu, and he was certain this happened before. He reached for the pendant, took it, brought it to his chest and compared it with the one hanging there.

"They're exactly the same," Dayton said.

"I didn't expect you to have one already," the old man told him. "I take it as a sign that we're doing the right thing here. The Lord said that together we'll do the world a great service. Um......you too, ma'am."

Tricks glared back at him, both suspicious and slightly dumbfounded.

Dayton responded, "So.....you're supposed to give this to me, then I slip back in time through this hole in the ground to give this to myself the night I was taken away to join the Black Heroes."

"Bingo," said the old man, "but you must do it right so you're not seen by just anyone, especially not yourself back then. Give it to your sister when no one is around, instruct her to give it to your other self somehow. And then get the hell out of there and back up here. Back in that time, when you go through the Black Heroes thing, none of them will hurt you. The most intuitive of them will know by looking at it that if they do anything to interfere with your destiny, it'll create a deadly paradox that could destroy us all. And your destiny is to deliver it back then so everything that has happened comes full circle. Tonight's the night, son."

"Why an alien face?" Dayton asked.

The horse grunted.

"No reason," the man shrugged his shoulders. "It could have been anything, but it made sense that you'd be least likely to lose it if it was something you could wear at all times. I bought the thing at a flea market in Bakersfield for twenty dollars from a little girl who said she was hungry and that was all she had to sell."

"So," Dayton continued, "who are *you*?"

The old man reached out his hand to shake Day's, and Dayton obliged. "I am the Reverend Samuel Hall, clairvoyant who dabbles in a little wizardry you might say, ex-television evangelist and homeless person. I killed a man so they said, and they hung me for it, but that was in a past life and I'm redeemed now. A soldier for Jesus all the way, man."

244

"*The* Sam Hall?" Tricks stared in disbelief.

"Yeah," said Sam, "that same guy whose face was seen in skies all over the world. I had the country rigged up so I could spread the word of Jesus before it was too late and those goddamn terrorist nukes struck, but apparently nobody listened, and they think *I* am the Messiah, the ones who survived. Like you. Hell, I heard the Heroes were even playing my song when the end came."

"Who else survived?" Tricks interjected.

"Some of the small towns," Sam said. "Clifton's a journey, but it's the closest......."

Dayton asked, turning to Tricks to present the same question to her, "Why is it that freaky shit waits until I've downed a half bottle of 90 proof to happen? This is all too much for me at once. It's evident I have to go back. I get it. When I return, we can all roast marshmallows and get to know each other, and I can allow everything to sink in, then we can figure out how to save the rest of the world. Right now, I don't care what you say......if this is a doorway that can take me back to see my family, to a time before the world ended........I'm going through it."

Dayton stuffed the other pendant into his front pants pocket, and without further hesitation, nor paying any mind to the reverend's increasingly fervent warnings, he crawled into the hole and disappeared into the mud.

But not before stealing a soft kiss from Tricks and promising to return, which was the clearest positive indication he'd given her so far that everything between them was what she was hoping for, and after a whispered plea for her not to eat Sam Hall while he was away.

15.

THE VAMPIRE SAVIOR

So it's a game?
Yes, it's a game, and we're gonna win it......
***

The vampire Dayton had bid Kira, his little sister, a solemn goodbye, left her standing in front of the closed door to his bedroom, in the hallway, with his alien face pendant in her hand and dumbfounded by her encounter with him shirtless and soaking wet and with lots of hair. He'd instructed her to give the pendant to the friend in his room, that it was all part of the Black Heroes initiation she was privy to, that he loved her and to tell his parents he loved them, too.

"So it's a game?" she had asked.......

Dayton had been awestruck when he'd emerged from out of the waters of the above-ground patio fish pond and fountain out back beneath the awning. He knew what he needed to do, and to do it quickly.

But when he emerged from the hallway into the livingroom, mission accomplished, he halted, stood for a moment, and withdrew from his front pants pocket the *other* alien face pendant. He felt Kira watching him, knew he had to move quickly before she opened his bedroom door and did a double-take, and for him to run into his vampire abductors would risk certain catastrophe.

A deadly paradox.

But then, he got to thinking.....

He was with his family again......he could *do* something, maybe even make a difference after all, which is why he joined the Black Heroes in the first place......

......and if everything happened before, according to his déjà vu feeling, he certainly didn't have another of what he now held in his hands.....

......a second chance......

....and he thought, *surely if I decided to do something, any deadly paradox can't be much worse than what I'm headed back to.*

And then he thought of the bright lights he could not prevent from coming, and how he *truly* had no time to lose......

***

"Kira!" he shouted. *"Wait!"*

A very determined Dayton marched right back down the hallway, sidestepping his sister, and opened the bedroom door. The younger Dayton was beside himself in all literal terms when he rose against the intrusion from his desk, and the sight knocked him onto his bed as he hurriedly backed away.

Kira's eyes riveted from one Dayton to the other, and screamed. The Dayton upon the bed didn't recognize the vampire, thought it was someone Bobby Lee had sent to take him prematurely, caught him so off guard he panicked for fear his parents would come rushing in from all the noise. He tried to hush Kira down with whispered cursing and by throwing a Fangoria magazine at her. The vampire Dayton shut the door, placed the pendant from his pocket around his own neck, took the one he'd given Kira and personally gave it to his earlier self.

"Put this around your neck," the vampire said. "It'll protect you, I think."

Earlier Self did as he said, after which he was more vocal to his sister. "Kira, stop screaming!"

By that time, it was too late. Dayton's pajama-clad father barged into the room, followed by his mother in an oversized Looney Tunes t-shirt.

Kira stopped screaming.

"What the hell is this all about?" his father roared.

"Now honey," his mother said to Dad, always the peacekeeper. Then, to the stranger, "who are *you*?"

Vampire Dayton wanted to embrace them when he turned, but his desperation focused upon Kira. He darted over to her, lifted her tightly into his arms, and ran with her out the bedroom door.

Kira began screaming all over again, fighting against her abductor. He held her fast.

The parents followed after him, Dayton's earlier self rushing from behind, their belated reactions giving vampire Dayton the

247

advantage to push through them and make it out into the patio with his terrified sister. As he ran to the above-ground pond, he lifted Kira as high as he could and plunged her into the waters before Mom or Dad could restrain him. When Dad pulled him away, Kira was no longer there. His parents diverted their attentions into the pond, desperately reaching into its shallow depths, splashing about, and Dayton's earlier self arrived and halted, not knowing what to do.

Vampire Dayton rose from a stumble backwards, went straight after his father from behind, thrusting with all his strength forward and plunging him into the water, face-first, lifting, pushing him altogether in. Mom attacked him, and Dayton's earlier self attempted a rescue. Dad had been pulled into the water fully, disappeared. Mom was next, and in the scuffle between her and the two Daytons, she was forced fully into the pond as well. Vampire Dayton grabbed Earlier Self by the collar of his shirt, swung him around, drove his back against the stucco of the exterior wall of the house, and hollered directly into his face.

"Listen to me!!! I'm *on your side*, and I just saved our family!"

Two figures approached them from both sides, and Vampire Dayton addressed them. They had not expected this. They stood still, and listened.

Earlier Self looked into Dayton's eyes, much like a glossy-eyed sorrowful puppy gazing into the person who was choking it to death. "Is this.....this a part of the initiation???"

***

Bobby Lee "Toad" Horton was just about ready to retire from watering his front lawn with the garden hose, had been at it for a while now, his intentions wrestling against the desire to keep watering just a little bit longer, wondering how his boys were doing in the Monday home across the street hogtying Dayton and bringing him out. He finished what remained of the joint he smoked, dabbing it with a fingertip's worth of hose water and pocketing it. He caught sight again of his wife at the kitchen window, and he motioned to her that he'll be in promptly.

As soon as he twisted the faucet handle that turned off the water, his ear caught the sounds of commotion from his friend's house and he turned, expecting to see Wars and Tendon carrying Day to their Ford Focus.

Instead, four figures approached from out of Dayton's side gate, traversed the street pavement and started across his manicured and well-drenched lawn, in equally determined strides. Two of them were the Brothers he'd sent out to *get* Dayton, but who they brought *back* with them, was.....

......was....

Toad threw the hose to the ground, and for the first time in perhaps centuries, he stepped backwards in a panic and nearly lost his footing, fear-stricken, if only for a moment and with a moment afterwards to spare that allowed him to regain his composure and demonstrate that he *had* no fear.

Wars and Tendon ceased their approach to allow the two Daytons to have word with Toad by themselves.

Toad saw who they were. His eyes went to one and then the other, and they together stood side by side, one the human he knew and one without a doubt a vampire through and through, both impossibly the same person, both wearing an article about their necks which he sensed had traveled through time and knew better than to fuck with.

The vampire Dayton lifted his pendant from his chest, up and over his head, took one step forward and held the alien face out to him. Toad cowered away from it noticeably, until the vampire spoke with an authority that transcended everything Toad was supposed to be.

"Later tonight the world as we know it will end," Dayton proclaimed. "I've been living in years way past this moment, and I tell you, if you stay here, you'll die. All of the Brotherhood, this neighborhood, this state, most of this *country* from sea to shining sea, will die. The blinding lights will come, and your beloved brethren and their ungodly camp meeting where *you* made me what I am will be obliterated as will most everything else, unless you do *exactly what I say........*"

Toad was all ears. Nothing needed to convince him of the authenticity of the situation, nor of the urgency.

"You must send a decree that all of the Brotherhood of the Black Heroes will never again harm a human being," Dayton instructed him, "and they must spare all those they've taken away from their homes to kill in sport at that infernal initiation tonight. Our Brotherhood will live up to its reputation, and help heal the world, instead of whatever all you guys are tripping on. I will save all of you, but only if you do this and help me save as many more as I can."

"I'm with you, buddy," was Toad's reply.

"*Promise me*, on your word as a Brother on your royal authority," Dayton persisted.

Toad sighed. He knew of the repercussions, the disappointments, all the bitching his kind would carry on about, but he also knew that if exerted his status, the Brotherhood was bound by blood to carry out his orders for as long as their immortality remained intact, and immortality, for vampires, depending upon its meaning, was just a word as with anything else.

"I give you my solemn oath," was Toad's response. "So, what's the plan?"

***

Hundreds of vampires.....the Heroes, the ancient bat-like ones, the humans they had stolen away to make carnal use of throughout the night, even Triad and Basics and the twenty other initiates including Wayne and Trish—Trick's earlier self.....all of them....evacuated the Arizona desert canyon where they held their festivities and formed a single-file line that stretched from the Monday's rear patio, through their livingroom and out the front door, down the street and around the block, and further down the highway a half mile or so.

Toad and the two Daytons had positioned themselves below the backyard awning, directing each who stood in line to wait for the other one at a time like ride attendants at a theme park. When one dove into the fish pond face-forward with hands and arms clamped to their sides, the next in line would be directed to wait a few seconds before doing the same, and so on. It took no time at all for things to get started. As soon as the first of them dove in and disappeared, everyone else was convinced that this was not bullshit and that made the line move along a lot faster.

At one point, Earlier Self Dayton swiveled to his knees to vomit, probably because his mind couldn't fully absorb what was going on about him, and the efforts his future vampire self made to console him only disturbed him further, so Earlier Self had to sit things out on a folding chair for awhile.

Toad had offered vampire Dayton a few questions about the future, which Day refused to answer, except to say he had a girl waiting for him when he gets back.

"How long do we have?" was one of them.

Dayton really didn't know. He wasn't even sure how long this time porthole thing would stay open.

Police arrived. They were expected, after awhile, what with this crowd winding through the neighborhood and with Dayton's insistence that all the neighbors be alerted and join them. Three helicopters, two news and one police, began circling the Monday's home and surrounding area like hawks.

Homes in the cul-de-sac and down the avenue came alive, the knocks on their doors by black-robed biker-looking dudes telling them to save themselves and outside commotion drawing many people to the streets, or to their cell phones in an effort to telephone nearby friends to venture out into the streets for them. Bizarre creatures were spotted, and an occasional naked person crawling with the line.

When the police *did* come, the first of them to embark upon the premises were told by those standing in line what was happening, and they set foot upon the patio to order whoever was in charge to disband the event, whatever it was, until they saw what was happening for themselves. They radioed to the others to hold their positions, that they couldn't believe what they were seeing.

The line ran for six hours until it deteriorated like the last trickle of trick-or-treaters on Halloween Night, into a large gathering outside the home who were too afraid to enter, some carrying banners and posterboard signs of protest because Headline News was watching, stating that the Anti-Christ lived there, that the Mondays were handing out passports to hell and that the damned were the first to go.

The four cops and reporter that remained around the patio because they were too spooked to take the plunge watched as Dayton decided it was time to go, told the stoic spectators that anyone was welcomed to follow while there was still time, allowed Earlier Self and then Toad to dive until, just before he dove in himself, he let out a sigh, and said to nobody in particular, "Finally I made a difference. Maybe I *did* send them all to hell, but at least I saved them."

And then a blinding light followed.

Cutting Edges

The original short
screenplay

FADE IN:

CREDITS ROLL OVER

INT. SHAVER'S HOME - KITCHEN

BETH SHAVER screams in a frustrated fury. She is a twentysomething wife who wears the pants, holds a full- time job and dominates the household, very dissatisfied with her marriage. She is yelling furiously at her husband BRUCE, who is OFF CAMERA. The kitchen is a mess, dishes waiting to be washed clutter the counter.

> BETH
> I thought I told you to have all
> this clean by the time I got home,
> you son of a bitch!

She throws a GLASS which barely misses Bruce and SHATTERS OFFSCREEN, continues raving AD LIB.

We go into an AD LIB MONTAGE of Beth screaming at Bruce around the house, for various reasons.

MONTAGE ENDS with Beth straddling Bruce on the bed during a lovemaking session in which she grows immediately tired and frustrated. Beth rises.

> BETH
> Goddammit, you can't get anything
> right, let alone *up*right, can you,
> you son of a bitch. I had a *cock*er
> spaniel that could lay me better.

She jumps off him and out of bed with a humph.

> BRUCE (O.C.)
> (to himself)
> What?!

> BETH (O.S.)
> And you should shave, too, it's like
> kissing goddamn sandpaper

> BRUCE (O.C.)
> (to himself)
> A cocker spaniel???

INT. SHAVER'S GARAGE - MORNING

The automatic garage door opens. Beth pulls out in her car, MUMBLES something harsh about her husband as she back up over driveway.

EXT. SHAVER'S FRONT DOOR

As we reveal BRUCE SHAVER, haggard and worn and just finishing smoking a cigarette, just outside the front door. He's a few years her superior, lazy, unemployed and unshaven, tattoos on his arms, timid and often cowering at her demands. He's happy to see her go, flicks the cigarette butt and retreats inside and closes the front door.

INT. SHAVER'S BATHROOM – DAY

Bruce steps before the bathroom mirror. He peers at his

unshaven reflection, rubs his palm over his darkening beard. He exhibits a series of spontaneous and lame martial arts moves, watches himself.

He FUMBLES through a drawer and finds a RAZOR, then a can of SHAVING CREAM. When he DEPRESSES the can, it JITTERS and he lets go. The can drops to the floor. Bruce gazes in disbelief as he draws in his breath with sudden anxiety.

The cream SPEWS spasmodically from the can and of its own accord onto the bathroom floor tiles, its WHITE FOAM from the can continues issuing forth an endless stream which accumulates and grows.

The FOAM rises from the floor gradually and forms into a three-foot-high SHAVING CREAM CREATURE with a bulbous head and solemn features, sporting a resolute and matter-of-fact personality all its own.

Bruce is awestruck, unbelieving. He wipes his eyes, strokes his beard.

                    SHAVING CREAM CREATURE
                    Hello. I believe you have some
                            problems.

                         BRUCE I___I

                    SHAVING CREAM CREATURE
                         (sarcastically)
                         I.......I.....

Bruce can barely contain himself, exits the bathroom, peers amazed back at the creature from behind the bathroom door.

> SHAVING CREAM CREATURE
> OhBrucey.....come here. Come on,
> I'm as real as your wife and
> believe me,
> you'd rather have me here than her.

INT. SHAVER'S BEDROOM

Bruce perambulates around the bed, not knowing what to do about the situation, panicked.

INT. SHAVER'S BATHROOM

Bruce pokes his head into the bathroom from behind the bathroom door.

> SHAVING CREAM CREATURE
> I'm still here.

> BRUCE
> No you're not.

> SHAVING CREAM CREATURE
> (enticingly)
> I can help you get rid of her.....

> BRUCE
> What? I'm going insane. I'm going
> fucking whackadoodle, that's what....

> SHAVING CREAM CREATURE
> Yeah, you're going... .whackadoodle.

(Sighs) Ya see, Brucey,
Ya gotta get some balls here. You
can eradicate her. Wipe the slate
clean off. And all her lovers, too.

BRUCE
(dumbfounded)
Lovers???

SHAVING CREAM CREATURE
She's such a bitch, isn't she?

Bruce opens the bathroom door fully.

SHAVING CREAM CREATURE
(cont.)
But what do I know? I'm shaving
cream. With a purpose.

BRUCE
What do you want from me? I've
got enough problems!

Bruce drops to his knees.

SHAVING CREAM CREATURE
Listen, I'll clue you in. Razors. That's
the ticket.

Bruce situates himself crosslegged on the floor before the
creature.

SHAVING CREAM CREATURE
(cont.)
Kill 'em with straight-edged
razor blades.

You know, like the ones
you used to scrape all that white
powder together into lines back
in the day. But you can even use
double-edged.

BRUCE
What do you mean?

SHAVING CREAM CREATURE
Just shut up and listen, man.....

The characters converse ad lib as camera pulls out of
bathroom.

We go into a MONTAGE of Bruce taking down the ceiling
fan in the bedroom and drilling razor blades onto the blades,
purchasing supplies from a hardware store, re-installing the fan,
etc.

SHAVING CREAM CREATURE
(cont., V.O. throughout
montage)
I endow you with the powers of
invincibility....as long as razors
are utilized in the slaying of others.

BRUCE
(V.O.)
....slaying?

SHAVING CREAM CREATURE
Razors are to you in the same way
as, say, the biblical Samson's hair was
to him. You know, when he cut it, he lost all
his strength. Anyway, kill your wife,

Bruce, and with razors you will rule the world. Oh, and be creative when you do.

BRUCE
(V.O.)
Will this do?
SHAVING CREAM CREATURE
Yes, that'll do, Brucey, that'll do.

MONTAGE ENDS with a FULL SHOT of the finished ceiling fan booby trap from the POV of the bed looking up.

INT. SHAVER'S GARAGE - NIGHT
Beth's car pulls up in the driveway and enters garage. Beth emerges from car.

INT. SHAVER'S BEDROOM - NIGHT
Beth enters the dark room without turning on the light and disrobes, tired and angrily MUMBLING AD LIB about a situation at her job that day.

We see Bruce as he watches on in the shadows, but she does not notice him.

Beth exits into the BATHROOM and remains there briefly, then re-enters the bedroom clothed in boxer shorts and very low-cut tank top that almost reveals her breasts and flops onto the bed atop its covers, onto her back.

Bruce still continues watching eerily, until he catches her eye with a start.

BETH
(startled)
Son of a bitch. You son of a bitch.

BRUCE
(with sweet sarcasm)
What did I do this time, my little
Honey Bunches of Raisin Flakes?

BETH
Standing there and scaring the shit out
of me like that, all quiet.

BRUCE
(after long pause)
I'm not all quiet.

BETH
Well anyway, go run off and watch
your t.v. and leave me alone. I
had a shitty day at the stress factory.....
(cont. O.S.)
.....and what do you know, you self-centered
unemployed son of a bitch.

Bruce is exiting the room even as she talks. He lifts a hand up
to the ceiling fan wall switch with a sly boldness.

BETH
(cont.)
Oh......

Bruce hesitates.

> BETH
> (cont.)
> .....and turn on the fucking ceiling
> fan. I'm getting heat blisters just
> lying here.

Bruce obliges as he continues to exit, grinning. He flips up the wall switch.

Beth relaxes and sighs.

> BETH
> (cont., under her breath)
> Son of a bitch.

The ceiling fan begins to turn. Bruce about-faces, leans against door frame, slips hands in pants pockets, watches and waits with anticipation, wondering whether his scheme will actually work.

An unsuspecting Beth snuggles on top of the bed. Faster the ceiling fan goes ....until the loosened screws give way ....and ELECTRIC SPARKS occur. The commotion draws Beth's attention at the last moment. She opens her eyes, can't believe what she sees and SCREAMS.

The fan plunges down upon her, spinning wildly. Bruce holds his breath and watches intensely. Beth struggles against the blades as they cut into her skin. Her panic increases, she writhes, spasms, arms caught between
the blades, razors cutting deeper, vital arteries severed. The red liquid flows over the quilts and down into the pool of blood forming on the carpet.

Bruce watches on from the bedroom doorway. He's elated, wide-eyed, like a mad scientist, breathing heavy, enraptured.

Beth now lies lifeless and bloody across the bed beneath the deadened fan.

A metal CLANKING SOUND from inside the bathroom disturbs Bruce away from the moment, and he turns toward the distraction.

The shaving cream can ROLLS from out of the bathroom into the bedroom. It disappears just beneath Beth's side of the bed. We then start to hear sounds of shaving cream spewing from a can.

A white shaving cream mound rises from the bedside and engulfs Beth, and the Shaving Cream Creature's head rises up to speak to Bruce while it FEEDS.

                    SHAVING CREAM CREATURE
                        That'll do, Brucey.

                            BRUCE
                      What are you doing?

                    SHAVING CREAM CREATURE
                    If I'd implied a sacrifice was one
                Of the terms of your new empowerment,
                I'd have wasted valuable time explaining it.
                    Mmmmm. She is delicious.
                      Like barbecue rib night.

                            BRUCE
                    So, what happens next?

SHAVING CREAM CREATURE
I'll take care of everything here.
You........go out on the town. Have some
fun for a change, celebrate your
emancipation. There's an underground
festivity taking place as we speak
in a building off of K Street.
You'll find your wife's boyfriends,
the ones who'd been banging her
there---

VERY TIGHT SHOT OF CREATURE'S MOUTH
SLURPING UP BLOOD, NIBBLING ON FLESH

SHAVING CREAM CREATURE (cont'd)
.. hell, she'd slept with the whole lot of
the crowd, come to think of it.....

BRUCE
(with mounting rage)
Well then there's things I gotta
do.....

While he talks, Bruce reaches down and nudges Beth's foot
with his hand, turns, then exits the bedroom, determined.

SHAVING CREAM CREATURE
(calling out to him)
Don't forget to do it with razors!

CUT TO:

We go into a MONTAGE of Bruce taking a large
MACHETE from his garage and drilling holes into it,

securing bolts over fastened razor blades along the perimeters of the blade.

EXT. K STREET BUILDING ALLEYWAY - NIGHT

Bruce waits in front of the back double doors of a building where we clearly hear the MUSIC and VOICES of a PARTY raging inside.

ESTABLISHING SHOT OF ALLEYWAY WITH IMAGE OF BRUCE STANDING IN FRONT OF DOORS

He smokes a cigarette. Bruce drops cigarette, stamps it out on the ground. He is garbed in a shirt and jeans that have ZIPPERS sewn into them along the outer sides of each pant leg.

Bruce opens the one of the double doors and steps inside. It's a fairly crowded place. PEOPLE are drinking, laughing, talking. Bruce starts walking into the party scene, going into the crowd, passing a number of partiers, slowly, scrutinizing, jealous of the intimacy his wife may have shared with each of them.

We pass a STONER propped against a wall eating a chicken drumstick. The stoner nods to Bruce as if to say "what's up."

TWO PARTY GIRLS drinking and clad in punk attire are talking to each other, both giving him brief glances.

Bruce passes a handful of groups of INTERESTING-LOOKING PARTIERS, some returning his gaze back with attitudes of their own.

A table can be seen set up as a bar with 1 6j a BARTENDER serving beverages and partiers helping themselves to a buffet. Bartender is pouring drinks out of familiar-labeled store-bought bottles of what looks like whiskey, vodka and such.

Some partiers reach for paper plates and fill them with chicken they've retrieved out of fast food boxes piled at the corner of table. Some of the partiers disperse from the table, revealing Bruce passing by very slowly, hesitating to catch a couple of quick glances of what is going on. The bartender is grabbing bottles aligned across the shelves of a book case behind them.
We see a CLOSE-UP of a half-empty whiskey bottle, its label design familiar except that it reads "INFIDELITY."

We see a close up of a vodka bottle, its label reading "YOUR WIFE WAS A WHORE."

We see a close up of another bottle, its label reading "THEY'RE ALL WHORES."

We see the label on a bottle held by 1 6r the bartender tilted to pour its contents into a cup held out by a thirsty partier. That label reads "FUCK 'EM ALL."

Bruce pulls his gaze away, leaves the table.

Not far from the table, a LADY holds an INFANT in her arms, seated in a corner, talking to a FRIEND, a drink in one hand.

Halfway into the crowd, Bruce spies a STEREO on a tabletop from which MUSIC BLARES.

He
switches the stereo OFF. The crowd goes silent along with
the music, except for the sounds of a cricket chirping which are
quickly stifled by the STONER PARTIER who all of a sudden
stomps on it.

> PARTIER FROM THE BACK OF CROWD
> Hey! That was a badass tune, dude!

An INTIMIDATING HARDCORE PARTIER steps up to
confront Bruce.

> INTIMIDATING HARDCORE PARTIER
> And we were all having such a good
> goddamn time. What's your problem, retard?

> BRUCE
> (yelling to crowd)
> I wanna know who here's been
> banging Beth Shaver! My wife!

The crowd MUMBLES her name in contemplation and
recognition. One by one, people matter-of-factly admit to it,
some even modestly raising their hands. It indeed seems like
everyone has had a piece of his wife.

One PARTIER whispers to ANOTHER.

> ONE PARTIER
> Hey, was she that bitchy chick who
> licked my anus Sunday?

Bruce is dumbfounded, maddened. He begins to turn to face the
stereo but turns back momentarily as the Intimidating Hardcore
Partier speaks.

INTIMIDATING HARDCORE PARTIER
(to Bruce)
So she's popular. What do you
care? She's a bitch.

BRUCE
Life's a bitch.

Bruce resumes to turn to face the stereo, lifts up his shirt and takes out a CD of his own he'd been keeping in his pants. Bruce switches the CD in the stereo with his own. He then flips the stereo switch back on and a NEW HARD ROCK SONG commences and fills the room.

He takes off his shirt. His body has MANY TATTOOS. He unzips his jean leg zippers, takes off his jeans. At his side, we can see the machete sheath tied to a belt and from the sheath he pulls out the razor- studded machete.

He is now clad in nothing but eccentric boxer shorts (just happens to be the same boxers Beth was wearing when she died). He flexes his body, readies his weapon. The crowd of partiers are taken aback by the sight, the circle around him widens as soon as he takes out the machete.

Within the pupil of one of Bruce's eyes, the Shaving Cream Creature appears.

SHAVING CREAM CREATURE
Use your razors. Kill them all.

In a violent flurry, Bruce single-handedly 16nn and systematically slaughters individuals in the crowd, mostly going for necks and faces. No one can stop him, even those brave enough to stand in his way. Many OUTCRIES, everyone PANICS, lots of BLOOD and senseless mayhem. People get killed in creative ways.

Massive Partier steps in his way. Before Bruce can bring the machete down on him, the Massive Partier manages to grab Bruce's wrist with both hands, tries to wrestle the weapon from his grip. Bruce gazes furiously into the Massive Partier's eyes. As he returns the gaze, glances at his firm grip on Bruce's wrist. The machete is almost free.

Bruce lets go of one hand and unsheathes a previously unseen HUNTING KNIFE studded in razors from the other side of his belt and from beneath his boxer shorts.

The knife blade cuts into Massive Partier's eye, popping it open. The partier lets go in a deafening cry of pain. Massive Partier steps backwards, hands over his eye. His eye drops, rolling onto the floor like a marble, and while people flee somebody's shoe steps on it, squashing its goo into the camera.

EXT. K STREET BUILDING ALLEYWAY

The double doors burst open as partiers struggle for a getaway. People escape into all directions.

> FLEEING PARTIER
> (screaming)
> Oh my god!!!!

> FLEEING PARTIER #2
> He's got razor blades!!!!

INT. K STREET BUILDING PARTY

People are lying bloodied and dead everywhere, Bruce now sitting on top of the stereo table, all is quiet.

The lady with child also lies dead .... her infant crawling curiously over the carnage.

One TWENTY-SOMETHING WOMAN is alive, picking herself up from toppled bar table and staggering. Bruce is distracted by the sounds of the woman, turns, looks in her direction.

EXT. K STREET BUILDING ALLEYWAY

Before YET ANOTHER PARTIER feverishly attempts an escape, bolting out down the alley, the TWENTY-SOMETHING WOMAN, who remarkably RESEMBLES BETH, is the last to vacate the building, wounded and bloodied and crawling out the doors and down the asphalt and mud puddles, inching her way desperately in hopes to evade the death and peril she'd left behind.

To her horror, Bruce emerges into the alley carrying his machete for another last kill or two, when he sees her.

                    BRUCE
            You! Hey sweetheart! You look
            like the bitch I married! You screw
               her too? Come here!

He chases her down, grabs her, slices her skin playfully with the machete as she persists in her attempt to get away. She cries, begs, pleads with him all the while.

A BUM drinking from a bottle in a paper bag staggers past them, stops to observe them.

                    BUM
              Lover's spat.

Bruce and the twenty-something woman pause to observe him, too. The bum then continues walking onward.

                    BUM
       Why can't we all just get along?

The twenty-something woman takes the opportunity to spring up and make a determined run for her life. Bruce switches his attention away from the bum to the woman and follows in pursuit with his machete.

EXT. PUBLIC SIDEWALK

She rounds a corner, and Bruce chases her past pedestrians and storefronts.

EXT. MOVIE THEATRE FRONT

She ultimately drops from exhaustion and blood loss before the ticket booth of a MOVIE THEATRE.
Bruce catches up to her, equally exhausted but twice as determined. She's out of energy, out of breath.

He grabs her by the hair, lifts her head, places the razor- studded machete up to her throat in full view of SPECTATORS who pass by and pay them no mind. The woman calls out to them but her voice is frail and weak.

TWENTY-SOMETHING WOMAN
(hoarsely)
Help me

Just then we hear the CLICK OF A HANDGUN. Bruce's eyes turn toward the sound. We see the gun pressed into Bruce's cheek, see the gun lifting away with each growth of Bruce's recognition, see the finger on its trigger as it's pulled with an accompanying GUN SHOT BLAST.

Bruce's head is shattered by the impact of the bullet and a forthcoming EXPLOSION of the other side of Bruce's face. Bruce's body falls limp and lifeless to the ground, dropping the machete beside him.

The twenty-something woman, traumatized, throws his body off of her and scoots away, attempts to stand, is greeted by the outstretched hand of the GUNMAN.
The gunman is clean shaven, his facial features resembling those of the Shaving Cream Creature, and the twenty-something woman notices a blotch of SHAVING CREAM on the side of the gunman's face.

GUNMAN
(to her)
Hey Missy, that was really
something, wasn't it? Come on, there's a
movie playing here you don't want to
miss.

Gunman helps her up. As they walk toward the ticket booth.... the gunman wipes the shaving cream from his face with one off-handed swipe. It SPLATS onto Bruce's body.

Shaving Cream begins to FROTH and expand, growing, FEEDING.

                    SHAVING CREAM CREATURE
                 Mmmmm, like barbecue rib night

WE PULL OUT SLOWLY from the scene until the entire theatre front is in FULL VIEW, and as we do so a COUPLE OF KIDS skateboarding down the sidewalk stop to pick up Bruce's machete from the ground beside him, examine it, SQUEAL IN DELIGHT of how cool it is, then skateboard away with it.

FULL SHOT THEATRE FRONT

as the THEATRE MARQUEE is revealed, and it reads: Now Playing: "CUTTING EDGES"

CUT TO BLACK

Extras:

Extracts from File Cabinet Hell

Dear Playboy Advisor

(Actually sent to Playboy, 1991, with response. Really, the author doesn't have this problem.)

Dear Playboy Advisor,

For quite a long period of time I have sought help concerning my ongoing problem, but no reasonable solution seems to exist. I've been reading your column for quite some time, but it never occurred to me to write until lately. Even now I'm not entirely sure I will be taken seriously.

When I was born, I had an unusual complication in that I carried between my legs two penises. The lesser, least developed of the two was removed by immediate surgery, and I have up until adolescence led a completely normal, healthy life.

The very first time I discovered masturbation, I also discovered that, unlike my friends, I could not secrete semen. The pleasure was there, the same sensations everyone else described, but there were no messy results. It's therefore obvious that I cannot have children.

The bizarre aspect also lies within the fact that, after countless medical examinations, the physical interior makeup of my organ is completely reversed. When I secrete seminal fluids, my testes divert them to the region where my second penis used to be. Mysteriously enough, the semen disappears. Despite examinations, however, no one seems to be able to locate the absorbed semen, nor can anyone reverse the problem.

Are you aware of anyone who can relate to this? So far, the doctors call me an "isolated case." Are you aware of any current treatments or therapy? Other than this, there is no danger or lack of pleasure or function.

I literally come inside myself, I come *backwards*, and there are times I feel like a freak.

Sincerely,

N. Randers

Response:

Nicholas Grabowsky

Dear Mr. Randers:

In all honesty, we've never heard of a situation exactly like yours. Absence of ejaculation isn't uncommon, and usually, the body absorbs semen that isn't expelled. Since you've already been examined by many doctors, there is not much we can offer in the way of advice. You might try contacting the American Urological Association for possible assistance. Thanks for your interest in PLAYBOY.

Sincerely,

MW for the Playboy Advisor

My Hamster Loo

(Written around 1984, high school senior year)

Loo, Loo, my hamster Loo
Stuck to the heal of my old grey shoe
Your face is all smeared
You look funny and blue
Loo, Loo, my dead hamster Loo

I went to clean your food dish But it
was all over the floor And
underneath the table Was the cat
from next door
I looked around the carpet

I thought my hamster was dead
I looked down at the heel of my shoe
And saw part of my hamster's head

And then I felt so sorry
I wiped your guts from the floor
I put you back in your cage
You still didn't move anymore
I looked around for my dinner
I was hungry before I saw you

276

I opened the cage, scraped your head off my shoe And
now I have hamster head stew

Loo, Loo, my hamster Loo
Floating around in my Campbell's stew
You're swirling around
With the vegetables too
Loo, Loo, my dead hamster Loo.

Write About the Ruler

(Written around 1979 for Jack and Jill Magazine, rejected)

Once I met a young boy who thought his ruler was a flight instrument to a land beyond the sun. He would take a pencil and insert it into the hole found in the ruler's center, then push the ruler until it spun like a propeller. The only thing that truly happened upon my observance was the ruler spun off the pencil as it twirled way too fast, flew into the air and across the room, smacking another young boy upside the head and sending him into an unconscious slump across the floor. When the stricken boy awoke, he spoke of a short vision he experienced of a bright light and flying beings surrounding it dancing in mid-air.

"That's the only problem I have with this ruler," the first boy explained afterward. "It's my ruler, but whenever I use it, it's always someone else who gets to go to the land beyond the sun."

The Adventure of Goldenfish

(Taken from a short screenplay written around 1980, ninth grade)

At a beach, four dead fish lie underneath a pier on the muddy sand. They lie facing one another, their eyes wide open.

Fish #1: "I am conducting this meeting today because I wish to tell you all something very important. Very important. Out there in the cities humans terrorize one another, pollute every possible place they can which isn't healthy for us fish and which is why we lie here dead ourselves."

Fish #2: "Then why are we talking if we're dead?" Fish #1: "Because we are superfishes, that's why!" Fish #3: (In an English accent) "I say, what in the bloody world are you talking about?"

Fish #1: "I am trying to explain that we should send out bands of superfishes all over the world to fight crime and pollution. We have lost the battle with humans eating us, so we must abide by the old saying that if you can't beat 'em, join 'em. We have to stand up for ourselves. We don't want just anybody eating us or keeping us as pets."

Fish #3: "Here, here!"

Fish #2: "Here, here!"

Fish #4: "Here, here!"

Fish #1: We will send out the only living super goldfish in the world Goldenfish....to lead the rest in an attack against evil. Oops, here comes someone!"

A small boy walks over to them. "Look, Mom! Dead fish!"

"Jimmy, leave them alone. Dead fish smell."

"Oh all right." He kicks one into the water, then runs away.

Not long after, two men come to the beach and dump a great big bucket of bacon grease into the ocean water to get rid of it.

Fish #1: "Guys, it's time! Send the word to Goldenfish, he must take care of the evil!"

Fish #2: "I'm worried about Sam, he got kicked over to the crabs."

Goldenfish hears their pleas. He's been waiting to do this for quite some time. He was just waking up and brushing his lips not far away when their telepathy signal stirred him into action. He knocked against the glass of his fish aquarium home, and a little eight-yearold girl playing a game of Pong on her black and white TV looks over to him. All he needs is for her to take him and throw him into the air, and he will come to the rescue of the environment promptly.

"Mom," she says, "my fish is scaring me."

"Well throw it out, sweetie."

"Okay."

Yes, yes, thought Goldenfish, *my will is bringing her to me. Soon I will fly, I will fight!*

The little girl dipped her hand in the aquarium water and lifted Goldenfish out by the tail. She opened her second-story apartment window and tossed him out.

Fish #1: "You all sense that?"

Fish #3: "I say, indeed! He's coming!"

All fish: "Fly, Goldenfish, fly!!!!"

Goldenfish flies, falls to the street pavement below. The two evil men, having done their mindless deed, drive straight over Goldenfish in their '57 Chevy. A cat then comes up to him, sniffs him for a moment, and then eats his head.

The end.

Russia Shocks World

(1983, for The Lamplighter, Nick's high school newspaper for which he was a reporter)

What was one of the biggest issues in the 1960's? If you can remember fairly recent United States history, one of the first things that comes to your mind would be the Cuban missile crisis. It was the time when the Russians secretly gave Fidel Castro missiles to set up in Cuba. When President Kennedy found out, there was a lot going on behind the closed doors of the White House.

As most people know, not long ago the Russians shot down a jetliner on its way to Korea. A great many passengers lost their lives. As soon as the news reached the United States, people began once again to talk more about the Russians, President Reagan ordered a boycott. Soon enough, other countries joined the boycott.

As everyone has heard, the jetliner shot down by the Russians was an ordinary civilian plane. The Russians say that the United States was using it as a spy plane. That is one of the many reasons for shooting it down.

Some people think the United States did use the jetliner as a spying device and endangered the lives of the aboard. Some people think it was all the Russians' fault and no one else's. But why was the jetliner flying so close and actually went into Russian territory? Or did it? All we know is what we hear on the news or what we read in the newspaper. Is there something really going on behind closed doors that we don't know about? My opinion is, yes. I tend to think both sides are in the wrong, but I also think the Russians are more in the wrong than we are.

You're a Pretty Boston Fern
(Written around 1986)

You're a pretty Boston fern
And you know it's true
But there's something you must learn
I can't keep you in my shoe

'cause shoes are meant for feet
to walk on hard concrete it
won't be very neat
to see you growing there

Well, I've heard of a green thumb
But it does sound kinda dumb
To have a green toe
Don't you know
That's not where you belong

You're a dainty pickled prune
And I cannot tell a lie
But I resemble an obscene loon
So get off of my fly

How can people have their fun

And say my fly's undone
When you're in the way, so son,
That's not where you belong

Bepto Pismal

(Seventh grade creative writing assignment)

When you look in your neighborhood pharmacy, what is the latest product you see? That's right! It's the new mint-flavored Bepto Pismal. It's a fun remedy for upset stomachs. Imagine: you are lying in your bed at one a.m. when all of a sudden you wake up and barf all over the place all the Quaker Oat Meal (graham cracker flavor) you had for dinner. You go into the kitchen, and among the packages of Cool Aide you find the mint- flavored Bepto Pismal. As you grab that spoon and take your first taste, you guzzle down the whole bottle and go back to bed.

It's now 2 a.m. You wake up and begin barfing all over the place again. You realize to your ultimate horror that there is no more mint-flavored Bepto Pismal. You run into the kitchen and barf up the rest of the Bepto Pismal back into the bottle. As soon as you go back to bed, your sick sister goes into the kitchen for her mint- flavored Bepto Pismal.

The Chloroform Angel

*(Undated, but probably late 1980's, inspired by
intoxicating substances)*

Peaceful now. Serenity lost within the confines of an endless minute, waiting for that minute's final deathcry of seconds to be echoed by the new minute's birthcry. Much the same for me, this serenity shall pass in a deathcry and then echoed by reality's pain. Which is the place where I dwell. To me, serenity is an all-expense-paid vacation away from the place I dwell. Often, like now, it arrives unexpectedly like the damp white crumpled tissue of chloroform imposed by the force of an angel's hand. Instant serenity. But any minute the angel will take me back home to the pain, just you wait and see.

Back at home, I have but a single piece of furniture. It never occurred to me that I needed anything else. I sleep on the rug in the bedroom. I set my plate and drinking glass down on a mat when I settle down for supper. I store most of my belongings in closets. I have plenty of space to move about freely without fear of stumbling into anything or knocking over a vase. I don't need that kind of fear. I have enough fear fueling my pain in the one item that shares my space.

A bar stool.

A nagging bar stool.

It nags me indeed, follows me around like a pestering child wherever I walk, unnervingly bumping into the backs of my knees and thighs pushing insistently in constant effort to force me backwards and sit, to bring me down.

I turn to face it, but that only makes matters worse.

There's no limit to my vulnerability in facing this menace, to look it straight down and speak my mind. But I did, I really let myself go, told it how I truly felt. Bad mistake. It was thoroughly offended, picked itself up off the floor and starting beating me.

Senseless.

In front of company.

The company was even entertained by it, called their friends on their cell phones to come by and witness the cool magic show. They didn't know how I did it, but they drank all my beer and marveled and laughed at my spectacle of pain, walking about and flailing their hands every which way in the air to see if they could detect strings or discover the great secret as to how it was done. Someone telephoned KCWR to get me and that goddamn bar stool on their morning show to do it all over again. Nobody cared about the way I felt, nor of my broken bones.

I made a resolution: next time, I'll pay it no mind but to give in and sit down...even before company and all......and make it not a mere bar stool which steers me towards insanity....

I will sit down and make it my throne. I figure, if I must live with all this, I might as well rule it instead of it ruling me.

As the chloroform angel approaches, I think a final thought as serenity is about to hit me once again, stealing away the pain:

Chloroform angels don't exist, and neither do I, but the stool remains forever real.

Sixth Grade Poetry

Poor Charlie Chean
Thinks he's so keen
Now the poor guy's green He
drank some Mister Clean

Poor Mary Murk
Waiting for coffee to perk In the
forest she does lurk She's such a
jerk

Little Joe Strat Such
a brat
Kicks my cat
 I hit him with a bat

Karl Keech
In the church he does preach In the
class he does teach He looks like a
leech

Little Timmy Tars
Chasing after cars
Looking through plastic jars He's
from Mars.

Nicholas Grabowsky

Story Going Nowhere and Left That Way

(written roughly around 2005 before I lost interest, and exhumed from file cabinet hell)

I wasn't sure exactly what it was I contracted or precisely how I contracted it. It was a complete mystery to me. If I were a rich fellow, or at least semi-rich, like a cross between whoever's responsible for Walmart and one of the least popular consistently paid Hollywood actors, I'd sponsor a competition where contestants would race to get down to the bottom of it all for me, find out the true nature of my disease. The first one wins a lump sum worthy of going through all that trouble and the runners up would win everything from cool Rocky Mountain vacation getaways to sun visors and tin containers of curiously strong mints.

At first, I mistook what plagued me for the symptoms of poison ivy or oak. The rashes were similar, the excessive itching. Damn the itching all to hell. But the symptoms developed to the point that a friend at the office (where I worked—Bowers, Price & Associates, an affiliate of a prestigious commodities firm) became quite concerned, ran to the nearest phone when I protested, insisting to him it was no big deal after all, and he held up his right hand with three fingers extended into the air.

Those were his 911 fingers.

He was determined to use them should I refuse, as he put it, to vow to see enough doctors until one gave me the opinion that something was wrong with me.

His personal prognosis was that I was becoming a leper. I don't know if he'd ever seen a leper before, and I know I never had, but I knew what one was from the stories of Jesus I'd heard in church and saw in movies like *The Greatest Story Ever Told*. But I was honestly convinced he didn't know his asshole from a bath tub drain.

284

I made the vow to see enough doctors alright, just to keep the bastard quiet, but, I tell you, when the itching subsided so did my determination. I mean, it seemed to be getting all better. Then it started up again. It made me realize my office buddy could have been right, that I should've taken him a little more seriously.

One hellish night last month the horrible itching started up again and then some. I couldn't sleep, needless to say, and I relinquished my t-shirt and boxers to the corner of my bedroom because my clothing felt to me like I was wearing wet leather, from what I can describe of it. I became deathly afraid of my condition, of what was happening to my body.

When it's warm and humid at night, so warm and humid that you have to open your windows in a neighborhood infamous for rampant crime and home burglaries because your air conditioner is out of order (that goddamn repairman never showed up that day) and you itch and itch and scratch and scratch at yourself with such relentless abandon that you feel a sticky wetness on your fingertips that just might be blood, you begin to go a little south of the border in the mental stability department.

I got myself up and went to the bathroom. My intent was to take a bath.

Epson Salts.

Mr. Bubbles.

Calamine Lotion, many bottles, like Cartman on South Park with chicken pox.

Anything to bathe in, I just needed a bath.

Yes, nice, bath, good.

I hobbled to the bathtub and with a desperate equal turn of both knobs released upon the porcelain basin the wellsprings of relief, then rose to face myself in the medicine cabinet mirror overlooking the sink, still fiendishly scratching, itching, scratching.

I suppose I would have seen what I looked like in that mirror, at least for a fleeting moment, but the opportunity of even catching a glimpse was stolen from me by fate as my feet suddenly slid against the slippery goo I'd left a trail of from out the bathroom door.

I fell.

I fell hard, the side of my head coming down against the outer edge of the bathtub with all the impact of a sweet juicy melon tossed with great force onto an asphalt back road from a Ford pick-up truck full of rednecks.

The consequences of this calamity gave me great relief in that, for awhile there as my being swam marathon backstrokes in the Carnival cruise swimming pool of blissful unconsciousness, I didn't itch. Not at all.

Nor did I care whether I still itched or not. I couldn't feel a thing.

I think it was because I was dead.

Now neither of us will ever know the rest of my story.

What I *do* know is that my blood emptied out from the point of impact on the back of my head and into the bath waters which tumbled and swirled down the unplugged drain, through the house plumbing and into the rest of the world around me. If I indeed contracted a truly alarming disease, maybe my death's blood unleashed a ton of pain into the world. I suppose we'll never know, though, because I'm dead.

I Got Drunk and Wrote This

(Late 1980's)

Fly, fly away, oh Tsetse
And feast not on thine unclean fruit
For the never and the unseen not yet Shall
stunt thine existence
And your essence shall be like that
Of the numerous flies
Which dwell in the world
Of the ceased-to-exist.

Mourn, mourn by night and day, oh Taoist
For the very reason that thine offspring
Are lying naked and barren
In the forbidden tent
And the ultrasonic moonbeams bounce off
Of thine own religion

Red Wet Dirt

Where the thoughts of imagination and experience
Have divided the child in the wasteland
Into sections of eight.

Beasts of the sea, fowl stenches of the air And
women in plates of paper and acid hair On thee
and more I shalt not stare
For the hour has come when in my prayer Forests
shall tumble everywhere
And the things I have thought will be.....will be
in my care.

Now nothing more shall I say
But take heart and mind and always soul
That the treacherous whores and lone princes
Shall be thine undoing
In a sink filled with broken glass.

I got drunk and wrote this.

Class Autograph

*(Sixth grade graduation yearbook, 1978, 'what we'll be
doing this summer')*

I will be on stage with some comedians. I will also go to
karate. I will sell things.

ABOUT THE AUTHOR

Nicholas Grabowsky's novels of horror/fantasy, both as himself, as Nicholas Randers, and as Marsena Shane, have generated worldwide acclaim for over two decades and praised by many of today's most popular horror gurus in the literary world. He began his career in traditional publishing houses with brisk sellers in mass market paperback horror, and known by many as a mentor and advocate to the smaller presses, which has become to him a passion.

His body of work includes the award-winning macabre aliens-among-us epic *The Everborn*, *The Rag Man*, *Pray Serpent's Prey*, *Halloween IV* (and its special edition), *Diverse Tales, Reads & Reviews* and *The Wicked Haze, Sweet Dreams Lady Moon*, numerous anthologies and magazine articles, with projects extending to screenplays, poetry, songs, film, and a wide variety of short fiction and nonfiction since the 1980's.

He's a veteran special guest at numerous genre conventions and makes appearances and signings across the United States. He has been in the limelight as a radical gospel preacher right out of high school and in the following years a rock vocalist, teacher, lecturer and activist, editor, publisher and founder of the Sacramento-based Diverse Media small press, which has recently blossomed into the subdivisions of Black Bed Sheet Books, which publishes local talent, and Black Bed Sheet Productions, which produces independent film, and Blue Bed Sheet Books, which publishes children's books..

Currently, Nicholas is at work with numerous anthologies, graphic novels and comic books, an *Everborn* sequel and the novels *The Downwardens* and *The Sirens of Knowland*. His independent film projects include the upcoming slasher creature feature *Cutting Edges*.

For more on the author and his works, visit

Downwarden.com

www.downwarden.com,
the official site of all things Grabowsky.

The world of Black Bed Sheet Books awaits you.
www.downwarden.com/blackbedsheet

Wherewolf by Franchisca Weatherman. 978-0-9833773-7-5

When a pack of werewolves hits a small southern town, the local Sheriff realizes this is one case he can not solve alone. He calls in the F.B.I. to help him take down the killers that are taking the lives of the local teens. When the wolves abandon the town for the streets of New Orleans during Mardi-Gras celebrations, the hunters become the hunted in an all-out war where no one may survive....

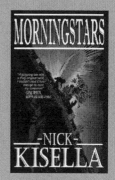
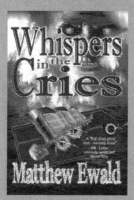
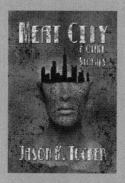

We employ and recommend:

Foreign Translations

Cinta García de la Rosa
(Spanish Translation)
Writer, Editor, Proofreader, Translator
cintagarciadelarosa@gmail.com
http://www.cintagarciadelarosa.com
http://cintascorner.com

Bianca Johnson
(Italian Translation)
Writer, Editor, Proofreader, Translator
http://facebook.com/bianca.cicciarelli

EDITOR STAFF

Felicia Aman
http://www.abttoday.com
http://facebook.com/felicia.aman

Kelly J. Koch
http://dressingyourbook.com

Tyson Mauermann
http://speculativebookreview.blogspot.com

Kareema S. Griest
http://facebook.com/kareema.griest

Mary Genevieve Fortier
https://www.facebook.com/MaryGenevieveFortierWriter
http://www.stayingscared.com/Nighty%20Nightmare.html

Shawna Platt
www.angelshadowauthor.webs.com/

Adrienne Dellwo
http://facebook.com/adriennedellwo
http://chronicfatigue.about.com/

William Cook
http://lnkd.in/bnC-yMd
http://www.amazon.com/Blood-Related

and HORNS

Look for us wherever books are sold.

If you thought *this book* was cool, check out these other titles from the #1 source for the best in independent horror fiction,

BLACK BED SHEET

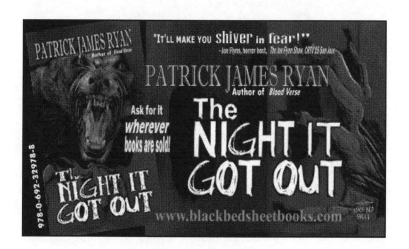

www.blackbedsheetbooks.com

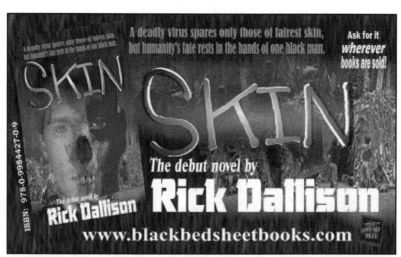

"POWERFUL!"
--Dead Men Talk Podcast

Family Man

The Unreal Story of
Charles Manson's Right-hand Man

Chuck W. Chapman